“O[illegible] r read. The bala[illegible] action is just p[illegible] author. You won’t [illegible]”

~Denyse Cohen, author of
Witch’s Soulmate, Book 1
of the *Living Energy* Trilogy

“Splendidly written in a wonderful voice, drew me in immediately. Ms. Peace’s imagination alone gets 5 stars. Spectacular worlds and enchanting scenes. Anyone who enjoys losing themselves in a world of a charming fantasy with plenty of layers and a host of intriguing characters won’t be disappointed!”

~Rosary McQuestion, author of
Once Upon Another Time

“As soon as I finished this book, I was eager to start the next. I highly recommend this book. Great Job!”

~Janus Gangi, author of
Elizabeth Rose and *That Morning After*

Rhemalda Publishing, Inc. (USA)
P.O. Box 1790, Moses Lake, WA 98837, USA
www.rhemalda.com

First American Paperback Edition

This is a work of fiction. Names, characters, places, and incidents either are the product of the author's imagination or are used fictitiously. Any resemblance to actual events, locales, or persons, living or dead, is entirely coincidental. The publisher does not have any control and does not assume responsibility for author or third-party Web sites or their content.

Editing by Diane Dalton
Text design by Rhemalda Publishing
Cover design by Melissa Williams
Cover art image by Fotokostic
Author photo by Martin Saban-Smith www.saban.co.uk

ISBN-13: 978-1-936850-22-8
ePUB ISBN: 978-1-936850-23-5
Library of Congress Control Number: 2013946786

Printed in the United States of America
10 9 8 7 6 5 4 3 2 1

The paper used in this publication meets the minimum requirements of the American National Standards of Information Services - Permanence of Paper for Printed Library Materials, ASNI Z39.48-1992.

Visit Caroline Peace at her author Web site www.caspeace.com

Dedication

To my much-loved parents, Barbara and Dennis. Thank you for all you have done for me; from a wonderful childhood to all the love and support you have given me over the years. Also for your unflagging faith in my writing skills!

To Richard,

Happy reading!

Cas Peace 18-12-2013

Artesans of Albia Trilogy

King's Envoy: Artesans of Albia, Book 1

King's Champion: Artesans of Albia, Book 2

King's Artesan: Artesans of Albia, Book 3

Acknowledgments

With the publication of *King's Artesan*, the final book in this first *Artesans of Albia* trilogy, I would like to thank and acknowledge everyone who has had a hand in its development, evolution, birth, and progress. Apologies if I miss anyone!

First to Dave, my husband, and to Mum and Dad. Also to Jan Church for early encouragement and enthusiasm. To Barry Tighe, for giving me my first online presence and also for editing and story suggestions (and *very* funny pictures and comments!). Then to the Authonomy community, for many valuable suggestions and for voting *King's Envoy* onto the Editor's Desk, where it gained its Gold Medal Award. Next, to Gerry Dailey, once again and always, for her love, thoughtfulness, excellent suggestions, and editing. I will never forget you, dear heart. To Gordon Long, for friendship, excellent edits, and suggestions. To NTN (my brother, David Snell, and David Shepherd) for ongoing song-writing and recording help and expertise. (For song details, see below.) To Sarah Gray and the Basingstoke Discovery Centre, and also Waterstones in Basingstoke, for all their support. To my fellow Rhemalda authors, my friends and contacts on Facebook, and anyone who has interviewed me, featured me and my books on their blog, or allowed me to guest post. You all have my sincerest thanks. And finally, to everyone at Rhemalda Publishing, namely Rhett, Emmaline, Diane, Kat, and Melissa, for helping me produce and publicize these three wonderful books with fabulous covers and layout.

A huge Thank You must also go to everyone who has read and loved this first Artesans trilogy. Especially if you were kind enough to write an Amazon, Goodreads, or blog review. I hope you are all looking forward to the next trilogy: *Circle of Conspiracy*.

I would also like to remind readers about the songs that accompany my books. For *King's Envoy*, there is "The Wheel Will Turn," which features in Chapter 14. For *King's Champion*, there is "The Ballad of Tallimore," first mentioned in Chapter

19. The song associated with *King's Artesan* is "Morgan's Song (All That We Are)," a song that is featured in the book and also appears numerous times throughout the entire triple-trilogy series. These songs are available for free download from my website, www.caspeace.com. I hope you enjoy them.

King's Artesan

Artesans of Albia

Book Three

Cas Peace

Rhemalda Publishing

Stone Circle
Port Loxton
Loxton Bay
Loxton Forest
Inn
Stone Circle
Inn
Canstown
The Manor
The Downs
Tolk
Inn
Shenton
Hyecombe
N
Central Albia

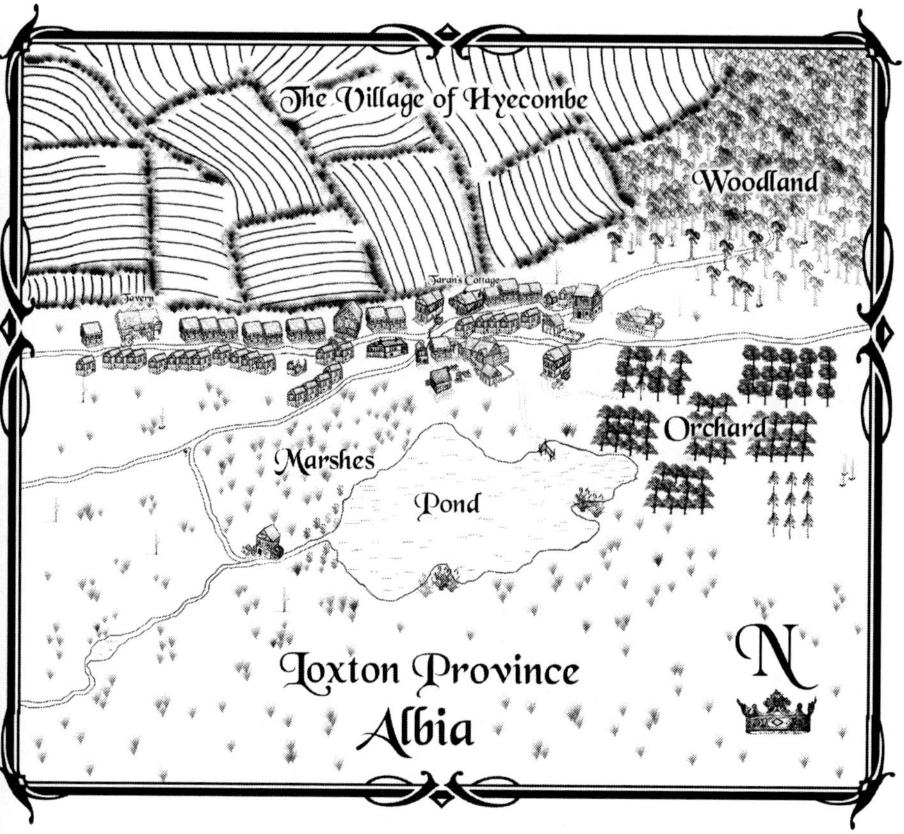
The Village of Hyecombe
Woodland
Taran's Cottage
Tavern
Orchard
Marshes
Pond
Loxton Province
Albia
N

Chapter One

The horse's jolting shook Taran's very bones, the sensation making him nauseous. He struggled to calm his heaving stomach, but it was impossible with his head bumping against the horse's shoulder. There was a gag across his mouth, so being sick could well prove fatal, and he was in enough discomfort already without choking on his own vomit.

He dangled helplessly, his hands tied tightly behind him. A peculiar buzzing invaded his brain and sapped his strength. It came from the spellsilver knife thrust through the ropes against his skin, cutting him off from his power. He hardly knew how to bear it, so he hung on and endured as best he could, trying not to groan.

There were horses all around him. Out of the corner of his eye, he saw Cal's mount. The young Apprentice was lying over its neck, similarly bound and gagged. Taran sympathized. The men who had taken them clearly knew they were Artesans, so Cal would also be suffering the effects of the spellsilver. Despite his fear at their situation, Taran couldn't suppress his guilty relief at Cal's presence.

The swordsmen talked as they rode, making crude jokes punctuated by rough laughter. The buzzing in Taran's skull prevented him from hearing clearly, and the blood rushing through his ears due to hanging upside down only added to the fog in his brain. Yet, as he listened, he gleaned enough to know that this group's commander was a man named Heron, and that they anticipated a rich reward for capturing Taran and Cal.

He tried not to guess the reason for their capture, but when he heard mention of fighting in Albia, he wondered if these men had been involved in the demon invasion. Then he cursed himself for slow thinking. Of course they had, they were Rykan's men. He knew Rykan had set up the invasion in order to get Sullyan sent to Count Marik, so it should hardly surprise him that this group had taken part. Yet knowing this brought him no nearer to understanding why he had been taken.

Serious though his predicament was, Taran couldn't help worrying about Bull and Rienne. He hadn't seen them when he was hustled off the hill, and he couldn't see them now. Was this a good thing, or a bad thing? It could mean they were still free—which seemed unlikely—or it could mean they had been killed. They might be somewhere behind him. He had no way of knowing, and speculation was futile. It probably wouldn't be long before he found out, though. Someone had targeted him and Cal, and he very much feared this meant Sullyan was dead. He had seen Rykan defeat her, and the vengeful Duke would hardly allow her to live, even if losing her powers meant she was no longer a threat. She would still be capable of wielding a blade, and Taran knew Rykan would never take the chance that she, or one of her friends, might come after him one day. Taran could only hope her death had been swift, not brutally drawn out to feed Rykan's lust.

He thrust that thought away, the lump in his throat threatening to choke him under the gag.

Taran felt the ground level out and knew they were clear of the hill. As the swordsmen set their mounts to a canter, the jolting grew worse. Taran was thrown violently about, and it was all he could do not to lose consciousness. A moan escaped him, muffled by the gag, but no one took any notice. He was in no danger of falling, tied securely to the saddle, but he was thoroughly battered and bruised by the time the horses slowed once more.

Breathing heavily around the gag, he tried to calm his spinning brain. As his horse halted the sound of voices grew, but Taran was in no state to understand the words. He only vaguely registered someone approach him, looking him over. Then a hand grasped his chin and roughly raised his head.

"Yes, this looks like the one. He fits the General's description."

The hand let go, and Taran's nose connected painfully with the horse's shoulder, making him moan. He felt someone tug at his bonds and thought they were going to release him, but they were only checking the knife. They knew what they were doing, his captors, and they knew not to let him access his powers. Sick and sore, he closed his eyes.

"Why are there two of them?"

The voice came indistinctly to Taran, as though muffled by wool. The speaker was clearly unhappy, and Taran struggled to hear the reply. He now knew that *he* was the target, not Cal. Anything he learned might help him. He strained his ears as men crowded around him.

The answer came from a gruff voice. "There were four of them on the hill, Commander. They weren't keeping watch and they didn't see us. We ignored the other two. One was an older man, the other a woman. But these two were standing together, so we couldn't take just one without alerting the other. If we had killed him, the other two would have seen. We thought bringing both was the best way. If the dark one's not wanted, we can always leave him on the battlefield. Cut his throat or stick him in the back. One more corpse won't make any difference."

Taran heard movement followed by the sound of Cal groaning. He guessed the Commander was looking Cal over now. He prayed they wouldn't kill him. He couldn't bear it if his Apprentice died just because he had been standing too close to Taran. Of all the failures in Taran's life, that would be the worst. His heart trembled as he waited for the decision.

"Bring them both." Relief flooded Taran. "If nothing else, he might be useful as leverage. What one knows, the other probably does too. But don't think you're getting double the reward. Now get on with you, Arif. Take them to the General. And once you've done that, get straight back here. I've other duties for you."

Taran's body jerked as his horse moved forward again. Nausea swamped him and he tried not to pass out. He caught a glimpse of Cal's face and thought his Apprentice was out cold. He envied Cal the oblivion, but no matter how deeply he craved unconsciousness, he knew he must stay awake. With Bull and Rienne still safe, there might be a chance of rescue.

*****

From their vantage point, Rienne and Bull watched the final, shocking move that ended Rykan's challenge. Unaware of Sullyan's desperate plan, Rienne hadn't been prepared for it. She had been terrified, devoid of hope while Sullyan lay defeated at the rebel lord's feet. She could hear Bull's labored breathing, and knew he felt the same. He had all but crushed her to his chest, but she was too distraught to feel pain. Her heart nearly burst when she saw Sullyan play her trump card. By the time Sullyan forced the Duke to yield, both Rienne and Bull were exhausted, overwhelmed by strong emotions.

As Sullyan struck off Rykan's head, Rienne sobbed with relief. She couldn't imagine how the Major was holding herself upright, let alone wielding a sword. The amount of blood she had lost worried Rienne deeply. She could almost feel Sullyan's agony and was desperate to help her. Sullyan was too far away, though, and they were not safe yet.

Closing her eyes, Rienne let herself sag. She and Bull were still locked in his feverish grip, and they clung to each other in relief. The big man's breathing still sounded constricted, but the panting was easing. They watched as the Hierarch tended to Sullyan and saw Robin kneel to gather her into his arms. Seeing her safe brought a lump into Rienne's throat.

Bull huffed out a great breath. "Thank the gods that's over!"

Rienne knew it was far from finished. Sullyan had collapsed from blood loss, shock, and exhaustion and was lucky to be alive. Rienne knew her friend would receive the best of care in the Hierarch's palace, but it was Sullyan's last despairing words that bothered Rienne.

"What did she mean, Bull, that Rykan's power was not enough?"

He shook his head. "I don't know. It looked to me like she managed to absorb his life force before she killed him, although how she did it without his consent, I've no idea. He was a Master-elite, like her, so he should have had an equal amount of power. We'll have to ask her what she meant by it not being enough."

Rienne turned pleading eyes on him. "Can we go down there now?"

He smiled back, unlacing stiff fingers from around her waist. "I think we'll be safe enough now, as long as we—" He stopped and glanced about the clearing. "Hello. Where have Cal and Taran got to?"

Rienne spun round. "They were here a moment ago." Softly, still mindful of possible danger, she called their names. There was no reply.

"That's odd." Bull sounded strained. "I'll just go and see if they're with the horses. Stay here."

He walked off into the trees to where they had tethered the horses. His startled shout brought Rienne running, her heart in her mouth.

"The horses have gone!"

She went cold. "What? Why would Cal and Taran move the horses?"

"They wouldn't." His expression frightened her. "Let me concentrate, see if I can pick them up."

She waited, wringing her hands, while he searched the substrate for any trace of their patterns. After a few moments, he shook his head.

She stared at him, tears blurring her sight. "But they can't just have vanished! They were standing right by us. Oh, Bull, I don't like this."

His tone was grim. "Neither do I. The thought that someone has been here and lured them or taken them without me knowing is frightening. And the fact that the horses are missing means they don't want to be followed."

He swore and punched a fist into the trunk of the nearest tree, making Rienne jump. "Why didn't I keep better watch? This is all my fault."

She put her arms around him. "There were four of us here, Bull. It wasn't just your responsibility."

"That's not how Sullyan will see it. Gods, I'm in for a double roasting now."

"But who can have taken them, and why? What could anyone

want with Cal and Taran? Why take them and not us? Rykan's dead, his faction has lost, so it can't be anything to do with him. Can it?"

Bull spread his hands. "I don't know. I can't answer any of that. All I know is I can't sense either of them, and that means spellsilver." He passed a shaky hand over his face. "We can't do anything about it now, not without horses. And I'm not going to put you in any more danger. I'm in enough trouble already. We need to get down to the Citadel and talk to Robin. Come on, lass, we had better start walking. Just pray that our bad luck's over and we meet up with troops of the right side first."

*****

Robin lifted the unconscious Sullyan carefully, thankful she couldn't feel her many wounds. He didn't like to look at her burned left hand. He doubted even a Master-elite could completely repair such damage. Surrounded by sounds of celebration, none of which eased his fear, he carried her toward the pavilion. There was only one thought in his mind—get her to Deshan as soon as he could.

No one paid Robin any attention. Pharikian was speaking with Sonten, giving instructions for the removal of Rykan's body and the dispersal of his forces. Anjer was beside him, and none of the other war leaders were visible. Desperate for help, Robin glanced round.

"Robin!"

It was Marik, gesturing urgently. Thankful for his support, Robin carried Sullyan to the Count's carriage.

Marik turned to Idrimar. "Take her, Idri, and give me the reins."

Idrimar frowned. Marik was in no condition to drive.

"Idri!" he barked, his sharpness making her jump. She obeyed, passing him the reins and taking Sullyan into her arms. Marik used his good hand to flick the little chestnut into a canter. Robin caught the back rail and vaulted onto the footplate. The carriage rattled back to the Citadel, the Princess casting admiring glances at Marik as they went.

Robin's heart ached. He couldn't believe how quickly his relief at Sullyan's survival and euphoria at her triumph could turn to despair. He would deliver her straight to Deshan so work on her wounds could begin, although if she was right and the power she had absorbed from Rykan was insufficient to counter the poison, all this urgency was futile.

*****

After what seemed like an age of discomfort, Taran's horse halted once more. He opened bleary eyes, unaware they had been closed. He could see only his horse's hide, for the spellsilver rendered him too weak to turn his head. Remaining limp, he strained to hear through the metal's nauseating buzz.

He heard the swordsmen dismounting and their horses being led away. There seemed to be many men, and Taran guessed that he and Cal were now in the midst of Rykan's army. The noise was muted, and this puzzled him. He knew these men had been defeated in battle, but surely the Duke's victory over Sullyan was cause for celebration? Shouldn't there be shouting and laughing? Shouldn't there at least be the sounds of men drinking, the smell of cooking? All he could hear were vague and sullen murmurs, low voices, and the tramp of feet.

He gave up. Perhaps they were too tired. Perhaps Rykan didn't believe in celebration. Taran imagined there would be much work to do. Despite what Sullyan had told him of the Codes concerning rivalry among Andaryon nobles, Taran couldn't imagine the Duke allowing his enemies to live. If he was now the new Hierarch, no one would dare task him with breaking the Codes, so perhaps his men had postponed their festivities until Rykan's takeover was complete.

"General Sonten? They're over here, my Lord."

There was movement close by, and the blurred image of two booted feet appeared before Taran's eyes. He heard the rasp of a heavy man's breath and smelled sweat. He glimpsed a cloak, black velvet trimmed with pale blue. The sight triggered a memory, but his head ached too fiercely to pursue it.

"Oh, that's good, Lieutenant, that's very good. There are two of them, you say?"

"Yes, my Lord. They were standing together, so we brought them both. The other one's over here."

The feet disappeared and Taran tried to crane his neck, but his strength had gone and his muscles wouldn't work. Then the feet reappeared.

"Two Albian bastards, eh? In it together, do you think?"

"Bound to be, my Lord."

"Hmm. Raise his head for me, I want to look in his eyes."

A hand grabbed Taran's hair, painfully forcing his head up. He tried to stifle a moan, but failed. A dark shape appeared, and he had the impression of a thick, fleshy body and a wide, leering face. Something about the face pricked Taran's brain, but the memory wouldn't surface. He screwed up his eyes against the discomfort and the buzzing as he tried to remember.

"You don't recognize me, Albian, do you?"

It was the voice rather than the face. He hadn't clearly seen the man during the duel with Jaskin, and only fleetingly at Rykan's palace with Marik. Yet that thick, imperious voice brought memories flooding back, memories of killing, pain, and death. Only then did Taran realize that this man was connected to the noble he had killed. The blood that had run to his head now drained completely away, and he stared, helpless, into Sonten's triumphant eyes.

"Ah, now you remember." The General thrust his face unpleasantly close, and Taran felt spittle as he hissed, "You took something from me, you murdering scum. You destroyed my plans and damn near cost me my life. Do you have any idea what you put me through? Any idea of the chaos you caused? Well, now you're going to pay. You're going to tell me what you did with it, and you're going to help me get it back. If you do, your death will be swift. Refuse and you won't believe how slow it will be. And in case you think that's an idle threat, just remember I also have your dark friend here. We'll see how cooperative you are when it's his screams you're hearing."

The man holding Taran's hair let go abruptly. For the second time, Taran's head fell against the horse's shoulder and agonizing pain shot up his nose. He cried out.

He vaguely heard Sonten snap, "Get the others and mount up. I want to be out of here before dark. We'll make for the forests and find a suitable spot to camp. Make sure none of Rykan's bloody rabble see you. I'm damned if I'll be responsible for their retreat now that Pharikian's annexed Kymer. Let his blasted men deal with Rykan's body! Now, where's that idiot messenger boy? Imris? *Imris!* Dammit, someone go find him. I want him to contact Heron. Well? What are you waiting for?"

Taran's horse stumbled into motion and the nightmare began again. The spellsilver sickness returned, but it was nothing compared to the sickness in Taran's heart. Torture and death awaited him now, and even if he managed to work out what his captor wanted, he doubted Cal would be spared. His Apprentice would die merely for being Taran's friend, and Taran knew he couldn't bear it.

*****

It was much later in the afternoon when the Major finally woke. Mercifully, she had remained unconscious while Deshan worked on the shattered bones of her wrist. He had done what he could, although the injury would need further attention. The damaged flesh needed time to settle before the more delicate work could begin. He had strapped the arm as firmly as he could without restricting her circulation.

The burned flesh of her hand had been cleaned, salved, and wrapped, and needed no further treatment for the moment. The wound in her side was long and deep, and had bled freely. It too had been cleaned and stitched, and would be sore and inflexible for days. Her other injuries were relatively minor, and all were now bandaged and clean. Her most serious problem was blood loss, and both Pharikian and Robin had donated some of theirs, while Deshan monitored Sullyan carefully for signs of adverse reaction to unfamiliar blood. The giving of blood was still an uncertain process, both here and in Albia. Physicians still didn't fully understand why some patients worsened and died when given someone else's blood. Fortunately, Sullyan showed no such symptoms and now lay conscious, although exhausted, against the pillows of the huge bed. Robin sat by her side, holding her undamaged hand, while Deshan and Pharikian looked on.

Noting the dullness of her eyes, the Captain felt deeply concerned. She really should be sleeping, but he and Pharikian had questions, and she was aware of their confusion. She could not rest while that confusion remained.

Robin squeezed her hand gently. "I don't pretend to understand much of what happened today, love. Can you explain it to me?"

She gave a weak smile. "I will do my best. What do you want to know?"

He tried to remember what had occurred in the arena. So much had happened so quickly that he found it hard to order his thoughts.

"Why did you agree to the spellsilver? When we left that drovers' hut, you couldn't possibly have known any of this would happen. Yet you made us bring it, and you had obviously told his Majesty about it before we left the Citadel today."

Too weary to hold her smile, Sullyan took a painful breath. "It was a gamble, my love. You are right, I had no foreknowledge that the spellsilver would play a part in Rykan's defeat. But as I had managed to breach its effects once already, it would have been foolish not to bring it. Do you remember what I said last night on the Tower? That I was trying to remember something? Well, when Timar said 'a gift freely given,' I suddenly knew what a potent weapon against Rykan the silver could be. One he would be powerless against even if he managed to win the duel. I realized how I could make use of it, for I suspected he might propose a condition stipulating that I wear it.

"My only worry was that his second would sense that the collar was Rykan's. Thankfully, he did not. I knew Rykan would not handle it himself, and as he had no idea I had managed to breach it while in his dungeon, it would give me an edge against him. Perhaps the only means I would have of saving my own life should he defeat me."

Her bloodshot gaze turned to the Hierarch. "You knew, of course, that I had no intention of abiding by the terms of the contract. Had I not been able to overpower Rykan's mind, I would have cast us both into the Void. The only thing that saved my honor was Rykan's failure to force me to acknowledge defeat before he took hold of the collar. I have Marik to thank for that, for distracting Rykan at the crucial moment."

Pharikian inclined his head, his lack of reaction telling Robin that he had known of her willingness to sacrifice herself in order to deny Rykan his victory.

Robin, though, was still confused. "So why did you insist on the Firefield? What good did that do you?"

The ghost of a smile crossed Sullyan's face. "As Rykan did not trust me, my love, so I did not trust him. But I was more concerned about his supporters, many of whom would not have scrupled to shoot me once they realized their lord was defeated. The Firefield guaranteed we would not be disturbed, whatever the outcome of the duel. It left me free to concentrate on absorbing Rykan's life force. I also gambled on being able to sense it during the duel, even through the spellsilver, and to use this against Rykan. Fortunately, that one paid off too."

Robin gave her a grim look. "It seems to me the whole affair was one huge gamble."

Again, she smiled. "Oh, my love! Of course it was. I thought you understood that."

Pharikian stirred. "It was a gamble that paid off handsomely. Every man, woman, and child in my realm is in your debt, Brynne. We could never—*I* could never—repay you, or thank you enough."

Her voice was a whisper. "Gratitude is neither necessary nor appropriate. It is I who should thank you, for allowing me my vengeance."

He moved closer, his expression sorrowful. "But has that vengeance gained you redress, child? From what you said on the field, I fear it has not."

Robin felt the blood leave his face as Sullyan closed her eyes. He knew she didn't want to think about this just yet, but her suspicion that the power she had stolen from Rykan was insufficient to save her life was tearing Robin apart. It would be the ultimate irony should Rykan triumph by default.

Her eyes opened and she gazed at the Hierarch. "I do not understand it, Timar. I took every last shred of his life force, every particle of his power. That he was a Master-elite is evident, and I can feel the skill and the strength. But the core of his power is missing, as if he had given fully half of it away. This puzzles me, because he was so sure of himself while gloating over me at the palace. How did he think he would overcome my skills, let alone defeat you, while laboring under such a disadvantage? I can think of no reason why his strength should be depleted, but I wish I had known it before. I need not have been so circumspect with my own metaforce on the field of battle."

No one had a viable theory, and Robin could see exhaustion overcoming her. He caught Pharikian's eye. Taking the hint, the Hierarch tried to convince her to rest.

"Not yet. I must return the donated life force," she said. "Please understand. Hosting Rykan's power is taxing what strength I have left. I cannot risk the poison overwhelming me before the life force is returned." She gazed up at the Hierarch. "I cannot rest until this is done."

The Hierarch immediately sent for those who had shared their life force. When they had gathered, Sullyan returned the borrowed power as gently as she had taken it. As she did so, Robin sensed an increasing lightness in her soul. Once it was over and the participants had left, he thought she would surely sleep. Yet there was one more task she was desperate to perform, and when she told him, the Hierarch studied her with grave concern.

"This is really not a good idea, Brynne."

Robin agreed. Sullyan shifted restlessly, impatient with their concern.

"I have no choice, Timar," she rasped, her urgency plain. "I *cannot* wait, much as I might wish to. I am too weak now to fight the poison. There is only one part of me left, one tiny, intimate part, still free of infection. If I do not attempt the purging now, if I leave it and try to grow stronger, I fear that this final part will be overwhelmed. If that happens, then I am truly damned. I have no strength to protect myself, and if I slept, not even you could guard that precious portion of my soul. But if you and Robin lend me strength, and Deshan guides me, I can use Rykan's power to cleanse as much of the poison as I can. The mystery of his missing strength will have to wait. Let us make an end, Timar. Please, I beg of you. I need to do this now."

Despite the warning in Deshan's eyes, and the terror of losing her in Robin's, Pharikian could not refuse. He nodded, and she sighed in relief.

The four of them linked psyches, with Pharikian as the driving force, sparing Sullyan any expenditure of power save what she needed for the cleansing. Deshan stood ready to help direct the flow of metaforce to where it would do most good. The Hierarch effortlessly drew Robin's offered strength into his control, and the Captain sensed his surprise at the younger man's potential capacity. He pushed away a brief flash of pride and gave himself fully to Sullyan's needs.

Gathering herself with an effort, Sullyan began the process. It was slow and painful, as the poison had to be physically burned out of her. Had it not been for Pharikian's skill and the support of both his and Robin's powerful life force, she could not have survived. Deshan showed her the vital areas, guiding her to the places that had to be cleansed if she were to live. For Robin, seeing each terrible black mass of poison wither and die before the onslaught of Rykan's power was immensely gratifying. Through their link, he felt Sullyan welcome even the sharp pain of it, for it was a cleansing pain, a healing pain, and what remained, although empty and raw, would eventually refill with her personal essence.

After a very long time, during which Pharikian had to bring her back from the brink of unconsciousness more than once and the sound of her agonized gasps caused Robin to break down in tears, Rykan's power finally gave out. The poison was burned away, the fibers of Sullyan's being cauterized, leaving her naked and hurting inside. The infection's inexorable creep had ceased, and her soul no longer felt the weight of imminent death. Only a small area of contamination remained, rooted in the deepest, most inaccessible regions of her soul. It was so strongly bonded to her essence that it would likely prove fatal to remove it, even with the full complement of Rykan's power. And that, as Robin knew, she did not have.

Physically and mentally drained, Robin and the two Andaryans held on to each other for support. Robin stared down at the fragile figure in the bed, oblivious now, sunk so far down after her last super human effort that even Pharikian was forced to let go. Wonderingly, he shook his head, unable to believe that so frail a frame had contained such vast, determined energies.

Her expression was serene, even though her face still bore traces of tears. Her last cry reverberated in Robin's ears. He had felt her triumph at beating Rykan's brutal legacy, much more intense even than her satisfaction at striking off his head. She might not be completely clean of him, but at least she was no longer in immediate danger of death.

All three men were shaking with exhaustion, but full of quiet admiration for what they had achieved. Pharikian passed a hand across his brow. "Oh, her father would have been so proud of her. If only he could have found the will to live. She would have been his strength, and what an invincible team they would have made."

Deshan gave a harsh laugh. "You wouldn't have stood a chance, Timar. No one would."

Robin saw Pharikian's wry answering smile as if through fog. Suddenly, his legs refused to hold him upright and he collapsed. Barely catching him, Pharikian eased him down onto the bed. Robin shuddered violently, and the Hierarch sat beside him, holding him while great, wracking sobs forced their way through his throat. It took some time, but eventually he grew calm.

The Hierarch gazed at him kindly. "Well done, son. You've been through a lot today, more than most considering how deeply you love her. You have helped her win her life back, at least for the time being, and you deserve your rest. No," he said, holding up a hand when Robin tried to protest, "you've done more than enough. There are others quite capable of taking care of things now. Get yourself into that bed and sleep." Grinning at Robin's expression, he added, "It's no use arguing with me, boy. You're not Master yet, and I could render you senseless with a thought, if I chose."

Robin smiled weakly, finally feeling at ease with this most powerful man. "I don't believe you, sir. I don't believe you have the strength to snuff a candle right now."

The Hierarch chuckled. "Enough of your insolence! But even if you're right, Deshan here makes a mean sleeping draft. Now, bed."

Wisely, Robin chose not to argue. He needed neither sleeping draft nor Pharikian's assistance to fall almost instantly into a deep, healing sleep.

Chapter Two

Slowly and gently, savoring every moment, Sullyan returned to wakefulness, feeling very nearly clean again and so thankful to be alive. Eyes still closed, she indulged in the luxury of spreading her senses throughout her body, delighting in the purity of places so recently occupied by infection. Yes, she hurt, felt ragged and empty, but her natural essence would reassert itself once the hurt had healed.

Instinctively, she avoided the one area of her soul where infection lingered, not wishing to be reminded that, despite her triumph, Rykan's legacy still meant that she couldn't cross the Veils, couldn't return home. She remained trapped in Andaryon, in an alien environment, and from this she would still die too early. She did not want to think of that. For now, she would just glory in being herself.

Too languid to open her eyes, she shifted her senses outward, exploring her other hurts. Every muscle ached, every tendon protested after her exhausting fight with Rykan. This was a small price to pay for victory, and one she was used to. The long slash in her side was troublesome. The stitches would pull, she knew, so she spent a few minutes in healing. She was a little surprised to find that the wound was already half-healed, and guessed Deshan must have helped it along.

Then she steeled herself to examine her wrist and hand, fearing to probe too deeply in case the damage was beyond repair. She could see where Deshan had worked on the small, shattered bones, bonding them together so no splinters remained. The wrist was swollen and extremely painful, but she could see that, given time, the bones would knit and the wrist would work again, possibly as well as before. She expended a little energy to reinforce Deshan's work, and the fierce pain subsided to a dull throb.

Her hand was another matter. The inner surfaces of the palm and fingers had escaped with minor burns, for she had reflexively balled her fist when Rykan trapped her in the fire. The back of her hand, though, had burned to the bone, and was a sorry mess. Although clear of infection, the area was raw and weeping and would take days, if not weeks, of Artesan healing before it was useable. It would never be the same. But then, she reflected, she wasn't the same since Rykan's abuse, so she could accept that. She did what she could for the moment to speed healing, then allowed her senses to roam the familiar room.

She had yet to open her eyes or move, so the person she could sense sitting beside her bed had no idea she was awake. Sullyan smiled to herself before opening her eyes, and had to swallow round a dry throat to speak.

"Rienne?"

The healer was lost in a reverie of some kind. Sullyan's voice, soft though it was, startled her. "Brynne!" she exclaimed, raising clouded eyes. "Oh, it's good to see you awake. How are you feeling?"

A tiny frown creased Sullyan's brows. There was deep unhappiness in her healer friend. She studied Rienne's face, seeing the anxious eyes, the capable hands clutched in her lap. Rienne was pale, there were dark rings under her eyes, and her long, dark hair had not been braided with the usual neatness, but then she had spent days out in the cold, with minimal rations and worry to contend with. It was not so surprising.

"Apart from the obvious, I am well. I am very pleased to see you, too."

Rienne unconsciously twisted her hands. "I hope you're not still angry with us. Bull told us what you said to him, but we just had to come. We were all so worried about you and we couldn't just sit around doing nothing while you risked your life against Rykan."

Sullyan watched her carefully. She could sense quite clearly that Rienne was attempting to hide something. "I am not angry with you, Rienne, not now. But you took a huge risk in coming here, and Bulldog went against my express command in bringing you. He should have known better, and he knows what to expect for disobedience. Where is he, by the way? And Robin?"

The high color that flushed Rienne's face and the way she cast down her eyes told Sullyan something was very wrong. "What is it, Rienne?"

The healer turned her head away, hands still twisting nervously.

"Rienne!" snapped Sullyan, fear making her sharp. The healer's head jerked back and Sullyan saw tears glittering in her eyes.

"The Hierarch made me promise not to tell you," she said, "not before he had seen you. But I knew I couldn't keep it from you. I told him you would sense it."

"Sense what? Tell me before I grow angry. What has happened?"

"It's Cal and Taran. They've disappeared. It happened while we were watching you fight Rykan. They were standing right next to us—well, almost—but Bull and I were so intent on you, we didn't see a thing. Bull couldn't even sense them, and there was nothing more we could do. Even the horses were gone. Bull and I came here, and he told Robin about it, and the two of them went looking for Cal and Taran and … and now Bull and Robin have vanished as well!"

Sullyan stared at Rienne in silence for a moment, then said darkly, "Give me the details."

Gathering herself with an effort, Rienne told Sullyan exactly what had happened on the hill. "After that," she said, "we gathered our things and began walking toward the Citadel. We didn't try to hide. It was getting dark and we wanted to be found by the Hierarch's men as quickly as possible. So we made for the high road and eventually ran into one of the patrols overseeing the dispersal of Rykan's forces. They were very suspicious at first, but our lack of weapons and horses and Bulldog's obvious knowledge of you and Robin convinced them. They escorted us into the Citadel where we were eventually summoned before the Hierarch.

"As soon as he heard the news, he sent for Robin. He told us Robin was exhausted after helping you burn out Rykan's poison, and when we saw him we felt terrible. He looked so drawn and tired. He was very glad to see us, but when Bull told him what had happened to Cal and Taran, he was all for leaving right away. He got quite angry, but the Hierarch made him wait until we had washed and eaten something. I think he was worried that Robin's exhaustion would affect his reasoning. He made sure Robin ate something too, and then he had Bull tell the story again. Afterward, he and Robin did a search for Cal and Taran, but they came to the same conclusion as Bull, that spellsilver was involved or … worse."

She took a shaky breath. "After that there was no stopping Robin. The only concession he made to the Hierarch was to take some extra men with him, but he and Bull left that same evening. Bull did come and see you first, but you were still asleep. Robin promised to report to the Lord General, Anjer, is it?" Sullyan nodded, her eyes distant. "But no one had heard anything from them by the middle of the next morning. That's when Pharikian discovered that he couldn't contact Bull or Robin either. And now … oh, gods, Brynne, I'm so frightened for them!"

Sullyan was about to murmur soothing words when something Rienne had said made her frown. Cold fear gripped her stomach. "Rienne, you said, 'by the next morning.' How long ago did they leave?"

The healer ducked her head. "The evening of the duel. It's now the third day since you killed Rykan."

Sullyan gaped at her. "Over two days ago? And they failed to report from the start?" She swore, startling the distressed healer. "Let me concentrate," she snapped, her pupils dilating as she flung out her senses to try to locate a familiar psyche.

Rienne sat unmoving, staring at her hands in her lap. At Sullyan's exasperated sigh, she jumped, fresh tears appearing in her eyes. The Major spared her some sympathy. She could see how wretched the healer felt. She had been under strict orders not to do what she had just done, but she had known she couldn't hide the news from Sullyan. They were too close, too attuned, for secrets, especially such emotive ones. Despite her current condition, Sullyan tried to convey an aura of competence, of comfort and capability, knowing Rienne badly needed them right now.

"Bull was right," she said, awkwardly pushing herself up in the bed and flinging back the covers. "I cannot contact any of them, and that can only mean one thing."

Rienne's eyes went wide. "They're not … dead, are they?"

Sullyan caught her breath. "Of course not! Did Timar not reassure you? You have not been sitting here all this time thinking they could be dead?"

"Well, I tried not to, but I couldn't get it out of my mind. No one mentioned the possibility, but I just thought they were being kind."

Sullyan snorted. "Kind? It was not kind to leave you worrying. Timar should have told you. No, Rienne, they are alive. If they had died there would be blankness, but I can faintly sense each psyche. Spellsilver blocks all contact, but it does not, thankfully, hide the pattern completely. It does mean, though, that I cannot use their patterns to track them. I am puzzled as to why someone would abduct Cal and Taran, but I assume Bulldog and Robin managed to find them. It appears they were careless enough to get caught too, but if they could track them, so can I." She slid carefully out of the bed and looked pointedly at the healer. "You will have to help me, Rienne. I cannot dress one-handed."

"What on earth are you doing? You've lost a lot of blood and you've been badly wounded. You can't possibly go after them yourself. You're not nearly fit enough!"

"Of course I can. Who else is there? Has Timar sent someone after them?"

"I don't know." Unhappily, Rienne eyed the dressings on Sullyan's thin body and the strapping on her arm. "I think he mentioned getting the patrols to look out for them. He's bound to come and check on you soon. Why don't you wait and ask him?"

"He will have other things on his mind right now." Sullyan's fear made her short-tempered. "Now, will you help me or must I call a page?"

Swiftly but reluctantly, the healer brushed and braided Sullyan's tawny hair. The Major indicated her combat leathers, neatly laid out on a chest along one wall. "What about your arm?" asked Rienne as she brought the clothes over.

"Bind it to my waist. Then I can still get my shirt on and it will be protected when I ride. Who guards my door?"

"It's one of the Hierarch's pages, a boy who reminds me a bit of Tad at the Manor. Apparently the leader of your group of pirates gave him the duty so they could all go and join the celebrations."

Rienne sounded disapproving, and Sullyan surmised she had heard about Vanyr's actions prior to the duel. She smiled despite her fear for her friends. Vanyr was no threat to her now, so Kyshan must have arranged for the boy to guard her suite as a joke, knowing it would irritate the Commander.

"His name is Norkis. Would you ask him to come in?"

The lad entered the room at Rienne's request, hurriedly averting his eyes from Sullyan's half-dressed state.

"Norkis, I want you to run down to the horse lines and tell the horse master to saddle Drum."

The lad cocked his head. "I was told to report back if you woke, Lady Brynne. I will go to the horse master, but I really ought to tell his Majesty as well."

She grinned at him. "Very well. But you don't have to hurry over the task, do you?"

Norkis scampered off, thoroughly understanding. Rienne finished strapping Sullyan's arm around her body and then helped the Major into her shirt, leathers, and boots. "I'm still not happy about this, Brynne. You're nowhere near fit. The Hierarch will be so angry with you. And with me."

Hearing her unhappiness, Sullyan captured her gaze. "We may be guests in his palace, but we are not his subjects. And I am not about to abandon my friends to whatever has befallen them." Her expression softened on seeing Rienne's distress. "Ah, do not worry so. I will not go courting danger. I do know I am not fully fit. I give you my word that if I need help, I will summon it. If it will make you feel better, give me half an hour and then find Timar. Tell him what I am doing, if Norkis has not already done so. Assure him I will keep in contact. And if you need something to take your mind off waiting, then you could offer your services to Deshan. He is over-occupied at the moment, and the two of you could learn much from each other.

"Now, pass me my sword belt."

Sullyan left the suite, a small pack slung over her shoulder. Stiffly, she strode through the corridors and out into the courtyard, noting with a wry grimace that the weather had turned. It was drizzling, the kind of persistent rain that got into all the warm, dry places under your clothes and soaked you to the skin.

With her good hand, she pulled up the hood of her cloak. At least it disguised who she was. The last thing she wanted was to be accosted before she reached the horse lines.

It was not her lucky day.

The barracks were deserted, but just when she thought she had escaped unnoticed, a lithe figure stepped out of a doorway in front of her and turned her way. Recognizing her immediately, Vanyr widened his eyes with surprise. Sullyan swore under her breath, annoyed that she might be delayed, especially by him. She was in no mood to play Vanyr's games right now.

"Major," he said in his clipped voice, "I didn't think we would see you around for a while yet. Where are you going?"

"About my own business, Commander."

She attempted to pass him by, but he planted himself in front of her. She glowered at him. "I have no time for your games, Commander Vanyr. If you delay me now, you will regret it. I know you bear me no love—although I thought we had made our peace before the duel—but if you bear me any respect at all you will stand aside."

Strangely, Vanyr seemed hurt by her words. "Respect?" he repeated. He looked puzzled, but there was no trace of hostility in his eyes. He made to step aside, but then changed his mind, his demeanor resolute. "No," he muttered, "I will say it."

Sullyan watched him impatiently.

"Major Sullyan, I will admit that I know little of love, but let me tell you that I bear you so much more than respect. Never before in my life or career have I seen such a consummate display of courage, skill, and strategy as you showed against Rykan. He was reputedly the finest swordsman in the realm, and I know of no one else—including myself—who could have stood against him as you did, especially considering what he had done to you. I offer you my heartfelt congratulations on your victory, and my sincerest apologies for acting against you. I allowed prejudice to rule me, and I am not proud of what I did.

"I am sorry to have delayed you. I've said what I wanted to say, so I'll detain you no longer." Abruptly, he turned away, his face flushing with embarrassment.

Sullyan's temper melted at his astonishing speech. Lowering her eyes, she sighed and passed a weary hand across her face. When she had regained her composure, her lips bore a faint smile. She called to him softly.

"Commander Vanyr?"

He turned reluctantly. She gazed up at him, seeing wariness in his eyes. "Commander, I beg your pardon for my harshness. Your gracious speech has touched me, and I thank you for the sentiments behind it. I wonder, would it please you if we forgot the history between us and began our acquaintance anew?"

He hesitated only a moment before inclining his head. His lips even formed a small smile, which considerably lightened a face rendered severe by his strange white eyes. "That sounds like a very civilized idea, Major."

She stepped toward him and, holding out her right hand, said, "Commander Vanyr, I am very pleased to meet you. I am Major Brynne Sullyan, and I am at your service."

Vanyr took her offered hand, but instead of shaking it as she had expected, he raised it and brushed it with his lips. She flushed.

"I am very pleased to make your acquaintance, Brynne Sullyan. My name is Torman, and if I can ever be of assistance to you, please don't hesitate to ask."

He released her hand and studied her, noting the pack on her shoulder. "Were you going to enquire after the captain and your other friends?"

She glanced up sharply. "Do you know who accompanied Robin when he left?"

"It was the big Albian who came with the healer, and two of Ky-shan's men. I couldn't spare anyone, and only two of Ky-shan's were sober. One was Xeer, the man who rescued Count Marik. The other I didn't know. Ky-shan could tell you, but he's probably still comatose."

Sullyan nodded her thanks and began to walk on, but he laid a hand on her arm. "Brynne, you can't possibly go after them. You're in no fit state."

She grimaced. "I cannot contact them. Would you have me sit idly here? What would you do if they were your men?"

He pursed his lips and opened his mouth, but made no reply.

"Yes," she said, "I thought as much. Not only are two of those who are missing under my command, but all of them are also my friends. I intend to ride out to the hill where they were last seen to see if I can pick up any clues as to who took them, and why. After that, we shall see. But if no one else can be spared to search for them, then yes, I will go myself." Turning, she walked on.

He kept pace with her. "Then I'm going with you. I'm surprised you can even walk with those wounds, let alone think of riding, and if I allowed anything to happen to you, the Hierarch would have my eyes. I'm already on a warning, so don't try to refuse me."

She gave him a sideways look. "I would not dream of it, Torman. I welcome your company. How good are your tracking skills?"

On reaching the horse lines, she found that Norkis had run his errand well. Drum was ready and waiting for her. He whickered when he saw her and stamped a hoof. Vanyr's horse was also there, kept in readiness whenever he was on duty. He turned to Sullyan, clearly intending to assist her into the saddle, but she mounted Drum before he had time to move, although she felt the pull of her stitches. She held the reins one-handed, and her sword was at her back as usual.

Vanyr regarded her, his expression wry. "You don't much like being helped, do you?"

She grinned, wheeling Drum away. "Maybe not, but I am not so stubborn as to refuse it when I really need it."

Touching Drum with her heels, she sent him clattering down the road to the south gate, Vanyr's mount in close pursuit.

It took them only a short time to reach the crest of the hill where she knew her four friends had camped. They passed two patrols on the way and stopped so both commanders could report to Vanyr, but neither had news. As they crested the brow of the hill, the rain still falling, Sullyan held up a hand for silence. Vanyr watched as she cast out her senses.

Immediately, she picked up an echo of her friends' psyches in the substrate and could even tell where Cal and Taran had been standing when they were taken. She also found Robin's pattern from when he had come up here to track them. She and Vanyr walked the horses over to where the four men had taken hold of Cal and Taran, and Vanyr dismounted to examine the ground.

Leaning over Drum's shoulder, eyes intent on the wet earth, Sullyan said, "Torman, do you ever mark your horses' shoes?"

"Those of officers, yes," he replied. "Two nicks on the off-hind."

"We use two on the near-fore and one on the off-hind," she said, continuing to quarter the ground.

Vanyr pointed. "I think this might be the Captain's horse."

Reining Drum over, Sullyan nodded. "Yes, those are Torka's tracks. He has one odd shaped hoof. The near-hind, do you see?"

Vanyr nodded and moved farther away to track where Robin had gone. Sullyan used the substrate, and Vanyr verified the direction when he returned.

"So they went southeast, toward the Haligan Forest," she mused. "Have they gone to meet up with some of Rykan's men, do you think?"

Vanyr shrugged. "Depends what they were wanted for. Don't you have any idea?"

"Not at present."

He remounted, and she eyed him pointedly. "I have to follow them."

"Yes," he said, "I thought you might. I'm coming with you." She tried to protest, but he cut her short. "It won't do you any good, so don't waste your breath. I'm due some leave now, and Barrin, my lieutenant, is a very capable man. I'll let Anjer know what I'm doing, and hopefully this time he'll approve."

The tone of his voice made her wonder if there was yet more

bad blood between him and the Lord General, but she didn't pursue it. Activity by the south gate had caught her attention, and grimly she watched the small band of horsemen galloping toward the hill.

"I can guess who sent them," she muttered.

Vanyr narrowed his eyes, unable to make them out at such distance.

"It will be Ky-shan," she sighed. "Rienne will have told Timar what I am doing, and he will have set my watchdogs on me." Noting the way Vanyr eyed the approaching pirates, she added, "I cannot refuse them, Torman. We have been through much together these past few weeks. There are debts on both sides."

"Don't worry," he said, his eyes never leaving the riders. "We understand each other well enough. I got what I deserved, and besides, I would probably do the same myself now."

She regarded him in astonishment and he grinned at her. She rather liked this easier aspect of him and found herself wishing they could have foregone their earlier mistrust and hostility.

"I know," he said ruefully, the fact that he had picked up her thoughts amazing her yet again. "The fault was mine and I behaved very badly. But that's behind us now. We've started afresh, yes?"

She cocked her head. "Are you sure you are only a Journeyman?"

He flushed with pleasure.

They waited under the sparse tree cover until the pirates arrived. Ky-shan, Ki-en, and Jay'el were there, as were the twin giants and five others of the band. They all looked a little worse for drink. Sullyan shook her head, but she greeted them warmly and raised her brows at the supply packs they carried.

Ky-shan saw the look. "The Hierarch's orders, Lady. We've been packed since yesterday. We wanted to go after the Skipper ourselves, but we were waiting for you. We knew you could track him better than anyone." He turned, pointing at Vanyr. "What in the Void's name is he doing here?"

"Torman has kindly offered to help search, and I have accepted his aid. I trust that meets with your approval?"

It did not, but Ky-shan didn't argue. He simply ignored Vanyr.

"Ky, who else went out with Xeer, Robin, and Bull?"

"As-ket," he replied.

She sighed with frustration. As-ket was no Artesan. "In that case, we shall just have to rely on our own eyes once the psyche trail runs out. Gentlemen, Torman and I have established they were heading toward Haligan Forest, and as they have a two-day lead on us, may I suggest we ride?"

With Drum and Vanyr's liver chestnut in the lead, they descended the hill at a gallop, Sullyan following Robin's trail in the substrate.

Chapter Three

All morning they rode hard, first across the rain-soaked Citadel Plains and then under the boughs of Haligan Forest. The trees in the forest grew dense and few trails wound between their tightly-packed trunks. This made tracking easier, and Sullyan followed Robin's pattern in the substrate while Vanyr used his eyes on the ground. Early on, he managed to find the prints of Taran's horse in a patch of muddy earth, confirming Sullyan's suspicion that all four of her friends had headed in the same direction.

She found herself wondering when they would come across the place where Taran's captors had ambushed Robin and Bull. It could not be far because they had failed to report to Anjer that first evening, and she knew they would not have ridden through the night. Robin would still have been exhausted, and he knew better than to push himself too hard. At least, she hoped he did. Maybe that was why he and Bull had failed to spot the danger, although Bull should have had more sense than to allow Robin to act so rashly. But then, she thought, Bull had disobeyed her express orders in bringing their friends through the Veils, and despite the tongue-lashing she had given him the night before the duel, she was still furious over that breach. Even more so now, for had he not disobeyed her they would not be in this predicament, and she would not be overstretching herself to find them.

Angrily, she shook her head, forcing down the fear surging through her heart.

Around midday she called a brief halt. She was surprised to find she was fitter than she had thought. She was only expending power to reduce the awful throbbing of her wrist and the sting of the sword slash in her side. The muscles that had ached earlier that morning seemed resigned to yet more activity and were not complaining. The stitches in her flank, though, were nagging, and she concentrated more power than was prudent on healing. She needed to be rid of them, although she could not imagine who among this rough band of men she could ask to perform that small favor.

When they resumed the search, she held them to a steadier pace, sure they were not far from where Robin and Bull had run into trouble. She and Vanyr took the lead again and rode well apart, she following Robin's pattern and he the prints of Taran's horse. After an hour or so they found a small clearing where Robin, Bull, Xeer, and As-ket had made their first night's camp.

With a surge of anger, she saw that Xeer and As-ket were still there. Calling to Ky-shan, she dismounted, letting Drum's reins drop. She moved to where the two bodies lay and kneeled beside the nearest, feeling a pang of grief as she gazed down at Xeer's lifeless face. Judging by their terrible wounds, he and As-ket had put up a valiant fight. As-ket lay several yards away, his body punctured by crossbow bolts. Xeer was covered in sword cuts, his throat gaping in a gory grin.

Ky-shan stopped beside her and stared silently down at his friend's immobile face. "I am so sorry, Ky," she murmured, reaching out to touch Xeer's cold hand. "Marik will be sorry, too. He thought much of Xeer for rescuing him."

The pirate's eyes glittered coldly as he turned back to his horse. "They did their duty."

Vanyr nudged his mount closer. "Is this where the psyche trail ends?"

Her pupils dilated as she checked the substrate. "Yes. They used spellsilver again. But Robin and Bull are both experienced men. Maybe they left me a clue …."

She quartered the campsite, studying what she could sense of the fight. It had happened swiftly, with Bull and Robin targeted instantly as hostages. They hadn't stood a chance. Xeer and As-ket had sold their lives dearly but uselessly. There were no other bodies to indicate who was responsible.

Vanyr dismounted, and together they sought tracks leading away from the campsite. The Commander found Torka's distinctive spoor immediately, still heading southeast. Sullyan swung up onto Drum again, stifling a gasp as her arm protested. This earned her a glance of concern from Vanyr, which she ignored. They had to travel slower now, as she could not track by psyche and the light was poor under the close-growing trees. At least the rain had let up, although the sky was still dark and the air much cooler.

They pushed on until it was too dark to see the tracks. Sullyan wanted to continue on foot with torches, but Vanyr overruled her. Unexpectedly, Ky-shan backed him up.

"You've gone white, Lady," he said. "You need to rest. If we stop now, we'll make better time in the morning. It'll do us no good if we miss their tracks in the dark."

"Who appointed you my nursemaid?" she grumbled, but she allowed Ki-en to see to Drum and accepted the mug of fellan Ky-shan gave her once the fire was lit. There was a generous measure of brine rum in it, and she shot him a hard glance.

He stared unrepentantly back. "You need the strength."

She decided not to refuse. Once seated by the fire, she realized how terribly weary she was. Two solid days of sleep, which either Deshan or Pharikian must have had a hand in, had gone a long way toward restoring her strength, but she was battling weeks of illness, strain, and worry, not to mention the subtler effects of taking and using Rykan's life force.

As she sat, silently cradling her cup, she became aware of Vanyr's eyes upon her. Because he lacked the definition of colored irises, it wasn't always easy to tell where the focus of his attention lay. Raising her face, she invited him to speak. He looked away immediately and she sighed.

"Speak, Torman, if you will. We are friends now."

He gazed resolutely into the fire. "Are we?"

She frowned, wishing he would stop playing games. "Are we not, then?"

He looked up and she realized he was harboring some doubt, some anxiety, over their relationship. She cocked her head in query.

"Will you answer me a question?" he asked.

She nodded, adding, "If you will do the same."

"Very well." He took a breath. "Why didn't you see Rykan's last move in the duel? We practiced it so much I thought you surely must see it. And yet, he caught you with it."

She glanced down, aware that he had a more important question than this. He was stalling, yet she chose to answer anyway.

"I did see it. You taught me well."

"You did? Then why …?" His expression changed to incredulity. "You never deliberately let him knock you down? That would have been a terrible risk!"

She sighed. "I know. It was not something I wished or planned to do, let me assure you. He was just too strong. He was fitter than I, taller, healthier, and faster. He was just too damned *good*!"

He stared at her. "So you took a gamble."

"What else could I do? What would you have done?"

He considered this. "I would never have had the skill to make use of him like that."

She snorted. "I think you belittle your own talents, man. But I had it in my mind before we began that I might need to do something desperate if I could not defeat him outright."

"Desperate is right! He could have killed you out of hand."

"No. I knew he would not do that. He coveted my powers too badly to kill me. And in that lay my second plan, the most desperate plan. The one I intended to use should he force me to yield."

"Which was?"

"To cast us both into the Void."

Understanding caused his face to turn pale. "I'm not sure I could have found the courage to do that."

She shrugged. "If you had been his captive for two weeks and suffered what I did, courage would have come, believe me. It would have been my only choice. As it was, Count Marik's timely distraction made Rykan forget the vital declaration of surrender, leaving me free to legitimately use my power."

Vanyr mulled over what he had heard. Then he raised his head again. "You have answered my question. What would you ask of me?"

Now it was her turn to look away. She hadn't planned to ask him this at all, let alone in company. Their easier relationship could be all too quickly spoiled if he took it the wrong way. She chose her words carefully, studying her hands as she did so.

"After your invaluable coaching before the duel, I thought we had made some sort of peace. I was a little surprised not to see you among the Artesans in Pharikian's chambers that morning. For the sharing of life force."

She let the small silence continue before glancing at him. He was staring at her oddly. Then he said, "I was told my contribution would not be required."

She frowned. She had hit an open wound. This was the matter behind his discomfort. "Who told you that?"

"Anjer."

"Anjer told you? What reason did he give?"

Vanyr's eyes were cold. "He said you didn't want anyone to contribute who was not completely willing."

"And were you willing?"

His head jerked up. "Of course I was! Like you said, I thought we had made our peace and put the enmity aside. Then you told him you didn't want me involved. Why did you do that?"

She spoke firmly, holding his gaze. "I did no such thing." Here was the reason for his doubt, she thought. She was surprised he had befriended her at all with this hanging over them. "I did ask his Majesty to make sure everyone involved was willing, but I did not ask Anjer to preclude anyone who wanted to participate. When will that man stop trying to protect me?"

Vanyr stared at her, clearly unsure what to believe.

"I would never have refused you, Torman," she said, her tone reflecting her sincerity. "I regret that you received that impression."

He averted his gaze and shook his head. "Maybe I just convinced myself Anjer was blaming you. Maybe it was all part of his punishment for what I did to you that day." He stared into the fire, his face flushed. "I deeply regret that now."

She waved it away. "I have forgotten it, it is not important." A mischievous thought occurred to her and she eyed him. "Although … there is a way you could atone for it, should you feel the need."

He looked at her sidelong. "Oh? And what would that be?"

"How steady is your hand with a small, sharp knife?"

He had no real choice. The pirates grinned, but turned their heads at Sullyan's pointed glare. Carefully, she shed her cloak, jacket, and shirt before the fire. Vanyr unbound the wrappings holding her left arm to her body, and then helped pull up her chemise, exposing the line of neat sutures. He sat cross-legged beside her, valiantly trying not to let his eyes stray from the stitches he was slitting. Sullyan smiled when she realized his trouble.

"Torman, my whole life has been lived among men. Your regard does not bother me."

He refused to meet her gaze. "That's as may be. It's not necessarily your feelings I'm thinking about."

Her brows shot up and her grin broadened. "Commander Vanyr, you amaze me at every turn!" She laughed, making him smile. "Do you not have a wife, then?" she asked.

His smile disappeared. "No." His terse tone warned her to pry no further.

When he was done, he helped her back into her chemise, clicking his tongue in dismay at the scars on her back made by Rykan's whip. He began to re-bind her left arm across her body, but stopped when he saw the pain in her eyes. "Do you need help with that? I may be only a Journeyman, but I do have strength. You need all yours at present."

Gratefully, she smiled. "It would be a relief."

He cast her cloak over her shoulders to keep her warm while they worked, then kneeled by her side, carefully unwrapping the bindings on her wrist. The pain was intense and her pupils dilated widely as she tried to block it. Beneath the wrappings, the skin was dark with bruising, but whole. The bones had splintered within the flesh rather than breaking through. Sullyan laid the arm across her lap and, ignoring the flesh of the hand for the moment, reached out to link with Vanyr. She said nothing, but what she saw within him surprised her.

They worked for some time, Vanyr allowing Sullyan to use his strength as she would. When she was done, the arm was throbbing anew but the bones were very much stronger. He lent her a little more strength to numb the pain before strapping the arm once more.

She was loath to expose the hand. It had been a mess the last time she had seen it, and she wasn't sure she had the nerve to look at it now. If it was to heal at all, though, she couldn't neglect it. Taking a deep breath, as much to brace against shock as pain, she let Vanyr unbind it.

It was as bad as she feared. Vanyr's face turned pale at the sight of it and Sullyan herself felt sick. Nevertheless, she schooled herself to deal with it, and once she was done, there was just the tiniest hint of healthy pink skin beneath the blackened scabs. Vanyr applied a fresh dressing and then strapped the entire arm across her body again. He helped her back into her shirt and jacket before replacing the cloak over her shoulders.

She felt drained, but smiled up at him in grateful thanks. "So, Torman, when will the Hierarch perform your confirmation?"

Arrested in the act of sitting down, he stared at her. "What?"

"Surely you know you are ready to become Adept?"

His jaw dropped. "Ready to …? Are you serious?"

"Did you not know? Do you not take note of your own status? Or maybe you do not wish to advance?"

"Of course I do! But lately, what with the threat of war and all our preparations, I haven't given it a thought. Anjer usually coaches us, but he's been busy, too." A sudden thought struck him. "You're a Master, Brynne, could you …?" He stopped, took a breath. "Would you be willing …?"

She dropped her eyes, sighing with genuine regret. "I ask your pardon, Torman. It is not my place. Not only is the Hierarch a level above me, he is also your ruler. We both owe him allegiance as Artesans. It is his duty. I cannot usurp his place."

Vanyr's disappointment showed. "I think you'll find you're his equal. I could feel it through our link just now."

She kept her voice firm but gentle. "Even if that were true, you are still his subject. You must speak to him on your return."

With that, he had to be content.

*****

Ky-shan's men prepared the evening meal, and then they all gathered companionably around the fire, watches set in case there were stragglers from Rykan's forces still around. As they settled with their food, the talk turned to a discussion over who would take control of Kymer and what Sonten's future might hold.

Vanyr's voice conveyed his disdain. "Sonten's always been ambitious, and he doesn't care who he tramples on to gain what he wants." He scooped up the last of his meat with a lump of bread. "His father was a noble, but Sonten's no Artesan, so he's had to fight to maintain his position. I've heard stories concerning his callousness, and he's made many enemies among his peers. He even managed to upset Lord Corbyn, one of Tikhal's nobles, a while ago. The man was angling for his own son to be declared Rykan's Heir, and he might have succeeded had Sonten not squeezed him out. Corbyn was livid and put the Lord of the North under severe pressure to exact revenge. In the end, Tikhal managed to convince Corbyn to drop it, but resentment like that is never forgotten. Sonten won't care. He's a conscienceless bastard, and he'll survive Rykan's demise. He might even welcome it. It isn't the first time he's had to change his plans."

"Why's that?" mumbled Ky-shan through a mouthful of food. He was losing his animosity for Vanyr in the light of Sullyan's trust.

The Commander took a gulp of fellan laced with brine rum. The pirates seemed to have an inexhaustible supply and they distributed it with liberal benevolence. Sullyan, who was feeling drowsy and mellow due to the liquor in her own fellan, was sitting comfortably with her back to a tree, rubbing shoulders with Jay'el. The men's low voices washed over her.

Warming to his tale, Vanyr went on. "As I said, Sonten doesn't have the Artesan gift, and this has plagued him all his life. His father, who was gifted, cast him off because of it. He went mad and eventually died a broken man. He never formally disinherited his son, though, so Sonten took over the province on his father's death. By this time, Durkos was badly in need of funds. Sonten's own marriage—which wasn't prestigious, for what lord wants his daughter to marry a powerless noble?—brought little in the way of wealth and nothing in the way of sons. Ironic, really, that Sonten's wife should prove as barren in her way as Sonten was in his."

Her eyes closed, Sullyan smiled at Vanyr's malevolent satisfaction.

"Sonten embarked on some very underhanded dealings in order to acquire capital. He married his sister off to a wealthy noble, but the man abused her dreadfully and she died of it. The poor woman had, however, managed to produce a son, and the child turned out to be gifted. Sonten, caring family man that he is, murdered the boy's father and took over his lands, holding them 'in trust' for his nephew. The boy, so I heard, had great potential as an Artesan, and under his uncle's devoted guidance"—Vanyr's voice dripped sarcasm—"he developed an ambition every bit as strong as Sonten's. I imagine the two of them were hoping to gain a leg-up on the back of Rykan's take-over, but I have no doubt that once the youth reached his full potential, he and his loving uncle would have found a way to remove Rykan and take his place. Just like Sonten ousted Lord Corbyn.

"Unfortunately for Sonten, his nephew was killed a few months ago. Rather suspicious circumstances too, in my opinion. The account I heard claims it happened during a peasant uprising in his province, but Sonten's peasants are far too downtrodden. They wouldn't have the strength to revolt. No. It's far more likely the young blade was raiding, or maybe dueling with an opponent too skilled for him. Sonten would have invented the story to save face."

He chuckled derisively. "Serves them both right. Sonten's a self-serving, vicious bastard, and Jaskin was turning out the same."

Drifting almost into sleep, Sullyan suddenly jerked awake. Her arm jarred and she gave a small cry of pain. Vanyr shot her a look of concern. "Are you alright, Brynne?"

"Torman, what did you say the nephew's name was?"

"Jaskin. Why?"

"Oh, gods. Sonten. It has to be."

She sank back against the tree, accepting Vanyr's help with the throbbing pain. Once it subsided, she told them her suspicions.

"The two men who were abducted from the hill came to me at our base in Albia a couple of months ago. One of them, Taran—he's now an Adept, although he was only a Journeyman then—had been trying for years to raise his status. Frustration made him reckless and he crossed the Veils by himself, intending to find and challenge an Andaryan Artesan. If he won the challenge, he was going to demand instruction as his prize."

Vanyr snorted. "What? That's insane."

She nodded. "So he found it, for he was captured by a young noble out hunting. When it became apparent that Taran was an Artesan, the noble challenged him. Surrounded as he was, Taran had to accept."

"Why on earth did the noble challenge him?" Vanyr asked. "Why not just kill him?"

"He gave no reason. He did not even give his name, and Taran was in no position to ask. He fought this young man, but because he had no second or witness, the noble was not bound to the Codes of Combat. When Taran proved too good a match, the noble used his power against him."

"No second?" Vanyr was incredulous. "Is the man stupid as well as insane?"

She smiled wearily. "No, Torman, just desperate. He knows better now."

"So I should hope!" The Commander shook his head. "Go on."

"This part is strange. The noble attacked Taran with some kind of artifact, something that channeled and magnified his metaforce. By all accounts, it was a terrible weapon. Taran was in desperate straits, and eventually his only option was to kill the noble. But then, of course, the man's entourage attacked him, and Taran had to flee for his life. They pursued him, but he managed to escape through the Veils. When he recovered from his wounds, he discovered he had unintentionally taken the artifact through to Albia with him. Bands of Andaryan raiders then began to plague the region, and Taran feared his actions had brought them. We now know this was coincidence, that Rykan ordered the raids as a way of persuading King Elias to send me as envoy to Count Marik. Taran, though, was convinced of his culpability, and he came to me looking for advice. When he told me what he had done, I discovered that the noble he had killed was Jaskin."

Ky-shan grunted. "There's your reason behind the abduction, then. Sonten must have been raging livid."

Vanyr looked doubtful. "Revenge? But how would abduction benefit Sonten? If he did want revenge on this man, why not just kill him? Why take him and the other one hostage, leaving two others behind? And why then take the Captain and your other friend as well? It doesn't make sense."

"I agree," said Sullyan. "If it is Sonten—and I think it has to be—then maybe he knows about the artifact. Maybe he wants it back, although as he is not an Artesan he cannot use it. I was not aware before today that he was Jaskin's uncle, or I might have suspected him sooner. But if Sonten is the connection, I still cannot explain how he knew it was Taran who killed Jaskin and took the weapon. They never met, and even if they had, how could Sonten know Taran was in Andaryon? From what Rienne told me, the men who came for Taran and Cal knew exactly who, where, and what they were. How can that be?"

Vanyr pursed his lips. "If this Taran and the noble never exchanged names, how do you even know it was Jaskin he fought?"

"Taran described him and I remembered Jaskin's family colors. I had encountered him before. Robin and I ran into him a couple of times a year or so ago. He was a prolific raider into our lands, so we gave him a few good reasons to steer clear of us."

Vanyr smiled. "I bet you did. So, that solves one part of the mystery, if it is Sonten. The only thing we don't know is exactly what he wants your friends for."

Sullyan shook her head, and they sat chewing over it a while longer. Without reaching a conclusion, they turned in to sleep, Vanyr and Ky-shan both insistent that Sullyan would not be woken under any circumstances for a turn on watch. She glared at them and used a few pithy words, but they remained unmoved. Grumbling at their amused expressions, she gave in and rolled herself carefully in her cloak to sleep by the fire.

Chapter Four

Dawn found them already mounted and moving through the dense trees. It was a crisp, cold day with only a few clouds crossing the weak sun. Vanyr and Sullyan once again took the lead, but this time they sent scouts ahead to keep watch for any sign of their quarry.

Almid and Kester were Sullyan's preferred scouts because she could track them through the substrate. If either of them found anything, they could alert her without returning. To save her energy, Vanyr tried to read them also, but his skills were not sufficient and he had to give up.

They made good time, pushing on through the day without stopping for a noon meal, only eating a little bread and dried meat in the saddle. Sullyan found riding much easier without the stitches in her side, and even her arm was less painful. She tried moving it once or twice, but soon desisted. It was still too early.

The hoof prints they followed hardly deviated from their southeasterly direction. The press of trees was clearly keeping their quarry to the trail. Vanyr found a spot where they must have stopped for food and rest, and Sullyan spent precious minutes searching the ground for any sign that her friends had been there. The prints of all the Manor horses were evident, but she could find no boot prints she recognized. She had hoped Robin or Bull might manage to leave her a clue, but there was nothing. She disliked the implications of that.

Again, they rode late into the evening gloom until they were unable to see the tracks. Sullyan fretted, sure their quarry could not be far away. The tracks were fresh, their spacing and depth indicating the band was moving at an unhurried pace. She surmised they did not intend going much farther with their prisoners, and Vanyr agreed. Once they stopped for the night, she contacted Almid and Kester, calling them back from their scouting.

After they had all eaten, she prepared to sweep the area with her metasenses. She was convinced Robin and Bull were close by and could not rest until she had searched as far as she could. Her reserves were still low, so she asked Vanyr to link with her in case she overtaxed herself. He readily agreed and sat beside her, staring into the fire to aid his concentration. Sullyan, buoyed by Vanyr's strength, cast out her senses, following the southeasterly trend.

The forest provided plenty of cover for anyone wishing to hide. With no pattern of psyche to follow, she was searching blind. Keeping the patterns of all four men firmly in her mind—it was possible that one of them might slip free for an instant or one of their captors make a mistake—she searched for signs of life.

The forest animals, such as there were in late winter, were mostly going about their usual business, undisturbed. She sought as far as she could, yet found nothing. Dispirited, she prepared for another sweep, knowing Vanyr thought she had already gone far enough. She pushed his half-formed protest aside and suddenly, faint within the substrate, caught the unmistakable signature of Fire. In such dense woodland there should be no fire, unless from some charcoal-burner's clamp. Yet the recent fighting would have frightened off any woodland workers, so she was sure she had found her quarry.

Eagerly following this imprint of Fire, she inched closer. Soon she found a spot where the substrate was considerably disturbed. Expending a touch more power, she was able to sense a group of men camped within the trees, around twenty-five or so, she thought. Now that she was focused, she could see the unmistakable flare in the substrate indicating the presence of Artesans, although the patterns were unknown to her. What made her heart leap with hope, though, were faint traces of other psyche patterns. Barely detectable patterns. Refining her probe as far as she could, she caught the characteristic tang of spellsilver.

Immediately, she withdrew, allowing Vanyr to provide the

strength to bring them both back. As he did so, she examined what she had seen, convinced this was the group they sought. Once she and Vanyr broke their link, she related her find to the pirates.

Ky-shan narrowed his eyes. "Twenty-five, Lady? Against our twelve?"

"Four of them are ours," she reminded him, "so sixteen against twenty-one, if we can free them. Surely not insurmountable odds?"

He rolled his eyes. "So, what now?"

Vanyr stirred, but Sullyan spoke first. "I need a proper look. I have to know what the situation is, how they are holding my friends, what their plans are. I will not be gone long."

"You're not going alone," said Vanyr. "Oh, it's no good looking at me like that. I won't try to stop you, but I'm not letting you go alone, and there's an end to it."

"Listen to him, Lady," urged Ky-shan. "I hate to admit it, but he's talking sense."

She knew it. "Very well, Torman. I just hope you are a silent tracker."

Mounting their horses, they rode cautiously into the darkness. Sullyan kept a link to Almid, so the pirates would know what was happening. She cast her senses forward, following the echo of Fire, and Vanyr kept his eyes open for scouts from the party ahead.

It took them over an hour to reach the camp, riding carefully through the dark woods. When they finally drew near, Vanyr was disgusted to find no proper sentries posted, just two men keeping a half-hearted watch and drinking from what looked suspiciously like ale cups. Whoever was leading this band did not expect to be followed.

Leaving the horses concealed behind a thick stand of hazel, Sullyan and Vanyr effortlessly skirted the sentries, creeping noiselessly toward the camp. For all Vanyr's height, he was slim and agile and he moved as silently as Sullyan. Eventually, they worked themselves into a position from which they could see the camp, but were not quite close enough to hear what was said.

There were twenty-one men in the group, including the careless sentries. As Sullyan had guessed, their leader was Sonten. She could see the General clearly, illuminated as he was by a huge roaring blaze. She shook her head. It was foolhardy to build such a large fire in enemy territory. The fact that he was still on Pharikian's land obviously didn't bother Sonten, who was lounging on a heap of his men's cloaks, eating from a plate piled with meat and bread. His men were scattered around the clearing and four were sitting by a smaller fire, as if guarding the dark shapes that lay on the ground.

Sullyan didn't yet try to establish whether those shapes were actually her friends. Her attention was fixed on what Sonten was watching while he ate his meal.

The General sat facing a large tree. Bound securely to it, his arms wrenched cruelly behind him and his feet lashed together, was Taran. His face was purple with bruises—he had clearly suffered repeated beatings—but Sullyan's professional instincts also noted that he bore no wounds. Whoever had administered the beatings had taken exquisite care not to damage him severely.

Taran was conscious, but from the way he half-hung in his bonds it seemed he was unable to bear his own weight. He was also uncomfortably near the fire, and Sullyan could see sweat drenching his face and clothes. Around the bruises his face was pale, and fear shadowed his darkened eyes. Looking closely, she could see a knife bound against the naked skin of his right arm. She guessed it was made of spellsilver. This gave her some hope, for ropes could loosen and knives fall to the ground. If each captive had been restrained in this manner, there might yet be a chance.

Gesturing silently to Vanyr, she withdrew. When it was safe, he asked, "Do they have your friends?"

She nodded. "The one bound to the tree is Taran. I think the others are across the clearing. Torman, I need to get closer to them to see what condition they are in. Poor Taran has been beaten pretty thoroughly, and Sonten is obviously not finished with him. If the others are in the same state … or worse … I need to know.

If we are to rescue them, we have to let them know that help is at hand."

"How on earth are you going to do that? You'll never get close enough to speak to them."

She smiled grimly. "There are more ways open to me than speech, my friend. Will you stay here and keep an eye on those lazy sentries?" She shook her head. "They would not last a day under my command."

"Nor mine," he agreed, and laid a hand on her arm. "Go carefully, Brynne."

Leaving him to return to their earlier vantage point, she slipped away into the darkness. Slowly, careful of her arm and mindful that with it strapped across her body she was not properly balanced, she circled the clearing. It was a simple matter to keep to the shadows cast by that huge fire, yet she kept her eyes and senses open for any sentries they might have missed. Encountering no one, she moved gradually to where the four guards sat. She crept as close as she dared, and could soon see three bodies on the ground, all bound hand and foot. Their guards were sitting across from them, not really watching them. Thankful for this sloppiness, she edged closer.

Now she could tell which man was which. Cal lay on the right, and he had also been severely beaten, bearing the same carefully administered bruises as Taran. His eyes were closed and she thought he was probably unconscious. Bull lay next to him, and she could see no signs of brutality on the big man. Even so, something about him bothered her, and she looked him over carefully. There might have been a faint blue tinge to his lips, but the light was poor and she couldn't be certain. His eyes were also closed, but she thought he was awake.

Robin lay at the far end, nearest the guards' small fire. She caught a glitter of reflected light from his eyes and felt a twinge of relief. He was the one she planned to alert.

As all three lay on their backs with their hands tied uncomfortably behind them, she couldn't see any more spellsilver. She knew it was there, though; she could taste it in the substrate. Keeping her eyes on the guards, she drew in her strength.

The four men sitting round the small fire were eating their supper, only occasionally glancing at their captives. One of them ripped the final piece of meat from a rabbit leg and tossed the bone into the fire. The flames flared and spat as if he had thrown alcohol, the sudden inferno causing him to scramble backward.

"What the hell?"

His companions laughed and told him not to be so careless. "It was only a bloody rabbit bone," he grumbled. "It shouldn't have done that."

To jeers and insults from the others, he moved farther away from the fire, farther away from Robin. Sullyan studied her lover's face to see if she had gained his attention. She had been wondering how to prick his soldier's senses, and the guard's careless bone-throwing was a piece of pure luck. Now, she was pleased to see that he was watching the guards, contempt on his features but no suspicion. She would see what she could do to change that.

The men soon tired of heckling their comrade and one of them produced some ale, passing it around to the rest. Sullyan waited until they had all taken a good swallow and were talking about something else. Then she reached out and made the fire flare again, although not as violently as before. The man closest to it jumped and swore, glaring irritably at the one who had thrown the bone.

"Moxy, you lackwit, what have you done to this fire? Put a spell on it or something?" Grumbling, he shuffled farther away.

Once again, Sullyan studied Robin. *Come on, love, think,* she urged silently. The incident had caught his attention, she could see that, but he wasn't puzzled enough by the fire's behavior to look for an outside source. Sighing, she decided to try another tack.

This time, it was not Fire she had to control but Air, the most capricious of all the elements. It had the whole world to move around in and was subject to all sorts of pressures and external influences. Being able to Master Air was the pinnacle of an Artesan's skill.

As Master-elite, Sullyan had been working on the complex nature of Air for some years now. She understood the paradox of working with this element. It needed a firm touch, not a light one, or it would simply slip away. Reaching out, she attuned her psyche and sent a faint zephyr to caress Robin's face before directing it to flare the fire again.

"What the bloody hell's the matter with this Void-damned fire?"

This time it wasn't the guards' reactions that caused a frown to appear on Robin's face. Sullyan exulted. *Yes, Robin! Come on, you know there has been no breath of wind all night.* To reinforce his growing suspicion, she caressed him with another breeze, this time leaving the fire alone. The last thing she wanted was to rouse the camp.

That final whisper of Air did it. She now had his full attention, and was thankful for his quick wits. It was fortunate that he had not been beaten senseless like poor Cal. He glanced around as unobtrusively as possible, trying to see where she was. Reaching out again, she caused a breath to brush at him from her direction. His gaze followed unerringly and she gently ruffled the dead bracken of her hiding place. She was relieved to see his tight smile.

Having alerted him, she sent a thought to Vanyr, telling him what she had done. Then she contacted Almid, asking him to have Ky-shan quietly bring the men. Backing carefully away, she circled the camp to rejoin the Commander and collect her horse.

*****

Robin wasted no time wondering what Sullyan's plan was or how she had found them. She had made her presence known, and he knew they had to be ready. Careful not to alert the disgruntled guards, he nudged Bull with his bound feet. The big man was resting, but the Captain knew he was awake. At his touch, Bull's eyes opened. They were dull and bloodshot, and Robin felt a pang of anxiety as he saw Bull's discomfort. He knew Bull's chest had been giving him trouble. Casting a cautionary eye-roll toward the guards, he mouthed, "Sullyan!"

Hope sprang into Bull's eyes, but having alerted him there was nothing else Robin could do. He had already tried loosening his bonds to no avail, and he couldn't even begin to slip past the spellsilver's dreadful effects. He had tried until he made himself vomit, and he now fully appreciated how desperate Sullyan must have been when she managed to breach Rykan's collar when he held her captive. All he could do was wait.

Earlier in the evening, he, Bull, and Taran had watched in helpless rage while the guards beat Cal senseless. They had carried out Sonten's orders with relish. The punishment seemed to have no purpose other than to render Cal unconscious, or perhaps it was meant to intimidate Taran. Cal had passed out quickly, and Robin knew there was no point trying to rouse him now.

He was very worried for Taran, though. The man had suffered the same treatment without breaking for two days. Robin was fearful of what Sonten had in mind. Until now, the four captives had been kept well apart, not even able to communicate by eye, and Robin had no idea what Sonten's goal was. It hadn't been lost on him that neither Cal nor Taran bore wounds that might prevent them from traveling the Veils, and he wondered if this was what Sonten intended. There was no guarantee, however, that the General's plans included Robin or Bull, and he might not be as restrained when dealing with them. Hoping desperately that Sullyan's rescue would succeed, and quickly, Robin turned his attention to Sonten. The bulky General had placed something in the blazing fire at the foot of Taran's tree.

*****

Sonten was beginning to lose what little patience he had. While needing to put some distance between himself and Rykan's unpredictable, leaderless men, he hadn't wanted to wait too long before questioning his captives. Time was limited because he knew they would be missed.

His first choice of campsite had been too close to the Citadel and was too easily discovered, much to his rage. The capture of Robin and Bull during the resulting skirmish was an unexpected bonus for which Commander Heron and his eagle-eyed scouts would be rewarded. Now, Sonten had all three of the men who had accompanied Sullyan to Marik's banquet, and he was certain of attaining his goal.

The human witch, Sullyan, held no great interest for Sonten, as he could not be sure she possessed the information he required. Besides, he was doubtful she had survived the duel with Rykan. Taran, however, certainly did possess this knowledge, and Sonten intended to enjoy himself extracting it. He felt again the satisfaction of seeing the sick look in Taran's eyes when he learned just what the Staff could do. The beatings his men had administered were only the preliminary stages of the damage Sonten was fully prepared to inflict.

The General had never even imagined gaining an opportunity like this after he had returned with Rykan to Marik's mansion to find that Taran had slipped the Duke's cunning net. Although this was probably for the best, Sonten was disappointed. The Albian's constant meddling in Sonten's delicately balanced plans had caused the General much suffering and fear. Sonten intended to repay Taran many times over for the torment he had endured.

Ruthless and conscienceless he might be, but unlike the late, unlamented Lord Rykan, Sonten wasn't wantonly cruel. He only used torture when it was necessary or justified, but he couldn't deny the enjoyment he found when inflicting it. If only Rykan had controlled his lust and allowed the General his way, Sonten knew he could have forced Sullyan to yield what Rykan craved. Yet, despite his deep misgivings and his contempt for the Baron, Rykan's so-called Albian 'ally,' it hadn't been in Sonten's interests to interfere with Rykan's plans. The Duke made it perfectly plain that he placed no value on Sonten's opinions, so the General held his peace and left Rykan to enjoy his brutal pleasure.

He huffed to himself. They all knew how that had turned out, and he wondered what the Baron would do now that Rykan was dead. He didn't think the Duke had communicated with the Baron since beginning his disastrous challenge, and Sonten reckoned the Baron would be apoplectic by now. Would he even know of Rykan's demise? What would his reaction be when he learned that Rykan's nemesis was none other than the very woman he had charged the Duke with killing?

Sonten grinned. Hadn't he said all along that the entire thing—the Albian invasion, the trip to Cardon, Sullyan's imprisonment—was a total waste of time? If the Baron had only waited until a victorious Rykan used the Staff to absorb the Hierarch's powers, then the young Albian witch would have stood no chance against him. Rykan could have stolen her metaforce and then slaked his lust for as long as he pleased. And the Staff would never have been stolen.

The General almost giggled. The Staff was as surely lost to the Baron as Rykan was to life. For should Sonten succeed in recovering the thing—and it was a virtual certainty now, he thought, mentally rubbing his hands—he certainly wouldn't make the Baron a gift of it. Although, he mused, he might be amenable to a deal, should the Baron put forward a sufficiently tempting offer.

Satisfied, Sonten dragged his thoughts back to the present. He might not casually indulge in torture, but right now, knowing Taran possessed the information he so desperately needed as well as Artesan powers which could be used to feed the Staff once he had it, Sonten wouldn't hold back.

Heron had explained why he must keep Taran whole if he wasn't to die when they crossed the Veils into Albia, so when Lieutenant Arif presented him with two captives, Sonten quickly realized that Cal was the ideal sacrifice. However, as Taran's companion, it was possible that Cal also possessed the information he wanted. Insurance was a useful commodity, so when Bull and Robin fortuitously fell into Sonten's hands, it gave the General other expendables to work with. Taran might not talk to save his own skin, but Sonten was pretty sure he would talk to save his friends.

Wheezing as he bent over the fire, the General removed the broad blade he had placed in its heart, holding it by its cloth-wrapped handle. It was glowing nicely. Stepping forward, he thrust it under Taran's nose, causing the man to twist his head aside and gasp in fear.

Sonten laughed. "Oh don't worry, my friend! This blade's not for you."

He turned to the guards round the smaller fire and snapped his fingers. They stood and laid hold of their largest captive, dragging the big man nearer. Despite the man's weakened state, it took three of them to do it and four of them to hold him down once he realized Sonten's intentions. The General merely smiled, waiting as his men subdued the captive.

*****

As Taran watched the greed and pleasure grow in Sonten's eyes, anguish swelled in his heart. He had taken the taunting, the beatings, and the awful numbing effects of the spellsilver, and he had watched in desperate silence while Cal endured the same brutal treatment. The younger man's dark eyes had warned Taran not to cry out or protest, asking him to trust that Cal could take the punishment just as well as Taran. Yet what Sonten intended for Bull was another matter entirely.

Taran knew he couldn't watch Bull being tortured or mutilated. He struggled vainly to dislodge the spellsilver. Yet even if he could get free of the knife, he didn't know who he could contact for help. During his first night as Sonten's captive, the General had told him that Sullyan was dead. However, when Robin and Bull were brought in, a swift glance from Robin gave Taran the impression she lived. He was sick and confused, beaten and frightened. He didn't know what to believe.

Sonten's leering face snatched him from his wretched thoughts. Smiling at the fresh sweat beading Taran's face and the abject terror in his eyes, the General brandished the red-hot knife. He indicated the struggling Bull. "Well, Albian? Are you going to tell me what you did with it? Or shall I play awhile with your big friend, here?" He brought the knife toward Bull's face.

The big man made a violent upward lunge, nearly dislodging the guards. "Don't tell him!" he panted at Taran. Two of Sonten's men wrenched his arm against its socket, and he let out a yell.

Taran struggled harder, staring in horror at the blue tinge to Bull's lips. "For the gods' sake, Sonten, don't do this!"

Sonten just smiled and laid the hot knife on Bull's arm. A harsh scream rang out across the clearing.

*****

Sullyan heard it from where she waited on Drum and her heart froze. She sent a searing thought to Almid, *Forget stealth, man. Come quickly!* She urged Drum forward, leaving Vanyr to rendezvous with the pirates. At a gallop, it should only take them minutes to reach the clearing.

Ducking her head to avoid low branches, she drew her long knife from the scabbard on her belt. She had to block out Bull's harsh roars of pain as Sonten once more applied the hot knife. She could hear Taran screaming, presumably trying to make Sonten stop, but she couldn't make out the words.

Once in position, she slipped from Drum's back. The two men still guarding the prisoners were intent on what Sonten was doing and weren't looking her way. Without giving herself time to think, she slid on her belly out of cover toward Robin, slitting the bonds on his wrists before he knew she was there. As the spellsilver knife fell away, she smothered his mind so he wouldn't startle, then passed him her blade.

Help is on its way, she told him, melting away again. She saw him move the knife toward his feet, hoping to slit the ropes that bound his ankles without alerting the guards. One of them must have heard him move, for he turned, eyes widening as he saw Robin's unbound hands. With a yell, he leaped for Robin and the Captain rolled, the knife coming up under the guard's ribs and plunging into his chest. He collapsed onto Robin with a gurgle of blood.

The entire camp reacted to the dying guard's cry and Sonten looked up from his grim work on Bull. The sound of galloping horses and the cries of approaching men filled the night. Rapping out commands, the General sent men flying for their horses. As they ran, Sullyan saw Ky-shan's band, Vanyr in the fore, come crashing into the clearing, cleaving a path through Sonten's scattering men.

The General dropped Bull's damaged arm and ran for his horse, leaping astride with surprising agility for such a heavy man. "Get him! Get him!" he yelled, indicating the unconscious Cal. The remaining guard grabbed Cal and slung him over his shoulder. Sullyan's heart sank. Robin couldn't stop him. He had only just managed to roll the dead man off his chest and still hadn't freed his feet. She watched helplessly as Cal was dumped across a horse's withers, the guard springing up behind. He spurred the animal toward Sonten.

The General sat his fretting horse just at the edge of the firelight, his expression furious. As the first of his men reached him, he turned in the saddle and flung the hot knife toward Taran. Sullyan gasped as it flew end over end, hearing the dreadful wet thunk as it buried itself in the Adept's shoulder, pinning him to the tree. Taran's shriek of agony pierced her ears.

Sonten dug his spurs into his horse's flanks and it shot away, carrying him into the night. Ky-shan's men thundered through the clearing, scattering sparks from the fire and mowing down those few men too slow to mount their horses. They too disappeared into the trees, chasing after Sonten. Robin gained his feet and sprang for Torka, leaping into the saddle. Sullyan ran into the clearing, heading toward Bull and Taran. Robin spotted her.

"Major," he yelled, "they've taken Cal! Will you be alright if I go after them?"

She waved a hand. *Go, Rob, but be careful.*

He wheeled the impatient chestnut and disappeared after the pirates.

As the frantic sounds died away, Sullyan dropped to her knees beside Bull. She quickly slit his bonds and removed the spellsilver. His breathing was ragged, and he was close to passing out. She heard movement behind her and turned, drawing her sword from over her shoulder, but it was only Vanyr. He spread his hands and she dropped the sword.

"Help him," she urged, indicating Taran, who was groaning with the pain of the knife in his shoulder. Vanyr crossed swiftly to him. Laying a supporting hand close to the wound, the Commander eased the knife from Taran's flesh. He hissed with pain, his face ashen. Once Vanyr cut his bonds, Taran collapsed. Vanyr had to take his weight and lower him gently to the ground. He promptly lost consciousness.

Leaving Vanyr to tend Taran, Sullyan turned her attention to Bull. His normally florid face was a nasty shade of grey, his lips blue and bloodless. She didn't like the sound of his breathing either, shallow and uneven. She reached into him to lend him some strength, but he didn't respond. With cold horror, she realized his heart was giving out.

She struggled with her jacket, desperate to free her left arm. "Quickly, Torman," she hissed, "help me! I need both hands."

The lithe man rushed to her side and helped her out of her jacket. He deftly slit the bindings holding her left arm to her side. Once it was free, she threw herself across Bull's hips. Ignoring the pain, she placed both hands on his chest and began pumping his heart with all her strength. He had stopped breathing, and she sobbed as she worked, desperate not to lose him. Vanyr looked on, helpless.

"Come on, man, breathe!" she gasped, still pumping Bull's heart. There was no response, so she cast her metasenses into him and forced his heart to beat, keeping the blood moving through his body and his organs alive. "Torman," she panted, "can you assist with his breathing? I can only spare attention for one function, and if I leave his heart, it might stop again."

Vanyr moved closer to place a hand on Bull's arm, the physical contact essential if he was to learn the man's pattern of psyche. Once attuned, he was able to find the mechanics of Bull's breathing and gently encourage his lungs to inhale.

Sullyan continued her work on Bull's overloaded heart. She wept openly, although she was only vaguely aware of it. The depth of her love for this huge, infuriating, wonderful, protective, disobedient man overwhelmed all else. Yet time was passing, and still he didn't respond. Sullyan's own breath grew harsh and ragged.

"Come on, Bull, you bloody great ox!" she screamed, panting in time with her heart massage. "How dare you do this to me? You dare die on me, you bloody useless fool! I need you, do you hear me? I will not let you go! Come on, man, just … breathe!"

The strain of keeping his heart going was draining her, as was the agony shooting through her damaged wrist. Sweat poured down her face and her strength was close to giving out. Yet she couldn't let up. Couldn't believe there was no hope. Wouldn't believe it. She would keep him going on sheer faith if that was what it took.

Just as despair was looming, just when she knew she would be forced to give up after all, his body gave a great lurch and he took a gasping breath by himself. Vanyr ceased his manipulation of Bull's lungs and sat back, passing a hand across his haggard face. Sullyan ceased pumping Bull's barrel chest, but remained sitting across his hips, her head hanging in exhaustion, sobbing from exertion and terror.

She withdrew her power, but kept a wary eye on his heart in case it should falter. It was beating by itself now, regular and slow, and his color improved. Easing herself off his body, she collapsed to the ground, hugging her throbbing arm and crying with relief. Vanyr reached over to squeeze her shoulder and she managed a wan smile.

"Well done, Brynne. I didn't think you could do it. I'd have given up on him long ago."

She took a shuddering breath, trying to slow her own frantic heartbeat. "You do not know Bulldog. He is not a man to give up on. But I could not have done it without you, and you have my deepest thanks. I could not bear to lose Bull. He is my oldest and dearest friend, and I love him more than words can say."

"You love him? But I thought you and the Captain …?" Vanyr stopped, his face flushing.

Sullyan wiped away the tears of her recent emotion. "Robin and I are lovers, yes, but Bulldog and I go back a long way. A very long way indeed. What I owe him can never be repaid."

She sat by Bull's side, holding his hand, listening to his breathing and feeling very thankful.

Chapter Five

Once she was sure Bull was sleeping peacefully and in no danger of his heart giving out, Sullyan turned her attention to Taran. Vanyr found her some water and set a pan to warm by the fire, ready for cleaning.

Taran was still unconscious, so she quickly cleaned the charred knife wound right below his collarbone, her damaged hand making her movements awkward. Taran would have cause to be thankful Sonten's aim had not improved, she thought. She was certain the knife had been aimed at his heart. As it was, the muscle was badly damaged. The heated blade had burned it extensively. Fortunately, it had also cauterized the flesh, so there was very little bleeding.

That task done, she set about checking the rest of him. With Vanyr's help, she removed his jacket and shirt, seeing with dismay the extensive bruising to his chest and abdomen. He would be sore and uncomfortable for days. Luckily, nothing was ruptured or broken. Sonten's bullyboys had known exactly what they were doing. She spared a thought for Cal, who would be in the same state, and hoped he would remain unconscious while slung over his captor's horse. If not, he would suffer considerable pain.

Thoughts of Cal led her to wondering about Robin. He and the pirates had been gone some time. She was about to reach for contact when his thoughts came to her.

They managed to escape us, love. It's too dark and too dense to go chasing after them now. We will have to wait for daylight.

She felt his disgust at the failure and his worry for Cal. *Alright, Robin. Bring them back here. You all need to rest, and we can discuss what to do when Taran wakes.*

He asked after Bull, but she didn't want to tell him how close the big man had come to death.

He is sleeping. He will be well enough.

She broke the link, knowing Robin would return as swiftly as he could. She needed his strength right now.

Vanyr was sitting by the fire, brewing fellan. The welcome aroma pervaded the clearing and Taran began to stir. Sullyan laid her hand on him to stop him moving, but he woke with a startled cry and began to struggle.

"Easy, man, easy," she soothed, using metaforce to reassure him. "You are safe now and among friends. There is nothing more to fear. Rest easy."

He slowly relaxed, a small sigh escaping his lips as she numbed some of his pain. She was too drained to do more. Her arm was throbbing and her exertions over Bull had left her empty of strength.

Taran opened his eyes. The lids were puffy and swollen from the beatings, and the whites were bloodshot. He looked truly dreadful. He obviously felt dreadful too, for moisture came into his eyes and his breath rasped painfully. Stretching out her hand, Sullyan smoothed perspiration from his brow. He moved his head away, refusing her comfort.

She frowned. "What is it, Taran? You are safe now, have no fear."

He gave his head a slight shake, refusing to look at her. Vanyr cast her a puzzled glance, which she could not answer. Instead, she rose stiffly to her feet, crossed to the fire, and poured a mug of fellan, adding a small dash of ale to it. A wry smile quirked her lips. Despite her disapproval of strong liquor, what she really needed was Ky-shan's brine rum, but right now there was none to be had. Ale would have to do. Coming back to Taran, she sat beside him, easing her right arm behind his shoulders for support. Holding the mug to his lips, she encouraged him to drink. For some reason he seemed reluctant and drank slowly, the closed expression still on his face.

When he was done, she asked, "Better now?"

He refused to answer, but he was still shuddering. She could feel it as he lay against her. She realized then that its root was deeper than the pain of his wounds. Leaning into him, she took his hand with her left. He gave a small sob.

"What is it, Taran?" she murmured. "Something pains your heart. Tell me what it is."

She felt him swallow, and when he spoke, his voice was harsh and raw with emotion. "I don't know why you're being so good to me."

"Because you are my friend. I care for you."

His trembling increased and she wondered at it.

"Well, you shouldn't. I don't deserve it. I've brought you nothing but trouble right from the start. All of this is my fault, and now Cal's life is in danger because of me and there's nothing I can do about it. What am I going to say to Rienne? She'll kill me for endangering him. And it'll only get worse. It'll start all over again when Sonten gets his hands on that bloody Staff. That's what he's after, and I told him where it is. I told him, Sullyan, even though I swore I wouldn't! I suffered the beatings and watched Cal go through the same, all for nothing. I should have told him straight away. I should have known it was useless to hold out. What he did to me was one thing, and I probably deserved it, but I couldn't bear what he was doing to Bulldog, what I knew he'd do to Robin. I had to tell him!"

Sullyan's eyes widened and she stared at Vanyr over Taran's head. Memories of their earlier conversation showed clearly on his face, and he nodded.

"Easy, Taran," she soothed, still holding his hand despite his feeble attempts to free it. "Go over it slowly. Tell me everything he said. Leave nothing out. This could be very important."

Taran was still trembling and it increased as he tried to order his thoughts. Putting aside all considerations for her own pain, Sullyan reached into him again and eased his aching body. She was surprised and gratified when Vanyr, unsolicited, did the same for her. She smiled her thanks.

Under this ministration, Taran calmed a little and drew a breath.

"It's that artifact, the one I came to the Manor to tell you about, the one I brought back through the Veils with me." His weakened voice was taut with shame and urgency. "Sonten calls it the Staff. It belonged to Rykan, and it's what Sonten's after. It can be used as a weapon, as I found out, but it was originally made as some kind of inanimate Powersink. Apparently, it can absorb indefinite amounts of metaforce and store it until the wielder requires it."

He took another breath. "But that's not all, as if it wasn't enough. Sonten said it is also capable of stealing life force. Sullyan, he says that terrible thing can drain life force and absorb it whether the victim is willing or not!"

Sullyan froze, her eyes fixed blankly on Vanyr. The Commander's brows drew down and he stared back, appalled. Neither of them spoke, and eventually Taran went on, unburdening his soul of its weight of blame.

"Sonten didn't say where Rykan got it from, but I do know it's very important to him, and he'll do anything to get it back. You remember that noble I told you I killed—Jaskin? Well, he was Sonten's nephew. The two of them had been working with the Staff without Rykan's knowledge, and Jaskin managed to figure out how to control it. Their next step was to see if they could use it to steal someone's life force. Sonten didn't say this outright, but he hinted they were going to use it on Rykan once he'd taken over the throne. Then Sonten would have been the Hierarch, with Jaskin to back him up."

Taran's voice caught and he coughed. Sullyan felt the jolt of it before he continued.

"That's why Jaskin challenged me that day instead of simply getting his huntsmen to kill me. If he had won that duel … if he had defeated me … he would have used that dreadful thing on me. I'd have ended up a drained and mindless shell. It appalls me even to think of it! They did it that way because they wanted to make sure their first victim didn't suspect what was coming. They wanted to test the Staff's power. And, like a complete fool, I walked into their clutches. Like some idiotic, willing sacrifice! I could hardly have made it easier for them if I'd tried. It was only pure luck that I managed to kill Jaskin and grab the Staff. I only held on to it because I was frightened someone else would use it on me. I never intended to steal it. Sonten must have been foaming at the mouth when he realized I'd escaped the tangwyr and taken it through the Veils."

He took a sobbing breath and Sullyan knew it wasn't over. She could feel the weight pressing on Taran's soul and willed him strength to tell her the rest. After a short pause, he did so.

"My killing—murdering—Jaskin that day ruined Sonten's plans. Part of the reason he took me was for revenge. But it seems I didn't ruin them enough. Sonten has another Artesan with him, a man called Heron who I think is one of his commanders. I don't know what his status is. Sonten intends for him to use the Staff now. He still has his sights on the throne. But what terrifies me, Sullyan, is that if he gets his hands on that terrible thing, no Artesan in the world will be safe!"

Taran's voice broke under the weight of his shame, and tears spilled from his eyes. "Oh, if only I'd had the courage to tell you everything from the start! But I was so concerned for my pride. I was so arrogant, thinking no one would understand my problems. I have caused all this, and now poor Cal could lose his life. He might already be dead for all I know. You really should have sent us packing once I finally told you about the Staff. You should have sent us away from the Manor, back into obscurity where we belonged. But you didn't, you befriended us. You spent precious time teaching me where I was going wrong, and then you raised my status. How undeserved was that? I'm not fit to be an Apprentice, let alone an Adept! It would have been better if you had never set eyes on me. No wonder my father never told me about you. I've been a failure all my life and he was right not to trust me. Hell, I don't trust me, and I don't think I'll ever use my powers again. If we get out of this alive, that is."

His shuddering increased once more as the emotion and self-pity flooded out.

Vanyr sat in stunned silence, and even Sullyan said nothing at first. Her heart had turned to stone when she heard what the artifact could do. How it existed, who had created it—certainly not Rykan!—she did not know. What she did know were the reasons behind some of Rykan's actions. His challenge made perfect sense now, and she also understood Sonten's determination to regain the Staff. He might not possess Artesan powers himself, but with a gifted subordinate under his control, he could easily revive his plans for advancement. In fact, she mused, this scenario might even work better for him, as he would not have to contend with Jaskin's own power and ambition. The young noble might well have decided to dispense with his uncle at some point, and even with the Staff Sonten would have had no defense against him.

With the Staff in his possession, however, and the Artesan wielding it firmly under his control, Sonten would be all-powerful. The mere threat of its use would buy him respect, and there would always be Artesans willing to serve him, even if it were with an eye to the main chance. A cold tremor ran through Sullyan. She had to stop Sonten at any cost. Not only for Pharikian's sake, a man she was growing to love, but for the sake of every Artesan in the five realms.

Concealing her fear, she sent a message for Robin to hurry. He and the pirates were not far from camp, but were returning with caution. Afterward, she rested her cheek against Taran's hair. Cradling his head to her breast, she murmured soothingly as the tide of his emotions ran its course. Vanyr sat in watchful silence. When Taran finally calmed and the tremors eased, she spoke quietly into his ear.

"My friend, will you hear me now?"

He was still too raw and closed his eyes and mind against her. With a sigh, she reached into his psyche, forcing him to hear her, willing him to see the truth of what she said. It was a breach of Artesan etiquette—and a lamentable breach of friendship—but it was necessary. As she was vastly stronger than Taran, even in her present exhausted state, he had no choice but to listen.

"Taran, you may not realize this, but if you think about it you will see that you saved my life the day you killed Jaskin." He opened his mouth to protest, but she continued. "Had you not met him that day—or fallen into his clutches, if you will—had you not fought him and had the skill at arms to defeat him, Rykan would surely have remained in possession of the Staff. Sonten and Jaskin were not ready to make their move, and so Rykan would have had it at his palace. Marik told you, did he not, that something caused Rykan to fly into a towering rage when he returned from that banquet to Kymer? Now we know the reason for that rage, and I can well believe he was furious enough to put some of his people to death. The purchase or creation of the artifact would have cost Rykan dearly. To think of it in the possession of another Artesan would have been intolerable."

She kept her mouth close to his ear, her cheek still resting against his hair. Such close contact must surely help him feel her sincerity. "Now that I understand what it is, I can tell you truly that had he used it against me, as was obviously his plan, I could never have withstood him, even without the spellsilver. You know this is true. Rykan would not have needed to resort to the desperate measures he used against me. He could have taken my life force and my power whether I was willing or not.

"Thanks to you, he did not have it and was forced to spend time he could ill-afford in trying to compel me, to break me down so completely that I surrendered. And I nearly did, my friend. My only hope, my only strength in that dark, fear-haunted place, was Marik and my memories of you, all my friends. They kept me going and enabled me to endure Rykan's torture. Terrible though that was, it gave you the opportunity to find me. And then, Taran, when you helped rescue me from the palace, you saved my life a second time. For your skills and care helped bring me out of the deep, dark place I had fled to, and you helped strengthen me for what came after, when I knew I would not survive Rykan's abuse. Your love and your friendship sustained me.

"This time, my friend, your bravery and strength in holding out for so long in the face of Sonten's brutality might well save my life a third time. And this is the most important of all."

"What do you mean?" he whispered.

She smiled. While he couldn't refute the truth of her words due to the link they were sharing, he didn't fully understand what she was saying.

"When I defeated Rykan in the arena, I was able to absorb his life force and his power, and later used them to burn out the poison. But I was puzzled, for some of his strength, the core of it, was missing. His rank was the same as mine"—she ignored

Vanyr's sudden snort—"so I know what his capacity should have been. And without this vital core, I could not completely eradicate the poison. There is still a tiny part left in my soul, and I had to accept I would never be free of it. But thanks to you, the mystery of where that core was stored has been solved. If we can stop Sonten and recover the Staff, it is just possible I can use it to destroy that last drop of Rykan's poison, the one thing preventing me from returning to Albia.

"For if I am forced to stay here, I will die. Rykan's poison will not kill me, Andaryon will. I could live, oh, maybe a year before this alien place begins to affect me badly, but after that, the end would be swift. So you see, my friend, far from causing me trouble, you have already saved my life twice and may yet do so a third time. Now tell me I was wasting my time coaching you and raising your status!"

She felt Taran stir, but continued before he could speak.

"I will have no more of your self-pity. You have strength and you have power, and it is your right to wield them. It is hardly your fault that your early training was flawed and incomplete. Such things, as you have seen, can be remedied. You have shown great courage and determination through a difficult life so far, Taran Elijah, and I am very proud to call you my friend."

The tremor of his body, which had lessened while she spoke, increased once more as his emotions overflowed. She kissed his cheek. "One thing I do not understand. Sonten's men were obviously looking for you and Cal when they took you from the hill. Was Sonten present when you fought and killed Jaskin?"

Taran nodded. "Yes. At least, I think it must have been him. He kept in the background and I never saw him clearly. Not even when he threw the Staff at Jaskin."

She sighed, and he flushed with renewed shame.

"I wish you had told me that before," she murmured. "Now, it all fits. Sonten was at Marik's banquet. Obviously, you did not see him. I am not surprised. He kept himself well out of Rykan's way. He must have seen you there with us. Had you thought to mention this mysterious figure when you told me of Jaskin, we might have been able to raise a memory of his family colors. Even a hint would have helped. Then I would have known to be wary that evening."

He hung his head. "I'm so sorry."

Sensing his remorse and distress, she kissed him again. "Forget it, Taran. What is done is done, and cannot be undone. Drink some more fellan, and then you should sleep. Robin will return soon. Then we can make arrangements for rescuing Cal and preventing Sonten from finding the Staff."

She felt Taran's jolt of fear on hearing his Apprentice's name. "I think you need not fear for Cal's immediate safety," she soothed. "Sonten needs him whole to travel the Veils, and to direct him to the Staff. That will give Robin plenty of time to intercept them and enlist the aid of General Blaine. Remember, we know exactly where they will go. Never fear, Taran, and have faith. All will turn out right."

Once Vanyr had helped her dress Taran's wound, Sullyan settled the Adept more comfortably and left him to doze by the fire. She also saw to Bull's burns while the big man was sleeping. Thankfully, he didn't stir. That done, she asked Vanyr to re-bind her arm. He also made them some food, for which she was very grateful. She was sitting by the fire sipping fellan when Robin and the pirates returned. There was a flurry of activity as the horses were cared for and men allotted watches.

The noise had woken Taran, and Sullyan made the formal introductions. Robin then gave Sullyan an account of the last two days, and expressed his regret to Ky-shan over the loss of As-ket and Xeer.

Ky-shan merely shrugged. "They were just doing their job," he said, but Sullyan could see the pain in his eyes.

She was about to initiate a discussion on plans for catching Sonten when she noticed Bull was awake. Earlier, following his introduction to Ky-shan and his men, Taran had told her how often over the past few days Bull had suffered from breathlessness. Sullyan, in her turn, told Robin the truth about Bull's heart seizure. She was exasperated beyond belief to learn that the big man hadn't mentioned his discomfort to Rienne, who could perhaps have helped him. She was even angrier now that he had disobeyed her orders to stay at the Manor. This, combined with the fear she still felt for him and her exhaustion, meant she was not in the best of moods.

She let Robin introduce the pirates this time. The banter and exchange of friendly insults between him, Taran, and Bull made it plain to both Vanyr and Ky-shan the tremendous depth of love, friendship, and camaraderie that existed between the Albians. This made her furious outburst all the more shocking.

Bull hadn't spoken to her since waking, but every now and then he cast glances her way. She kept her expression neutral. Conflicting emotions warred within her, a sure and ready recipe for igniting her volatile temper. Part of her was terrified he would have another seizure, and part was furious with him for endangering both himself and their friends. Bull knew her temper well and was clearly expecting some kind of backlash over his actions. Yet she steadfastly refused to speak and just sat staring coldly at him.

Finally, he could stand it no longer. When there was a lull in the conversation, he said, "Major, I'm sorry I disobeyed you in coming here. I take full responsibility for what's happened. And I'm sorry if I frightened you earlier tonight."

She felt herself freeze, the heat of her fury crystallizing into a painful lump of solid ice. How dared he sound so contrite? As if a simple 'sorry' would wipe out all her fear!

"Frightened me?" she hissed. "Frightened me? You were bloody *dead*, man! Why did you not tell Rienne you were having problems? How could you be so stupid? Do you know how hard we had to work to save your miserable life? Do you know how long it took us to get you back?"

Her vicious tone cut the air, and every head in the camp turned her way. Conversation died in the face of her fury, and even the fire seemed muted. Robin drew back slightly and Taran's face paled. Vanyr's mouth dropped open and he muttered, "Bloody hell."

Sullyan hadn't finished. "You deliberately disobeyed my direct orders. You put Taran, Cal, and Rienne in danger to come on some damned fool's errand. What good did you think it would do? How did you think it would help me? Would it have helped if you were caught by Rykan's men? Oh, yes! Can you imagine what would have happened then? I'll bloody tell you. He would have enjoyed playing with you, one by one, until I could stand it no longer. All that suffering would have been in vain. You might as well have left me to die in his palace! But did you think of that? No! You are a bloody fool, Bulldog, I should never have trusted you. Maybe Vanyr and I should not have exhausted ourselves to save you. Maybe we should have left you to breathe your bloody last!"

She paused for breath. Robin took a worried glance at Bull's bloodless face and unwisely tried to defend him. "Isn't that a little harsh, Major? Bull and the others were worried about you. They only came because they cared."

She rounded on him, her intense glare making him throw up his hands in defense. "Did I ask for your opinion, Captain? You are just as much at fault for keeping this folly from me. You encouraged it, and do not think I have forgotten. Now, I was not talking to you, so keep silent!"

Robin shrugged, giving Bull an apologetic glance. He knew when he was beaten.

The pirates watched this display of spleen with astonishment, and Vanyr's mouth remained open. Bull lay back, tears shining in his eyes. "The last thing I wanted was to distress you."

"*Distress* me?" she yelled. "How dare you speak of distress?" She flung out her good arm in Vanyr's direction. "There is someone who knows about distress. Ask him! Go on! Ask the Commander how distressed I was an hour ago. Ask him how panicked I was when you were lying there with no breath and no heartbeat. Ask him how much pain I went through to keep you alive. By all the heavens and hells, Bulldog, do not speak to *me* of *distress*!"

She stared at him through brimming eyes, her fear and her love for him plain on her face.

Her fury drained abruptly, leaving her shivering. The mental image of him lying there dead was enough to calm her temper and make her realize that the last thing he needed was more stress. Tears spilled down her cheeks and the smile she gave him was made of pure love.

"Bloody hell, Bulldog," she sighed, her voice trembling with exhaustion.

He wiped his eyes and regarded her sidelong. "Am I forgiven, then?"

She choked back a laugh. "You might at least have the grace to wait until I am through being mad at you!" Her eyes closed briefly. "You are a bloody great useless ox, Hal Bullen. I cannot think why I bother with you. It must be because I love you. But let me warn you, if you ever put me through anything like that again, I will have your balls for breakfast!"

Vanyr spluttered over his fellan, and Robin slapped him on the back. Sullyan turned to Ky-shan. "Have you any of that hideous rum about you, Ky?"

The pirate stared, amazed at the complete turn-around of her mood. Then he grinned and produced a small brown bottle. She took it and gulped down a healthy swallow straight from the neck. Coughing, she wiped it and passed the bottle back.

Bull gaped at her. "But Sully … you don't drink!"

"See what you have reduced me to?" she snapped, but her voice was warm.

Looking contrite, he held out his arm. She crossed to sit beside him, wrapped in his embrace. Ky-shan passed his bottle around the men and the atmosphere slowly returned to normal.

Chapter Six

Once the alcohol had mellowed her mood, and the memory of Bull's brush with death had lost some of its sting, Sullyan told Robin and the pirates what she had learned from Taran concerning Sonten and the Staff. When Robin heard how vital it was for Sullyan to gain possession of the Staff, it took all her powers of command to prevent him from rushing off into the night once more.

"Strategy and planning, Robin," she cautioned him. "Remember your training." He flushed and subsided, and she turned to the pirate leader beside her. "Ky-shan, can you spare some men to go with Robin in the morning?"

The pirate cocked his head at her. "They've already volunteered to go, Lady. All of them. Although, I'm going to leave at least one man here with you."

Ki-en spoke up. "I will stay, Ky-shan."

Jay'el glanced at him. "I'll stay too, Father."

Ky-shan nodded his approval.

Vanyr stirred by the fire, drawing their attention. Sullyan was astonished when he said, "I will go with the Captain too, if he'll have me. I have just spoken with Anjer, and he agrees with me—for once." He smiled wryly, and she grinned. "He is sending out a patrol at dawn to escort you back to the Citadel, Brynne. You'll need help with Bull and Taran here."

Bull opened his mouth to speak, and even Taran roused from his exhaustion, but Sullyan stared them both down. "Do not even think it. Neither of you can cross the Veils at present, and for once you will both obey orders." Glaring, she dared them to argue.

"Yes, ma'am," they chorused, drawing sympathetic chuckles from Ky-shan's men.

She turned back to Vanyr and clasped his arm. "Thank you, Torman."

He waved away her thanks, but sat watching her while she wound up the discussion.

It was very nearly midnight, and as none of them had had much sleep the night before or rest during the day, they began to turn in. Robin and Sullyan drew slightly apart from the others, leaving Taran and Bull together by the fire with Vanyr watching over them. Robin took Sullyan into the circle of his arms and they sat silently, communing with each other. This would be the first time they had been apart since Sullyan had sent Robin back to Albia from Marik's mansion, and she sensed he liked it even less now than he had then.

"I am not alone now, Robin," she murmured. "I will be quite safe. It is for me to fear for you this time. Please hear me, my love. Let Torman and Ky-shan counsel you. Make use of their strength, and take no unnecessary risks. Remember, your primary objective is to rescue Cal. Forget the Staff until after he is safe. If you must, let Sonten take it. He cannot use it himself, and I suspect it will take this other man, Heron, some time to learn its control. We can deal with them later. Keep yourself and your command safe and return to me as soon as you can. Now, I suggest we try to sleep. There is little enough left of the night, and you must leave by dawn."

Kissing, they held each other close, Robin mindful of her painful left arm. Then they wrapped themselves in shared blankets near the fire and settled to sleep, safe in the knowledge that Ky-shan's men were on watch.

*****

Sullyan's instinctive time-sense, developed over years of training, woke her well before dawn. The men of the camp roused efficiently and quietly, so quietly that neither Bull nor Taran, who still needed all the rest they could get, were disturbed. In very short order, the horses were saddled and those who were leaving for Albia stood grouped around Robin. Sullyan stood beside him as he prepared to mount Torka. He had recovered his sword from among the weapons left behind by Sonten's band, and had buckled a light crossbow to his saddle rings, along with a quiver full of short, deadly bolts. With a final tug at its straps, he turned to hug Sullyan.

"Go swiftly, Robin," she said. "Your powers are strong enough now to open a tunnel directly onto the river below the ridge behind the Manor. You remember the technique?" He nodded. "As soon as you can, contact General Blaine and explain the situation. Ask him to spare you a company. Our own, for preference. But Robin," she cautioned, seeing the hard look on his face, "mind you ask nicely."

He feigned a hurt expression. "Why wouldn't I?"

She smiled, appreciating his clumsy attempt to lighten the mood. "Sonten should not be too far ahead of you, and, with any luck, he will have a nasty shock when he prepares to cross the Veils. At least, he will if he expects Cal to supply the means."

Vanyr, already mounted, frowned. "Why's that, Major?"

She turned to him. "Cal is only Apprentice-elite, and newly fledged at that. He has neither the skills nor the strength to open a trans-Veil tunnel. Neither could he fix the destination of a portway. So, unless the two Artesans Sonten has with him are far more skilled, the General will have to take a chance on his point of entry into Albia. I doubt he is familiar with the lesser towns and villages of our land, and Taran only told him the name of his village, not its exact location. Your timely arrival last night prevented that. We, on the other hand, know precisely where he needs to go, so that should give you every chance of arriving before him.

"Do not forget that the villagers are vulnerable innocents. Do all you can to protect them. Engage Sonten in the fields, if you can." She swept them with a concerned gaze. "You should go. The light is increasing, and Sonten will be on the move. Do not fear for me. We will return to the Citadel. No doubt Anjer's escort will meet us on the way. Robin, my love, take care."

With a final clasp of her hand, Robin vaulted into Torka's

saddle. Wheeling the horses, the company disappeared through the trees. Ky-shan was last to go, and as he passed Sullyan, he said, "Don't worry, Lady, we'll watch out for him."

"Thank you, Ky," she murmured, watching him spur his horse after Robin.

*****

Followed by Vanyr and the pirates, Robin rode as fast as he dared through the dense woods. The light increased steadily. He was content to trail Sonten for now because he didn't hold out much hope of catching him before he crossed into Albia. Sonten would have quickly realized he had shaken his pursuers last night, and Robin was sure the General would have wasted no time discovering how little his remaining captive knew about traveling the Veils. What this had cost Cal, Robin dared not think.

It was what Robin himself would have done—learn your enemy's strengths and weaknesses before planning your final strategy. Therefore, despite last night's chaotic events and the darkness which would have made it tricky finding a suitable place to cross the Veils, Robin wouldn't be at all surprised to learn that Sonten was already in Albia. If that was the case, then he stood little chance of tracking the General directly. Had Robin known the patterns of either of the two Artesans in Sonten's party, he might have been able to follow their echo through the substrate. He did not. He didn't even know their rank, so it was entirely possible that at least one of them had the strength or knowledge to open a tunnel for Sonten, maybe even one large enough to take his whole party through at once. Therefore, Robin's plan was to find a suitable boundary, set up a tunnel, and pass through to the Manor as quickly as possible. Then, hopefully with Blaine's help, he could prevent Sonten from reaching Taran's village.

He told his thoughts to Vanyr and Ky-shan as they rode. Both men nodded. Vanyr then mentioned the factor that was taxing Robin. "If Sonten does need Cal to open the Veils, he'll have to take the spellsilver off him, won't he? We would be able to find him. He would surely try to contact one of you, tell you where he is."

"Perhaps," conceded Robin. "Trouble is, he doesn't know what has happened. He was unconscious all through last night. Sonten might have told him the rest of us are dead, and Cal won't know truth from lie. But Sonten won't use Cal unless both his own Artesans are Apprentices. Why take the risk? And I think this Heron we've heard about must be ranked higher than that. Otherwise he'd stand no chance of learning to use the Staff." He grimaced. "There are too many unknowns for me. I prefer to rely on facts. I know where Sonten's headed, and if I can get there first, so much the better. I like an ambush, Commander. They're neat, tidy, and usually very effective."

Vanyr smiled. "Do you think we could get hold of this Staff thing before Sonten even arrives? Can you imagine how furious he'd be if we did?"

Robin shrugged. "I doubt it. Taran says it's buried under tons of rubble and would take days to dig out. It sounds like it would take hours even if we had an entire company digging. No, Commander. Much as I would like to taunt Sonten with it, I want to concentrate on rescuing Cal. Once we have him safe, we can turn our attention to digging out the Staff. Now, have you any idea how much farther these damned woods extend?"

Having made the decision not to hunt Sonten on the Andaryan side of the Veils, they made better time. Vanyr knew where the forest boundary was and guided Robin toward it, the Captain's mind and nerves churning as he rode. Despite Sullyan's avowal that he was strong enough for this next task, Robin was anxious. Fixing the egress of a trans-Veil tunnel was a Master-level skill. He knew the mechanics of it—the theory was easy to learn. The problem was having the sheer strength of will to direct where it opened, and he knew he would need every ounce of concentration he could muster. At least Vanyr's Journeyman strength could help him if he faltered.

They didn't stop for a noon meal, but ate while riding. They slackened pace to allow the horses some rest for an hour or so, then Robin picked it up once more. By early evening they had reached the forest boundary on the border between the Hierarch's province and Kymer.

Robin called a halt to breathe the horses and sat regarding the land spread out before him. They had headed steadily southeast and, if they continued on, would eventually reach Rykan's palace. Briefly, Robin wondered if that was Sonten's immediate objective, rather than Taran's village. A secure base from which to extract more information from Cal in relative safety. Yet he soon dismissed the notion. Sonten must know he was being pursued, and he would also know that his destination was obvious to anyone who knew Cal and Taran. He would want to make all possible speed.

Despite his lack of confidence, Robin knew he had to attempt the crossing before camping for the night. Once back on Albian soil, he could contact General Blaine in safety and set things at the Manor in motion.

He turned to Ky-shan and Vanyr, both watching to see what he had decided. "It has to be tonight."

They nodded, having expected no less.

"I have to tell you," he added, the candor of his tone drawing their eyes, "that I have never done this before. Sullyan says I am capable, and she should know, but I'm not confident. I'm warning you now. I might need help with this, Commander, if you're willing."

"My name is Torman, Captain, and I am at your disposal," said Vanyr. "I don't believe the Major would have told you you're ready if you're not. But if my skills can help you, don't hesitate to ask."

Robin gave a sigh of relief. "Thanks."

He dismounted, taking a steadying breath. "This is a likely place for me to form the tunnel, because that line of rocks there will make a good barrier against leaks. This is what I propose. Most of these horses have never been through the Veils before, so I think we should blindfold them. Sometimes they spook, and I can do without loose horses ruining my concentration. Any of the men who are nervous can wear blindfolds too, if it helps. Going through the Veils can play tricks with your eyes. Ky-shan, will you organize that?"

The stocky seaman nodded. Turning to his men, he gave the

order to dismount. Vanyr also dismounted and laid a hand on Robin's shoulder. "I have faith in you, Adept-elite. If Brynne Sullyan has had a hand in your training, you know far more than you think. You do know she's Pharikian's metaphysical equal, don't you?"

Robin frowned. "What, Senior Master? You sure? She never mentioned it."

Vanyr shrugged. "She's not admitting it to herself yet. I suppose she's got other things on her mind. But I could feel it when we linked, and I know Pharikian's capabilities very well. If she comes through this, don't be surprised if he has something planned for her."

Sudden tears pricked Robin's eyes. There were too many 'ifs' to be resolved. These past few months had been the hardest, yet also some of the sweetest, of his short life. He had never known such emotional turmoil since his sister Jessy's illness and death. It was almost too much to bear.

As if in understanding, Vanyr squeezed his shoulder. "Come on, Captain. Let's get to work."

Ky-shan had organized his men well, and many of them already sported blindfolds. Most of the horses did too, and they stood quietly, lined up nose to tail for safety. Vanyr told Robin that neither his nor Ky-shan's mounts would baulk. On hearing this, Robin asked the Commander to lead the column through, with Ky-shan bringing up the rear. All that remained was for him to open the way.

He stood beside the blessedly steady Torka, the big chestnut's ears pricked and alert, sensing his master's tension. Robin looped the reins over one arm and took a few deep breaths. He was aware of Vanyr's encouraging eyes upon him and Ky-shan's expectant expression. Hoping he wouldn't show himself up, he began.

The first task was to isolate the portion of his complex psyche that related to Earth and attune himself to it. This was easy—it was a basic Apprentice skill. Once immersed in and surrounded by the signature of Earth, Robin sent his senses deep into the ground beneath his feet, feeling for the ponderous power, keeping the solid, symmetrical quality of it firmly in his mind. He felt relief as it responded to his will, rising smoothly up from the bedrock and soil to form the shimmering grey structure of a trans-Veil opening. As it took shape in the air above the natural rocky outcrop Robin had chosen as his starting point, the Captain fixed his thoughts very firmly on a specific area of the Manor's vast lands, namely the edge of the stream below the ridge where he and Bull had watched Taran take his final step toward the rank of Adept. Locking this location in his mind, he pushed forward on the power, easing it through the Veils.

As it slipped through each barrier, he anchored the structure, still holding firmly to his destination. Then the final barrier gave way and he smiled in relief when he saw a familiar landscape of water and a riverbank open out before him. Desperate not to lose his concentration, he gestured to Vanyr.

The tall Commander nudged his horse forward and rode slowly through the grey, color-shot tunnel. He had drawn his sword—Robin would have done the same—but once he was through, the Captain could see there was nothing to trouble him. Robin then signaled for the column to start moving, and they slowly shuffled forward in single file. Thanks to the blindfolds, all the horses went calmly. Robin allowed himself to relax. Even one spooking at the wrong moment could have caused him to lose control, and had the structure collapsed it would have stranded the column somewhere in another land. Finding them again would not necessarily be difficult, but it would be tiring and time-consuming.

The strain was beginning to tell on Robin, and he was thankful when Ky-shan, as rear-guard, finally reached Vanyr's side. He followed through with Torka, collapsing the tunnel as he went. Once safely on Albian soil he stood breathing deeply, trying to regain some strength. He accepted Vanyr's congratulatory slap on the back with a feeling of pride. Perhaps he was ready to become Master, after all.

While the Commander and Ky-shan saw to the removal of the blindfolds, Robin sent a questing thought to General Blaine. It was late in the evening, but not too late. The Captain knew Blaine never retired early. His tentative contact was swiftly accepted, but what Blaine had to tell him shocked him to the core. His dismay must have shown on his face. Vanyr was watching him closely, and as soon as Blaine broke the contact, he asked, "What is it, Captain? What's wrong?"

Robin swore. "We've badly underestimated Sonten, that's what's wrong. Far from relying on Cal to take him and his men through the Veils last night, or even this morning, he must have sent an advance force into Albia via one of his own Artesans. They could have been here for days, hiding out in the countryside, learning their way around, just waiting for Sonten's instructions. Once he'd made Taran tell him where the Staff was, he must have relayed the information to this advance force. They pinpointed Taran's village and surrounded it. He already has the place completely cut off."

"Triton's balls!" grunted Ky-shan.

The young Captain continued. "The good news is that Blaine got word of it. One of the villagers managed to get away and rode through the night for help. Two companies from the Manor are already on their way to Hyecombe. The bad news is that the village was taken at night, so all the villagers were in their homes. General Blaine has ordered our forces not to engage Sonten while the villagers are in danger."

"So Sonten and Cal are already there?" Vanyr's expression registered his disgust.

"We have to assume so, yes. With Sonten's advance party in control of the village, they would have directed him straight there. They probably even know which house to search and may already be digging out the Staff. Let's hope Taran was right about the amount of time it would take to retrieve the thing."

"Any news of Cal?"

Robin shook his head. "No doubt he'll be kept closely confined, if he's even still alive. My guess is that his life depends on whether Sonten knows where the Staff is. I don't know if Sonten's Artesans would be able to sense the thing, but even if Cal has held out on him—and if I know Cal, he'll have tried his damnedest—it won't take Sonten long to work out where the weapon is. Maybe Cal still has hostage value, and maybe he doesn't. That will depend on Sonten's plans for the Staff once he recovers it. If this man Heron is going to take Jaskin's place, then I'm guessing they'll need a victim to test the weapon on."

Vanyr turned pale. Robin tried not to imagine how being stripped of his powers by such a terrible method might feel. Another dreadful possibility occurred to him, and he stared at Vanyr in horror.

"What, Captain?"

Robin's voice shivered with dread. "Torman, what if Sonten knows Sullyan needs the Staff to survive? He knows what Rykan did to her. He must also know what she did to Rykan in the arena, and why she needed his life force. We all heard Rykan refuse to trade his life for hers, and Sonten must surely have heard her say that some of his power was missing. Oh, gods! Torman, if Sonten is ambitious and confident enough to mount his own challenge on the Hierarch, then he won't want Sullyan in the way any more than Rykan did. Especially now he knows she would be on Pharikian's side. He only has to keep us from recovering the Staff to be rid of her!"

Vanyr scowled. "Then we'll have to make damned sure he doesn't succeed."

Ky-shan nodded. "Don't you worry, Skip, Sonten won't slip through our fingers this time. He may think he has the upper hand for now, but he doesn't know we're coming in force against him. With any luck, we'll take him by surprise and slaughter the lot of them before they disappear with the Staff."

"I can't take any chances with the villagers," warned Robin, "but apart from that, I agree with you. I'm not going to jeopardize Cal's life if I can help it, but neither am I going to let Sonten deny Sullyan her chance of survival. Much as I want to leave for Hyecombe right away, I think we ought to call at the Manor tomorrow morning. I can brief General Blaine fully and try to convince him to send more men. Then, if we ride hard, we can make it to the village by nightfall, assess the situation, and rendezvous with the commanders of the units already there. Together, we'll work out what's best to do."

*****

Under low scudding clouds and intermittent rain, Robin led his band into the Manor. The sentries were expecting him, but even so, they looked askance at a group of Andaryans riding openly into their midst. After tactfully asking Solet to see to their comforts, Robin left the pirates at the horse lines, taking only Vanyr and Ky-shan to meet with General Blaine.

Blaine invited them into his office and shook hands gravely with both the tall Commander and the stocky seaman. Appreciating the irony of the situation, Vanyr and Ky-shan remained silent while Robin swiftly briefed the General. When he was done, Blaine sat back, his face impassive.

"You say this … artifact is vital to the Major's survival?"

"Yes, sir," said Robin.

"And if she can make use of it, she will be able to return and resume her life?"

"Presumably, sir."

Robin was unable to read Blaine's expression, but for once he was not rattled by it. The General seemed to be taking him seriously and treating the matter with the gravity it deserved. After his unprecedented display of emotion on taking his leave of Sullyan at Marik's mansion, much of Robin's dislike and mistrust of the man had vanished. His previous unflattering opinions had undergone a radical turn-around. Blaine had finally let his guard down, and Robin could understand why he acted as he did.

The General regarded him, eyes hard. "You're certain there's no other way for Sullyan to return? You're saying that if we don't recover this artifact, this Staff, we'll be as good as signing her death warrant?"

Robin's heart lurched at Blaine's blunt phrasing. "That's about it, sir."

"Very well. Captain, take the Major's company to Hyecombe. Sergeant Dexter has been leading them well enough, but I know he'll appreciate your return. I authorize you to do whatever you can to relieve the village and recover the Staff. Protect the villagers as best you can, but use all your resources to regain that artifact. Is that clear?"

"Perfectly, sir." Robin snapped a smart salute. "I'll succeed, sir. Don't worry."

"I don't doubt it, Captain," said the General, slapping Robin on the shoulder. The young man was astonished. Never before had Blaine shown such trust in him.

He still couldn't believe it as he led Vanyr and Ky-shan swiftly back, past the Major's office door, which he tried hard not to look at, and out toward the barracks. His heart racing at the thought of positive action, he yelled for Dexter to ready the Major's company.

*****

Escorted by Anjer's men and accompanied by the Lord General himself as an indication of her status, Sullyan arrived back at the Citadel by noon. Riding into the lower town, her party received the acclaim of the sentries and members of the Velletian Guard. Pharikian's people had not yet had the opportunity to honor the Champion of the Crown and were eager for festivities to celebrate Sullyan's achievement. As they rode along the Processional Way, Anjer told her that Pharikian would be organizing some kind of formality to mark the victory. Sullyan, however, only had thoughts for Rienne, and worries for Robin and Cal.

She dismounted in the palace courtyard, pleased to see that some of Anjer's men were assisting Taran and Bull. Both men looked about with interest as grooms led away their horses. A slim, dark-haired figure came running into the courtyard and threw herself into Taran's arms. Rienne was sobbing wildly, and the startled Adept held her as tightly as his bruised flesh would allow, murmuring words of encouragement and comfort.

Sullyan went over to add her own reassurance. "Cal will come back safe, Rienne, Robin will see to that. Sonten needs him too badly to harm him overmuch. Cal is not without defenses. He will be alright, I promise you."

Rienne pushed herself out of Taran's embrace. "How can you say that?" she snapped. "Look at Taran! Just look what's happened to him! Why couldn't you have got Cal away safely, too? Why did you leave him behind?"

Sobbing inconsolably, she turned and fled back into the palace. Sullyan watched her go, tears in her eyes.

Taran came close and put his arm around her thin shoulders. “Don’t worry,” he murmured, “she didn’t mean it. She’s just upset. I understand how she feels. I want to rage at someone too because of my fear for Cal. She’ll be better once she’s let it out. I’ll go after her. Maybe I can calm her down.”

“If there is anything I can do, Taran, please call me,” said Sullyan sadly, watching as he limped stiffly after Rienne.

He was right. The truth was that she was feeling guilty about what had happened to Cal, and she was undeniably responsible for his being caught up in her problems. She had known of her friends’ presence in Andaryon before the duel with Rykan. She really should have sent a patrol out to guide them into the Citadel. She had not, and now she was helpless to do anything to aid Cal and must leave others to do her fighting for her. It was not a situation she was used to, and it galled her.

Another figure emerged into the courtyard, interrupting her thoughts. He was walking slowly and carefully with a stick to aid him. Seeing him gladdened her heart after Rienne’s distress. She walked toward the Count and accepted his outstretched hand with a smile. He pulled her gently to him and planted a kiss on her lips. She felt herself flush and he laughed.

Bull walked past them and gave Marik a teasing glare. “You sly dog! You wouldn’t dare do that if Robin were here.”

Marik grinned.

Sullyan stood back to look at him. It was two weeks since he had been so gravely injured, and Deshan’s healing, along with Idrimar’s careful nursing, had brought him along nicely. His arm was no longer in a sling, but she could tell by the way he carried it that the shoulder was still tender. The wound in his back was clearly healing well, and the nerves and muscles were only stiff due to lack of use.

“How do you feel, Ty?”

“I am well enough, Brynne,” he assured her. “I have only to get my strength back, and it’s coming slowly. Idri still wants to keep me wrapped in blankets like a baby, and I suppose I shouldn’t blame her. But I'm getting bored, and I'm afraid I'll get fat on what she insists on feeding me. I'd give much to get back on the training ground and start working again."

"Not too soon," she cautioned. "That shoulder needs to strengthen before you tax it overmuch. Listen to the Princess. Let her pamper you for a while. You might as well enjoy it while you can."

He smiled, his eyes glittering. "Oh, I am, Brynne. Believe me, I am."

She smiled at his smugness. "Well, I hope you are both being careful. You are not married yet, you know."

He feigned a hurt expression. "I may not have much power, but I know enough not to let her get pregnant. I can at least get that right."

"I hope so. I can just imagine what Pharikian would say—not to mention her brother—if she went to her wedding swelling with child. I have heard that the Heir is a stickler for protocol and correctness, and he is apparently very protective of his sister. If he was to hear of your premarital … arrangements, it might prejudice him against you."

Marik's pale eyes widened. "Do you think so?"

"Definitely."

He stared at her a moment before breaking into a grin. "Damn you, Brynne Sullyan. I never know when you're being serious. When will I learn to stop falling for your innocent face and barbed comments?"

"When you are in your grave!"

She laughed, their easy banter lightening her soul. Taking his arm, she steered him slowly after the others.

Chapter Seven

Robin wasted little time marshaling the Major's company. Once Sergeant Dexter understood the seriousness of the situation, he swiftly alerted the men. They greeted Robin warmly and gathered around him as he entered the barracks, clamoring for news of Sullyan. The Andaryans trailed Robin nervously, uncertain of their reception, yet once Robin had explained their relationship with Sullyan and what they had done for her, they were accepted without rancor.

Vanyr was amazed and turned to murmur to Ky-shan beside him. "I've never seen anything like this. These men are treating their Captain more like a friend. The love they bear both him and the Major is obvious. I try to be a fair and firm commander, and all my men respect me, but this goes far beyond anything I've experienced. These Albian swordsmen sound more like a family than a company of fighting men."

Ky-shan grinned. "I'm sure the Skip will explain it to you if you ask him. For me, all I care about is how quickly they obey his orders."

Robin's orders were obeyed swiftly enough to satisfy the most critical of commanders. His briefing over, the men ran for their horses, mounting and forming up behind Robin with the seamen absorbed into their ranks. Robin moved them out and rode at their head, Vanyr and Ky-shan just behind him.

Once they were underway, Dexter nudged his horse up close to Robin's. Keeping his voice low, he asked, "How is the Major, Captain? What are her chances of returning to us?"

Robin glanced at him. He had not been completely candid in

his briefing, and the quick-witted Dexter had realized there was more to be told. His clear concern entitled him to the truth.

"That's partly up to us, Dex. The artifact Sonten is so desperate to get hold of is actually the key to her survival. If we want her back, we have to stop it falling into his hands. But he's still holding Cal hostage, as far as we know, and Sullyan will kill me if anything happens to him. Our two objectives are Cal and the Staff, but Cal takes priority. We also have to think about the safety of the villagers. We can't allow Sonten to hold them to ransom or do them any harm. If necessary, we'll let him take the Staff and run him down later. Those are her orders, backed up by the General. This time, I intend to obey them."

Dexter nodded. "Understood, Captain. But if the demon does take the Staff, let me and the boys hunt him down. It's the least we can do. They've been fretting about her all the time she's been gone. They need to do something to help."

Robin smiled grimly. "They'll get their chance, Dex, don't worry. They'll get their chance."

Robin was both pleased and proud that his men had taken little convincing to accept the Andaryans. He could hear snatches of conversation in the ranks of horsemen behind him, coupled with good-natured banter as the seamen told how they had helped Sullyan win her place in the Hierarch's forces. Their instant camaraderie took care of one of his main concerns. His one remaining fear revolved around Vanyr and Ky-shan. The pirate leader might have set aside his dislike of Vanyr for the moment, but it would only take one word from him, one hint of what Vanyr had done to Sullyan at the Hierarch's palace, to reach the ears of Robin's men, and the tall Commander might never see his homeland again. The Captain could only hope that their mission would keep them occupied, and that Ky-shan wouldn't let anything slip.

They arrived at the outskirts of Hyecombe just after nightfall. Using his intimate knowledge of the terrain, Robin had taken them cross-country, saving precious hours. When they were close enough, he slowed them and sent a couple of outriders ahead to contact the sentries of the other two units. On receiving their report, he led his men into the encampment to confer with the other two captains.

An outlying hay barn was doing duty as a makeshift command post. As he strode inside, Vanyr, Ky-shan, Almid, and Kester at his back, Robin immediately gained the attention of the two men waiting for him. He was ready, having been forewarned by General Blaine that one of the captains was Parren. The young man had been harshly disciplined by Colonel Vassa and stripped of privileges for weeks after their duel, but Robin knew that Parren was too good a field officer to lose. Vassa had decided not to transfer him, as he had threatened, but to give him a second chance. The other two men involved, Parren's corporal and sergeant, were summarily dismissed from the King's service, and the corporal was imprisoned for his attempted rape of Rienne, but Parren had gradually insinuated himself back into Vassa's good books.

Now he regarded Robin with barely concealed dislike. He had probably, thought Robin, convinced himself that neither his rival nor Sullyan would return from Andaryon, so this development would only embitter him further. Robin could sense that Vanyr had picked up Parren's aura of hatred, and he hoped the Commander wouldn't make trouble. This would be delicate enough without tempers getting frayed.

Parren, the purple line of his scar showing starkly against his pale cheek, feigned disinterest. He lounged indolently against the barn wall, his hands thrust through his sword belt. The other captain, who was also under Vassa's command, was a small, agile man called Baily, and he willingly briefed Robin on the current situation. Robin tried hard to concentrate on Baily's words, but all the time he could feel Parren's eyes scraping his back.

Trying to ignore it, he asked, "How are Sonten's men deployed?"

Baily brought both hands together. "In a cordon round the whole village. The area's sewn up tighter than a whore's purse. They had too much time to entrench before we got here."

Parren spat, making as much noise as possible. "Couldn't you have alerted us sooner, Tamsen? You must have known they were coming."

"Not in time, I didn't." Robin threw the other man a sour look, galled to have to admit this in front of him. "We knew nothing of Sonten's extra troops, or that he had already sent them through the Veils. We only rescued Bull and Taran yesterday. We thought we were on his heels and that he'd have trouble crossing the Veils. It seems we were wrong."

Parren straightened from his slouch. "Well, he's out-thought you properly for sure. We'll be hard pressed to budge him before he gets what he wants. Even then, he has enough men to keep us occupied while he slips away."

"We'll have to make counter plans if he tries," said Robin. "Commander Vanyr and Ky-shan here can take their men and go after him if necessary. They know their own lands best. The rest of us will hold as many of them as we can and do our best to make sure they don't escape."

Parren's flat gaze roved insultingly over the Andaryans. "And how can we trust that these … demons … will do as you say? What's to stop them from turning on us in the dark?"

"They won't turn on us, Parren, because they're friends. I'd trust any of them before I'd trust you, that's for sure!"

Vanyr's hand had dropped to his sword hilt, and Ky-shan's expression was bleak.

Parren went white and he even drew a short length of steel before the looming figures of Ky-shan and Vanyr forced him to snap it back home. He glared at them with clear hostility. Ignoring him, trying to stay calm, Robin turned back to Baily. "How many men do you think Sonten has?"

Baily shrugged. "About two hundred and fifty, I reckon. I have no idea how many are in the village itself, but if the numbers in the cordon are anything to go by, he must have at least that."

Robin stared at him, dismayed. His own command numbered eighty, and the other two units would have about the same. Equal odds were not what he had hoped for. Yet he could hardly expect Blaine to release any more men. It would leave the Manor dangerously low on defenses. He had to make do with what he had.

"Intelligence," he muttered, ignoring Parren's insulting snort, "that's what we need here." He turned to Ky-shan. "What are the chances of one of your men getting inside Sonten's cordon?"

Ky-shan's pale blue eyes gleamed in the lamplight. "I can call for volunteers, Skip. Do you want me to do it now?"

Robin nodded. "It has to be tonight if we're going to do it. Sonten might already have men digging out that Staff and I don't want to gift him more time than I have to. The darkness will hide our man and make it easier for him to move about unrecognized." He turned to include Vanyr, Parren, and Baily. "What we'll need is a distraction along the cordon, just enough to let someone slip through. Although how he'll get out again is anyone's guess."

Ky-shan grinned. "Don't worry about that, Skip. I think I know just the man. Let me see if I can persuade him."

As the seaman left the barn, Vanyr moved a step closer to Robin. Parren glared at them both and kept his hand on his sword hilt. Robin's heart fell, hoping the sour young captain wasn't going to jeopardize his plans. Parren had no loyalty to Sullyan—just the opposite, in fact—and now that Robin knew the significance of the Staff he wouldn't bet against Parren trying to sabotage their efforts to regain it.

Ky-shan soon returned, bringing with him a small, wiry man. Brown and weathered as all the pirates were, he had a thin, pointed nose and chin, and his tiny bright eyes were pale brown. Robin recognized him. His name was Zolt, and he had been an enthusiastic harrier of Rykan's forces. His face bore a mischievous grin, and he seemed more than willing to carry out Robin's plan. "What do you want to know once I'm in, Skip?" he asked.

Robin briefly outlined his main objectives.

"If possible, I want to know what's happened to Cal and where he's being held." He ticked the items off his fingers. "Then I need to know if Sonten has identified the Staff's position, and whether he's doing anything about recovering it. Next, I want to know what's happened to the villagers and whether any of them have been harmed. And lastly, a more accurate assessment of Sonten's numbers and how they're distributed within the village."

"Is that all?" Zolt grinned. "That won't take me long."

"Just be careful," warned Robin. "Without this knowledge our hands are tied. We need you in and out as soon as you can manage it."

The little man grinned again. "This is right up my rope, Skip. Don't worry."

Ky-shan clapped his man on the back. "He used to be a wharf rat," he said to Robin.

The term meant nothing to Robin, who had never seen a commercial port.

Ky-shan elaborated. "Wharf rat is what the port authorities call those who make their living by liberating items from the cargoes of merchant ships. They climb the hawsers by night, break into the holds, collect a store of goods, and then slip out again before anyone knows they've been. Very good at it, they are, if they live to be Zolt's age."

Parren leaned forward. "Oh, a common little thief," he sneered. He jumped backward as the wickedly sharp knife which had materialized in Zolt's hand was jammed against his belly, poised to slide home. He didn't even have time to grasp his sword hilt. He turned white with shock, and swore.

Zolt hissed into his face. "Less of the common, if you don't mind, my scarred friend."

Beads of sweat appeared on Parren's brow and he muttered a grudging apology. The little seaman stepped back and the knife disappeared. Robin shot Parren a look of disgust before turning to Zolt once more.

"We'll create a diversion by attacking part of the cordon. That should give you the chance to slip past. Once you're inside, though, getting out again will be your own problem."

"I'll be fine, Skip," said Zolt, throwing Parren a menacing look before leaving to make his preparations.

Robin turned to the other two captains. "Can we expect your help with the diversion?"

Baily nodded instantly, but Parren held Robin's eyes longer than he would have liked. "Who put you in charge?" he demanded.

Vanyr stiffened, but Baily moved quickly. "We're here to achieve the same end, aren't we? What does it matter who makes the decisions?"

Parren stared at him coldly, then shrugged. Too low for Baily to hear, he muttered, "Oh, it matters."

Robin wisely decided to let it drop.

The Captain briefed his men and gave them their orders. This might be a diversionary tactic, but it would also serve to test just how well organized and determined Sonten's defenses were. Baily and Parren had already failed to make an impression on the cordon in the short time they had been here, but if the Albians could account for some of Sonten's men in this feint it would increase their chances when the main assault began.

Moving silently, Robin joined the line of crossbowmen facing the outer houses of the village. Vanyr and Ky-shan—neither of whom were skilled with the weapon—looked on. The plan was for the bowmen to punch a hole in the cordon, which the swordsmen would then try to keep open just long enough for Zolt to slip through. Then they would retreat. Robin wasn't prepared to risk too many men in the darkness.

Once he was happy with their positions, Robin gave the order to pick targets. The men in Sonten's cordon were spread around the perimeter of the village, using outbuildings and sheds as cover, and Robin had instructed his bowmen to approach as stealthily as possible before loosing their bolts. So far, no alarm had been raised. The swordsmen were crouched behind the bowmen, weapons drawn, ready to move in once the bows discharged. Zolt was hiding somewhere in the darkness, wrapped in a dark cloak and armed only with his wicked knife. He had refused any other weapons, saying that if his knife was not sufficient then he would deserve whatever he got. Respecting his confidence, Robin did not argue.

From behind a large tree, Robin took careful aim at his chosen target. The man was half-hidden by the shed he was using as cover. Robin had spotted him when he moved a fraction, possibly easing cramped muscles. Robin could just draw a bead on his head.

Vanyr's voice came softly over Robin's shoulder. "You'll never hit him at that angle."

His voice tight with concentration, Robin said, "Would you

care to make a wager, Torman?" He let off a bolt that sped straight and true, killing the man instantly and pinning him to the side of the shed. He heard other crossbows discharging, followed by the grunts and cries of wounded men. The alarm was raised and Sonten's men began shooting back, but they aimed blindly because Robin had yet to release the swordsmen.

He rewound his bow, taking the bolt held out to him by an impressed Vanyr. "Where the Void did you learn to shoot like that?" the Commander murmured.

Dexter, crouched on the other side of the tree, heard him and chuckled. "Our Captain's the best shot in the King's forces."

Robin smiled grimly and took aim on another of Sonten's men, who had left himself exposed while searching for a target of his own. He never stood a chance.

After that, the opportunity for clear shots was over. Robin released his swordsmen and Sonten's defenders rushed toward them. The clash of steel and the cries of men sounded louder than normal in the darkness. Robin and Vanyr fought side by side, the Commander grunting hard with each stroke. Dexter fought on their right, his strokes rarely missing their target.

Despite their skill, it soon became clear that the defenders were too well entrenched for the Albian forces to make any real headway. They fell back on Robin's signal and regrouped, none of them having seen Zolt get through. Dexter thought he had seen a man on the roof of an outhouse, but couldn't be sure if it was Zolt or one of Sonten's men. Robin shrugged. He could only hope the man would return safely with his report.

He took stock of injuries and losses. They had got off lightly due to the surprise of their attack, and there were only minor wounds. The crossbows, however, had accounted for a good ten of Sonten's men, which was heartening. To prevent the besiegers from resting, Robin gave the order for the bowmen to continue shooting sporadically during the night. Then he retired to the barn.

Baily and Parren were already there. Vanyr, Ky-shan, Almid, and Kester followed Robin in. The two giants, much to Robin's surprise, stationed themselves on either side of him as he sat on a campstool, and Parren regarded them sourly, looking them up and down. "What's this, Tamsen?" he sneered. "Bodyguards?"

Robin smiled. "No, Parren, just loyal friends. Not virtues you have much experience of, are they, loyalty and friendship?"

Parren's expression hardened and he stared hungrily at Robin. He forbore to comment, but his demeanor promised retribution. Robin didn't dwell on it. He had more pressing matters to worry over. Once they had eaten and the camp settled for the night, he turned in.

*****

Dexter's hand on his shoulder woke him just before dawn. The barn was quiet, the others still asleep. Robin roused and followed Dexter at the Sergeant's beckon. A figure wrapped in a cloak was waiting for him outside, the little man's grin clearly visible in the predawn gloom.

"Zolt," exclaimed Robin softly, "I didn't expect you back so soon. Any luck?"

The small man nodded. "Told you it wouldn't take me long, Skip. Yes, I got your information."

"Come and tell me what you learned," said Robin, keen to hear the news and form a plan before Parren got wind of it. He guided Zolt over to the edge of the camp, Dexter following. "Right, let's have it. You obviously didn't have any trouble from Sonten's men."

The little man spat dismissively. "It was easy as stealing. Managed to slip past them and move about freely. I know how to be inconspicuous when I want. From what I could tell, pretty much all the villagers are being held in a large building to the west. It's a tavern. None of them have been harmed, as far as I could tell. Some of their jailors are a little worse for drink, but not enough to incapacitate them. I doubt they've paid for their grog, though, and your tavern keeper's none too happy! Your mate Cal isn't with them. He and Sonten, along with about five guards, are holed up in a small cottage near where the two streets cross. It's in a right state. There's rubble all over the deck and it looks like someone's been digging up the floor."

Robin frowned. Had Sonten already found the Staff? "Do you think the rubble's fresh, or does it look like it's been there for weeks?"

"Dunno." Zolt shrugged. "There's plaster dust everywhere. Could be fresh, could be old. Dust is dust."

"I suppose so. Alright, what else did you learn? I take it Cal's still alive?"

"He's alive. I saw him through the window. He's in a bad way, though. Broken arm at least, and he's been beaten and burned. I reckon Sonten's not finished with him yet either, because one of the guards was giving him water. He's safe enough for now."

Robin forced down his concern for Cal. He could not afford the distraction. "What about their numbers?"

The little man replied after a moment's hesitation. "I reckon two-fifty's about right, Skip. I couldn't see any more concealed anywhere. Most of Sonten's strength's in the cordon. There're only a few score inside the village as guards. My guess is that the villagers' good behavior is surety for Cal's life, and they're mindful of that. But they didn't look like they were cowed or frightened, so I don't think they'd hesitate to fight back if they thought it would do any good."

Robin pondered this before realizing he had to tell the others. Much as he hated to admit it, Parren was right. Blaine had not put anyone in overall charge, and he, Baily, and Parren were all the same rank. Without their cooperation he couldn't command them, and he needed their cooperation if the village was to be saved. Taking Zolt back inside the barn, he woke the others and told them the news.

Parren was unimpressed by Zolt's suggestion that the villagers would support them from the inside. "I think we ought to wait for this Sonten to dig up what he wants and let him leave the village," he said. "That way he's done all the hard work, none of the villagers are endangered, and we can engage him out in the fields."

Cautious as always, Baily shook his head. "Don't forget he has equal numbers. It wouldn't be an easy fight, out in the open with no cover."

"And there's no guarantee he'll leave the villagers unharmed," added Robin. "He's bound to kill Cal, at least, and I wouldn't put it past him to fire the houses as a diversion. Even kill the lot of them as revenge for Rykan's death."

Parren glared at him. "That was your doing, Tamsen, not ours. It has nothing to do with Albia."

"He's made it Albia's business by invading Hyecombe," Robin shot back.

"And anyway," said Baily, "since when have we let demons run roughshod over our countryside without giving them a taste of our steel?" He flushed, suddenly remembering there were five armed demons in the barn with him. He glanced hastily at them. "Begging your pardon, of course."

Vanyr showed his teeth and Ky-shan glowered.

Robin sighed. He couldn't afford to let them argue. "Gentlemen, all this bickering is getting us nowhere. General Blaine's orders are that we do whatever we can to prevent Sonten from escaping with the Staff, and to rescue Cal. Protecting the villagers is a given, but we mustn't let Sonten leave. Are you two going to help me or not?"

"Of course we are," said Baily. He glared pointedly at Parren.

The sallow captain didn't take his empty eyes from Robin's face. "Oh yes, of course. Can't leave the Queen of Darkness in trouble, can we?"

Robin reacted immediately, but Vanyr was quicker. The Andaryan loomed over Parren, his lithe form hovering dangerously, his hand on his sword hilt. "Are you referring to Major Sullyan?"

Parren was unfazed by Vanyr's menace and spat back at him, "What's it to you? You another witch-lover, are you?"

Vanyr's white eyes narrowed. "How dare you? She's a friend, and a good one. If I hear any more insults from your mouth, I'll stop it for good."

Parren snarled, surging forward with his sword half-drawn. "I'd like to see you try!"

Dismayed, Robin stepped between them. Almid and Kester moved swiftly to either side of Parren, ready to take his arms if necessary. Glowering at them, recognizing his peril, Parren spat on the ground by Vanyr's feet. His sword slid home.

Robin stared at both of them, trying to keep his tone level. "Gentlemen, please! Surely we have more important concerns right now than arguing and insulting each other? There'll be time enough for settling personal scores once we've accomplished our task." He turned to Vanyr. "Commander, may I remind you of the reason we're here? The Major is relying on us. Let's keep our minds on that."

Vanyr backed off slowly, his eyes still fixed on Parren. "Very well, Captain. But once we're done here, I intend to have an accounting for his insults."

"My pleasure." Parren spat again. "If you live long enough."

The tension in the barn subsided as they made their plans. The dawn light brought confirmation that their night raid, coupled with the sporadic attacks that had continued through the dark hours, had caused Sonten to tighten his cordon. He had fired some of the outlying buildings, presumably to prevent them being used by the Albians, and had withdrawn farther into the village. The smoke gave the Albians some cover, but also meant it was harder to see Sonten's men.

Robin, his memories of the village from his brief acquaintance with Paulus, Hyecombe's Elder and tavern keeper, having been refreshed by Zolt, drew its layout in the dust for the others to see. "There's one central street," he said, "running east to west, like this. The tavern where the villagers are being held is at the western end—here. There's another lane running at a tangent to the main one. Taran's house, where Cal and Sonten are, is here, just before that lane bisects the main one. There are houses and shops along both streets, but they're probably deserted, if the villagers are all in the tavern as Zolt says. That means they can be used as cover by Sonten's men, and we can't let that happen or we'll never flush them out.

"I suggest we expand on last night's tactics. If we detail about a third of our strength to mount an attack at the eastern end of the village, the Andaryans will have to counter it. Once they're committed, the rest of us will make an all-out assault on the western end, forcing Sonten to split his men. With any luck, we'll capture the tavern before they can stop us. If we do, I think the villagers will lend us their support by fighting back. It's a gamble, but if we time it right, I think we stand a good chance of success. Any thoughts?"

He glanced around, inviting comment. Parren remained silent, and Robin suppressed a sigh. The man was going to keep any thoughts, helpful or otherwise, to himself. Judging by his expression, he was still seething, and probably hoping either that Robin would be killed in the fighting or that the plan would fail, causing Robin to lose face with Blaine. Either way, Robin knew, Parren would be happy. He certainly wouldn't lose any sleep if they lost the Staff.

By the look on Baily's face, he was going over the plan in his mind. Naturally cautious, he was not given to spontaneous action. While his courage was never in doubt, he wasn't known for making quick decisions. Robin suspected the man would never rise higher than captain, but he knew Baily wasn't worried. He was quite content with his life. He eventually shook his head, seeing no flaws in the plan.

After giving the Albians time to speak, Vanyr voiced his thoughts. "Captain, it occurs to me that the house where Cal is being held is some distance from the tavern. As the villagers are your first objective, might I suggest that Ky-shan and I make the house our target? If Sonten has not yet recovered the Staff then he's likely to use Cal against you. And if he gains it over the next few hours he'll want to slip away as quickly as possible. He may very well kill Cal once he's served his purpose. If Ky-shan's men and I head directly for the house, using your attacks as cover, we can be in a position to prevent Sonten's escape and hopefully offer Cal some protection as well."

Robin glanced at Ky-shan, who nodded, before turning back to Vanyr. "That sounds good to me, Commander. You and Ky-shan will hold yourselves in readiness. Wait for us to gain you access to the village. You will then concentrate on the cottage. Baily, how many men do you think you would need to cause a good diversion at the eastern edge of the village? If you circle north round the fields and come up through the trees, you can get pretty close to the end of the main street before you risk being seen. Remember, we need enough to make them think you're a decent attack-force."

Baily thought about it while Robin suppressed his impatience. "I'll need them all, Robin. To make it look like there's more of us, some could cut south and come up through the orchards as well, although we'll have to take care to avoid the marshes and the pond."

Robin nodded, indicating the marshes on his drawing. "We should all avoid that area, although if we can get Sonten on the run, we can push his men that way. They don't know the terrain, and the ground looks solid enough until you step on it. Right then, Baily will split his command and come at the eastern end of the village from the trees and the orchards. The rest will come with Parren and me. Torman, it might be better if you and Ky-shan go through the fields to the north and approach Taran's house from the back. Once you hear the fighting start and the cordon begins to fragment, you can make straight for the house. And if Sonten's men don't all leave their posts, you should still be able to slip through by working your way closer to the tavern and driving in with us. But the field route would be better because it would save you having to cut through the mêlée. Are we all agreed?"

There were no objections, so it only remained to decide the timing of the attack. Parren wanted to go in straight away, and Baily recommended waiting until the evening. Robin and Vanyr, however, were both in accord.

"Unless Sonten finds the Staff beforehand and shows signs of trying to leave," the Andaryan Commander said, "I recommend just before dawn tomorrow. They'll be cold, hungry, and sleepy. We'll have the advantage of knowing it will get lighter, so if the fighting's fierce, we won't have to worry about losing them in the dark. The last thing we want is for Sonten to slip the net."

Parren's eyes betrayed his thoughts on that, but he kept his counsel and no one but Robin noticed.

"We should mount occasional raids on the cordon throughout the rest of the day and night," continued Vanyr, "to keep Sonten unsettled and hopefully account for a few more of his men. Even the odds a little before we strike."

"I agree," Robin said, "although I hate the thought of leaving Cal so long in Sonten's hands. I dread to think what state he'll be in. Zolt, do you think there's any chance of you getting back into the village and passing a message to Cal? At least to alert him to the possibility of rescue? It might just give him the strength to hold out."

Zolt shook his head. "I could get back in alright, but there's no way I can guarantee getting a message to your mate without jeopardizing the whole operation. Not in daylight, anyhow. He was pretty closely guarded last night and, from what I could see, he was in a bad way. I'd have to risk entering the house to make sure he saw me, and that would have been tricky enough last night. Nothing will have changed today to make it any easier. I think you should stick to the plan, Skip. Keep them on their toes today to let them know we've not given up. With any luck, and if he's conscious, your friend will hear us and know help is at hand. Let Sonten think he's held us off successfully, then drive in hard and fast at dawn."

Still unhappy about Cal's precarious situation, Robin couldn't improve on the plan. They parted, Parren still muttering about wasting time.

Throughout the rest of the day the Albians subjected Sonten's men to sporadic raids. Although this kept them awake and alert, it didn't do much else. Robin tried to curb his impatience by going over the plan again and again in his mind. He felt frustrated that he was unable to do more. He tried contacting Cal on more than one occasion, but spellsilver was still blocking his mind. All Robin could glean from his efforts was that the dark-skinned young Apprentice was alive and, for the most part, conscious.

Chapter Eight

At that moment, Cal would have been more than happy to be thoroughly oblivious. His broken right arm was in agony, and his entire body was one vast bruise. He knew that if they started on him again, he would have no strength left for resistance. He wasn't even sure why he was bothering to resist at all. According to Sonten, Taran, Bull, and Robin were dead, as was Sullyan. She had been killed by Rykan, who even now was lording it over the Hierarch, whom he had deposed and would soon execute. Sonten would be his right-hand man once he returned to Andaryon with the Staff, a priceless artifact that Taran had willfully stolen from Sonten's nephew, murdering him most foully in the process.

Cal might be dazed and confused from the pain, but he knew very well that the last two statements were false. Taran had never stolen anything in his entire life—unlike Cal himself—and the young man was well aware of the story behind Jaskin's killing. So, he reasoned, if these two things were false, what about the rest?

He didn't know. All he did know was that after Sonten's men had taken them, he and Taran had been severely beaten. Then Robin and Bull had been captured too, and Sonten had tormented Taran with graphic descriptions of what he would do to his friends if Taran didn't tell him what he wanted to know.

Now Cal was on his own, so Sonten's story about the others being dead could very well be true. And from what he had seen of the duel between Rykan and Sullyan, well, none of them had held out much hope for her survival. Sonten was here, in Albia, and clearly in control. If the Major had triumphed, surely Sonten would now be the Hierarch's prisoner.

Bewildered, in pain, and afraid, Cal very much feared that most of what Sonten had said was true. He knew the General would see the killing of his nephew as murder no matter what the circumstances, and Taran must somehow have been persuaded to give Sonten the information he wanted, because the General hadn't needed Cal's assistance to find their village. When they had arrived, Cal was dismayed to find that Sonten's men were already in control of Hyecombe, and that the villagers had all been imprisoned. This had very nearly broken what remained of Cal's spirit. There seemed little point in holding out any longer.

Only … one piece of the puzzle didn't quite fit. Despite the rubble in Taran's cottage and the energetic searching Sonten had forced his men to perform, Sonten didn't yet have the Staff. He clearly didn't know exactly where it lay. Maybe Taran had tricked him at the end—maybe he had been rescued before Sonten pried the final bit of information from him. Or maybe he had died under Sonten's torture.

If any of those were true, then Cal didn't feel like giving up that vital piece of information without a fight. He owed it to Taran. He had come this far and held out this long, why not a little longer? Perhaps help would come. Surely some of the villagers had managed to escape and alert someone? Surely someone had noticed that all was not right in Hyecombe? Cal knew he had to hold on to that hope and pray that Sonten didn't start on him again.

Unfortunately, his hope was in vain.

*****

"Bloody damned Albians!"

Sonten's patience was running out. His foresight in having Commander Heron take the vast majority of his company through the Veils well in advance of Sonten's own arrival was a stroke of genius, although it had left him dangerously vulnerable when Sullyan and the pirates unexpectedly attacked him. The outcome of that skirmish might not have gone Sonten's way had Sullyan brought more men with her. The General knew he had been fortunate to escape, especially as Taran had divulged the name of his village scant seconds before Sullyan's arrival.

Both Sonten and his Commander, Heron, were well aware of the swordsmen stationed at the Manor. Any Andaryan commander worth his pay found out early in his career where the enemy's garrisons were and what their strength was. Plus, Heron had already fought Manor swordsmen during Rykan's feigned invasion. These facts had led Sonten to order Heron through the Veils into Albia with instructions to head for the Manor's vicinity. His reasoning was that as Taran was associated with Sullyan, his home village should not be too far away. Admittedly, this was a gamble, but it had paid off. Once Sonten had shaken Robin and the pirates off his tail, he had instructed his young Artesan messenger, Imris, to contact Heron and tell him the name of the village. It was then a simple matter for Heron to learn its exact location. As soon as Heron relayed this information to a jubilant Sonten, he received the General's orders to take control of the village and wait for Sonten's arrival. If he found the Staff before Sonten got there, he was not to touch it.

Heron had performed his task well, the only slip-up being the escape of two villagers. The pair, surprised in the middle of a romantic liaison in one of the outlying hay barns, had somehow managed to slip the cordon Heron threw around Hyecombe and raise the alarm.

Now, much to Sonten's fury, the village was surrounded by angry Albian swordsmen. He had cursed freely when told of their arrival, as he had planned to be in and out before the province's defenders learned of his occupation. Sullyan's earlier attack on his camp meant he hadn't had time to torture the Staff's exact location out of Taran, and his current captive was proving reticent, despite vigorous persuasion.

Frowning with impatience, Sonten dropped heavily into a comfortable chair by the fire, just across from Cal. He regarded the half-conscious young man with a calculating eye. Should he apply more pressure to the man himself, or should he use one of the villagers? He decided on the latter merely as a matter of expedience. He didn't want the young Albian to die just yet.

He was aware of the sporadic attacks from outside the village, but Heron had held them off with very few losses. Sonten wasn't worried about being overrun. Had the defenders of this area wanted to send more men against him, they would surely have done so by now. He had only fired a few houses and wasn't threatening anyone else, so they were obviously content to keep harrying him and watch what he did. They must think they had him pinned down. This made Sonten smile. How surprised they would be when he and his men disappeared from under their noses overnight!

Sonten decided he had waited long enough. He snapped his fingers at one of Cal's guards. "Fetch one of the younger village women. Make sure she doesn't scream before you get her here."

He gave the order in a low voice so Cal wouldn't hear. He was pretty sure the dark-skinned young man was too confused to make sense of what he might hear, but he didn't want his surprise revealed too soon.

As the guard left, Sonten sauntered over to Cal. He was bound securely to the high-backed chair, both arms wrenched behind him. Naked to the waist, his upper body showed the signs of Sonten's persuasive methods. His eyes were closed, the lids puffy and swollen, his dark skin unhealthily pale. His head was hanging, but Sonten could tell by his breathing that he was conscious. He leaned over Cal and rested his hands on the arms of the chair. Cal groaned.

"This is your last chance, lad," said Sonten, his tone reasonable. "Why hold out any longer? It's only a matter of time. All your friends are dead, and I know the Staff's here somewhere. You have nothing to lose by telling me where it is. You might even save your own skin. And why not—haven't you suffered enough? Why prolong this? What use is the Staff to you, anyway? You can't wield it, you haven't the skill. It's obviously wrought some damage here. Do you want to leave such a dangerous item loose where anyone might pick it up? Who knows what could happen? Why not let me take it back to its rightful owner, and get it out of harm's way?"

Grinning, staring into Cal's bloodshot eyes, he waited for the Albian to answer.

*****

Cal heard Sonten's voice as though through muffling fog. He couldn't think straight. Hadn't he and Taran tried to return the Staff? Wasn't that what Taran had wanted? So why shouldn't he do exactly as Sonten suggested and let the demon take it? He was on the verge of opening his mouth to do just that when an image of Rykan came into his mind. He remembered that Sonten was Rykan's man, and whatever he could do to inconvenience Rykan had to be good. Why else had Sullyan fought him and given her life, if she had indeed died? Could he do any less?

Thoughts of Rienne flooded his mind, and his heart clenched. He had no idea what had become of her after he and Taran had been taken. His fervent hope was that Bull had left her safely at the Citadel. Yet even if she was at the Citadel, with Sullyan dead, as Sonten claimed, Rienne would be all alone in an alien environment with no means of returning home. Cal simply had to survive this and deny Sonten his desire, if only to protect Rienne.

His intended revelation concerning the cellar died in his throat. Instead, he groaned again.

He saw the cottage door open, revealing the guard who had been sent to the tavern. He was accompanied by a girl of about fifteen, who he was dragging by the arm. She was struggling, but Cal didn't immediately realize what her presence meant. She gave a gasp of shock when she saw him, and froze. Sonten took her arm, not too roughly, and propelled her toward Cal's chair. She stood looking down at him with fear-widened eyes, one trembling fist held to her mouth. Cal stared at her, bewildered, then cried out as Sonten kicked his leg.

"Well, lad," said the General, his voice maddeningly cheerful, "what do you think? Is it a fair trade, her safety for your cooperation? What will her mother think if you allow her to be beaten and abused, all for something that is useless to you and belongs rightfully to me? Speak up. Do you understand me?"

Cal understood only too well. He knew the girl, now that he

could see her clearly. She was one of his neighbor's daughters, and this was his worst nightmare come true. Watching Sonten torture Taran and being beaten himself was one thing. To let it happen to this innocent girl was another. He just couldn't do it. He had been dreading this ever since waking in this familiar room with an aching body and sinking heart. The fact that it had taken Sonten so long to get around to it only meant that the man wasn't wantonly cruel. That was something, at least. Cal could hope that if he told Sonten where the Staff was, the girl might be released unharmed.

"You're taking too long," warned Sonten. He ran a meaty hand over the girl's breasts. She cried out and struggled, but he held her firm.

A heavy despair descended on Cal. He couldn't let Sonten go on. He moistened dry lips, but still could not speak.

Sonten scowled. "Get him some water!"

One of the guards hastened to obey. Once the dribble of water had eased his parched throat, Cal managed to rasp, "In the cellar."

Sonten grunted. "There! That wasn't too hard, was it? You could have saved us both a lot of time and trouble, my friend. Now, where's the access to the cellar?"

"Under that lot," rasped Cal, nodding painfully toward the mess of rubble in the hall.

Sonten swung round. "What? Are you telling me the truth?" He slapped the girl's face, causing her to scream in terror.

"Yes, yes!" croaked Cal. "It was the Staff brought the ceiling down. We couldn't touch it, and the backlash caused the cellar to cave in."

He collapsed back, his energy spent. With a vicious oath, Sonten flung the terrified girl at one of his men. "Take her back to the tavern. Get as many men as Heron can spare and find spades, shovels, whatever you can. It's going to take hours to clear this bloody lot. Go on. Get on with it!"

The man leaped to obey, dragging the sobbing girl with him. Sonten lunged toward Cal and gave his broken arm a vicious twist. Cal screamed.

"I'll teach you to play games with me, lad!" the General hissed.

"Don't think you'll get out of this with your life. I'm not finished yet, either with you or your pox-ridden village!"

He lumbered away toward the cottage door, roaring for the remaining guards to begin removing the rubble from the cellar entrance. Cal, thankful to be left alone, allowed his pain and the awful, droning buzz of the spellsilver to carry him into oblivion.

*****

For the rest of that day, Sonten drove the men Commander Heron reluctantly spared from the cordon as hard as he could. They worked feverishly, urged on by the lash of Sonten's tongue. Forming a chain from the cellar entrance to the cottage door, they slung rubble and masonry out into the street. Heavier pieces that couldn't be lifted were hauled out on ropes pulled by horses.

All the while, the enemy made life difficult for the besiegers, causing Commander Heron to request the return of the men he had detailed to help Sonten. The General refused, sending Heron's runner rudely away. He would not allow the clearance work to slacken, not even when two of the men in the chain were hit by random crossbow bolts as they emerged into the street to dump their burdens. One of them was Imris, Sonten's young messenger-Artesan. The General cursed his loss, although the lad's death was an inconvenience rather than a tragedy.

To prevent further losses, Sonten ordered the men to build the rubble up into a protective wall. This took more precious time, but once it was done they were able to work in relative safety. Heron refused point-blank to release any more men from the cordon to replace those Sonten had lost, so finally the General ordered the villagers to be herded together into the tavern's largest common room and locked in, leaving only two men to guard them. This meant he had twenty able bodies shifting rubble. What was left of the cellar entrance was narrow, and only two men could get down the stairwell at a time to pass rubble out. Sonten organized his workforce into two shifts to work more efficiently.

By late evening, one man approached him and said, "We've reached floor level, General, but there's still heaps more rubble. It would help if we knew how far in the weapon is likely to be. Save us shifting more than we need."

Sonten grunted and walked toward Cal. He had left a guard on the young man, but it was hardly necessary. He had drifted in and out of consciousness all day and had been given no food or water save that mere trickle preceding his confession. He sat in his own ordure and the smell was becoming oppressive, but Sonten ignored it as he slapped Cal hard across the face. Cal's head snapped back and his eyes opened.

"Whereabouts in the cellar?" demanded Sonten. "Come on, man! Do I need to fetch the girl again? I will, you know, if you don't cooperate. Resistance is hardly worth it now. We're down at floor level. Where is the Staff?"

Cal, weak and confused, didn't immediately grasp what Sonten was saying. Lack of food and water, and the effects of the spellsilver, had finally rendered him witless. Exasperated, Sonten swore. He was so close now! If the Staff was across the other side of the cellar, it could still take his men hours to reach it. Cal could save them that time. Sonten slapped him again, more in frustration than with any hope of gaining answers.

He snapped at Cal's guard, "Tend to him, you snuffwit! See if you can get him to come around a bit. I still need him, do you hear?"

The guard reached for some water and held it to Cal's lips, but most of it spilled down his chin. Angrily, Sonten left him to it and went back to the cellar door, as near to the collapsed area as he dared.

"Stop slacking, you useless lot! If we have to clear it all, we'll do it, so get back to work."

*****

As the night advanced, Robin made his preparations. He showed Vanyr and Ky-shan the route through the fields by which he hoped they could gain access to Taran's house. They would have to avoid the main street and approach the cottage from the rear, but at least the hedges round the fields would afford them some cover. With luck, the defenders would be too busy dealing with the attack Robin and Parren intended to unleash and wouldn't notice Vanyr's small band.

Baily had strict instructions to hold as many of Sonten's men as he could at the eastern end of the village. The last thing Robin needed was for all the Andaryans to come at him from up the main street, preventing him from liberating the villagers in the tavern. He hoped to push through swiftly and decisively, and dividing Sonten's men was crucial.

By the time everyone was briefed and in place, it was well past midnight. Robin checked with Vanyr through the substrate, even though they had agreed to keep metaphysical contact to a minimum in case either of Sonten's Artesans should sense them. Robin had tried again but was unable to sense Cal. The spellsilver was still doing its job.

Robin crouched with his men in the darkness. He couldn't stop wondering how far he could trust Parren. All he could do was hope the sly young man would keep to the plan. He was impatient for Baily to commence his attack, but there were still a couple of hours to go. Only when the first rush was well under way would Robin give the order to engage.

He searched the darkness, trying to spot the men in the cordon. Not for the first time, he wished he had some influence over the element of Air. The buildings Sonten had fired were still smoldering, and the resulting smoke was fogging the area. It would work against defenders and attackers alike, and Robin wished he could provide his forces with some advantage.

This was the first time since Sullyan had left the Manor that Robin had spared any thought for his potential to become a Master Artesan. His excitement on learning he was ready had been buried by the events that had followed, and his dread that Sullyan might never return had killed any desire for advancement. Or so he had thought. She had a chance now, and the rekindling of his hopes for her had reignited his own ambitions.

For the moment, though, that had to wait. All he could do was watch and prepare. His crossbow was wound and loaded, and he thought he knew where his first target would come from. He had managed to use a few bolts to good effect earlier on in the day when Sonten had rashly allowed his men to drop their masonry outside Taran's front door. It was too good an opportunity to miss, and he had earned more admiration from Vanyr for his skill.

Parren, predictably, had been unimpressed. "Weapon of stealth," he sniffed disdainfully. "A coward's weapon."

Robin didn't bother to reply. Vanyr didn't speak either. He simply stared hungrily at Parren. Robin sighed. He wouldn't give much for the sallow man's chances if the two came together during the battle, and he certainly wouldn't have any regrets if the Commander's sword found its way into Parren's guts.

Another hour of waiting passed. Suddenly, Robin detected the unmistakable sounds of engagement coming from the other end of the village. He frowned in concern. It was too soon! There was still another hour to go until dawn, and they had agreed to wait until the moon was down before engaging. Something had obviously gone wrong, but it was too late to worry about it now. Baily must be supported and the Andaryan forces must be split or none of them stood any chance. Robin turned to give the order to engage, but Parren grabbed his arm.

"Not yet, you bloody fool! We'll be striking blind. It's far too early!"

"I know that, Parren, but Baily's in trouble. Can't you hear it? We can't let him take them on by himself. Whatever's gone wrong, he's in the thick of it and needs our help. And what about Vanyr and Ky-shan? If they go in on the back of this, they'll walk slap into Sonten's men. Come on, Parren, we must go now!"

Parren stared angrily at him. "Alright, but it's on your head. I take no responsibility, and I want it noted that I object to this course of action. If that bloody fool Baily's got himself killed, then it's no fault of mine."

"Gods," snapped Robin, furious that Parren would stall him like this. "Your objections are noted, Captain. Now, let's get on with it!"

He gave the order for the bowmen to begin their salvos as the swordsmen behind got ready to rush the cordon. It was hard to see properly in the darkness, and all was noise and confusion. Under cover of the crossbows, the Manor forces at the western end of the village crept closer to the Andaryan cordon. They suffered losses from the defenders' return volleys before Robin judged they were close enough for the charge. Slinging his bow across his back, he drew his sword and yelled, "Go, men! Go now!"

His men surged forward to engage the enemy.

*****

Sonten was so close. His taskforce had cleared most of the rubble from the cellar doorway and was making a path through the middle of the floor. Peering down into the small circle of light given off by the lantern below, the General became quite excited when he realized they had uncovered the beginnings of a depression in the floor. He might not have any Artesan power of his own, but he had witnessed Rykan working often enough to know that this was the likeliest resting place for the missing artifact.

"There, you lackwits, there!" he yelled, pointing. "Concentrate on where the floor dips."

They were tired and flagging, and Sonten urged them on with threats and promises. They renewed their efforts, staggering under the weight of the rubble and plaster they were handing up the chain in buckets. Eventually, one of them straightened an aching back.

"My Lord, I think we have it!"

"Let me see," snapped Sonten, shoving his way past the men at the head of the ladder. Awkwardly descending—his unwieldy bulk was never meant for ladders—he gave a predatory grin. Amid the wreckage he could see the Staff's unmistakable shimmer.

It lay innocently in the center of the depression, glittering very gently, completely unaffected by its dusty incarceration. Sonten knew that its main component was a form of spellsilver, one in which the effect was somehow reversed so that instead of blocking or repulsing metaphysical function, it actually attracted and amplified it. He didn't understand it and experienced a momentary twinge of regret for the untimely demise of his nephew, remembering the many secret hours it had taken Jaskin to learn how to use the priceless weapon. Sonten would have to start over again, and once more in secret, for if the Hierarch learned of his plotting then Sonten's head would go the way of Rykan's.

He grimaced. It was a drawback that Commander Heron had no familial ties to him, but at least Heron's current level of skill was greater than Jaskin's, so that should be an advantage. Promotion and an increase in pay would place the Commander ever more firmly in Sonten's debt, and maybe the General could find some other, tastier rewards for the man once he learned his particular weaknesses. Every man had them, as Sonten well knew, and he was adept at exploitation.

Now, however, possession of the Staff was enough. Wary, mindful of its lethal potential, Sonten stretched out his hand and grasped the metal rod.

A shock ran through him and he almost dropped the weapon. He had half expected a reaction from it, but he realized almost instantly that it wasn't the weapon creating the noise he had heard. It was his men. Hearing the cries and the unmistakable ring of steel, Sonten understood what was happening. His men were under attack from the Albians.

Angry with his shaking fingers, he secured the Staff within a specially designed scabbard on his belt. "Out of the way," he growled, and shoved roughly at the men in the cellar. Heads appeared above him and a hand was extended to help him out of the hole. He batted it away. "Find out what's happening!" he barked, and the heads disappeared.

He hauled himself out, panting his fury. If this was an all-out attack rather than another feint, he would have to disappear sooner than planned. Yet for that he needed Heron, and presumably the man would now be directing a counter-attack. Cursing the loss of Imris, Sonten sent a man scurrying for Heron while he urged the rest out of the cellar.

Chapter Nine

Vanyr, Ky-shan, and the seamen had made their way successfully toward the edge of the village without raising the alarm. Finding an unoccupied, burned-out house they crouched in the darkness, awaiting the sounds that would confirm Baily's attack had begun. When it came, Vanyr shot Ky-shan a glance. Surely it was too soon? The seaman merely shrugged and raised his sword, indicating it was time to go. Vanyr followed as the others surged from the shell of the house, running through the darkness, alert for Sonten's men.

They heard yells from the western end, telling them that Robin's forces had joined the attack. A quick movement in the gloom beside him warned Vanyr just in time as a swordsman aimed a lunge at his breast. Vanyr raised his blade to parry the stroke, and Ky-shan ran the man through. He dropped and they pounded on, following Zolt's lead toward Taran's cottage.

Another man ran across their line of sight, but he either didn't see them or he thought they were his comrades, for he carried on, heading for the western end of the village. Vanyr had seen where he had come from and he grabbed Zolt by the arm. "Is that the one?" he hissed, pointing at the small house.

Zolt nodded. They pitched up against the back wall of the house and crouched down. There was a wooden door to their left and a window above them, through which lamplight and the flickering silhouettes of men showed. Zolt raised his head and glanced into the room beyond.

"Cal's still there, tied to a chair. I can't tell if he's alive. There's at least one other man in the room, and there are others just outside."

Vanyr nodded to Ky-shan, who turned to the hulking forms of Almid and Kester. "Go on, boys."

The giants stood either side of the wooden door and delivered simultaneous kicks with their huge boots. The door splintered and shot back, one hinge shattered. The twins surged into the room, followed by Ky-shan, Vanyr, and the rest of the men. Vanyr could see the inert form of Cal slumped in the chair, but ignored him. Ky-shan had instructed Almid and Kester to guard the young Albian, and Vanyr had other prey on his mind. While Almid casually dispatched the man closest to Cal with one sweep of his huge sword, Vanyr scanned the cottage.

He caught sight of a heavily-built figure and roared with fury when he saw the artifact hanging from Sonten's belt. It could only be the Staff. Sonten heard him and turned, his eyes widening as he recognized the Commander of the Hierarch's personal guard. Shoving frantically through his men, the General fled the house. Vanyr lunged after him and Ky-shan ordered his men to follow. Bellowing, they spilled out into the street, the seamen's blades ringing against those of Sonten's men.

*****

Robin and Parren, at the head of their men, had punched through the enemy cordon and were making headway toward the tavern. Robin gave a tight grin of satisfaction. The smoke, the darkness, and the sound of two separate battles was clearly confusing the Andaryans. Their Commander, whom Robin recognized from his short time as Sonten's prisoner, had seemingly deserted his men. Robin had seen him go running off in the opposite direction. Maybe, he thought, the man was going to help lead the second battle, against Baily's attack force. Whatever the reason, their Commander's desertion had left this half of Sonten's militia leaderless and lacking clear orders. They were milling, unsure whether to defend or fall back.

A swordsman lunged at Robin and the Captain blocked the stroke, turning the enemy blade aside with a twist of his sword. The man stumbled into his neighbor and Robin immediately chopped forward, shearing through the man's sword arm. There was a harsh scream as the Andaryan dropped to the ground, and Robin leaped over him, looking for his next opponent.

The space before Robin was suddenly clear. A gap was beginning to open on his side of the battle. Yelling, he urged his unit forward, opening the gap wider. The Andaryans' disarray and lack of cohesion suited him just fine, but he found a moment to hope that Baily wasn't suffering as a consequence.

Seeing Sergeant Dexter's flushed face beside him, Robin yelled, "Keep herding them away from the tavern, Dex. Push them back toward the eastern end."

Dexter nodded and relayed the order. Robin took a moment to glance over his shoulder through the gloom, trying to check on Parren's whereabouts. There was another mass of bodies behind him to his left. It seemed the sallow Captain had managed to draw the other Andaryans away from those fighting Robin's band. Nodding in satisfaction and trusting that Parren would continue to keep them occupied, Robin concentrated on pushing farther into the village.

*****

On his stool beside the tavern bar, Elder Paulus stirred uneasily. He frowned at the empty beer kegs and upended tankards, using his disgust at the mess to keep himself from showing fear. The villagers looked to him for guidance. So far, none of them had been hurt—at least, not seriously—and Paulus wanted to keep it that way. Nonetheless, all this passive sitting around, waiting for others to determine their fate, was grating on his nerves.

Penned in the tavern for many hours now, the villagers had caused no real trouble. They knew they were far outnumbered by the demons that had invaded their village, and on Paulus's advice hadn't even rebelled when the girl was taken. Her mother had gone into hysterics when she realized they were going to sit by and watch her daughter be taken away, and many of the men had raged at Paulus, unable to understand his stricture against resistance. Yet Paulus knew there were too many armed guards for the villagers to take on, and he believed the girl would be returned unharmed if they behaved themselves, as the man who took her told him.

Paulus had won the argument and the men sat tight, doing their best to calm the girl's mother. Their mood, though, had turned ugly. When the girl was returned, terrified but mercifully unharmed, Paulus felt sick with relief. He accepted the villagers' grudging apologies, but realized the girl's wellbeing didn't mean the demons would leave without harming anyone.

Once the girl had calmed down, he quietly questioned her, telling her to pretend she was still weeping and distraught, and to whisper her answers so the guards wouldn't overhear what she had to tell him. From her replies, he guessed that Sonten was looking for the artifact Taran had told him about before leaving the village. What it was and what the demon intended to do with it, Paulus had no idea. He decided not to tell the villagers that the invasion of their homes was Taran's fault. Neither Taran nor Cal had been popular before they left, and if the villagers learned that this was their doing, neither man would ever be able to show his face in Hyecombe again. They might even turn on Cal, should the demons leave him alive. After cautioning the girl not to reveal this information to the others, all Paulus could do was keep alert and be ready to react to whatever happened next.

When the demons had roughly herded all their prisoners together in the main room and left only two of their comrades on guard duty, Paulus took the opportunity to prime his fellow captives. They had all heard the sporadic noises during the night and guessed there were Albian swordsmen outside the village trying to dislodge the demons. The villagers might only be farmhands, bakers, and shopkeepers, rather than trained fighters, but surely they could overcome two lone demons if they worked together? Using whispered comments and concealed gestures, Paulus directed them to whatever might be used as a weapon. Broken ale jars—or even whole ones—could do a lot of damage, and ale tankards were nice and weighty, handy for women to throw. So stealthily did Paulus work that when the noise of attack broke out in the street, he and the villagers were fully prepared to help their rescuers win the day.

He leaped off his bar stool yelling, and the other men quickly snatched up their chosen weapons. They charged the two demons standing by the locked door and overwhelmed them, attacking whatever part of their bodies they could reach. The crunch of bone and the shattering of stoneware almost drowned out the screams. Then they turned their attention to the tavern door, and Paulus couldn't help but wince as it gave way under their kicks. The women grabbed tankards, stools, brooms, whatever came to hand, and poured out of the tavern behind their men.

It was still dark and the noise outside was deafening. Paulus wanted to yell at the villagers, to form them into some kind of cohesive band, but their blood was up. Some of them raced toward a mass of fighters on one side of the street while others split away, heading for a second battle raging farther on. Whooping and roaring their anger, they added their weight to the fight.

*****

Sonten's impatience was turning to panic. His men were only just holding Vanyr and the seamen. His feverish eyes raked the predawn gloom. Where in the Void was Heron? Sonten might have possession of the Staff, but he couldn't use it. He needed Heron if he was to escape as planned. Protected by about fifteen of his men, he retreated slowly before Vanyr's onslaught, making for the main street where the horses were. When Heron finally came running, bringing welcome reinforcements, Sonten thrust the Staff into his hands.

"Do it now," he grated, his eyes wild. "I've told you what I want you to do, so get on with it. Let's get out of here!"

Despite the chaos around him, Heron eyed the Staff. "I don't like this, General. It goes against the grain to sacrifice so many of our men. And I'm not sure I'm capable of doing what you want. I've only opened a large trans-Veil tunnel once before, and I don't have the strength or skill to fix its destination."

Sonten couldn't believe this. Couldn't the man see how desperate their situation was?

"For the Void's sake, man, get on with it! This thing amplifies metaforce, remember? You'll be at least twice as powerful as you were before—I've already told you that."

"But the people, General. The risk is—"

"Sod the bloody risk, Heron! They're only Albians. This is our lives we're talking about."

Sonten was furious. Heron had raised this objection before when he had first heard about the plan. Despite the General's assurance that the Staff would vastly amplify his power, Heron wasn't confident. He had blathered on about the risks involved in opening any kind of rent in the Veils so close to occupied dwellings. Sonten had laughed in his face. He had no regard for the human population of Hyecombe and couldn't understand why Heron would bring it up again.

Despite his General's anger, Heron tried one last time. "But it's not just—"

Sonten shifted slightly. Heron's eyes widened in shock as he stared down the length of the General's sword, its tip pressed just below his sternum.

"Do it, Heron! Just do it."

The Commander swallowed and nodded. Sonten removed his blade and watched avidly as Heron concentrated his will on the Staff.

Sonten had deliberately not told his Commander how long it had taken Jaskin to learn to use the Staff. He assumed that Heron's Adept-elite rank would overcome that problem, and anyway, he was only going to use it to open the Veils. Once they were back in Durkos, there would be time aplenty for Heron to fine tune his control.

After a few seconds of intense concentration from Heron, the Staff began to glow. Ripples of blue, green, and grey light raced up and down its length. Heron glanced up at Sonten, his face alive with power. Forgetting the fight raging around them, the yells and screams and roars of angry men, the General grinned. His plan was going to work.

Heron turned and raised the Staff. He gestured with both hands. The grey gloom of early dawn began to shimmer in front of him. Suddenly, Sonten could make out the outline of a portway. He clenched his fists in triumph. Let the rest of his men perish along with the thrice-damned human villagers! He could easily glean more from Rykan's estates before the Hierarch annexed the lot. Despite the failure of Rykan's challenge and the disastrous war with the Hierarch's forces, there were plenty who would follow Sonten's banner, plenty who would cleave to his cause. Especially once he had outlined his plans and made Heron demonstrate what the Staff was capable of. Rykan had never been liked, either by his peers or his men—he had been too cruel for that—but Sonten was known as a fair lord and a generous one, provided his orders were followed.

He shook his head. Rykan had been such a fool. If only he had listened to Sonten instead of allying himself with that scheming Albian Baron. If he hadn't wasted time pleasuring himself with the human witch, he would have been Hierarch by now, without any of that messy dueling business. Yet that had been Rykan all over. The obvious and brutal approach when subtlety would have been more apt.

Yelling above the din for his bodyguard, Sonten told them to grab the horses.

*****

Captain Baily pounded past the backs of the houses, his men crowding his heels. They had had a hard time of it at the eastern end of the village. The light of the lowering moon had betrayed them, and they had been spotted by a sharp-eyed demon scout before they were fully in position. Baily had been forced to engage the enemy far earlier than Robin had planned.

They suffered significant losses before recovering from the resulting disarray. The demons fought hard, harder than Baily had expected, refusing to be distracted by the sounds of another attack coming from the western end of the village. Baily's men were rapidly outnumbered and lost ground fast in the darkness. He knew he had to pull out or risk losing his entire command. Making his decision, he yelled, "Fall back, lads. Retreat."

They obeyed and followed Baily, who decided to slip back through the fields and come through the houses from the north, to provide backup for Vanyr and Ky-shan. He knew his men would be massacred if they stayed where they were.

Glancing over his shoulder into the growing light, Baily felt relief when the demons decided not to pursue him but instead ran to help their fellows in the main street. Calling to his men to rally them, Baily plunged back between the houses to rejoin the fighting.

*****

Sonten's defenders jostled around him and Heron, the horses whinnying and curveting as men yelled and swords clashed close by. One of Heron's underlings bellowed in Sonten's ear, "There's another unit of Albians coming, General! They're forcing our lads back up the street toward us. I don't think we can hold them off."

Sonten cursed. The man was right. They were on the verge of being overwhelmed. His orderly escape was in danger of falling apart, and he abruptly decided on a radical change of plan. Heron was still concentrating on expanding his tunnel and could spare no attention for the General. Screaming at his men to abandon the horses, Sonten barked a command to retreat.

"Heron," he yelled, "finish that damned tunnel!"

The Commander was concentrating so hard he barely acknowledged Sonten. He made an ambiguous gesture that Sonten chose to interpret as readiness. Giving Heron no further thought, the General shoved the nearest men into the shimmering portway. No chance he was going first.

The trans-Veil structure shot sparks and Heron reacted wildly, grabbing the General's arm. Sonten angrily shook him off.

"It's not ready, General," cried Heron. "I don't have full control … it won't come out where you—"

"Doesn't bloody matter," spat Sonten. "Just hold the damned thing open."

Heron's eyes were wild and his face deathly pale. The General ignored him. The Staff had plenty of power, and it didn't really matter where the tunnel opened as long as it was somewhere in Andaryon. Once the first men to enter had proved it was safe, Sonten could make his escape.

*****

With a savage cut to the throat, Robin dispatched his opponent and drew a breath, using the brief lull to glance around him. He was pleased with the progress they were making, but could not understand what had happened to Parren. He and Parren were supposed to be supporting each other, driving Sonten's forces away from the village and out into the marshy ground around the pond, yet Robin's command were doing all the work themselves. There was no sign of Parren.

A sudden commotion to his left caused Robin to spin round. With relief, he saw the remnants of Baily's command come pouring down through the houses to engage Sonten's flank. This gave him respite to try to locate either Parren or Vanyr. He could see neither man, but what he did see, to his dismay, was the unmistakable shimmer of a trans-Veil portway. Limned against it like a blue halo was a tall figure wielding what could only be the Staff.

Robin went cold. Summoning his strength, he yelled, "Torman!" There was an answering shout from somewhere in front of him. Abandoning caution, Robin linked with Vanyr.

Sonten's man is opening a tunnel. He's got the Staff and he's getting away!

Vanyr's response was tight with strain. *Don't worry, I'm on him. If he tries to use the tunnel, we'll follow, but it's not ready yet.*

Reassured that Vanyr had the situation covered, Robin again scanned the mêlée for Parren. There was still no sign of him, but in the slowly growing light Robin could just make out some of his men outside the tavern. Before he could wonder what the sallow captain was doing back there, an Andaryan swordsman aimed a lunge at Robin's chest. Whirling, he deflected the stroke, his blade ringing on his opponent's as he sidestepped, avoiding the backslash. There were more Andaryans facing his command now as those from the eastern end were rallying the ones surrounding Sonten. The battle was turning desperate.

*****

Sonten screamed at Heron to hurry even as he continued to shovel men into the portway. He knew nothing about the mechanics of anchoring such structures and had no understanding of the risks or pressure Heron was under. All Sonten knew was that Vanyr and the seamen were bearing down on him, battling their way ever closer. Without warning, he grabbed at the Staff in Heron's hand.

"Quickly, man, it must be now!"

He dived into the dangerously unstable tunnel, dragging Heron behind him. Struggling to maintain the structure, Heron tried to resist. He pulled back on Sonten's grip, desperately holding on to his connection with the Staff.

"No, General! It's too early! If I don't anchor the portway, it could implode with all—"

Sonten wasn't listening, furious that his carefully prepared escape was being jeopardized. First he had lost Imris, and now he had to leave the horses. Maddening though this was, it was incidental compared to his and Heron's safety. And if it came down to priorities, even Heron could be sacrificed provided Sonten escaped with the Staff. He could always find another Artesan open to bribery—or coercion. Heron's frantic resistance was earning him no favors. Sonten wasn't about to relinquish his grip on the Staff.

Neither was he going to listen to Heron lecture on how an Artesan's power worked. All he knew was that his escape route was in existence. Seeing Vanyr and the seamen closing rapidly, Sonten bolted as fast as his bulk and Heron's resistance allowed.

With Vanyr's furious roar echoing in his ears, Sonten fled.

*****

Cal opened bleary eyes. The bearded face of a huge man loomed over him. He would have flinched had he not been so exhausted. The man quickly introduced himself, and Almid's low murmur reassured Cal. He felt the giant's hands working loose the bonds around him, and prepared himself for pain as the circulation returned to his broken arm. What he wasn't prepared for was the return of his Artesan powers when the spellsilver knife blocking them fell to the ground. It was as if a thick cocoon of wool had been abruptly ripped away.

Hot agony shot up Cal's shattered arm. His scream of anguish was echoed and amplified by his suddenly accessible metaforce. Cal grabbed for power to dampen the pain. He was only half-conscious and so didn't wonder at the vast amount of power that flooded through his broken body. Still screaming, he pulled at it, soaked it up, and reached for more. His use of power was uncontrolled, uncontained, and metaforce leaked wildly into the substrate, fueled by his anguished screams.

*****

Vanyr knew he was gaining on the General. He also realized that Heron was not fully in control of the portway. He could feel its instability through the element of Earth from which it was formed. Casting aside thoughts of his own safety, he had eyes only for the two fleeing men and the artifact they carried. As he ran, he tried reaching out with his own metaforce, wondering if he could disrupt Heron's concentration. If he could wrest control of the Staff from Heron, he might be able to seal the end of the tunnel, trapping Sonten inside. He was aware that Heron was metaphysically stronger than him, but Sullyan's words concerning his ranking five days ago had given him new confidence.

Exerting his will, Vanyr latched on to the strange signature of the Staff. He could now feel Heron's pattern of psyche and sense how tenuous his grip on the Staff was. Ignoring the weird sensations the Staff sent crawling through his body, Vanyr succeeded in severing Heron's connection to the weapon. Triumphant, he saw the enemy commander stumble and then glance fearfully over his shoulder.

Vanyr grinned, but his triumph faded as a strange and ominous rumbling came from behind him. Glancing over his own shoulder, he frowned at the eerie ripples advancing toward him, warping the air. The figures of men seemed to bleed, their shapes flowing like muddy water. Sound warped too, the cries and screams of men swelling and ebbing in his ears. He felt sick.

He grabbed for the substrate, trying to control the strangely fluctuating power. Before he could act, a shockwave barreled into him. The sound of a thousand souls screaming in agony whipped Vanyr around like fluff in a gale, making him gasp in pain. He stared, helpless, as the weirdly augmented scream rebounded wildly through the tunnel, blasting over Sonten and his fleeing men. Vanyr's eyes widened in horror as the tunnel wavered on the verge of collapse.

He shielded instinctively, turning to yell furiously over his shoulder at Ky-shan and the seamen. "Cover your ears! The tunnel's collapsing! Go back! GET OUT!"

Without waiting to see if they obeyed him, he plunged his metasenses into the Staff, grasping at the vat of power with no restraint. He took a deep breath, for the ripples of the shockwave had reached the far end and were racing back toward him with mindless fury. He saw Sonten and Heron fall, both men crumpling like slaughtered deer. Clapping his hands over his ears as the wave raced over him, Vanyr fell to his knees. His body was blasted and shaken like a rag, yet his mind clamped desperately over the tunnel's structure as it shuddered around him, threatening to fall apart. It ripped at his senses and he screamed, fighting to hold it together. The sound wave bounced back once more, punching him flat to the ground, searing his nerves and burning them raw. In anguish, he called upon the power of the Staff, just enough to direct the tunnel's opening. He forced himself to crawl forward, desperate to snatch the Staff from Heron's hand. He had to make it out before the tunnel collapsed completely.

Holding his connection to the Staff was agony. Its power charred his barely shielded mind. Needles of hot pain lanced into his eyes and boiling liquid spilled down his face, making him shriek. On hands and knees, he blindly forced himself forward, pace by tortured pace, crying with pain as he grimly held on to the tunnel.

One thought kept him going, distracted him from his agony. It was the image of Sullyan fighting for Bull's life as the big man lay unresponsive after his heart seizure. She would never have given up on him, and Vanyr knew he could not give up now. Everything she had suffered—at Rykan's palace, in the arena, and then to save her friends—could not be wasted. Without the Staff, she stood no chance of life.

Vanyr could not let her down. Setting his teeth in a rictus of urgency, he clamped his mind around the disintegrating tunnel.

He had no idea if anyone else was left in the structure. He had no thoughts, no time to speculate, no capacity for anything but this bitter battle for survival. He felt it like a sword in his back when the Albian end of the tunnel fractured, broke, and collapsed. He shrieked aloud as it raced up behind him, tumbling and buffeting his body as it imploded, shattering all around him.

Flinging himself forward with a last, muscle-wrenching effort, he clawed desperately for the tunnel's end.

*****

The structure's collapse sent a vast sound wave booming through the village. Every window was shattered and buildings were flattened. Once the aftershock had died, there wasn't a single person left standing in the ruin that had once been Hyecombe.

Chapter Ten

Even while she slept, Sullyan's metaforce surrounded her psyche with gentle healing. Moving through her blood and flesh, the amber essence encouraged bones to knit and new skin to grow. It was a soothing process, an unconscious process once set in motion, and Sullyan's dreaming mind lay cocooned in power.

The onset of searing agony ripped through her, shattering her dream. The force of a loud boom pressed against her ears. She thrashed and yelled, gripping her head in her hands to stop her skull from splitting apart. She instinctively burrowed into her psyche, blindly seeking refuge in the depths of her power.

It lapped about her, protecting her from the worst of the pain. Ignorant of its cause, Sullyan lay gasping. The sudden movement had made her injured wrist throb and she feared she had undone some of the healing. When she was certain her body had sustained no further damage, she opened her eyes, blinking and shying away from a dark shape looming over her.

She felt a hand touch her shoulder—Rienne's hand. As her vision cleared, Sullyan could see the healer was speaking, but she still had her hands clamped over her ringing ears. She forced her hands down, wincing as the healer's worried tones echoed in her mind.

"Sullyan, are you alright? What on earth was that noise? Surely it can't have been thunder?"

Still struggling to recover, Sullyan didn't reply. The blast—if that's what it was—must have been truly huge if Rienne had felt it. Or maybe the healer was only getting an echo of what Sullyan had felt. Rienne's arm slid around Sullyan's shoulders, and she used the support to help her sit.

"What is it, Brynne? What's happened?"

Soothed by her metaforce, the pain in her head was subsiding. Sullyan rose with Rienne's aid, mindful of her throbbing left arm. "Pass me my robe," she croaked. Rienne complied and helped her tie it around her waist.

"Please tell me what's wrong!"

Rienne's voice wavered with fear, yet reassurance would have to wait. Sullyan knew time was of the essence. If the shock was what she feared, others would be in desperate need of her aid. She had been lucky; her metaforce had shielded her.

"Oh," she moaned, "I hope the others shielded in time!"

She staggered toward the door as Rienne grabbed her own robe to follow her out.

The passageway was in uproar. Servants with torches rushed about, and somewhere someone was screaming. Ignoring the confusion, Sullyan made straight for the room allotted to Bull and Taran. She flung the door open and rushed in. Both men lay collapsed in their beds, Bull moaning softly and Taran deathly still. Panting with exertion, Sullyan sought their minds, giving a huge sigh of relief when she found that Taran was merely stunned. Bull was in pain but essentially undamaged.

"Rienne, stay with them. They are alright, but if you have any willow extract to numb their pain, they will be in your debt forever. Save some for me, if you can." She turned to leave the room.

"Where are you going?" cried Rienne, but Sullyan had no time for explanations.

She ran to Pharikian's chambers, pushing past his page and barging in without ceremony. She went cold when she saw the ruler of Andaryon laid out on the floor, blood coming from his ears. She bent to examine him, immediately realizing that he had protected his mind at the expense of his body. It was only his eardrums that had suffered. Gently, she helped him back to consciousness and got him sitting up. The door swung open and his senior page appeared, white faced, shocked, and frightened.

"Norkis, tend to his Majesty. He will be alright in a few moments. Get him something to drink. Tell him I am dealing with it."

Without waiting for his nod, she left.

Marik's rooms were next, but neither he nor Idrimar were there.

She ran on through the dimly lit corridors, wondering where she would find any of the generals at this early hour. Not all of them would have been abed, of that she was sure. The problem was solved for her when she suddenly saw one of Kryp's lieutenants running toward her.

He skidded to a gasping halt. "Oh, Lady, can you come? General Kryp's had some kind of attack. Ephan, too. I think they could be dead."

She urged the man on and soon found Kryp and Ephan both lying silent and ominously still on the council chamber floor. Examining Kryp first, she could see there was no hope. The man's brain was charred; clearly he had not been quick enough to shield. Ephan was another matter; he was in a bad way, but she thought there might be enough to salvage.

Working fast, ignoring the blinding, jagged migraine stabbing in her own head, she cocooned and sealed Ephan's damaged mind within a protective barrier of his own metaforce. He would have to wait until she felt stronger before she could help him any further.

The lieutenant was bending over Kryp, clearly distraught. Roughly, she pulled him upright, too urgent for soft words. "Kryp is dead, man, but Ephan needs your help. Keep him warm and comfortable and move him to his bedchamber as soon as you can. We will do more for him later." She gave the traumatized man a shake. "Can you do that?"

He nodded dumbly.

"Where will I find Anjer?" she asked, but the lieutenant shook his head. She bit back a curse and left the chamber at a run.

Back out in the corridor the wall sconces were being lit. Clearly someone was trying to restore order. One of the calmer servants directed Sullyan to Anjer's private chambers. Entering the suite without knocking, she opened the bedchamber door, startling a naked Torien who was weeping by her husband's side. Anjer, also naked, lay unconscious in the great bed, and it was all too obvious to Sullyan what the two had been doing when the shockwave had struck.

Torien was hysterical and completely unaware of her state of undress.

"Oh, Lady Brynne, thank the gods!" she wailed, throwing herself into Sullyan's arms. "Anjer's collapsed! I don't know what happened. We weren't doing anything … excessive. He just screamed and went still. I think he's dead! What am I going to do?"

Sullyan pushed her away and went to Anjer's side, placing her hands on his sweat-sheened face. She shot Torien a sharp look. "Get a robe on."

The young woman whimpered and stumbled toward her robe, one hand clamped to her mouth.

Turning back to Anjer, Sullyan had to probe deeply to find his consciousness. Because he had been otherwise occupied at the time of the blast, he had not shielded his mind and by rights should be dead. Sullyan's probing, however, revealed a surprising fact. Anjer had been expending power to prevent Torien from conceiving as a result of their lovemaking. Unable to understand why he would—they were married, after all—Sullyan realized that this use of power had inadvertently protected Anjer's mind. Although his consciousness was buried deep, it was still there.

She ran a weary hand over her face and sat on the bed, her mind still linked to Anjer. She absently covered Anjer's rather magnificent body with the comforter. Torien had now belted her robe, which was just as well because the Hierarch suddenly entered the room. He was unsteady on his feet and looked haggard and old. Seeing that Sullyan was working he didn't disturb her, but turned instead to the still-weeping Torien. Anjer's wife flew into his arms and he murmured words of comfort.

Once Sullyan had done for Anjer what she had already done for Ephan, she turned to Pharikian. "How are you, Majesty?"

He managed a smile over Torien's head. "I'm alright, Brynne. Or I will be, given time. How is Anjer?"

Sullyan glanced back down at the Lord General's ashen face. "He will be well with expert care. Although I fear that none of the Artesans in the palace will be fit to give it for a while." She paused. "Majesty, I regret to tell you that General Kryp is dead. He died instantly. Ephan is still with us, though. Do you know where I might find Marik and Deshan?"

The Hierarch's face showed pain over the news about Kryp,

but he replied steadily enough. “Deshan will be in the infirmary, I expect. Marik and Idri should be in their chambers. But what about you, Brynne? And have you any idea what caused all this?”

“I have a hellish headache, Majesty, as we all will for some time. As to what caused the shockwave, I very much fear that someone was attempting to use Rykan’s Staff, and lost control while working. They will almost certainly be dead, as will anyone else caught too close.”

She rose, trying to force down the pain. “I am afraid for Robin, Timar. Very afraid.”

As the Hierarch had said, Sullyan found Deshan in the infirmary. Because of the large number of Artesans in the Citadel, the infirmary was shielded by walls coated with spellsilver, just enough to block the effects of a substrate scream should an injured Artesan lose control. This protection meant that not only was Deshan unharmed, he was also completely unaware of events. Mercifully, Marik and Idrimar were also there, giving Deshan the opportunity to check Marik’s shoulder before the day’s work began.

Once Deshan learned what had happened, he abandoned his examination of Marik, gathered his healers, and went to tend the injured. He left strict instructions for Sullyan to stay there and rest, but she ignored him. She made her way back to Anjer’s chambers, this time knocking politely on the door.

Torien opened it, her face blotchy and streaked with tears. She ushered Sullyan into the room. “Oh, Brynne, he’s no better.”

“He will not be, Torien, not yet,” she soothed. “I had to shut him away inside himself for protection. Come, sit with him and take his hand. Let us see if we can wake him. Poor man, he will have a fearsome headache for days.”

The young woman anxiously followed Sullyan into the bedchamber and sat on the bed beside her husband, looking tiny and frail beside his massive frame. Sullyan sat on his other side, placing her hands on his temples. Probing deeply into Anjer’s mind, she let loose the bonds of his psyche and reached down to his consciousness. She could sense he was holding memories of the sudden, searing pain and was unwilling to surface. Sullyan coaxed and led and, eventually, he opened his eyes.

Torien immediately covered his face with kisses. "Oh, my love!"

Anjer looked bemused, then startled when he realized Sullyan was sitting next to him. She smiled faintly as she saw him glance down, relieved to find the bedclothes in place.

"You will be well," she told him gently. "Sleep now. Let me help you. When you wake, you will have nothing more than a sore head. Do you understand?"

He gave a slight nod, and she turned to Torien. "Lady Torien, he needs to rest. You can stay by him, but let him sleep."

Anjer's tiny wife moved away as Sullyan effortlessly sent Anjer into a deep and healing sleep. She stood up to leave but then, struck by a thought, said, "Lady Torien, might I ask you a personal question?"

Torien nodded hesitantly.

"I do not mean to pry, but I confess I was surprised to learn that Anjer is preventing you from conceiving. Why is that? Do you not want children?"

Torien flushed in embarrassment and wrung her hands. "Anjer says I'm too small."

"To bear his child?"

Torien nodded unhappily.

"But you both want children?"

"Oh, yes, Lady Brynne! I want to give him a son more than anything. I told him we weren't suited when we wed, but we were so much in love. We still are, but now I feel I'm letting him down. And he's not getting any younger, and I'm so afraid that he …" Blushing brightly, she trailed off.

Sullyan gave an indelicate snort. "You need have no fear for your husband's capabilities, Torien. He will remain lusty for many years yet."

The young woman flushed even deeper and looked away. Sullyan smiled. "Forgive me for being so forthright, but I have lived among men my whole life. Such things hold no embarrassment for me. Let me assure you, it would be perfectly safe for you to bear the Lord General a child. It would likely be a robust child, especially if it was male, but it should not be too much for you. Deshan could have confirmed this for you had you asked. My advice would be for you and Anjer to pick up where you left off, this time without the restrictions. Tell him so when he wakes, Torien. It might just take the edge off his headache!"

She left, an image of Torien's flaming face and blissfully happy smile in her mind. It gladdened her to think that someone in this Citadel would find happiness today.

She returned to Bull and Taran, who had both taken Marik's old suite across the passage. When Sullyan entered, Rienne was mixing a concoction of willow extract. The healer glanced up as Sullyan appeared, took one look at her, and wordlessly handed her the cup. Sullyan took it and regarded the mixture dubiously. She knew how bad it would taste.

"Go on," growled Bull from where he sat propped and pale among the pillows. "We've all had to. Why should you be different?"

Knowing he was right, she swallowed the cup's contents in one go. The flavor caused her to glance in startlement at Rienne. The healer and the two men burst out laughing, although Taran groaned afterwards.

"You should see your face!" said Rienne.

Sullyan grinned ruefully. "At last someone has found a decent use for that firewater you love so much, Bull. I have never heard of medicine tasting pleasant. Rienne, you must give Deshan the idea. Most of his potions taste foul."

She sat on Taran's bed while the willow took effect, her metasenses helping it through her system. As she waited, she explained what she thought must have happened. She was unable to hide her fear for Robin, which prompted Bull to ask, "Do you have any idea who was using the Staff at the time?"

She shook her head, and then wished she had not. The pain was abating, but she was still very sore. "It was not Robin, that is all I can say. Bull, I hesitate to ask this—your head must be as tender as mine—but can you sense him at all? Anyone who was in close proximity to that blast must surely have been injured, at the very least. And if it occurred within a substrate structure …" She trailed off, too appalled to say it.

She watched as Bull gathered his wits and tried a tentative call to Robin. He shook his head; no response. Breathing heavily, he tried again while Sullyan absently massaged her aching left hand.

After a few minutes, he grimaced. "No, there's nothing. Wait! Was that a glimpse of his pattern?"

He closed his eyes to aid concentration. Sullyan held her breath.

Bull's urgency showed on his face as he stretched himself to the limit. "It's gone. Maybe I imagined … No! I've got it. He's there. But he's not conscious. And I can't tell if he's damaged or not."

Relieved, Sullyan nodded. At least he was still alive.

Rienne fidgeted in her chair. "Bull? Any trace of Cal?"

"Oh, dear heart, forgive me! I should have thought. Let me just …" After a few more minutes, he smiled. "Yes, Rienne, I can sense him. He's unconscious too, though. Sully, what the Void has happened?"

But Sullyan could only speculate. She hated feeling so intensely helpless.

*****

Only three people in the entire village of Hyecombe were undamaged by the implosion of Heron's tunnel. One of them was the man responsible for the catastrophe, and he was in no state to worry about it.

Following his calamitous expenditure of power, Cal had once again lapsed into unconsciousness. He was totally unaware of the devastation he had caused. The tiny portion of his mind that had retained the ability to reason had been surprised by the depth of power he had managed to call up. Had he been lucid at the time, he would have realized it wasn't his own. However, as well as dampening his pain and protecting his mind, the intense rush of metaforce had put him to sleep, so Cal was blissfully unaware of the destruction around him.

The twin giants, Almid and Kester, were protected by their proximity to Cal. They had ducked to the floor when the windows blew in and were showered with glass and rubble, but due to Cal's instinctive blanket shield they were otherwise unharmed.

After shaking dust and debris from their backs and releasing Cal from the rest of the ropes binding him, they lifted him carefully from the chair and carried him into Taran's sleeping room. Almid cleared glass shards from the bed and Kester laid Cal down. Then they went outside to look at the carnage. It was not quite daylight, but they could see that the street containing Taran's house was not as damaged as the main street. Sonten's wall of rubble had collapsed, and all the houses had broken windows, but only one of the buildings had come down.

The main street was another matter. Those houses directly in the path of the blast had been completely destroyed, and all the rest had lost doors, windows, and most of their roofs. There was dust, rubble, glass, and splintered wood everywhere. A gritty, musty smell hung in the air. There were also bodies, some lying still, some twitching or staggering to their feet. There was the sound of groaning, coughing, and spluttering. Some of the bodies were buried or half-buried by fallen masonry.

With unspoken agreement, Kester returned to the cottage to watch over Cal while Almid searched for Ky-shan.

Frowning in confusion, Almid picked his way toward what looked like a large crater in the ground. This marked the center of the blast, and there were dead horses and dead men inside it. All of the men were Andaryans, but none of them were seamen.

Almid turned away. Walking gingerly up the street toward the tavern, he suddenly heard a shout. Looking up quickly, he saw a crowd of villagers and half a dozen soldiers coming down the street toward him. As they came closer, he recognized Captain Parren at their head. The man was grinning savagely.

Baring his teeth, Almid reached for his sword.

*****

Parren could hardly believe his luck. He, along with some fifty of his men and a handful of villagers, were inside the tavern at the time of the blast. Though they had all been blown to the floor, they had all suffered only temporary deafness and pain. Ears still ringing, Parren had led them outside and saw that things could have been much, much worse. He smiled at the thought. With any luck, the troublesome Robin Tamsen had been caught by the blast and might already be dead. And if he wasn't, then who was to say that the hole in his hide—the one Parren intended to give him—had not come from an enemy blade? There would be no witnesses to gainsay Parren's account.

Striding down the street with the bewildered villagers and some of his men at his back, Parren was intent on searching for his quarry. Then one of his men shouted, pointing at a huge demon walking brazenly through the rubble. Parren waved them on and they ran forward to intercept the giant. The demon made ready to defend himself, unsure of their intentions.

That was enough for Parren. He recognized the man as one of Robin's party and remembered that the giant was mute. Here was his chance to be seen taking a prisoner, one he could claim was an invader, and he fully intended to round up any surviving demons and put them to the sword in front of the villagers. With Robin dead and Baily denounced as being responsible for botching the plan in the first place, Parren would be hailed as Hyecombe's savior. He had already ensured, by the simple expedient of being first into the inn, that the villagers saw him as such.

He congratulated himself on having done the right thing in forcing Robin to take the brunt of the fighting while he, Parren, convinced the villagers that he was in sole command of those responsible for ending the siege. Now was his chance to cement that belief.

He called orders to his men as they advanced on the giant.

*****

Robin lay half-covered by fallen debris and a dead body. He felt stiff and bruised but could feel all his limbs and didn't think he had any broken bones. The blast had stunned him, but he was largely unhurt. He had realized what was happening in the vicinity of the tunnel and had sensed the struggle for control going on within it. Deciding it might be prudent to shield, he had protected himself just in time, so fortunately his mind was undamaged. But he had been close to the site of the blast and was knocked off his feet by its force, as was everyone else around him. He thought he had seen Ky-shan and some of the seamen fleeing from the tunnel mouth before the whole thing shattered, but it had happened so fast. He didn't know if they had escaped alive.

Opening gritty eyes, Robin gazed at the rubble all around him. There was a dead man pinning his legs, and the Andaryan was a horrific sight. Blood had streamed from his eyes, ears, and nose, and his face was contorted in a frozen scream. Repulsed, Robin sat up and heaved the body from him. A startled curse sounded close by and he stared up, straight into the furious eyes of Captain Parren.

Struggling to his feet, Robin was suddenly aware of Almid behind him, sword at the ready. His immediate thought was that Almid was protecting him, but Robin soon saw that the giant was more concerned for his own safety. He stared in astonishment at the obvious animosity between Parren, his men, and Almid, unable to believe that even the vicious Parren would attack an ally. Then he registered Parren's fresh appearance and realized that the man had slyly avoided the worst of the fighting. This made him angry.

"What the hell do you think you're doing, Parren?" he demanded, dust clogging his throat and making him cough. "Back off, this man's a friend!"

"So *you* say," snarled Parren. "*I* say he's a demon, one of the invaders. The good people of this village want rid of these outlanders and I intend to oblige them. Stand aside."

Robin glared at Parren and at the swordsmen with him, one or two of whom looked confused. No one could fail to recognize Almid, even if they couldn't tell the twins apart. They had all seen them with Robin before the attack and knew them to be allies. Yet Parren's authority couldn't be denied and his men were bound to obey him. The villagers had no idea that some of the demons had come here to help them—Robin would have wagered a year's pay on Parren concealing that fact—and were urging the swordsmen on, baying noisily for Almid's blood.

Drawing his sword, Robin went to stand beside Almid. He faced Parren. "Back off," he commanded, his voice stronger. "I'm telling you, this man is on our side and we'll need his strength if we're going to sort this mess out. We should be tending to our people, Parren, not fighting our friends."

Parren spat in the dirt. "*Your* friends, Tamsen. You seem to have defected to the other side. What are you doing in the company of demons, anyway? Look what they've done to this place!"

Robin knew what Parren was trying to do. He and Almid were alone against Parren's trained swordsmen and a crowd of frightened villagers. This could get ugly. Casting about for recognizable faces, he suddenly caught sight of Paulus emerging from the tavern. The businessman had probably been counting the cost of the damage to his livelihood, and his expression said he didn't like what he saw. But he came up the street at Robin's call, looking bemused by the standoff.

"Captain Tamsen," he exclaimed when he finally recognized Robin. "I had no idea you were here. What's going on?"

The young man breathed a sigh of relief. As both Elder and tavern-keeper, Paulus was well respected by the villagers and Robin knew they would listen to him. At his very appearance their raucous shouts died down.

"Paulus, thank the gods! Listen, I want you to tell everyone that not all of the Andaryans here are invaders. Some of them came here with me to help relieve you. You wouldn't want to see them mistaken for enemies and killed, would you?"

Paulus frowned at Parren and Almid before looking back at Robin. "No, of course not. But how will we know which are which?"

"Almid here can identify them. He might not be able to talk, but you can trust him. I don't have time for this. I have to find Cal. I need to know what happened to the rest of the men who came here with me, and I need to know what became of the invaders' leader. Would you and some of the villagers help Almid search for survivors?"

Receiving Paulus's dubious nod, Robin turned to the giant. "Almid, is Cal alright?"

The giant's eyes were still fixed on Parren's dangerously flushed face, but he nodded, giving Robin a brief account of what had occurred in Taran's house. Robin didn't hear Almid as clearly as Sullyan could, but he got the gist of it. Paulus, reassured by

Robin's manner, began calming the villagers, telling them not to fear Almid or any demons he indicated were friends.

Parren, clearly realizing his moment had passed, tossed a venomous look at Robin. "This isn't over, Tamsen. You put your own desires before the safety of the villagers, and I intend to see that the General hears of it. You left me to ensure their well-being and we could all have been killed. Blaine won't be too happy when he hears of your conduct."

Robin's mouth dropped open. The threat of denouncement didn't bother him—Blaine knew exactly what he had come here for. But the villagers just might back Parren, as he had undoubtedly helped them escape their jailors and events could easily be twisted with a few well-chosen words. However, Robin had other things on his mind right now. More men were gaining their feet, friend and foe alike, and he could hear the sounds of renewed fighting coming from the other street.

"Drop it, Parren," he snapped. "Now is not the time. Our men need help and direction. We need to know where Baily is, and I must find Cal. I suggest you gather your men and do your job."

Leaving Almid with Paulus, Robin let Parren deal with the recovering people in the main street. He made for Taran's house, where he found Kester awaiting him, his huge sword in his beefy hands. Leaving the giant by the door, Robin found Cal still blissfully unconscious on the bed, looking as pale as someone with such dark skin could. Checking him over, Robin was relieved to find no damage other than the physical. He re-emerged from the house to see Baily and about thirty of his command desperately fighting the remnants of the demon forces farther up the street. Calling Kester, he rushed to help.

Although the Andaryans were fighting, they were thoroughly demoralized, as much by the desertion of their lord and commander as by the effects of the explosion. Their hearts were not in their resistance and they were flagging. Baily's men, still smarting from having the tables of ambush turned upon them earlier, were using their anger to good effect. Their foes were all but subdued by the time Robin and Kester added their swords.

Seeing this, Baily roared for the Andaryans to surrender their arms. With one or two exceptions, they did so, morosely allowing themselves to be herded into an outbuilding at the far end of the street. It had but two windows and one door, and was easily guarded by half a dozen men. A panting but triumphant Baily accepted Robin's praise before the two captains ran back to the main street.

The fighting here was sporadic. Most of the demons not already put to the sword had been herded into buildings. Only a few individuals were left to resist. As Robin and Baily watched, the last of these surrendered and half a dozen Manor swordsmen manhandled them into temporary prisons. It was then that Robin realized there was no sign of Parren or the bulk of his men. He frowned.

Kester gripped his arm with crushing force and spun him about, pointing to the far end of the village. Almid was already sprinting for the tight knot of men just visible in the distance. They were being harried by Parren's forces, pushed slowly but inexorably toward the treacherous marshy ground around the pond. Robin saw Ky-shan's unmistakable form, his few remaining men around him, struggling to fend off a furious Parren. Cursing, Robin and Kester rushed to their aid.

"Parren!" roared Robin. "Stand off! He's a friend."

Parren ignored him, clearly in no mood to relent now that he had a demon in his sights. His bloodlust was up, and as far as he was concerned Ky-shan was a legitimate target.

The pirates were giving ground, totally outnumbered by Parren's men, only a few of which had heard Robin's call and backed off. Still yelling, Robin fought his way through to Parren and barged heavily into him, knocking him off-balance.

"Put up, *put up*!" he roared. But Parren, enraged by the interference, bellowed at his men to carry on. Unsure who to obey, some continued fighting. Now, however, Kester and Almid had rejoined Ky-shan and their vast strength forced a stand-off.

Regaining his balance, Parren whipped round to face Robin. His sword wove in the air menacingly. The two forces stood panting and watching warily, neither side entirely sure what would happen next. Robin and Parren glared at each other, both breathing heavily. Parren's eyes were hooded and vicious, Robin's concerned and wary. He was getting tired of this, and desperately needed to know what had happened to Sonten, Heron, and Vanyr.

He spoke quietly, trying to calm the situation. "Leave it, Parren. I told you, now is not the time."

"Oh, I don't know." Parren's voice was dangerously low. "Maybe now is exactly the time. What better opportunity to be rid of a traitor?"

"What are you talking about?" demanded Robin.

Baily pushed his way through the press of men and came to stand at Robin's side. "Come on, Parren, Tamsen's no traitor. You've no grounds for an accusation like that."

"Oh, haven't I?" The dark line of Parren's scar stood out starkly against his sallow skin. His sword ceased its weaving. "Who was it brought more demons here? Who is obviously friendly with our enemies? Who is defending them, even fighting alongside them? Look at him, Baily! He's just itching to be gone, to follow his slit-eyed friends! Are those the actions of a loyal Albian? I don't think so!" He aimed his sword tip at Robin's breast.

To Robin's amazement—and relief—Baily brought his own weapon up, knocking Parren's aside. "Enough!" he barked.

Parren stared at him, and Robin smiled faintly. It took a lot to rile Baily.

"I won't listen to your spiteful defamations, Parren," he said. "You're being ridiculous. Blaine has no reservations about Tamsen's loyalty, and neither do I." Turning to Robin, he said, "Go and do what you have to, Rob. Parren and I will clear up here and report back to the General. And don't worry, I'll see the correct story gets told. If needs be, your friend Paulus will back me up."

"Thanks, Baily, I appreciate it." Robin eyed the silent but furious Parren as he would a poisonous toad. Then he turned to the stocky pirate. "Ky-shan, what can you tell me about Sonten and Vanyr?"

Chapter Eleven

Robin and the pirates walked slowly back to Taran's cottage to the sound of a vicious row erupting behind them. Ignoring Baily and Parren, Ky-shan told Robin what he had seen inside the tunnel and how he and most of his men had managed to flee the structure before it imploded. Only three seamen had failed to emerge, and those who had escaped were immediately swept off their feet by the blast. Thanks to Vanyr's warning they had all covered their ears, saving them from permanent damage. Even so, some were still partially deaf and they all had splitting headaches. Robin could sympathize—his own head was throbbing like a drum.

"So Vanyr, Sonten, and Heron were all caught inside the tunnel?" he asked. "With the Staff?" Ky-shan nodded, and Robin's heart quailed. "Oh, gods. Let me see if I can sense Vanyr, though I don't suppose he could have survived."

On entering the cottage, Robin dropped wearily into a dust-covered chair. He calmed his aching mind, sorting Vanyr's psyche pattern from the others he knew and longed to contact. His senses ranged through the Veils, easily following the disruption caused by the imploding tunnel. Its echoes were everywhere, and he knew that every realm would have felt the aftershock, although none as intensely as Albia and Andaryon.

Finding the tunnel's intended exit, he cast about for signs of life. There were no traces of Sonten or Heron in the substrate, and Robin hadn't expected to find any, but neither could he detect Vanyr. He reluctantly concluded they had all perished inside the tunnel, as Ky-shan had indicated. Withdrawing, he sat with his splitting head in his hands, wondering how on earth he was going to tell Sullyan the precious Staff was lost.

He began to tremble as tears pricked his sore eyes. He was going to lose her after all. He couldn't believe they had come this far, gone through so much, only to be defeated like this. If only he hadn't underestimated Sonten so badly. If only he had arrived sooner. If only he had been nearer to Sonten when the tunnel had opened. He had never even considered the possibility that Sonten might force Heron to open a trans-Veil structure right in the middle of the village. It was suicidal madness, and Heron should have known better. But Robin had completely failed to understand the depths of Sonten's ruthlessness, and now Sullyan would pay the price. He didn't know how he would bear it.

The pirates moved around the little cottage, throwing out more rubble and clearing the fireplace. One of them gathered splintered wood and lit a fire. It was full daylight now, but it was still early and the sky was cloudy, promising rain. The cheerful blaze dispelled some of the gloom and lamps were lit so that the little house soon resembled the cozy home it had once been. A couple of the pirates went to round up their scattered horses, bringing the nervous animals to the front of the house, including Robin's Torka. From their supplies, they produced the inevitable bottles of brine rum and some food. Robin accepted what he was offered, although his head was still pounding and depression was making him nauseous.

Ky-shan put a hand on his shoulder. "Why don't you get some rest, lad?" He sounded so much like Bull that Robin's vision blurred. "We'll watch here. You grab a bit of sleep. We'll wake you if anything happens or your friend rouses. Though, by the looks of him, he needs a week of solid sleep."

Robin could think of no good reason to refuse. It was still too early to contact either Blaine or Bull, and he would feel better after a couple of hours sleep. Thanking Ky-shan for his thoughtfulness—and cautioning him unnecessarily to be wary of Parren—Robin went into Taran's room, rolled himself in a blanket, and lay down on the floor by Cal's bed. He fell instantly asleep.

*****

Sullyan, Rienne, Bull, and Taran stayed together, waiting for dawn and willing their headaches away. Rienne lay curled in Taran's arms on the bed for comfort. Servants brought them fresh fellan and food, but only the fellan was consumed. Sullyan remained silent and withdrawn, not knowing what to do. She was unable to cross the Veils to see for herself what had happened, and Taran also was unfit to travel. Bull could have gone, but she was unwilling to send him alone, and her other allies, Kyshan and Vanyr, were with Robin and probably caught up in the catastrophe. Jay'el was totally untrained, although she toyed with the idea of sending him and Ki-en with Bull to stand for the big man if he needed them. But the near-miss of Bull's heart seizure made her doubly protective of him and she was reluctant to part with him, although she knew he would go if she asked him. She was helpless, and hated it.

Dawn was just breaking over the inner courtyard gardens when she made up her mind to send Bull. She knew Robin and Cal were in trouble and could bear it no longer. She would ask Bull to cross the Veils and contact General Blaine as soon as possible to see if he had any details. She was drawing breath to speak when the faintest touch on her mind made her freeze. Her gaze was an enormous black void as she used all her strength to hear the frail and tenuous call.

Brynne.

There it was again, although she had to strain to hear it. Its tone was suffused with pain and suffering, as if the caller was near to death. She couldn't tell who it was. Following the faint trace in the substrate, she tried to strengthen the mind of whoever was so desperate to reach her.

Brynne.

It came a third time, weaker now. But she was ready for it and held firmly to the fading psyche as it slipped, supporting it steadily.

Hold on, she urged. *Do not try to call again. I have heard you. Just stay conscious if you can. Rest, be easy. I am coming.*

As she leaped from her chair, the sudden movement startled the others. Bull rose with her and she briefly considered ordering him to stay, but then thought better of it. Glancing at Rienne and Taran, she said, "You two stay here. Bull and I are going out. We will be in touch when we can. Rienne, will you do what you can to help Anjer and Ephan? They both need attention. If you see Pharikian, tell him we will return as soon as we may, but I do not know how long this will take."

"Why, what is it?" demanded Rienne, worry for Cal clear in her tone.

Sullyan dropped her eyes. "It is Vanyr," she murmured. "I fear he is dying."

Striding from the room, Sullyan called for servants to run ahead and order their horses saddled. There was no time to gather packs or supplies. The faint trace of Vanyr's psyche was weakening all the time despite Sullyan's soothing and strengthening hold. She was very much afraid she would lose him before she could reach him.

On their way through the palace, they picked up Ki-en and Jay'el. The two young men fell in beside them without a word, and Sullyan merely nodded as they strode at her shoulder. Bull spared them a glance, no doubt keen to hear the full story of Sullyan's sojourn at the palace, but he kept his thoughts to himself as they approached the horse lines.

Drum and Bull's horse were saddled and waiting and grooms hastened to ready mounts for Jay'el and Ki-en. Wasting no time, they mounted, the Major casting a covert glance at Bull to satisfy herself he was fit for the ride. She was unable to determine Vanyr's exact location because the link was too tenuous, but she knew he wasn't close by. In all probability they had hard ride ahead of them, and she could do without Bull having problems on the way.

She led them at a fast pace down to the Citadel's west gate and was recognized instantly by the sentries. They all knew Drum by sight now, and the gate was being opened before she could request it. Leaning over the big stallion's neck as they passed through, she headed him west of the Citadel hill and urged him into a mile-eating gallop. The others followed suit, and soon they were among the trees. The spires of Caer Vellet disappeared behind them.

Sullyan briefed Jay'el and Ki-en on what had happened, explaining why they were riding out just after dawn on an early spring day in pale, intermittent sunshine. Fear and concern shone in the young men's eyes for Ky-shan and their comrades, but she could do nothing to reassure them. Her only thought was for Vanyr. The fading nature of his psyche was forcing her to expend more and more power to keep him alive.

Following it like a beacon, she held a fast pace for the best part of four hours. The countryside to the west of the Citadel was more thickly populated than the east. There were more in the way of villages and towns, and there were open fields and farmlands instead of forests. These fertile lands supplied Caer Vellet with its staples, foodstuffs, herbs, cloth, wool, and leather. The craftsmen and workers were already out in their fields and workshops, and farmers were making the most of the better weather to get on with the spring planting. Many curious eyes were raised as the four riders galloped past, and more than once Sullyan felt the tentative touch of a trained or semi-trained mind probing hers. But her shields were down tight, as she needed all her concentration to follow that faint and frantic presence in her mind. He was still trying to reach to her, still calling her name. He was failing and desperate, and she was desperate to reach him in time.

*****

Someone was shaking his arm and Robin roused instantly, seeing Kester looming over him. Judging by the light, it was some time in the afternoon. Robin hadn't intended to sleep so long. As he sat up his head began to throb again, and he spent a few minutes expending power to try to ease the pain. It was something of a trade-off because the more he used his power, the more his head hurt. Eventually, he felt he had achieved a balance of sorts and was able to stand.

As he did so he met Cal's dark eyes, the young man's return to consciousness clearly the reason for Kester waking him. The mute knew Cal would be puzzled and maybe alarmed and would welcome a familiar face. As Robin stood, Kester gestured to the pot of fresh fellan on the dust-covered table and then withdrew.

Robin poured himself a welcome cup and sat on the edge of the bed, noting Cal's unhealthily pale face. Despite his low spirits he managed a grin. "I never knew you dark-skinned types could go that pale."

He was rewarded by Cal's weak smile. "Neither did I."

"How are you feeling? You look awful, if you don't mind me saying."

Cal gave a snort, and then winced. "Thanks, mate! I'll remember that the next time you get beaten up and have your arm twisted half off. Who did this, by the way?" He indicated his bandaged arm. "And who the hell was that huge man? I take it he's on our side? I seem to recall him from yesterday, but that was before all hell broke loose."

Now it was Robin's turn to snort. Should he tell Cal, he wondered, that the hell which broke loose had been the Apprentice's own doing? Maybe not, if the Staff was lost for good. He shied away from that thought—it was too raw. He would save the information for later. Instead, he spent a few minutes describing what had happened since dawn that morning while Cal listened, open-mouthed.

Shocked and stunned, all Cal could say was, "Bloody hell! Taran's going to be very grateful to Sonten for clearing out his cellar."

The young Captain sighed. "Then he'll be the only one who is."

Cal struggled to sit. "What happens now?"

Putting aside his cup, Robin helped him. "We'd better get you back to the Manor, I think. Unless you want to stay here, of course. This is your home, after all."

Cal stared around the ruined room, the glass, the dust, the mess. "Home? No, I don't think so. Taran and I were only ever tolerated here, and that was mainly because of Rienne. After this, I don't think we would be able to show our faces without someone spitting at us. None of the villagers would lift a finger to help me now, except maybe Paulus, and I wouldn't want to burden him.

So I'll take your offer, if you don't mind. I know Rienne would be happier if I was at the Manor. I take it she's alright?"

His tone was casual, but there was a plaintive note behind it, and Robin cursed himself for not thinking. "Yes, yes, she's fine. She's with Sullyan, Bull, and Taran at the Citadel. I'll contact them later once I've made arrangements to get you back to the Manor. I'll be going back to Andaryon myself soon, with Ky-shan and the rest, and I imagine that Bull, Taran, and Rienne will come back here."

Cal gave a huge sigh of relief. "They're all alive then? I didn't think Sonten was telling the truth, but …."

Robin suddenly remembered that Cal was totally unaware of everything that had happened since Sullyan's duel with Rykan. He quickly related the events, and also told Cal the significance of the Staff and the reason why both he and Sonten had been so desperate to recover it. Cal was silent when he learned what had happened to it. Robin poured him some fellan and sat in silence while he drank it, not letting himself dwell on what would happen to Sullyan now that the Staff was lost. He was thankful when Cal didn't ask.

Robin went out into the street looking for Baily and Parren. He found Paulus instead, at the tavern surveying the damage his premises had sustained. Despite the mess, the innkeeper wasn't too unhappy. The building had escaped relatively unscathed, and doors and windows were easily replaced. His liquor supplies were also largely intact, and both villagers and swordsmen alike would be happy to spend a few coppers drowning their sorrows in ale. He had fired up his big range and some of the women were busy organizing food and warm drinks for those whose houses had been destroyed. The tavern would be a welcome haven and place of comfort while the village was rebuilt.

With approval, Robin saw some of the Manor swordsmen helping the villagers clean up. The dead were also being dealt with. The Albians—all Kingsmen—were being loaded onto a cart for transportation back to the Manor, but the demons were unceremoniously taken out to the marshlands around the pond and flung uncaringly into their sucking, brown depths. Ky-shan had identified his own dead and had made a large pyre out in the fields. Its smoke drifted lazily away from the village.

Robin finally located Baily and Parren in one of the least damaged houses, where they were being fed by some of the women. They looked up as he came in, Baily with a tight smile and Parren with a look of undisguised hatred. Ignoring him, Robin addressed the smaller man.

"Baily, will you see to it that Cal gets back to the Manor? He'll need a litter or cart, I think, and he'll have to go slowly. I was going to come myself, but Ky-shan wants to get back and I have to report to the Major."

Before Baily had a chance to answer, Parren sneered, "Have to tell her you've failed, won't you, Tamsen?" There was a sly grin on his sallow face. "The Queen of Darkness will have to stay where she is now, won't she? To die among her own kind."

With a suddenness that shocked even him, Robin snapped. He lunged at Parren, slamming him to the ground, sending chairs and food plates flying. The women shrieked and ran from the house. Heaving himself astride Parren's thrashing body, Robin used his knees to pin the man's arms while his hands found Parren's straining throat. He felt the pounding of the other man's heart and drank in the fear and hatred in his blazing eyes. Robin wished he could find the determination to tighten his hands and squeeze the life from Parren, but his prior impetuousness was gone, replaced by a cooler head and more measured reactions. Had Parren only realized it, despair had made Robin a much more dangerous opponent.

The Captain smiled down at his rival, his voice low and deadly.

"I could do it, you know. It's not fear of you or Blaine that stays my hand." He exerted just enough pressure to cause Parren considerable discomfort. "I want you to know that. I am totally under control, and if I wished to take your life, I would. But I don't. There's enough blood on my hands, and I don't want any more. Not even yours, you miserable excuse for a man."

He leaned down, allowing his hot breath to warm Parren's already sweating skin. "You're right, I do have friends in Andaryon, friends who would defend me to the death and who

I would defend in my turn. I'm not ashamed of that. I'm not ashamed to call them friends, even if they are from a different race. The very least of them is worth twenty of you, you sick bastard. So you can ride back to the Manor in triumph if you want, and you can spread your lies. Blaine will never believe you. I'm going to contact him before ever you get the chance, and he'll hear the tale from me. Yes, even of my failure. Baily knows what happened here, as does Elder Paulus, so just you try denouncing me and see what happens. I no longer care."

Giving Parren's bruised throat one last vicious squeeze, causing the man to choke and cough, Robin rose. He ignored Parren's spluttering curses and turned to Baily. "Sorry, Baily, I didn't mean to sleep for so long. Will you be alright if I leave you here to clean up? Dexter and the rest of my command will stay too, and you can all go back together once you've done what you can."

Baily nodded, watching Parren, who was still lying on the ground, making much of his bruised throat. "You go, Rob. He won't give me any trouble."

Robin thanked him and took his leave, disdaining to notice the thoroughly poisonous look Parren gave him as he rose from the floor. Returning to Cal, Robin told him about the arrangements.

"I'd rather come with you," the Apprentice said.

"I know, Cal, but you're not even fit to go as far as the Manor yet, let alone across the Veils. I'll contact you as soon as I know what's happening. Don't worry, I'll tell Rienne you're alright."

"Thanks." Cal closed his eyes. "Tell her I miss her."

"I will. She'll be back soon."

Going outside, Robin composed himself to report to General Blaine. He hadn't intended to put it off this long. He walked away from where the pirates were getting ready to leave and sat on a pile of rubble. His quest for contact got the General's attention immediately, and he ran through the events leading up to his arrival in Hyecombe succinctly. Blaine heard it all without comment. Then Robin described the battle for the Staff. He omitted any mention of Parren's obstructive behavior, trusting Baily to bear him out. He managed to keep his emotions at bay until he reached the part where the tunnel collapsed. He got as far as describing the Andaryan General's desperate scramble through the structure and Vanyr's heroic pursuit. When he tried to continue, however, he choked.

There was a short silence before the General asked, *What became of them, Captain? Do you have the artifact?*

Shame and sorrow colored Robin's tone. *I'm afraid not, sir. They were all inside when the tunnel collapsed. It would have killed them, sir. I think the Staff is lost.*

Lost? Do you mean permanently?

I don't know, sir. I searched, but I couldn't find any trace of Sonten, his Artesan, or Vanyr. If they were trapped inside the tunnel when it blew, as I'm sure they were, then it's gone for good.

Blaine was silent. When he did finally speak, he sounded weary and old.

And Major Sullyan?

Robin sidestepped the question. He didn't trust himself not to break down. *I haven't told her yet.*

He heard Blaine sigh. *Then you better had, Captain. I take it you're going back?*

With your permission, sir.

I've already told you you're free to stay as long as she needs you. Just remember to report now and then.

Of course, sir, and thank you. By the way, I'm sending Cal Tyler back with Dexter and the others, once the village has been cleaned up. He'll need medical attention, but he should be alright. I imagine Bull, Rienne, and Taran will return soon too.

Very well, Captain.

What do you want done with the prisoners, sir?

The General's tone was hard. *Herd them back through the Veils, Captain, and leave them. I don't care where.*

Robin thought the General had finished, but Blaine didn't break the link. Robin waited, wondering. And then Blaine's voice came again, as if from very far away, and Robin could barely hear the whispered words.

Tell Sullyan ... tell her that I ... oh, dammit, just take care of her, will you?

He broke off abruptly before Robin could reply.

*****

Sullyan had no time to wonder how or why Vanyr was dying way out here in the Andaryan countryside. She also didn't know why he was so desperate to reach her. All she knew was that he needed her badly and she wasn't about to fail him. She had come to value his friendship highly and acknowledged that without his expert tutoring she would never have been able to manipulate Rykan during their duel. If only she had been a bit stronger, held out a fraction longer, she might have saved herself considerable agony. But she couldn't dwell on that now. She had to concentrate on reaching Vanyr in time, and so she pushed herself and her companions ever westward as they rode on into the afternoon.

After another couple of hours, she allowed them to slow. The trained and muscular stallions had kept the pace well, but they were blowing now and she wouldn't risk their wind. She slowed Drum to a regular, easy trot and cast about with her metasenses, trying to pinpoint Vanyr's location.

His presence was now a barely perceived spark in her mind. He had not called her name for some time, and she prayed this was because he knew she was coming. He was still conscious—just—and she kept up a soothing flow of metaforce, desperate to keep him from slipping away.

A smudge of smoke in the distance caught her eye and she pointed, drawing Bull's attention. "Over there," she said, urging Drum into a canter. How she knew this stain in the sky was significant, she couldn't say. She only knew it marked Vanyr's location.

They skirted a village, a very small one with only a handful of crude houses. At least, they had once been houses. Now only ruined, mud-spattered walls were left, along with clumps of old thatch and scattered debris. It looked as if a tornado had ripped right through it. There was no one in sight. Sullyan pursed her lips and forbore to comment, but the sight twisted her guts with fear.

Riding through the fields toward the faint column of smoke, they began to see bodies. The first one, a farmer, lay spread-eagled on his back, arms outflung. Blood had congealed where it had poured from his eyes, ears, nose, and mouth. He was a grim sight, and he wasn't the only one. Stony-faced, Sullyan counted over twenty more peasants all in the same condition, some with expressions of extreme agony stamped on their frozen faces.

The dead villagers weren't the only indications of disaster. Trees had blown down, all facing in the same direction. Hedges had holes blasted through them, and there were dead animals everywhere. Mainly rabbits, but one field was full of dead sheep, all tumbled over as if some vast wind had mown them down.

And then they saw the crater. It was huge, fully fifty feet in diameter and at least ten deep in the middle. From its charred center a pall of smoke rose lazily into the afternoon sky. They halted on its edge, Jay'el and Ki-en with their mouths hanging open. Under his breath, Bull muttered, "Bloody hellfire!" but Sullyan, tears standing in her eyes, stared urgently about her. Her metasenses picked over the area as she sought Vanyr's almost imperceptible trace.

"Torman, I am here," she called. "Where are you? Can you speak to me?"

Dismounting from Drum, she walked about the place, avoiding the huge crater, looking for traces of someone having walked or crawled away. Softly, she called again. "Torman, where are you? Guide me, if you can."

She opened her mind, sensitive to the merest touch. Bull and the two lads watched in silence, unwilling to disturb her. She stilled herself, so still that even the beat of her heart and the pulse at her throat were muted.

At last she heard it. The faintest trace of a call, the merest breath of her name. Swinging unerringly toward it, she followed it around the crater to a small copse of thin trees which had miraculously withstood the blast. Branches and shredded leaves lay everywhere, but as she came closer she could just make out a body lying huddled under the thin, whippy trunks.

"Bulldog!" she snapped, and the big man hurried over. Together, they approached the man on the ground. Lying on his right side, he was curled up as if at the last he had sought to protect himself from the explosion. His arms were wrapped tightly about his chest and his face was hidden from view, buried under leaves and dirt.

Kneeling by his side, Sullyan placed her hands on his back. Gently she sent her senses into him, soothing, strengthening, cocooning. He had terrible internal injuries. How he had survived this long, she didn't know. Barely conscious, he didn't respond at first. She gently began to clear away the leaves and detritus covering his face. Jay'el and Ki-en came over to help, leaving the horses to stand.

When she finally uncovered his face, she went white and cold with shock. Jay'el gave a gasp of horror and Ki-en rushed behind the nearest tree, where they could hear him noisily heaving. Bull and Sullyan had seen many such sights on the battlefield and were hardened to gore, but even they felt their stomachs turn at the sight of Vanyr's ruined face.

The all-white eyes were gone, only bloody empty sockets remaining. Their liquid had boiled down Vanyr's face, melting and searing the flesh. He would have suffered unbearable agonies. His ears and nose had also bled heavily, and he was totally unrecognizable.

Her heart aching, Sullyan reached out her senses again, making very sure that he would feel no pain when his consciousness returned. She could feel him swimming up from the depths of his psyche toward her, every little advancement an effort to his damaged mind. Enveloping him in her own vast strength, she let him use her powers instead of his own. With Bull's help, she gently took hold of his body, lifting and turning him so that he lay in her lap, his ruined head cradled to her breast.

He made a small sound in his throat and a shudder ran through his body. "Bull," she murmured, "get him some water."

The big man fetched a water skin from Ki-en's saddle and managed to dribble a little liquid into Vanyr's damaged mouth. He swallowed with difficulty.

"Brynne," he croaked. "You came."

"Of course I did, my friend. I would never refuse you, you know that."

"I did my best," he whispered, desperation coloring his tone.

"I knew I had to save it for you, and I did my best. But it was too strong … I wasn't quick enough. I don't know if the others got out in time. I tried to hold it, but I couldn't …."

"Hush, Torman, hush," she soothed. "You have been so strong. Can you tell us what happened? You do not need to speak. Only open your mind and let me see. Lie easy and let me do the work. Rest now."

He sighed as she entered his mind, her presence a soothing balm to his hurts. Relaxing, he let her take control. She linked with Bull so that he too could see what Vanyr had experienced.

Chapter Twelve

Sullyan watched quietly as Vanyr's mind replayed the scene. She saw him and the pirates battling with Sonten's men, watched as Commander Heron was given the Staff and ordered to open the tunnel. She heard Robin's shout and Vanyr's reply as he pushed toward Sonten. Grimacing, she saw Sonten thrust first his men and then Heron into the unstable tunnel. Cal's scream, both vocal and metaphysical, made her wince as it reverberated through the tunnel, rampant metaforce overbalancing its precarious existence. And she felt Vanyr's agony as he valiantly tried to hold the tunnel together by channeling his own power through the Staff.

She shared his urgency as he sent Ky-shan and the seamen scuttling for safety, but she couldn't tell if the pirates got out or not. Of Robin there was no further sign. Frowning, she saw both Sonten and Heron go down, Heron's mind instantly obliterated by raging forces he couldn't control. Sullyan gasped as she felt the power's backlash rip through Vanyr's body, destroying his face even as he doggedly clung to his lifeline. Large, bitter tears rolled down her cheeks as she realized that his feelings for her had enabled him to hold on, even through such unimaginable torture. Thoughts of her had caused him to reach out, trying desperately to grab the Staff as he hurtled past the lifeless Heron, pain wracking him as the tunnel imploded.

She was amazed he had found the strength to open the tunnel and release that final blast, but that strength had enabled him to shield a tiny portion of his mind as the soil of Andaryan exploded, sending the contents of the crater skyward and flattening the poor village. And then he had somehow found the will to call her, fulfilling his final self-imposed task, the one he had given his life for.

Feeling him stir, she looked down, her sight blurred by tears. She saw him unclench his arms, revealing the object he had been holding so tightly.

It lay gleaming, totally untouched by the ruin it had caused. Shimmering blue and green along its length, it was innocuous, quiescent, beautiful, and strange. She was loath to touch its deadly beauty, but he had wrecked himself for this, striven for it, endured agony for it, and she must not show her revulsion at touching something that was still such an intimate part of Rykan. Accepting the artifact from Vanyr's nerveless fingers, she could almost feel Rykan's hands upon her naked body, experienced the sick helplessness she had felt as he forced himself inside her time and time again. Biting back a sob, she accepted that the consequences of Rykan's brutality were far from over.

She managed to hide this from the dying man she cradled so tenderly. Suffusing him with her love, she let him see how proud she was, how highly she valued him. She told him how they would revere him back at the Citadel, and how carefully they would tend him once she got him home.

He stirred again.

"No, Brynne." His voice was a harsh murmur. "There is no home for me now. Yet I am content. The Staff would have been lost forever, and it is enough for me to know that you have it safe." He sighed, his chest barely rising. "I'm dying. I know that. It doesn't matter. I don't wish it any different. If I have one regret, it's not being able to see your face again …."

She blinked, tears rolling freely. As she looked in mute appeal toward Bull, the big man guessed what she was asking. They were still linked, so he sent her image into Vanyr's fading mind, a peaceful image of her smiling serenely down at him as he lay in her arms. Tactfully, he omitted showing the Commander's ruined face.

Vanyr's bloody lips moved, trying to form a smile, and Sullyan's heart nearly broke. She sat in silence, gently stroking Vanyr's hair, letting her friendship and pride wash through him. With his hand clasped in her good one, she tried to ease his discomfort as best she could.

"Brynne?" His voice was so faint she could hardly hear him. "Will you do me one last favor?"

She took a trembling breath. "Anything, my friend. Just ask."

"Will you open the way for me?"

Feeling the blood drain from her face, she closed her eyes. Bull gave a sharp intake of breath. What Vanyr was asking for was the ultimate gift, the most precious gift one Artesan could give to another, although it took nothing less than a Master's skill. To open the Void, the Gateway to death, to help the consciousness slip slowly and painlessly through in dignity and in peace. For the dying it was a welcome release, but for the giver it was hard. It left such scars on the soul as would never fade away. Such an intimate thing could only be asked of the most loving and faithful friend. Or, perhaps, the bitterest enemy.

Sullyan bowed her head. Unbeknownst to any of them, she had already done this once before. Even Robin didn't know that this was how Jessy, his beloved sister, had left the world. Harrowing as it was, she knew what it felt like.

"Of course I will, Torman, if that is truly your wish."

"It is," he said. His breath rasped. "Brynne, I do regret that we were not friends sooner. Can you forgive me for what I put you through? I can't believe how petty I was. I couldn't see what you were, couldn't believe you could do what you claimed. I was blind then, but now, when it is too late, I can see. Will you forgive me?"

Through her tears she whispered, "Hush, my friend, you were forgiven long ago. Today you have given me a wonderful gift, the gift of hope, and I love you for it. You have nothing to reproach yourself with, and you have the gratitude of all those I love. Your name will be remembered forever, and you will be accorded the highest of honors for what you have done. I was right when I told you that your strength was greater than you knew, but today you surpassed even my expectations. You are a very powerful Artesan, my friend. Not many could have done what you did."

Biting back sobs, she squeezed his hand. The tall Andaryan

smiled faintly, his lips oozing fresh blood. "I am ready now," he breathed, and she could feel him relaxing, opening his soul and life force fully to her, giving himself up to her control. Taking a deep breath, she reached her senses into him, surrounding his soul with a cocoon of his own psyche.

"Farewell, my friend," she whispered, and bent to place a soft kiss on his ruined lips. As she did so, the Void of oblivion opened to her command and she helped him slip slowly through, watching with silent tears as the glowing pattern of his psyche flared briefly and then faded, falling down into darkness until she could see it no more.

For a long time she sat there just holding his body, head lowered, eyes closed. Bull, Jay'el, and Ki-en left her in peace, for which she was grateful. She vaguely heard them tending the horses, setting out supplies, lighting a fire to brew fellan. Bull's murmured request that Jay'el should relate the story behind her friendship with Vanyr did not disturb her, and neither did the lad's soft voice as he complied. Memories swam gently through her mind to the cadence of Jay'el's tale, slowly soothing her aching heart. Gradually, she brought herself up from her grief, passing through gratitude, and finally into acceptance of what had happened.

Easing herself from under Vanyr's cooling body, she wrapped him in his cloak, hiding his ruined face. She reluctantly took up the Staff and looked down at him for a little longer. Then she moved over to the fire, sitting cross-legged and accepting the steaming mug held out to her by Bull. She didn't speak, and he watched her expectantly as she communed with the Hierarch, informing him of Vanyr's demise. When she was done, she walled off her grief for the moment.

"Pharikian asks that we bear Torman home," she told him. "He wants to give him a full military funeral and has asked me to participate. We will camp here for tonight and return in the morning. An honor guard will be sent to meet us."

Bull nodded. "How are they all at the Citadel?"

"Pharikian is well enough. He needs further attention but should quickly heal. Anjer is undamaged but weak. Ephan still has not regained consciousness but is expected to fully recover. Deshan and Rienne are caring for them."

She broke off and Bull waited for the rest. She was holding herself in check, but he knew what was troubling her.

"Do you want me to go back?" he eventually asked. She knew he meant to Albia. "Ki-en and Jay'el could come with me."

She shook her head. "No, Hal. I thank you but … not yet. We must convey Torman home first. And I do not want to send you into what could be trouble." She looked him in the eyes. "But I would ask you to try for contact, if you would. I cannot help but be worried for Robin."

*****

Aided by Dexter and forty of his command, Robin herded the Andaryans together at the far end of the main village street. Parren's and Baily's commands stood well back, leaving the clean-up until this was over. A few of the villagers had come to watch, but most stayed away. They were uncomfortable watching Artesans work.

Having first made sure there were no stray villagers to get in the way, Robin opened a tunnel. He was heedless of where it led. His only concern was that it should not open anywhere he knew. Once it was stable, his men herded the prisoners through, many of the Andaryans complaining bitterly about the lack of horses or supplies. They only desisted when Dexter bluntly offered to ensure that they never needed either again. Robin didn't care. He just wanted to be rid of them so he could get back to Sullyan. Time was passing and evening was drawing on, and he wanted to be back in Andaryon by nightfall.

As soon as Dexter had shepherded the last stragglers through, Robin collapsed the structure, massaging his aching temples. His headache was making him snappy. It was just as well, he thought, that Parren had kept himself occupied elsewhere.

He took his leave of Dexter and the men, promising to return sometime in the future, although he shied away from thinking about the circumstances that would enable him to keep that promise. Dexter understood and gripped his shoulder. "Tell her … well, just tell her, Captain."

"I will, Dex. Now I really must go. I'm sorry to leave you with all this. Take care of Cal, and watch out for Parren. I have a nasty feeling he's going to try to make more trouble."

"Don't worry," said Dexter darkly, "I've got my eye on that one."

Giving Cal a final wave through the cottage door, Robin swung up onto Torka. The pirates were already mounted and moving out of the village. Taking them into the fields, Robin gathered his woolly wits and aching head and once more called up the power of Earth. Passing through the Veils without incident, they emerged onto the Plains below the Citadel just as night was falling.

The tunnel's grey shimmer slowly faded, dying away to nothing.

*****

Sullyan sat fretting, her eyes on the flames of their fire. How she resented not being able to cast her senses through the Veils to contact Robin! She may have rid her body of the majority of Rykan's poison, but that last tiny residue lodged deep in her soul meant instant agony if she tried to force even the smallest part of her mind through the barriers. So she had to rely on Bull, and after his recent exposure to the substrate blast, his strength was limited. He had also not completely recovered from his heart seizure, and the last thing Sullyan wanted was for him to have a relapse. So she accepted his failure to contact Robin with as much good grace as she could muster, which wasn't much.

She knew that Bull was aware of her feelings. They were so used to each other that, despite her prowess in guarding her expressions and thoughts, she was doubtless being all too transparent to him. It was the price you paid for such closeness, and even Robin didn't know her as well as Bull did. The brilliance of the swaying flames before her sent many vivid images into her mind, some painful, some bitter, some pleasant.

Bull watched her sitting there in silence, drinking yet another cup of fellan and staring into the fire as if it was a window on the world.

"Sully?"

She didn't take her eyes from the dancing flames. "Mmm?"

"Can you summon images in Fire the way you can in Water?"

Bull had always been wary of Fire. He was an Adept-elite, and so could influence the element, but deep down Fire frightened him. It touched something primal in his soul and he had never been able to overcome his fear. It was one of the reasons he had never been able to progress above his Artesan rank, one of the reasons Sullyan had gone looking for someone like Robin. Bull would never sit as she could and watch his memories come to life in the flames.

Her gaze flickered but did not leave the fire. "Sometimes. Why do you ask?"

"Oh, just wondering. You're staring so hard, I wondered what you were seeing."

"Nothing important, Hal," she sighed. "Just keeping warm."

She could tell he wasn't sure whether to believe her, but he didn't press the point. He was about to speak again when she suddenly stiffened, her eyes dilating wide in the dusk. Then Bull stiffened too.

"Robin!" she exclaimed, linking with Bull so he could also hear the Captain.

They sat immobile while Robin told his tale. Both could hear Robin's despair as he related what had happened to the tunnel and the village, and how he believed the Staff was lost. Sullyan sensed Bull's pride in the young man for the forthright way Robin told them about his failure to secure the weapon. She immediately put his mind at rest, telling him of Vanyr's heroic sacrifice. Despite his sorrow at Vanyr's death, Robin couldn't disguise his relief and elation on learning that she possessed the precious Staff.

We will return to the Citadel tomorrow, she told him. *We are bearing Commander Vanyr home where he will be sent off with full military honors. We will start out early in the morning. You get back to the Citadel and reassure Rienne about Cal. She and Taran will be pleased to see you. We will be there by late afternoon, I think. And, Robin?*

Yes?

I am very proud of you, my love. It was no fault of yours that you could not secure the Staff. If it had been lost, you would have borne no blame. Do you hear me?

I hear you, replied Robin, although they all knew the young man would have blamed himself for the rest of his life had the artifact been lost for good.

Breaking the link, Sullyan sighed. Jay'el held a plate of meat out to her and stared hard at her until she accepted it. Smiling ruefully, she began to eat.

*****

Vanyr's body was returned to the Citadel in somber style. The honor guard, led by a recovered Anjer and Vanyr's lieutenant, Barrin, comprised some fifty Velletian Guardsmen. All had volunteered for this sad duty and were soberly resplendent in ceremonial dress. Sullyan and her party met them around midday. Bull, who had been carrying Vanyr's wrapped body in his arms, gave his burden to the Lord General, who placed Vanyr carefully on the bier they had brought with them. It was drawn by two white horses and draped with a sumptuous purple banner bearing the Hierarch's tangwyr emblem. They all formed up around it, Anjer and Sullyan riding beside the bier with Bull, Ki-en, and Jay'el just behind.

On entering the city, they were greeted by a rousing fanfare from the heralds and a clashing of weapons from the swordsmen thronging the battlements. It seemed the entire population had turned out to witness the homecoming of the Commander of the Velletian Guard. Sullyan, seeing tears and sorrow on many faces, thought how amazed Vanyr would have been to see such signs of respect. Knowing intimately how they felt, she bowed her head.

The cortege slowly mounted the Processional Way, trumpets marking its progress, and came to rest in the palace courtyard. From there, Vanyr's body was taken away to be prepared for his funeral and Sullyan and Bull were reunited with Robin.

It was an emotional time, especially for Robin and Sullyan. The young Captain had returned to the Citadel before full dark the previous evening and wasted no time in telling Rienne and

Taran the tale of the siege. He also gave Rienne the message from Cal, which caused the healer to break down in sobs. They eventually managed to calm her, once Robin had reassured her that Cal should make a full recovery. He even offered to contact Cal and pass on a message for her, but Rienne demurred with a mischievous smile, saying she didn't think Robin was capable of passing the sort of message she wanted to give. His blushes finally made her laugh.

Now, gathered in Sullyan and Robin's chambers, they sat gazing at the Staff which lay on the table, innocently gleaming in the firelight. Rienne shuddered at the sight of it. Taran could hardly bear to look at it, no doubt remembering how he had felt when using it.

Robin, however, saw things in a very different light and sat staring hungrily at the artifact. "So, what happens now?"

Sullyan sighed, not sharing Robin's optimism. "For the moment," she said, "I am not thinking past Vanyr's funeral. Once that is over, I will have much to discuss with Timar and Deshan. And Taran."

The Adept started then flushed. Robin frowned at him before turning back to Sullyan. "But what do you need to discuss? Surely you can use the Staff as you did Rykan's life force? Why should you need to talk to Taran?"

Hearing the tiniest hint of jealousy in his voice, Sullyan closed her eyes. "Because Taran is the only person living who has used the Staff. I will need him to tell me everything he can remember. This final process will not be simple. You recall how difficult it was for me to purge the poison? Well, that was the easy part."

Robin turned pale, memories of the agony and anguish she had gone through passing across his features. She smiled ruefully at him, understanding his confusion.

"The rest of the poison is lodged deep in my soul. It has become part of my being. I do not know if it is possible to remove it now, and even if it is, there is a danger I might damage my psyche."

Robin looked shocked. "What? You never told me that! I thought once you had the Staff—"

"It would be a simple matter of using it to burn out the poison?

No, Robin. I wish it was, but the truth is, it might not be possible at all."

An uneasy silence fell.

Holding Robin's dark and troubled gaze, Sullyan said, "I did not tell you this before because I do not know what will happen. Something like this has never been done before. I might not even be strong enough to make the attempt. If it is possible, it will be very arduous. And there could be other … complications."

"Complications? What complications?" Robin's optimism drained away. He had clearly thought that gaining the Staff was the final battle. Now she was telling him the war was far from over.

She shook her head. "I do not know yet. I must discuss it with Timar and Deshan. Let us not dwell on it now. Tomorrow will be a sad day. Let us honor a good man and a true friend and leave the other matter for later. It will keep."

Chapter Thirteen

Vanyr's funeral was a state occasion held on a bright, clear day with the promise of spring. Sullyan and Robin were to be part of the honor guard accompanying the bier and felt privileged to be so included. The Major had also been asked to participate in the ceremony itself, along with Pharikian, Anjer, and Barrin. She had demurred at first, protesting that it was Ephan's place, but he had been more than happy for her to represent him as he was not fully recovered from the substrate blast.

At midday they gathered in the courtyard. Vanyr's body once again lay on a bier drawn by two white horses, the Hierarch's standard covering his form. Sullyan and Robin, mounted on Drum and Torka, fell in beside Pharikian, Anjer, and Barrin. Rienne, Taran, and Bull were traveling with Marik in Idrimar's carriage while Ephan and Baron Gaslek, the Hierarch's secretary, traveled together in another. The rest of the palace household followed.

As the cavalcade passed through the north gate, the horns of the Velletian Guard resounded in honor of Torman Vanyr. To the north of the Citadel a small hill could be seen, crowned with an ancient ring of standing stones. Within this ring a huge pyre had been built, and toward this hill they wound their way. The towering monoliths dwarfed even the tallest mourners. Those with the power to sense it could feel their elemental puissance singing through their souls.

The bier drew to a halt beside the pyre. Six Guardsmen lifted Vanyr's body and placed it on the platform above the logs. The Hierarch's standard was removed and Sullyan saw that Vanyr had been well-prepared for this farewell. Someone had carefully washed his damaged face, making it as presentable as possible.

A light strip of cloth covered the ruin of his eyes, and his face appeared calm. He was dressed in ceremonial uniform, his sword lying on his breast. One of the honor guard reached up to remove it but Sullyan held up her hand. “Let it be.”

The guard frowned at her. “Lady, it won’t burn. And we can’t leave it here. It will be taken to be melted down by the swordsmith.”

Sullyan glanced at Pharikian and received his nod. “Let it be,” she repeated, and the guard shrugged, removing his hand.

The honor guard stationed themselves around the crest of the hill just outside the circle, enclosing the pyre and those who stood near it. The Hierarch, Anjer, Sullyan, and Barrin took their places, one at each corner of the pyre, with the four Cardinal Stones at their backs. After a reflective pause, Pharikian raised his head and addressed the assembly. He spoke of Vanyr, telling how he had come to be in his ruler’s service and what that service had meant. The Hierarch told them that in honor of Vanyr’s bravery, he was posthumously awarding him the rank of Artesan Adept. Sullyan saw many heads nod in recognition.

Anjer took up the tale, speaking of Vanyr’s military career and training, his leadership and battle strategy, and his weaponry skills. Barrin followed the Lord General, and he spoke of serving under Vanyr; how the commander had discharged his duties and trained his men, and how he was respected by all who had served with him.

Then it was Sullyan’s turn, and she spoke of friendship and loyalty, trust and love. She made no effort to hide her feelings, and there was many a damp eye when she was finished. There was a final stirring fanfare from the trumpeters, and Vanyr’s warhorse, a large liver-chestnut stallion which had been brought back from Albia by Robin, suddenly raised its head and pealed out a long call to its fallen rider. The trumpets fell silent and the Hierarch gestured for Barrin to begin.

The Lieutenant stood at the western Cardinal, representing Earth. Raising his arms, he said, “Torman Vanyr, tutor and Commander. By the power of Earth, we honor you.”

Barrin called power from the stones and it thrummed through

them, rumbling under the mourners' feet. Pharikian nodded his approval and Barrin lowered his arms.

Anjer stood at the northern Cardinal, representing Water. He too raised his arms. "Torman Vanyr, Commander and battle leader. By the power of Water, we honor you."

Anjer's hold and control caused a great wreath of mist to form in the air around the pyre. Glittering in the sunlight, it slowly settled onto Vanyr's body, bedewing him with pearly drops. They shimmered in the light before fading. Bowing his head, Anjer lowered his arms.

Sullyan stood for the east, representing Fire. Lifting her clear voice, she almost sang the words. "Torman Vanyr, true friend, giver of life by your sacrifice. With the power and force of Fire, I honor you."

Sullyan's power rushed through the circle as she summoned Fire from its source. Tiny flames appeared in the air over Vanyr's body, slowly settling to touch his face, his hands, his breast. Fingers of flame appeared at each corner of the pyre, dancing around the logs but not yet consuming them.

With Sullyan's Fire unquenched, the Hierarch raised his voice. "Torman Vanyr, Artesan Adept, loyal and true subject. We bid you farewell. We send you on your journey buoyed by the powers of Earth, Water, Fire, and Air. We honor your memory and commend you to the powers that be. Torman Vanyr, with the power of Air, we honor you!"

A great roaring assailed their ears as the Hierarch of Andaryon, Senior Master Artesan, called Air. A warm, strong wind raced toward the hill at great speed, flowing through, around, and over the mourners. It caught at Sullyan's Fire as it danced among the logs. All at once, with a vast, hungry roar, the wood ignited. Fanned by Air and fed by Earth, flames rocketed into the sky. It was spectacular but confined as the flames fed hungrily on the seasoned logs. The power of Earth, drawn from the western Cardinal Stone, roared sunwise around the ancient circle, the ground shuddering and quaking with force. The air within wept a fine mist.

Within minutes, the pyre was consumed. It fell in on itself, showering sparks. Reaching out again, Sullyan caused the flames to rage even hotter, melting and vaporizing the steel of Vanyr's sword. Melding with his bones, it would travel with him on his final journey.

Glancing again at Pharikian, Sullyan reached out her right hand. He smiled and took it. Linked, they pooled their strength, and the watchers saw a tiny, perfectly-formed funnel of Air appear directly over the pile of ash. It swirled sunwise until, gently, it touched the ash, whirling it up into a spiral. Black eyes ringed with gold and slit-pupilled yellow eyes watched and controlled the spiral together as it broke away from the earth, ascending high into the sky above their heads. Then, with a wisp of thought, it was borne away by a swift wind, disappearing to scatter over the forests to the east.

*****

Later that same afternoon, Pharikian came to Brynne Sullyan where she sat with her friends in the chambers she shared with Robin. The Captain had reported back to Blaine, telling him that the Staff was not lost and promising to keep him informed of any developments. Blaine reported that Cal had arrived safely back at the Manor and was in the capable hands of Chief Healer Hanan, who had confidently predicted he would make a full recovery. Dexter had told the General of the trouble caused by Captain Parren, but Blaine wished to speak with Robin privately before he would consider taking any action. He saw no need to address the problem while Robin was absent from the Manor. Robin was content with that.

Determined to ensure that Taran and Bull would be fully fit to return to the Manor, Sullyan had just finished an intense healing session when Norkis, Pharikian's page, tapped at the door. Bull's heart was stronger and his burns were fading. Taran's knife wound was healing well and there was no trace of infection to prevent him from traveling. Her own hurts were also improving. The bones of her left wrist had knitted well and she had more control over her fingers. The back of the hand was shiny and pink with new flesh, and she had at last been able to replace Robin's ring on her middle finger. She could not yet tell whether she would regain full use of the hand and suffered pangs of regret when she thought she might never again play her harp, but she wasn't going to give up until she knew she had done all she could. She fully intended to start gentle sword practice the next day.

As Norkis bowed Pharikian into the room, they all stood. Waving them down, he said, "We are all friends here, and I have had quite enough formality for one day."

He accepted the fellan Bull passed him, and sat on the couch next to Rienne. He had developed a liking for her in the few days he had known her, and Deshan had told him how highly he rated her healing skills. Smiling at her, he asked, "How is your young man doing, my dear? Well, I hope. I would like the chance to meet him one day."

Rienne assured him of Cal's recovery, and he nodded in relief. Then his expression clouded and he glanced at Sullyan where she sat in the circle of Robin's arms by the fire.

"Brynne, my child, we have much to discuss concerning Rykan's Staff. Both Deshan and I have thoughts on the matter. However, I have come to ask if you would consider waiting one more day. I have just received word that my son is returning from the north tomorrow, and considering what Rykan would have done had he won his challenge, this is a doubly welcome event. My people will expect a celebration, especially after the sadness of Vanyr's passing. I know that my son is keen to meet you, and a day of relaxation, music, good company, and cheer is just what we all need after the events of the past few weeks.

"What do you say, Brynne? I shall understand if you would prefer not to delay. Both Deshan and I can spare some time today to begin our discussions, but I had hoped you would not mind too much waiting until after Aeyron's return."

Sullyan smiled, guilty relief stealing through her. "Timar, I would be honored indeed to meet Prince Aeyron. How could I deny your people their celebration? They are right to rejoice at the safe return of your Heir, and I would not miss his first meeting with Ty Marik, nor his reaction when the Princess asks his permission to marry! A day of celebration would be welcome indeed, for each and every one of us has much to be thankful for. Except, perhaps, the Lady Falina."

The Hierarch's face clouded at the mention of General Kryp's widow. "Yes," he agreed sadly, "she has been inconsolable. But Aeyron was always a favorite of hers, so perhaps his arrival will cheer her.

"Very well, Brynne. You are all invited—no, required—to attend tomorrow's festivities, and we will save our conversation for the day after, when you will have our full attention. I believe Deshan has something particular to say concerning your … circumstances."

She gave him an enquiring look, but he shook his head. "It's no use asking me, child, he hasn't told me what it is. We will have to wait, but I am sure he will tell you when he is ready."

*****

The feast day was a balm and a tonic to all. The fears and frustrations, fighting and killing, were all forgotten as the entire Citadel gave itself up to celebrating the Heir's return. When Rykan's hostile intentions had become clear, Pharikian had immediately sent the young man into Morvaigne, the mountainous region ruled by Tikhal, the Lord of the North. Now, his homecoming was seen as the final promise of peace in the realm.

Pharikian spent much of the morning on the Tower battlements, eagerly watching for the cavalcade heralding his son's imminent arrival. Sullyan joined him in the cool spring sunshine, accompanied by her friends. It was mid-morning before they finally heard the trumpets and caught sight of the banners carried by the heralds riding in the fore. The pale sun glinted from swords and lances, and Sullyan was surprised at the size of the party. The banners proclaimed that Lord Tikhal himself had accompanied the Heir, bringing a large number of his own household to swell the Prince's retinue. There must have been over three hundred people in their entourage.

The Prince and the Lord of the North rode at the head of the company, just behind the heralds. They were surrounded by an honor guard whose cloaks bore the colors of both noble Houses, and whose rank badges shone in the sunlight. The horses were caparisoned in the colors of their riders' families, and there was a palpable air of gaiety and festivity over all.

Sullyan remained on the battlements as Pharikian descended to greet his son. He had asked her to accompany him, but she firmly demurred, saying that his first greeting should be private. This was their moment and their triumph, and she would have ample opportunity to meet the Prince later. She watched from the Tower as Pharikian and Idrimar, flanked by Barrin and the Velletian Guard, rode down to the northern gate to welcome the returning Heir.

Even from her lofty vantage point, she could see that Aeyron was a tall, lean young man, very like his father and sister in build. But whereas Idrimar's hair was dark, as her father's must have been when he was younger, Aeyron's was a bright and shining blond. There was no mistaking him among Tikhal's entourage. It seemed to Sullyan that he was not as mindful of protocol as Pharikian had led her to believe, for as soon as he saw his father, he leapt down from his tall bay stallion and ran toward him. The Hierarch also dismounted, and the pair embraced fondly, unembarrassed by the show of emotion. Then Aeyron turned to his sister and swept her up in a huge bear-hug which must have left her breathless. Even on the battlements, Sullyan heard their delighted laughter.

She noticed that Marik had also remained in the Citadel, and guessed he was too unsure of his position or his welcome to intrude upon this family reunion. She smiled. She was sure Aeyron would willingly accept the Count, as the young man was clearly very fond of his sister.

The first rush of emotion over, Pharikian then greeted Lord Tikhal, who was now his most powerful noble since the demise of Rykan. Sullyan was interested and relived to see that the handshakes these two mighty lords exchanged were informal and friendly. Tikhal was trusted implicitly. If not, Aeyron would never have been sent into his care.

Formalities over, the cavalcade moved at a stately pace around the Citadel walls, entering via the south gate so they could ride up the Processional Way in front of the townspeople. The roar of the crowds, the cheering and acclaim they accorded their Prince, reached clearly up to the battlements, telling Sullyan just how deeply the populace loved the Heir. A general holiday had been declared by the palace and the townsfolk were making the most of it. Street parties and feasting were already underway in many parts of the town.

Once the cavalcade was well on its way, Sullyan suggested that she and her companions should return to their rooms to begin preparing for the celebrations. There was to be a huge banquet in the Great Hall with music, dancing, singing, and all manner of entertainments which would continue all afternoon and evening—probably until there was no one left who could eat, sing, or dance any longer.

The men retired to Bull and Taran's chambers while Sullyan and Rienne helped each other in the Major's suite. Pharikian had seen to it that both women had new gowns for the occasion, and that the men had fine shirts, tunics, and breeches. Sullyan's gown was of spring-green satin. It clung to her and flowed around her body like a shimmering jade waterfall. She was still thinner than usual and it showed, but she was slowly regaining her health and strength. She left her wealth of tawny hair loose, binding it simply around her brow with a single fillet of gold. Her fire opal flashed at her throat, and she had begged a subtle, flowery perfume from Idrimar that just hinted at summer meadows.

Rienne's gown was also satin; a deep, royal blue that accentuated the darkness of her hair and the soft grey of her eyes. She had a silver clasp in her hair to hold it out of her eyes, and Idrimar had lent her a heavy rope of silver for her throat. She looked regal in her new attire, and her only sadness was that Cal was not there to see her.

"That might be just as well," observed Sullyan dryly when Rienne voiced her regret. "If he saw you looking like that, the pair of you would not make it to the banquet at all!"

Rienne smiled coyly.

When the men entered after politely tapping on the door, there were gasps of admiration all round. Bull, already very fond of

Rienne, instantly fell in love with her, never having seen her dressed so finely before. Robin, however, only had eyes for his lady, and Sullyan's prediction concerning Cal's reaction was also true of the Captain. Her smile promised shared delights later.

Poor Taran was as badly affected as ever by the sight of Sullyan and was nearly overcome by the strength of his desire. He valiantly tried to conceal it, but it was naked in his hazel eyes whenever he looked at her, and obvious in the way he studiously avoided looking at her. She was aware of his feelings—his emanations were too plain to miss—but there was nothing she could do to help him. Robin gave no sign of noticing Taran's hopeless infatuation, but Sullyan knew he was aware of it too.

The men were simply dressed in fine lawn shirts of various hues, sleeveless tunics that showed off their muscular forms, and dark breeches. Sullyan commented on how handsome they looked, knowing that the unattached ladies in the palace would find both Bull and Taran irresistible. However, she decided against warning them both to be careful; it would remind them too forcibly of the last banquet they had attended. Bull was well versed in such occasions, and she knew she could trust him to keep an eye on Taran. Although, she reflected ruefully, if the Adept's expression was anything to go by, he would pay little attention to anyone else that evening.

She sighed. That particular problem would have to wait.

At the appointed hour, a page arrived to escort them to the Great Hall. The huge vaulted room was hung with bright banners and bedecked with lavish tapestries. The tables were laden with all manner of foods, fruits, and sweets, and positively glittered with gold and silver plate, jeweled cutlery, and whatever early flowers and greenery the gardeners had been able to procure. Every noble, every palace dignitary and lady was there, and all were presented to the Heir and Lord Tikhal as they arrived. Pharikian had asked Sullyan and her friends to enter next to last. As the Champion of the Crown he felt it was her due, and she could hardly refuse.

So it was that they made a grand entrance at the top of the marble stairs leading down into the Great Hall. Baron Gaslek, acting as Master of Ceremonies, caused the huge silver gong to boom when he saw Sullyan and her party approaching. The Major paced serenely forward on Robin's arm, his dark blue shirt and gold trimmed tunic complementing her green gown to perfection. Gaslek formally announced their names, adding Champion of the Crown to Sullyan's other titles. Rienne and Taran were both surprised to find the epithet Captain attributed to them, as they had virtually forgotten their honorary and temporary Manor rank.

Bull had begged and been granted the right to escort Rienne, and he looked as proud as he could be leading her down the stairs behind Sullyan and Robin. Taran walked at Rienne's other side. They were then presented to Lord Tikhal, a man in his late thirties with long, dark, curling hair and pale blue eyes. He greeted them warmly, his slit-pupilled gaze lingering appreciatively over Sullyan's and Rienne's slim forms. Then they moved to stand before the Heir, and Pharikian himself made the introductions.

Master Artesan Aeyron Pharikian was possibly an inch or two taller than his father and had the same long, straight nose and generous mouth. His eyes were a shade paler than the Hierarch's, reflecting the light blond of his hair. His manner was open and friendly, his voice a pleasant baritone. Taking Sullyan's hand as she made him a deep obeisance, he raised it to his lips. "I am very pleased to meet you at last, Lady Brynne." Smiling into her eyes, he raised her. "My father and I are deeply in your debt. If there is ever anything we can do for you, you must not hesitate to ask."

She replied demurely. "Your Highness is most kind. I was pleased to be able to give service to Andaryon's Crown."

As the others were introduced, Sullyan and Robin moved on down the line. When they had all completed this part of the proceedings, a trilling fanfare sounded from the double doors at the top of the marble stairs. All conversation ceased, every head turned. Sullyan watched the Prince's expression closely as the final pair of guests stepped through the doors. She smiled with real pleasure to see Ty Marik with the Princess Idrimar on his arm, proud of his steady gait. She was well aware that his legs had lost all strength.

Marik had taken great care over his attire and wore his customary maroon velvet, trimmed now with gold. His clothes were cut to accentuate his lean height, and on his breast lay the heavy gold chain that was a gift from Pharikian for his part in Rykan's defeat. He stood straight and tall with Idrimar by his side, the stately Princess looking serene and happy in an extravagant gown of purple and gold. Her color choice did rather clash with that of her intended, but no one attending this special occasion was going to quibble over the niceties of fashion.

Baron Gaslek sang out their names, and the pair paced regally down the marble stairs.

They came to a halt before the Prince, and Sullyan watched Aeyron closely. The Heir wore a carefully neutral expression rather than the smile she might have expected, and she caught a flicker of uncertainty in Idrimar's eyes. Gaslek, who had followed them down, now formally introduced the Count, and Marik executed a deep and courtly bow before holding out his hand to the Prince, who took it.

"I am honored indeed to make your acquaintance, Count Marik," said the Heir, his voice curiously devoid of inflection. "I tender my heartfelt thanks for your aid in averting Lord Rykan's threat. Andaryon's Crown stands forever in your debt."

His tone was neutral, even cold, and Sullyan saw Princess Idrimar fix her brother with a pleading, desperate gaze. According to the customs of Andaryon's ruling House, she had to obtain both her father's and her brother's permission before she could wed. She already had Pharikian's blessing, but the Prince could block the union if he didn't approve her choice.

Looking pale, her voice trembling slightly, she said, "Your Highness, my brother. I formally ask your permission to marry this man, Ty Marik, Count and Lord of the lands of Cardon, within the fiefdom of Kymer. My father has already given me his blessing and approval. Will you do the same?"

Aeyron turned pale yellow eyes upon his sister. He seemed to consider a moment before saying clearly, "I do deeply regret it, my sister, but I cannot approve this match."

Chapter Fourteen

A shocked gasp sounded from the assembled guests. Idrimar turned white, while Marik stood there trembling, his eyes a little wild. Rienne clutched at Sullyan's arm and hissed, "What's the matter with him? He can't do this, it'll break her heart!"

Sullyan didn't take her eyes off the Hierarch. She murmured, "Hush, Rienne. Just wait."

Pharikian stepped forward. "My son and Heir," he said formally, "by what reason do you reject this match?"

The younger man glanced from Marik to Idrimar, noting their stricken expressions. "I reject it by reason of status, Majesty. My sister is a Princess of the ruling House of Pharikian. This man is merely a Count. There is no parity in the match."

Guessing what was coming, Sullyan smiled. Marik and Idrimar must have caught on too, because they both visibly relaxed.

Pharikian turned to Gaslek, who approached his ruler bearing a highly polished ceremonial blade. He offered it to the Hierarch, who took it and turned to Marik. "Count Ty Marik, step forth."

Marik released the Princess's arm and moved forward to stand before the Hierarch. He was still trembling, but now with anticipation.

Pharikian's deep voice rang out, true and strong. "Ty Marik, for seven years you held the lands of Cardon under your liege-lord, the rebel Rykan, Duke of Kymer. Rykan died a traitor's death by the hand of the Crown, and so all his lands and fiefs are forfeit. They have reverted to the Crown, and thus I proclaim you landless."

Despite his hope for the Hierarch's intentions, Marik turned pale. For a noble, even a lowly one, to be proclaimed landless was tantamount to becoming outcast.

"On the field of battle," continued Pharikian, "you did of your own free will forsake your former allegiance, swearing fealty instead to the House of Pharikian, even to the pledging of your life. I ask you now; do you here, before these Witnesses, aver and declare that oath to be true?"

Marik swallowed before replying clearly, "Majesty, I so swear. I am a humble servant of your House and will uphold your supremacy all my days."

The assembled guests roared with one voice, causing the walls and floor to vibrate with the strength of their approval, "Heard and Witnessed!"

Stepping closer, the Hierarch raised his sword, and Marik went down on one knee, bowing his head. Pharikian leveled the naked blade and offered it to Marik's lips. "Ty Marik, you have sworn allegiance to the ruling House and to the Crown of Andaryon before Witnesses. Will you serve faithfully and sincerely for as long as you have life?"

Marik kissed the blade and replied, "Majesty, I will."

"Ty Marik, it is the Crown's pleasure to bestow upon you the title of Duke. Will you swear to govern your people wisely and well, pledging to raise troops from your lands as required by your ruler, in defense of the Crown and the realm?"

Once more kissing the blade, his voice reflecting the gravity of the moment, Marik responded, "Majesty, I will."

Pharikian passed the sword back to Gaslek and held out his right hand for Marik to kiss the royal amethyst seal upon his finger. Raising Marik, he said, "Ty Marik, the Crown confirms and avers that you hold the title of Duke to the province of Kymer. It is also our wish that the lands of Cardon be joined seamlessly to this fief, these lands to be united under you and your heirs in perpetuity. May their people serve the Crown better than under their former liege."

This was clearly more than Marik had expected, and he looked stunned as the Hierarch turned him to face the assembly. Without exception, the gathered nobles made obeisance as Pharikian's voice rang out once more.

"My Lords and Ladies, nobles all, the Crown presents Lord Marik, Duke of Cardon and Kymer."

A great wave of cheering and applause rose from the assembled guests. Idrimar's eyes were shining, the Prince was smiling, and Marik was so proud that he didn't know what to do next. His problem was solved by Pharikian, who embraced him whole-heartedly, slapping him on the back. Then Idrimar reclaimed his hand, leading him once again before her brother. They stood smiling at each other before the Princess repeated her request. "Your Highness, my brother, I wish to formally ask your permission to wed this man, Lord Marik, Duke of Cardon and Kymer. Will you give us your blessing?"

"Dearest sister, with all my heart."

Whatever they said to each other as Idrimar's loving arms fastened around his neck was lost in the cheers and roars of approval that rang around the joyful Hall.

*****

The rest of the day passed pleasantly in feasting, music, and good company. Sullyan found time to approach the newly invested Duke of Kymer, adding her congratulations to the many others he had received. Marik was still struggling to take it all in and was thoroughly embarrassed by the deeply reverent curtsey she made him.

"So, my Lord Duke," she said, giving him an impish look, "are we mere mortals permitted to address your Grace?"

Marik grabbed her hand and raised her. "Stop that, Brynne," he scolded, glancing wildly about to see if anyone had seen. "You'll make people think I'm giving myself airs."

"You?" she murmured. "Never!"

Mindful of her damaged arm, he swept her into a hug, then glanced at Robin for permission before guiding her onto the dance floor. "I never dreamed he would give me Rykan's lands as well as my own, you know. It was quite a shock."

As the musicians struck up, she melted into his arms. "He was right to do so. You will govern them well, Ty. And you are part of the royal family now, or will be once you and Idri are wed, so you will need lands and status enough to be worthy of her."

"I suppose so. But I'll tell you one thing, Brynne." His tone had turned cold. "I'm going to raze that cursed palace of Rykan's to the ground. I'm going to burn the lot. There'll not be a single trace left, especially of those thrice damned cells."

She was overcome by his vehemence. "Oh, Ty, you do not have to worry on my account."

"I want to," he said grimly. "There's no way I could ever live there, and my old mansion is far too small to accommodate Idri's household, no matter how finely it was renovated. So I've decided to build a new palace, somewhere between the two, one that will be a symbol for the merging of two lands and two families."

She smiled, loving him for his sentiments, and after another dance gave him up again to the arms of his betrothed.

During the latter part of the evening, Sullyan was approached by Anjer and Torien. She was sitting at her ease, watching Robin partner one of the court ladies. Anjer and his tiny wife sat down beside her, and Sullyan smiled pleasantly at Torien. The woman blushed crimson every time the Major looked her way. Sullyan couldn't help but be amused. The incident in their bedchamber and the personal nature of her advice to Torien raised no awkwardness in Sullyan. She had never been embarrassed by intimate matters, having lived most of her life among men. She had been inured at an early age to innuendo and frank talk. Even had she not been, the necessity of attending to bodily functions alongside the men of her company when out in the field would soon have swept any shyness away, as privacy was rarely possible. Her early experiences had ensured she was never troubled by shyness.

Torien, however, had been more delicately raised, and it was no surprise to Sullyan that she found such topics difficult to broach. What did surprise her was that Anjer also seemed less than comfortable discussing the subject.

Avoiding her direct gaze, he said, "My lady tells me that we have cause to be grateful to you, Brynne."

This was a glad topic, and as the events of the evening had further lifted her spirits, Sullyan mischievously chose to misunderstand him. "I only helped ward you from further damage, my Lord," she said. "You would have recovered by yourself, only more slowly."

He stared hard at her innocent expression. "I wasn't referring to that! I was talking about the other matter."

Her eyes on Taran, who was being guided through the steps of a stately pavane by an attractive young lady from Tikhal's retinue, Sullyan asked, "What matter would that be, my Lord?"

"You know what I'm talking about, dammit!"

She ceased her teasing and smiled. "My Lord General, you and Lady Torien will make excellent parents. I wish you every joy of your future offspring. I am sure you will both more than enjoy your efforts to obtain them!"

Anjer's face flushed. "Witch!" he accused. Torien's face was flaming too, but she couldn't hide her smile. "You just wait," continued Anjer. "I bet it won't be long before that handsome young captain of yours wants to start a family."

Her happy mood fell instantly away and she glanced across at Robin. "Yes," she murmured, absently rubbing her aching wrist, "I am sure you are right."

There was one other surprise before that pleasurable evening finally drew to a close. It was one that Sullyan whole heartedly approved of, although she hadn't known of it beforehand. Ky-shan and his men had been invited to the Great Hall to join in the celebrations, although most of his band had chosen to remain with the soldiers and join in their rowdy festivities. Ky-shan himself, however, with Jay'el, Ki-en, and the twins, had consented to attend the Hierarch's gathering and had not disgraced themselves. Sullyan had danced with them all, as had Rienne, but at this late hour only the younger members of the gathering still had energy for dancing. The older seamen had retired to the sidelines.

As she sat peacefully listening to the minstrels, Sullyan noticed that Pharikian and Aeyron seemed to be conducting a deep discussion, and that their eyes repeatedly fell on Ky-shan's stocky form. She was intrigued, so when they rose and approached the seaman, she managed to creep close enough to overhear their conversation without being observed. Ky-shan was watching his son's creditable performance in the close embrace of one of Tikhal's young ladies and didn't immediately see the two men. When he did, he glanced at Pharikian sharply.

"Ky-shan," began the Hierarch, "I wanted to tell you personally how grateful I am for your efforts against Lord Rykan. Not least for the assistance and support you gave Major Sullyan at a most difficult time. Your … care of her here at the Citadel was also noted and appreciated."

Ky-shan's swarthy complexion deepened under Pharikian's praise. "We only did our duty, Majesty."

Pharikian smiled. "Then you did it very well." He changed the subject. "I won't prevaricate, Ky-shan. Aeyron and I have a proposition to put to you, and we would be obliged if you would consider it very carefully before coming to a decision."

The seaman's eyes narrowed as he glanced from Hierarch to Heir. Pharikian traded a look with Aeyron before continuing. "We have some shipping interests on the eastern seaboard which we want to expand. We have employed a succession of factors to manage these interests for us, but they have all been land-based and this has proved a problem. It seems there are too many ways in which ships can be lost or taken on the open ocean, and we are reluctant to sink much more investment into the venture without firmer assurances of a return on our expenditure. What we need is a factor who understands the sea. A man who can speak with authority on the best design of cargo vessels, and the safest, most profitable routes those vessels should take. A man who can hire the right captains for those ships, who will manage and oversee the entire venture in return for a share of the profits. What do you think, Ky-shan? Could you be the man we're looking for?"

The pirate had remained silent throughout the Hierarch's speech, his eyes growing wider and his expression more amazed. When Pharikian finished, the stocky seaman barked out his gruff laughter and grasped the Hierarch's arm.

"By the Triple Sea, Majesty, I never expected this! You want me to turn legitimate and run your shipping business for you? Ha! I tell you, there would be many a frightened man on the high seas if I agreed to that!"

His rough and loud amusement turned many heads close by. The Hierarch's face fell, but the stocky pirate wasn't done. Eyes glowing with malicious humor, he grinned at the ruler of Andaryon. "By the Triton's teeth, Majesty, I believe I'll do it. There are some old scores to be settled and some favors to be called in, and more than a few noses will be put out of joint, believe me! But you couldn't have found a more knowledgeable seaman to run your venture for you. And if I don't turn a healthy profit in the first year, I swear you can toss me over the side and feed me to the fishes!"

Sullyan saw Pharikian sigh with relief as he offered the seaman his hand. "I hope it won't come to that, Ky-shan. Welcome to my court."

The festivities carried on well into the early hours of the following morning, but despite her pleasure in Ky-shan's good fortune, Sullyan had lost all appetite for gaiety. She had tried hard to forget, just for one day, the sword of Fate hanging over her, but her conversation with Anjer had reminded her of it. The plain and simple truth was that she was terrified. Terrified she wouldn't have the strength to do what her friends—and especially Robin—wanted her to do. She badly needed to talk with Deshan about the practicalities and, more importantly, the feasibility of using Rykan's Staff. The terrible experience of purging his poison had made her all too aware of how precarious her hold on life was. She feared that an attempt to rid herself of it completely might well prove beyond her capabilities. She already knew that if she did it at all, she had to do it alone. Neither Pharikian nor Deshan could help her this time. She needed advice, needed someone else to make the decision for her, whether she should attempt it or not. So, after making her excuses to Pharikian and Aeyron, pleading her scarcely recovered health, she went alone to her chambers. In the uncaring darkness, she cried herself to sleep.

*****

The following morning, still feeling low and oppressed, Sullyan took Robin with her to the palace training ground. She needed to clear her mind of the depressing dreams that had crowded her sleep, and sword play was the only anodyne she knew. They had the arena to themselves as most of the revelers were still sleeping off the previous night's excesses. She started slowly, using her father's lighter sword and her right hand, giving herself time to recondition her muscles to the disciplines of sword play. She and Robin sparred gently for half an hour before Sullyan called a rest.

So absorbed had she been, sharp steel and exercise working its usual charm upon her mind, that she had not noticed the small group of people watching from the sidelines. Rienne, Taran, and Bull were there, along with Prince Aeyron, who had Norkis, the Hierarch's young page, with him. As soon as Sullyan glanced his way, Norkis came running across the training ground toward her. Skidding to a halt, he grinned impishly and gave her a courtly bow.

"Good morning, Lady Brynne. His Majesty sends his compliments, and would you and your companions be pleased to join him and the Master Physician in his Majesty's private chambers? He will provide you with refreshment."

She nodded. "Thank you, Norkis. Please inform his Majesty that we will attend him once we have made ourselves presentable."

The page scampered off, and they made their way back into the palace so she and Robin could change. Although the Hierarch's invitation had included them all, Rienne asked softly, "Brynne? Would you rather speak to his Majesty alone?"

Sullyan glanced at her. "I would be very happy to have your company, Rienne. I may well need your support today." She turned to Aeyron. "Highness, will you join us also?"

He seemed surprised, but looked pleased. "As you wish, Lady."

When they finally gathered in Pharikian's private chambers, Deshan was already there. After greeting both men, they ranged themselves around the room. Aeyron chose to sit by the large window, slightly apart from the rest. The Staff was lying on a small side table, but no one even glanced at it, concentrating instead on the food and wine brought in by servants. When they had all eaten their fill, the Hierarch nodded to Norkis and the young page brought the Staff closer. He then served everyone with fresh fellan and withdrew to his post by the door.

Pharikian leaned forward in his chair, capturing their attention. "Brynne, my child, Deshan and I have been discussing your problem and we have examined this artifact in as much detail as we can. There are a few points we wish to make before we turn to the practicalities of your situation. First, my dear, are you aware of the properties of this artifact, and how it was made?"

Sullyan glanced at the innocent-looking metal rod on the table and tried to suppress a shudder. She shared a brief look with Taran, who was sitting as far from the thing as he could get while still being part of the group. He would know exactly how she felt.

She took a steadying breath. "I know that its main component is a form of spellsilver, which instead of nullifying or blocking metaforce actually attracts and amplifies it. I have not had a chance to examine it more thoroughly."

Pharikian nodded. "It is mostly made of what is known as reversed polarity spellsilver. This in itself is remarkable, for despite the fact that spellsilver occurs naturally in our realm, it is extremely rare. Known stocks of the normal ore are closely and jealously guarded. I would have been amazed enough to learn that Rykan possessed a sufficient amount of positive spellsilver to make such an object, but the fact that he laid his hands on this quantity of reversed polarity ore is astounding. It does exist in a natural state, but it is extremely hard to come by.

"However, that is not the weapon's only remarkable aspect. The silver is encased by a type of ceramic which is notoriously tricky to manufacture. It requires a highly sophisticated method of construction. It must be combined with a particular type of silica and melded in a furnace which must be controllable to a precise and extreme temperature. Not only do I have no knowledge of anyone possessing such a furnace, but if one did exist then the cost of its hiring would be prohibitive. Add to that the incalculable cost of the raw materials—not to mention the almost unimaginable skill necessary to combine them so precisely—and what you have is an artifact not only beyond Rykan's skills to create but also worth the price of several kingdoms.

"Wealthy as he was, there is absolutely no possibility that Rykan could have funded such a device."

Everyone except Sullyan bore expressions of confusion and astonishment. She was staring at the Staff with a contemplative look. Then she raised her eyes to Pharikian's face.

"You are saying that Rykan had allies. Rich and powerful allies who were prepared to put their weight and wealth behind him in return for … what?"

She cocked her head at Andaryon's ruler, her eyes widening as her thoughts raced ahead. Silently, he waited for her to answer her own question.

"Timar, if what you say about the rarity and value of this artifact is true, then we have been looking at far too narrow a motive for Rykan's actions. Taking into account the more sinister aspects of the Staff's capabilities, we must conclude that his allies, whoever they are, created it for a very specific reason. Surely they would not beggar themselves simply so Rykan could usurp the throne?"

The aging monarch remained silent, his yellow eyes locked on hers. Sullyan held his gaze, and he frowned as she drew a slight breath.

"The crucial question here is what was Rykan's—and his allies'—true objective? Was the throne of Andaryon their ultimate goal, or was it their intention to place him and themselves in a position where they could dominate or—oh, dear gods—*eliminate* every other Artesan in existence?"

There were gasps of horror. Clearly none of them, except maybe Pharikian, had thought of this before Sullyan voiced it. Reluctantly, the Hierarch nodded. "The throne was secondary, I think."

Still staring at him, she shook her head. "Not secondary. I think the throne was vital. It would have been Rykan's reward, the bait that won him to their cause. With the authority of the Hierarchy behind him and the enhancing properties of the Staff under his control, he would have had the power to compel every Andaryan Artesan to submit to his will. But if what you say about its creation is true, Rykan was not the architect of this plan. Once he had the throne, and had subjugated all the Artesans in your realm, he would surely have had to return the Staff to its maker. I think the backing of his challenge for rulership and his eventual inauguration as Hierarch was the price he claimed—or was offered—for the risks he would run."

She paused, giving them time to assimilate the true horror these deliberations had raised. Her face taut, her eyes wide, she continued. "Given these conclusions, our next question is: Who else is involved? Who is wealthy and powerful enough not only to have created such a terrible weapon, but also to be certain of controlling Rykan once he had the power he desired? And—oh, gods, Timar, to what lengths might they go to recover it now?"

All eyes turned in renewed consternation to the shimmering device on the table. Taran and Bull had drawn farther away from it, as if it could steal their metaforce simply by being there. Marik, sitting close to Aeyron, shifted uneasily and cleared his throat. Sullyan turned to look at him. He returned her gaze unsteadily, plainly uncomfortable with what he had to say.

She raised her brows, encouraging him.

He swallowed. "During the time I was held at his palace, I did hear rumors about Rykan having powerful allies. There was always an undercurrent to the gossip, as if his actions, or the allies themselves, were not trustworthy. It was nothing more than furtive whispers. I never heard any names. And I had other things on my mind at the time, I'm afraid. I never paid the gossip much attention."

Sullyan smiled and shook her head. He could hardly be blamed for not obtaining information which only now turned out to be important. And she knew what had been on his mind at the time. Yet he still dropped his gaze and sat staring at his hands, no doubt wishing he had listened more closely.

Robin stirred at the Major's side, glancing from her to Pharikian. "I suppose these allies don't necessarily have to be Andaryan, either. With Rykan's false invasion of our realm in mind, maybe they are Albian."

Sullyan considered this before nodding. "We cannot rule it out. If Rykan did ally himself with outlanders, it would certainly generate resentment among his nobles. It could also explain why I was targeted. I am probably the best known Artesan in Albia, and there are some powerful people in King Elias's court who would delight in the demise of the Artesan gift and the death of anyone who carried it. There was considerable opposition to my appointment as captain when I finished my training, and even more when I was promoted to major. We are fortunate that King Elias is sympathetic to our kind and supports our craft, but some of his nobles vehemently oppose his tolerance and protest our inclusion in military or state matters."

Rienne interjected, the subject overcoming her usual shyness. "But why should they? I've never understood this. Surely it would be beneficial to the realm if our rulers employed people with powers such as yours?"

Sullyan gave her a smile. "Of course, Rienne, provided you trust them! But you must know that there are a great many devious and unscrupulous people at court. People with their own agendas, their own spies and networks. Artesans would be considered a threat because it is widely believed that we can read people's minds. Why do you think our kind have become so reviled and mistrusted by the Albian populace? It is an understandable reaction, to fear those with powers you do not possess and cannot control. How much more would you fear them if you thought they were threatening your own position or rise to power? No, it is no surprise that there is such strong opposition."

Rienne frowned and shrugged, her every move betraying what she thought of such suspicious and power hungry people.

Sullyan continued. "There must be some highly influential people indeed behind this plot. If the weapon's components are as priceless as Timar says, then those behind it have access to almost unlimited funds. And that points to the involvement of some extremely powerful nobles—"

She broke off and looked over at Pharikian, who sat watching her with admiration. "Timar, one thing is certain. We cannot permit this artifact to be used as its makers intended. It must be destroyed."

He nodded. "Yes. I'm not sure how it can be done, but you are right."

She considered this, her gaze resting blankly on the Staff.

"Normal spellsilver will melt, and you said that the ceramic is formed by very high temperatures."

"That's true. Very precisely controlled, extreme temperatures."

"Then maybe you and I acting together could destroy it."

He thought for a few seconds and was about to reply when her expression caught his attention. Her words had pricked her memory and another piece of the puzzle fell into place, a piece she should have understood long before. Speaking slowly, she said, "You say you know of no craft smith capable of building a furnace to manufacture the silicon-ceramic—no one capable of controlling a fire so precisely?"

He frowned. "That's right. Not in Andaryon, anyway."

She felt her face drain and her eyes cloud over. "Then there is only one kind of craft master who could."

He stared at her, shocked as he caught her meaning. Its full import staggered him. "No, Brynne! I can't believe that."

"It must be so," she replied. Realizing that the others were still puzzled, she turned to explain. "Any Master Smith who can forge a sword could probably have worked the silver. Maybe even the special ceramic, given time to study its properties. But not even a Master Smith would possess the type of forge necessary to control such extremes of temperatures. Neither would any other ordinary craftsman. There is only one way in which all the elements of this device could have been brought together so precisely. Only one type of craft master with the knowledge and skill to perform such a feat. This terrible device had to be created by an extremely skilled Master Artesan."

Maybe they should have seen it sooner, but her suggestion that the Staff had been created with the destruction of Artesans in mind had deflected them from the obvious. Once the initial shock died down, Rienne said, "I can understand Rykan's desire to usurp the throne. I can probably even understand why he might wish to control other Artesans. But why would one Artesan want to *destroy* others?"

"A very good point, my dear," said Pharikian, "although we cannot answer it yet."

"Ultimate power," murmured Sullyan. "That was Rykan's

obsession. And if there is one who craves such dominance, you may be sure there are others. There is, however, another possibility." She paused, gazing at the Hierarch. "The possibility that the Staff's original creator—whoever it was—did *not* want to control or destroy the others."

Pharikian looked thoughtful. "Someone was forced to create it, you mean? I suppose it's possible."

"So it is also possible that he had no idea what his creation was intended for," she said. "If he was coerced, he might well be blameless. Having created it, he might then have been killed. But if not …." She trailed off, apprehension in her eyes.

"If not," said Pharikian grimly, "then we have an unknown renegade Artesan on our hands."

"A rare and powerful one, Timar. Senior Master at the very least."

Chapter Fifteen

When the implications of this discussion finally sank in, the talk turned to the matter at hand. Namely, whether Sullyan was physically capable of using the Staff to rid her soul of contamination. Pharikian and Deshan exchanged glances, causing Sullyan to wonder what was on their minds. Deshan seemed uncomfortable, and even the Hierarch appeared unsure of himself. This, she could do without.

"Gentlemen, I beg you to speak plainly. I am in no mood for guessing games."

If Andaryon's ruler was offended by her tone, he showed no sign. His yellow eyes flicked from her to Robin, and he took a steadying breath before he replied.

"My dear, there is a particular aspect to your problem which has taxed both Deshan and myself. But before we tell you what it is, Deshan has a request for you."

The Major turned to the Master Physician, who gave her a smile.

"It has been two weeks since you defeated Rykan and used his life force to purge your body, and it has been well over two months since you were last in Albia." He paused as she nodded. "The effects of Rykan's maltreatment aside, your body could already be showing signs of deterioration due to Andaryon's alien environment."

"Yes," she agreed. "I fear you are right."

"Therefore, I feel it would be prudent to ascertain the exact state of your health before discussing how, or if, you can make use of the Staff."

"Deshan," she sighed, "that is a very roundabout way of asking me to agree to an examination."

He grinned wryly. "Do I take it you are amenable?"

Rolling her eyes, she held out her right hand. As he took it, she afforded him access to her psyche and her state of health. Everyone sat in silence while the Master Physician conducted his examination. When he finally released her hand, Deshan exchanged a glance with Pharikian. "It is as I suspected, Timar. There is no discernible change."

Pharikian's expression betrayed hope at these findings. Sullyan, however, wanted clarification. "Deshan, are you saying that my protracted stay in Andaryon has had no adverse effect on my health?"

He nodded. "None whatsoever."

"But that should not be possible."

Rienne was frowning, intrigued by the medical turn to the discussion. "So why has this happened?" she asked, eagerly leaning forward. "And what does it mean for Brynne's chances with the Staff?"

Robin held his breath, and both Bull's and Taran's eyes were fixed on Deshan.

"As for her chances of ridding herself of contamination, there is nothing to prevent her except her own strength and determination." The Master Physician flicked a glance at Sullyan. "As to the how or why, Pharikian and I have had several discussions on the subject. What we have been forced to conclude, Brynne, is that the blood Timar gave your mother all those years ago somehow affected you in the womb. It became part of your physical being. It is unprecedented in any records I can find, but the theory is supported by the color of your eyes, which are so like Timar's. I cannot fully explain it, but it seems that you are a hybrid, and your blood, which is partly Andaryan, is protecting you from harm. If that is so, then I cannot see any reason why it should not continue to do so indefinitely. Living in our realm should affect you as little as living in your own."

He fell silent. Sullyan was silent too, a strange mix of emotions surging through her. Her skin felt taut and drained, and she knew her face was white. Seeing this, Pharikian leaned forward in his chair and took hold of her damaged left hand. He stroked the soft new skin and looked deeply into her eyes, eyes that but for their round pupils could be his own.

"Brynne, my dear," he murmured, "we had to tell you. We wanted you to know that you do not have to risk your life yet again. There is no reason for you to suffer the undeniable agonies which must accompany any use of the Staff, irrespective of failure or success. You have an alternative, and I urge you to consider it carefully. Child, there is a place for you here, in my House and in my heart, should you wish to remain among us. You have become as dear and close to me as my own daughter, and my whole family would be happy to welcome you into our midst. I know it is what your father would have wanted, but I offer you this out of my love for you, not just the love and friendship I felt for Morgan.

"If you are concerned about your career then I can put your mind at ease there too. Anjer has asked me to say that he would value your experience and professional skills, and indeed there is a military post vacant now that we have lost General Kryp. What do you say? Will you think about it?"

His tone was soft and pleading, but her eyes were blank and lost. It was clearly all too much, and he sighed. Releasing her hand, he said, "We have given you much to consider. Perhaps you should leave us now, take some time to discuss this with your friends. Even your general, should you wish. Return to us once you have made your decision. Deshan will be happy to advise you about the procedure should you decide to use the Staff. Just—please—assure me that you will give full consideration to what I have said."

She looked him full in the eyes, unable to hide the turmoil his astonishing offer had stirred in her. She simply could not comprehend the consequences of what she had heard, and found herself unable to speak. She had to leave, had to be alone with her thoughts. She stood, nodding dumbly. Without a word, she left, her gaze unseeing.

*****

Rienne had tears in her eyes. With shaking fingers, she fumbled for a handkerchief. The Hierarch's words were echoing round her head, like a chant with no meaning, and she realized she was holding her breath. Sullyan had just been handed the answer to all their prayers, but Rienne had no idea what the younger woman would do. How could she turn her back on her life at the Manor? Yet what Pharikian was offering was the love of a true family, something Sullyan had never known. Surely she would accept?

Taran and Bull were rising, preparing to follow Sullyan, and Rienne hastened to clear her vision. Before she could stand too, Robin moved in front of her, his body stiff and tense.

"Let her be."

Forgetting her handkerchief, Rienne stared at him. His gaze was fixed on the door through which Sullyan had passed, lines of deep concern on his face. Turning, he faced the Hierarch. There was a moment of silence within the chamber before he spoke again, and his tone carried a sadness and maturity she had not heard from him before.

"Majesty, that was not well done. I wish you had spoken to me before placing such burdens on her. I might have been able to prepare her, and I too would have appreciated some forewarning. This affects us all and will change our lives. After what she's been through, it was unkind to place the responsibility solely on her shoulders."

Without waiting for a response he headed for the door, casting a glance at Rienne, Bull, Taran, and Marik. "Come. We'll leave her to think for a while, but she'll need us later. We ought to talk about this among ourselves before that happens."

The men followed without question, but Rienne hesitated. Pharikian was staring at the open door, his face pale and his mouth slightly open. She could tell he was devastated. Noticing her, he shook himself and gave her a pale smile.

Aeyron spoke quietly into the awkward silence. "That's a very mature young man, and one who is deeply in love."

Pharikian sighed, slumping back into his chair. "I know, I know. I value him highly too, and now I have unwittingly given them both unnecessary pain when I sought only to give them hope."

He bowed his head into his hands, and Rienne crept softly from the room.

*****

With no real knowledge of what she was doing or where she was headed, Sullyan made her way up the Tower stairs. She didn't register her surroundings until she opened the heavy double doors and felt the strong westerly wind catch at her hair. It was chilly up here and she hadn't brought a cloak. Hugging her arms about her body as if to contain her pain, she leaned against the battlements and stared unseeing over the landscape.

She didn't know what to think. Before Deshan's startling revelation and Pharikian's totally unexpected offer, she had swung uncomfortably between the desire to return to Albia and terror in case she could not. Now she had a third choice, and it was hard not to jump at such an easy solution. Yet that had never been her way. She had always met trouble head-on, and besides, staying in Andaryon was not the easy option it might at first seem—not while there was Robin to consider. He had no Andaryan blood and could not remain here with her, and she knew now that her life would not be complete without him.

Yes, she could continue her military career in Andaryon—if she had fully understood, Pharikian had actually offered her the position of general—and she knew she could serve the Hierarch as wholeheartedly as she had served Albia's High King, Elias. Moreover, the Hierarch was the nearest she would ever come now to having a father. He had opened up a whole new aspect to her life with his tales of her parents and the history that existed between them. This, coupled with his care for her, had birthed an embryo love in her heart, and his offer to accept her into his family proved that he felt the same.

Friendship—Anjer's, Marik's, Idrimar's, and Aeyron's—would provide her with the companionship she would need until she felt more at home. Yet friendship could never replace the love she had found with Robin, and she could only imagine what it would do to him should she decide to stay. She understood the depth of his love for her. They might not have had the most promising of starts, but once he had recovered from his sister's tragic death and come to the Manor, they had been virtually inseparable.

She sighed, deeply regretting that it had taken Rykan's abuse to make her fully appreciate the importance of Robin's place in her heart. Her irresolution, however, didn't seem to have caused any lasting damage. Simply put, she couldn't conceive of life without him, and she knew he felt the same way.

Yet that brought up another matter, one she would have to discuss with him openly and honestly before they made any binding commitments. She knew she had been permanently scarred by what Rykan had done to her, and this damage had been exacerbated by the poison of his seed. If—or when—she used the Staff she would run the risk of further damage, quite aside from the question of success or failure—or death. She didn't know how Robin felt about the possibility of having children, but she did know she was now incapable of conceiving. It would be unfair not to tell him. He had a right to know.

As if to leave her disquiet behind, she began to walk slowly around the battlements. Looking out over the Citadel Plains, she could see the great raw scars in the earth where the pyres of Pharikian's dead had burned. Soon, with the advent of warmer weather, they would become softened with grasses and starred with wild flowers, a fitting tribute to those who had given their lives for their realm. Moving on, she gazed down on the spot where she had fought and triumphed over Rykan, absently massaging the bones of her left wrist as she remembered the day. She could also see the small hill where Bull, Cal, Taran, and Rienne had watched the combat, and from where Taran and Cal had been abducted by Sonten's men.

She mused on that, her golden eyes unseeing. Just what was Sonten's role in all this? She remembered seeing him at Rykan's palace, noting that he had taken no obvious pleasure or part in the Duke's brutal abuse. But neither had he intervened, and she wondered now, in the light of what they knew about the Staff and Sonten's frantic efforts to retrieve it, whether he had been involved in the suspected plot to control or eliminate powerful Artesans. If so, where had his and Jaskin's ill-fated experiments with the weapon fitted in? Had he been connected to whoever had made the Staff, or had he merely seen an opportunity to further his own self-serving greed? She would probably never know. Sonten hadn't been gifted with Artesan powers, and as both he and his ambitious nephew were dead, along with the commander he had hoped to use in Jaskin's place, speculation was futile.

Walking on, she made out the other small hill to the north, crowned with its ancient wreath of standing stones—the site of Vanyr's funeral pyre. Her heart ached at his memory. She recollected their brief and awkward conversation on this very roof when she had tried to apologize for the beating he had received at the pirates' hands. She also remembered his reluctant concern for her when the sight of Rykan on the battlefield had nearly crippled her with pain. She suddenly wondered what he would have made of the Hierarch's offer and how he might have advised her. Raising tear-filled eyes to the cloudy sky, she sent a message of love to his memory on the wind. There was no reply.

Completing her circular tour of the battlements, she suddenly came face to face with Robin. Startled by his silent appearance, she halted. He stood unmoving and unspeaking, just watching her with no expression on his face. He had brought her cloak with him, and she suddenly realized she was shivering.

*****

Her startlement told Robin how preoccupied she was. Never before had he been able to come near her without her sensing him, and he experienced a pang of anxiety. Should he have given her more time? But she smiled gently at him and let him place her warm cloak about her shoulders. Although he badly wanted to, he didn't take her into his arms. Instead, he stood at her side, asking nothing, offering his presence for comfort. She looked over the Plains in silence. Eventually, he had to speak.

"Sullyan." He was still not entirely at ease with her given name, so in his uncertainty he fell back on the familiar. "I want you to know that should you decide to stay here, should you not want to risk using the Staff, I'll understand."

His voice was unsteady and rough, but he got the words out. He surprised himself by doing so. This was one of the hardest things he had ever done.

She turned to look at him, her pupils dilating.

"Will you, Robin?"

Her mind brushed his, but her delicate probe was too much for him and he shut her out, immediately revealing what he was trying to hide.

"Ah." She looked away again. "I thought not."

The silence continued. He was ashamed that she had seen through him so easily, but it was his own fault. They were just too close and his control was imperfect where his feelings for her were concerned. After a moment, he tried again.

"Alright. Maybe 'understand' was the wrong word." His own eyes filled with tears and he cursed his lack of self-control. "What I meant was I would never ask you to do something just because it was what I wanted." He swallowed, fumbling with his sentiments. "My love, you know how I feel about you. I would do anything for you—anything! If saving you from certain agony and the risk of death means giving you up, then I'll do it. I won't pretend it'll be easy and I know it won't make me happy, but I'll do it."

He heard her sigh and saw a tear slide down her cheek. "But what would be the point?" Her whisper was so soft he hardly heard it. "For I could never be happy if I gave you up, no matter what Timar offered me. I cannot deny that I have found more of myself here than I could ever have imagined, but it would all mean less than nothing without you. We belong together, Robin, I know that now. I will not relinquish that without a fight, whatever the risk."

Joy flared in his heart and he turned to stare at her. Before the emotion of the moment overwhelmed them both, she stepped back, holding up the hand that bore his ring.

"All is not yet settled," she warned. "There is something I must tell you before you commit to me too deeply."

His voice was deep and husky. "Oh, you're far too late."

Looking away from the naked emotion in his eyes, she continued resolutely. "Nevertheless, this is not a thing we have discussed before. The need has not arisen. Yet if we are to take each other for life, I must tell you—"

"You believe you are unable to bear children." Seeing her startled expression, he said, "Pharikian and Deshan made sure I was aware of the possibility when they helped you purge yourself after Rykan's death. And I have to admit, when I first knew exactly what that bastard had done to you, the thought came into my mind.

"But it doesn't matter!" He took her by the shoulders, gazing earnestly into her eyes. "Your love and commitment are all I've ever wanted. Just to be with you and know that you're mine is enough for me. What's in the future is in the future. We'll face it together. And if it has to be just the two of us for the rest of our lives, then so be it. I've never wished for anything more."

She took a gulp of breath and he feared she would dissolve into tears. Instead, she stepped into his embrace and nestled her head on his chest. He felt the rapid thud of her pulse and the warm clasp of her arms around him. He thought his heart would burst.

"Will you come with me and tell the others, love?" he murmured. "Bull and Rienne are so very worried. And poor Taran—I just don't know what we're going to do with him. He's so helplessly in love with you, you know."

She raised her head and smiled, dashing tears from her eyes. "Yes, I had noticed. He is very obvious with it. We will have to pay some attention to finding him a partner. He has so much to give, so much passion in his soul, and I would hate to see it wasted. Very well, we will go and find the others and then tell Pharikian our decision. But I warn you, if I am going to attempt this then I need some time to prepare and think. It is not something to be undertaken lightly. And someone has to inform General Blaine. I think, under the circumstances, it had better come from you. You and the others should return to Albia for a while anyway. You do not have the advantage of my hybrid blood. Poor Cal must be desperate to see Rienne, and I know she has been missing him. You can come back and help me prepare once you have spoken to the General. But I am still very afraid, Robin, and success is by no means guaranteed. This may well prove to be beyond my powers."

"Don't worry, love," soothed Robin. "We'll all help and support you, you know that. Together, we can cope with anything. I just know you're going to succeed."

Putting his arm around her, he guided her toward the Tower doors.

*****

It was a chilly, rainy, windswept day when Robin, Bull, Taran, and Rienne prepared to leave Andaryon for the Manor. Rienne was torn, for eager as she was to see Cal and hold him in her arms, she couldn't help but feel she was deserting her friend again just when she was needed. Sullyan understood her turmoil and took the healer aside to reassure her. They talked at length and, eventually, Rienne was pacified. But as they gathered on the Citadel Plains just outside the south gate, she still felt more than a little disloyal.

Bull was also feeling ambiguous about the trip. He had no real need to return to Albia as his duties would only resume if and when the Major returned. But she was concerned about his heart, so Bull didn't voice his reluctance. After the last time, he didn't intend to disobey her orders ever again. She already had enough to think about, and only Robin could help her now. So he made no protest, merely accepted her wishes, and saw the grateful thanks in her eyes.

Taran was uneasy for quite a different reason, and this time his feelings had nothing to do with Sullyan. He was unsure of the reception he would find at the Manor. After all, good swordsmen had lost their lives in lifting Sonten's siege of Hyecombe, and blame for their deaths could be laid literally and squarely at Taran's door. He didn't speak of his concern, but Robin had a flash of intuition, realizing what was troubling the older man.

"No one blames you, Taran," he assured the Adept. "All of our company were impressed with you and Cal when you helped us repel the invasion, and that hasn't changed. And Blaine has said nothing, as far as I know. So put it out of your mind, man. You're one of us now. Just think how relieved Cal will be to have you and Rienne back. You all deserve a rest. We'll think about the future later."

Surprised and grateful for this reassurance, Taran resolved to heed Robin's words. He certainly didn't want to cause any more problems.

Gathering outside the Citadel gates, they once more bade farewell to Sullyan. The circumstances were not so different from the last time and they were all reminded of it, but no one let their emotions overspill. The Major stood back while Robin opened the tunnel, and her pride in his growing skills and strength filtered through to the handsome young man.

The little company mounted their horses and rode through the Veils. Looking back, they could see her standing by the gate, sentries of the Velletian Guard behind her, her left hand raised in farewell. Then Robin allowed the structure to fade and they found themselves back in Albia.

Their reception at the Manor was more intense than any of them could have foreseen. Bull had always been popular—although more so since he had ceased to be an active Sergeant-Major—and the men of Sullyan's command were gratifyingly enthusiastic in their welcome. When Taran found himself included in the raucous cheering and hearty back-slapping, he was left in no doubt as to their wholehearted inclusion of him into their ranks. Rienne was also greeted with pleasure, as her work in the infirmary had benefited most of the men in one way or another.

The most enthusiastic greeting of the day came from the young kitchen boy, Tad. He had been waiting for days for Robin's return, and when the Captain finally swung down from Torka's back in the stableyard, the boy barely restrained himself from flying into Robin's arms. Whooping with delight, he skidded to a halt in front of Robin and, instead of the childish hug he really wanted to give, he snapped a very passable salute which he had obviously been practicing. Robin returned his homage gravely, causing Tad's young face to flush crimson, and then, to the boy's everlasting delight, scooped him up and set him on Torka's high back, giving the reins into the boy's proud hands.

"Walk him around a bit, lad," said Robin with a grin. "Just don't let him eat too much grass."

"I won't, sir! I'll take care of him!" breathed Tad, pure, undying hero-worship in his shining eyes as he gently nudged Torka into a walk.

"Will he be alright on that huge stallion?" asked Rienne as they walked away.

Grinning impishly, Robin cast the rapt lad a glance over his shoulder. "He'll be fine, Rienne. Torka's very gentle with youngsters."

They went up to the manor-house, passing the barracks and acknowledging the waves, cat-calls, and cheers from the men of the other companies. Seeing them, Baily came over, slapped Robin on the back, and grinned up at Bull. "Come back to do some work at last, have you, old soldier?"

Bull scowled at him. "I'll give you 'old soldier,' you insolent young pup. I could still teach you a thing or two, and don't you forget it!"

There was no sign of Parren as they made their way up the stairs and through the maze of corridors and halls toward the private quarters. Robin knew that Cal was no longer in the infirmary, and he silently communed with Bull and Taran as they neared their rooms. Tactfully, they left Rienne outside the door of her apartment to be reunited with Cal in private. Then they made for Bull's rooms, feeling in need of some brandy.

Chapter Sixteen

Later that morning, Robin had an interview with General Blaine. Despite the gravity of the subject, it was by far the most comfortable meeting he had ever had with the man, and their discussions were unmarred by resentment. Knowing enough about what could happen when Sullyan used the Staff, Robin realized she might need Blaine's metaphysical help with the procedure, but he also wanted the General to know their suspicions concerning the Staff's creation and the hypothetical reason behind Rykan's challenge to Andaryon's throne. Blaine listened gravely while Robin repeated the discussion they had had with Pharikian. He was obviously appalled at the thought of such a high-level plot against Artesans, but immediately grasped the reasoning behind their suspicions.

"It is true that there was considerable opposition at court to Sullyan's inclusion in our ranks," he mused once Robin had fallen silent. He glanced up, briefly nodding his thanks as his aide, Hyram, placed cups of fellan on the table. "At each promotion I had to fight for permission to advance her. But it was never very clear whether the opposition was because of her gender or her other talents. She always had Elias's approval, of course, or he would never have accepted her Oath, let alone appointed her King's Envoy. But it is undeniable that there are nobles at court who are … less than happy, shall we say, about her rank and position."

He eyed Robin frankly. "You do realize that this is the reason I've always been so hard on her? The slightest slip or hint of misconduct and those nobles would have petitioned the King for her removal. Despite his support, he couldn't have ignored them. It could all have gotten very awkward."

Robin set down his cup. "I didn't really, sir, no, although I suppose I should have. I did know that she and Artesans in general, of course, had powerful enemies at court. She told me so when I first came here, but I never really considered how it might affect your relationship with her."

Blaine looked down at his hands. "We deliberately never made an issue of it."

Robin sighed. "Then perhaps the misunderstanding was not entirely my fault. Still, I behaved very badly, sir. I was too deeply involved to see things objectively, and I admit I have a tendency to be judgmental. I always resented her defense of your actions, and I could never understand why she didn't resent your attitude. I was too simplistic, sir. All I could see was that although she'd saved your life some years ago, you seemed to be totally ungrateful. I know now that I had no business passing judgment. Please accept my heartfelt apologies for any lack of respect I may have shown you."

Blaine appraised the young captain, a small smile playing about his habitually stern mouth. "Well, well, you seem to have grown up at last. I'll admit, I had my doubts when the Major first asked permission to bring you here, and I've regretted giving her that permission a good few times over the past two and a half years, as I'm sure you know! But you've finally justified her faith in you and all the effort she put into your training. I will have no reservations about your confirmation as a Master Artesan, or in approving your promotion, when it becomes appropriate."

Robin was stunned by Blaine's open reversal of a long-held opinion. "Thank you, sir," he said, trying not to stammer.

His thanks were waved away. "I will keep in mind what you've told me about a possible alliance between this Lord Rykan and some high-powered noble," the General continued, "although I can't imagine any of the narrow-minded bigots in Elias's court allying themselves with an outlander. None of them have the Artesan gift, so it's highly unlikely that your suspected renegade is among their number. However, I will send a runner to First

Minister Levant asking him to make some discreet enquiries. I will not burden the King with this unless we have firm evidence.

"In the meantime, Captain, we should concentrate on getting Sullyan back where she belongs. You can tell her she will have my full support in whatever capacity she needs it. I value her, you know—maybe more than either of you know—and I've missed her more than I care to admit. But you can keep that last bit to yourself, Captain, and that's an order!"

Robin grinned broadly. "Yes, sir!"

On returning to Bull's rooms, he found all his friends gathered there. Cal was looking much more his usual self now that Rienne was back, and Robin greeted him warmly. He and the others had been discussing the immediate future, and as soon as Robin finished his greeting, Rienne demanded to know what Blaine's reaction was. After accepting a glass of firewater from Bull, Robin relayed the General's comments.

"When are you going back?" Cal asked.

"Tonight. I'll bathe and change and collect a few things, and then I'll be off. I don't want to leave her too long."

"You know you can count on us for help and support, don't you?" said Rienne. "If I can help Brynne at all before she decides to attempt this, you only have to come fetch me."

Robin gave her a warm smile. "Thanks, Rienne. We both appreciate it. I can't say how long it'll be before she's ready, but you can be sure I'll keep you informed. Now I'd better go change and get back to my horse before Tad rides him into the ground!"

Robin needn't have worried. When he finally reached the horse lines, he found his mount's coat gleaming, curried to within an inch of its life. The leather harness had been cleaned and oiled, and the bit and buckles polished. Even Torka's hooves had been picked out and rubbed with oil so they shone. Tad was sitting on the railing next to the tethered chestnut, talking quietly to the horse and feeding him pieces of apple, which the big beast took with gentle lips.

Robin stood unobserved for a moment, smiling as he watched the young boy petting his horse. When Tad finally saw him, he jumped off the rail.

"He's all ready for you, sir. He's had a light feed and some water, and your gear's all ready. Shall I tie that pack on for you?" He took the small pack from Robin and secured it deftly to Torka's saddle rings.

Walking around the stallion, Robin eyed Tad's work. "Did you do all this by yourself?"

Tad glanced up at him, concern in his eyes. "Have I missed something, sir? Did I do something wrong?"

Robin shook his head. "No, no, lad, quite the opposite. This would pass muster on parade day. How old are you, Tad? I think it's time we spoke to the General about starting your cadet training."

The young lad flushed and puffed his chest proudly. "I'm thirteen, sir."

"Well old enough, then. Did you know that Major Sullyan was only ten when she began training?"

Tad's eyes grew large. "No, sir, I didn't."

Robin smiled. "I have to go back to Andaryon right now, Tad, and I may be gone a few more days. But when I return we'll put things in motion. How does that sound?"

"Oh, thank you, sir, that would be wonderful," breathed Tad. "But … sir?"

"What is it?"

The boy flushed again and stared down at his shuffling feet. Hiding a grin, Robin urged, "Speak up."

Tad raised adoring eyes and managed to whisper, "I want to be in your company, sir. I want to be under your command."

Robin let the grin out and ruffled the boy's straw-colored hair. "Well, Tad, work hard at your training and do the very best you can. Remember, I will only take top class cadets. Now, be off with you. I'm sure Goran has duties for you."

This reminder of his current station caused Tad's face to fall. Seeing the slump of his shoulders as he walked away, Robin called, "Just remember, lad, we all had to start somewhere. You can learn to work hard and obey orders in any situation. Don't worry. It won't be for much longer."

The boy turned and gave Robin a quick salute. "Yes, sir," he said as he scampered off. Robin swung onto his gleaming mount and nudged Torka out of the yard, a foolish grin on his face.

*****

Almost a week passed before Sullyan felt she was as ready as she would ever be to attempt purging herself of the last bit of Rykan's poison. Most of that time was spent in getting herself as physically fit as possible. She fenced with whoever would spare her the time, and Marik, Anjer, Ephan, Barrin, Aeyron, Robin, and even Pharikian himself were all pressed into her service. That the Hierarch should acquiesce was a surprise, as no one had seen him wield a sword for years. Yet he was fitter than he looked and seemed to thoroughly enjoy the few sessions he shared with Sullyan, the years falling away from him as he remembered his old skills.

When she was not fencing, Sullyan was talking with Deshan or discussing the Citadel's defenses with Anjer or schooling Drum—who needed regular strenuous exercise to take his mind off the Citadel's many mares. She did, however, allow herself and Robin some relaxation, and they took to riding over the countryside in the afternoons as a means of forgetting the coming event.

Inevitably, there came a day when she could put it off no longer. With Deshan and Pharikian, she had discussed every possible angle, every development and contingency she could imagine, attempting every experiment they could devise short of actually using the power in the Staff. She had even tried to attune herself to it one afternoon, the experience convincing her to leave well alone until it was unavoidable.

One of her immediate concerns had been cleverly resolved by Pharikian. Their agreement that the artifact should be destroyed once she had recovered from her use of it still stood. Sullyan was confident that she could destroy it—provided she didn't kill herself while using it—but was concerned about how the Staff might react. It had already caused untold damage in two separate realms, not to mention the men it had killed. The risk to Sullyan's safety was something she had to accept—risk to her friends, she would not.

It was unthinkable that she should attempt to use the Staff out in the open. The energies it contained were far too potent to risk unleashing them without some form of containment. She also knew that no shield created by an Artesan—not even the Hierarch, Senior Master though he was—would be strong enough to withstand the backlash which might occur if those energies broke loose. The only substance strong enough to resist and contain the potential power surge was that of the Veils, but she could not cross the Veils while carrying the taint of Rykan's seed.

Understanding her concerns, Pharikian proposed a way to overcome them. Sullyan could enter the Veils surrounded by a closed and shielded Andaryan structure maintained by the Hierarch himself. Robin, in Albia, would be on hand to lend his strength if needed. This would provide several benefits. First, it would be a neutral environment which would cause her no pain. Second, it would protect her from external disturbances. Third and most important as far as Sullyan was concerned, either the Hierarch or Robin would be able to maintain the shield should she lose control of the Staff, containing any fallout within the Veils and allowing it to dissipate harmlessly.

After considering this suggestion, Sullyan approved it with one proviso. Despite her faith in Robin's powers, she didn't want him taking the responsibility for providing the Hierarch with back up by himself. If anything went wrong, she knew he would blame himself for the rest of his life, and she couldn't countenance that. She stipulated that Blaine be asked to support Robin. Two Master-ranked Artesans would surely be strong enough to hold the construct firm in the event of a disaster.

It was settled that they would use this method when Sullyan attempted the purging, and if all went well, they could duplicate the process when the time came to destroy the Staff. Having made this decision, she could find no more reason to delay. Robin would travel back to Albia to inform the General of their plan. Once Blaine had agreed, Pharikian and Deshan would stand at the Andaryan end of the structure, with Robin and Blaine at the Albian end. Sullyan would enter with the Staff and finally purge herself of Rykan's lethal legacy. This, of course, was the only part of the procedure over which no one had any control. They had covered all the angles. It only remained to be seen whether Sullyan was strong enough or determined enough to succeed.

Her last night in the Citadel before the purging attempt was spent under a somber, uncertain air. In an attempt to distract her from her fears, Pharikian invited her friends to supper in his private chambers. Only Ky-shan and his band were missing, as the pirates had left a few days earlier to take up their new duties on the east coast.

Gathered that night in the comfortable privacy of Pharikian's rooms were the Hierarch himself, Prince Aeyron, Deshan, Idrimar and an emotional Marik, Anjer and Torien, Ephan and Hollett, the Lady Falina, Baron Gaslek, and Robin. They spent a quiet evening with gentle music and good food. Sullyan had even managed to regain a little of the weight she had lost and no longer looked quite so thin. Her color was good, and she astonished Robin by accepting a glass of the Hierarch's best red wine, a much sought-after Cheosian vintage, after Deshan told her that a small amount would do her good. The mood was relaxed and easy, and no one mentioned the coming trial.

Once the meal was over and before the atmosphere became strained, the guests made their farewells, filling their voices with encouragement and their eyes with optimism. Pharikian tried to persuade Sullyan to stay on a while, but as soon as she decently could she left him to his family, desiring to be alone with Robin. Once their chamber door had closed and they laid themselves together on the bed, there was an urgency, almost a desperation, to Sullyan's lovemaking that had never been there before. Alarmed, Robin did his best to calm her, showing her the depth of his love and distracting her as well as he could. But once they were spent her tears came, and he held her close in loving silence.

Her trembling only eased when he finally helped her slip into sleep.

*****

In the morning, Robin was pleased to find her serene. Showing no apprehension, she bathed and dressed, then packed her belongings for him to take back to Albia. It felt strange to Robin to be leaving the suite, and as Sullyan took a last lingering look before closing the door he knew she thought the same. This felt wrong somehow, and he hoped it wasn't an omen. Sullyan's parents had used these rooms—she had been born, and her mother had died here—and he knew she felt very close to them. It would surely wrench her heart to leave.

He and Sullyan broke their fast with Pharikian and Aeyron, and no one referred to what she was about to do. Relaxed and friendly, the conversation followed trivial lines. Robin was due to return to the Manor at mid-morning, taking Drum with him and reporting to General Blaine to inform him of the final preparations. Once all was in place, they could begin.

Pharikian accompanied them to the Citadel's south gate to see Robin off. The Captain had Drum on a lead-rein and all their gear in packs. Pharikian had decided that the best place to construct the Andaryan tunnel would be far out on the Plains, well away from any habitation. Robin and Blaine would decide for themselves where the Albian end would be. Despite Pharikian's assurances that no damage would occur in either realm should Sullyan lose control of the Staff, Robin's experience in Hyecombe had left him nervous. He intended to make certain there were no buildings or people anywhere near the vicinity of the Albian structure.

Bowing to Pharikian, he kissed Sullyan before vaulting onto Torka. "Go swiftly, Robin," she said. "I am anxious to get this over with now. I have waited long enough."

With no further ceremony, Robin constructed a trans-Veil tunnel and rode through it into Albia. Drum's protesting whinny echoed back through the substrate as his rider faded from view.

General Blaine was waiting at the Manor. Hearing what Robin had to say, he wasted no time. He had already told Bull what was to happen, asking him to alert the infirmary in case their services should be needed. Taran and Cal were also aware, but Blaine had decided against making it common knowledge in case of disaster. Rienne, however, had insisted on attending and suggested that Bull and Taran be present as back-up. Robin agreed, knowing Sullyan wouldn't mind having her closest friends nearby.

The party rode out, Blaine and Robin choosing their site carefully. They didn't want to be too far from the Manor should they need help, but there was plenty of open countryside on the far side of the ridge and it was far enough away from the Manor farmlands to be clear of people. When they were satisfied, Robin and Blaine took up their places. Bull, Rienne, and Taran waited some way off with the horses, close enough to be within call but far enough away to feel safe. Robin sensed Bull and Taran linking psyches, sheltering with Rienne beneath a solid shield of Earth.

All was ready. Trying to control the nervousness creeping treacherously into his heart, Robin sent a call to Pharikian. The Hierarch's reply was instant. Before they could begin, however, there was an unexpected delay. Sullyan had requested a private word with the General. Blaine frowned and glanced at Robin, who shrugged. He had no idea what she wanted.

*****

Sullyan waited anxiously until the General emerged into the sunlight over the Citadel Plains. Mathias Blaine bowed gravely to Pharikian and shook Deshan's hand before turning to the woman by their side. He raised his brows.

In a low voice, she said, "I would speak with you a moment, Mathias, if you please."

Blaine traded a glance with the two Andaryans and followed her as she moved away, stopping just out of earshot. She saw him looking at her hands and realized she was distractedly massaging her left wrist.

"What is it, Brynne?"

She took a deep breath, aware that her uncertainty would be showing in her eyes.

"There is something I wish to ask you, Mathias. Forgive me for placing this burden on you, but there is no one else I can trust."

He arched his brows, clearly disliking like the sound of this. "Go on."

She sighed. "I do not know how much Robin has told you about the Staff, but I want you to understand that I am not at all sure I can use it as he hopes."

Blaine sucked in a breath. "Then why risk it? I understand you could stay here indefinitely."

She caught his gaze. "That is true. But it is not what I wish. My life is elsewhere, my heart and loyalties also. I would not be happy, and neither would Robin. So I must take my chances. Pharikian thinks I am strong enough, and perhaps he is right. Only time will tell. But I must ask you this favor, Mathias. I want you to promise me something, if you will."

He folded his arms across his powerful chest. "Name it."

As unemotionally as possible, she continued. "I can see three possible outcomes to this trial. The first is complete success." She smiled briefly up at him. "That is what Robin hopes for."

He did not respond, and she looked away again. "The second is complete failure, and I cannot discount it. It may be impossible to remove the poison. I can only try."

She stopped.

"And the third?" he asked, knowing this was what she feared.

She ducked her head. "The third would be something between the two."

Raising her eyes, she took a breath, meeting her fears head-on as usual. "Mathias, I very much fear that I will succeed in cleansing my body at the expense of my mind. When I took Rykan's life force in the arena, he was left with nothing but a physical shell. He would have lived the rest of his days a mindless husk. Before he lost all conscious thought he begged me to kill him, not to leave him like that. When I struck off his head, I did so for mercy's sake, not from hate or vengeance."

Blaine was appalled; she could feel it radiating from him. "And you're asking me to do the same for you?"

She turned away, and her voice was barely a whisper. "Like Rykan, I cannot bear the thought of a living death. I may succeed today, all may yet be well. Or it might be that some partial damage will occur and I would need a few days to recover. But if the damage was too great … if the coma went on and on … ah, that I could not bear. I am asking you to ensure that my friends—and especially Robin—do not prolong the inevitable if the situation is hopeless. I cannot ask them, Mathias, I cannot burden any of them with this. And so, I must ask you."

Distressed, he hissed, "You want me to kill you if you destroy your mind? Oh, Sullyan! Even if I agreed, do you think I'd get the chance? Robin would never stand for it—I'd never get near you!"

"Robin need never know!" she said, pleading. "You are a Master Artesan, for all you rarely use your powers. You know how to be discreet. No one need ever know. You know my psyche pattern well, and I would never fight you, you know that."

His face was stern, his psyche closed to her, and she became distraught.

"Please, Mathias, do not make me beg! I cannot go through with this unless you agree to help me. I would hate to live like that, and deep in his heart, Robin knows it. You are the only one I can trust. Forgive me for asking, but I must have your answer."

He turned away, but not before she had seen the moisture in his eyes. She watched him taking deep breaths, struggling to regain his composure. Giving him time, she waited silently until he was calm.

When he finally turned round, his eyes were dry and hard. "Very well," he growled. "I don't like it, but I'll do as you wish. If it comes to that, how long do you want me to wait before I … act?"

Relief swamped her. "A few days, Mathias, no more. You will know if it is hopeless." On impulse, she took his hands, feeling him start. Like Taran, he found such physical contact difficult due to the depth of feelings he didn't often acknowledge. "I thank you, my friend, for agreeing to this. I know I have put you in an impossible situation, but I had no choice. I am truly grateful."

He stood looking down into her eyes for a moment before awkwardly embracing her. "Just you make damned sure I don't have to do it!" he said. She gave a wan smile as he turned away, and she watched him cross the Veils, Robin's tunnel compressing behind him. As he emerged next to Robin, she saw him ignore the Captain's quizzical look.

When the two Albian men were ready, Robin nodded to Pharikian. Sullyan sensed the Hierarch reaching down into his psyche, gathering the fabric of the Veils and weaving it strongly. Soon, she could see where the two structures—Robin's in Albia and Pharikian's there in Andaryon—would meet and mesh. Like filaments of pearly mist, the two substrate structures sought each other, coming together and linking seamlessly until the construction was complete. Right in the middle, separate from the main tunnel, was an area of neutral ground just large enough to contain one person.

Sullyan felt weak but composed, and she gave Robin a small smile. Then she turned to Pharikian and he embraced her, bowing his face to her hair. But she could not risk her emotions spilling over, and so she broke away, taking deep breaths to steady herself. Then, with a nod to Deshan, she walked into the tunnel's grey shimmer, the Master Physician following behind. She was relieved to feel no pain. Pharikian's theory was correct. Reaching the area of neutrality, she stopped, instinctively knowing that if she took one more step, it would be too far. She turned to Deshan, who had halted beside her.

Placing his hand on her shoulder, he smiled encouragingly. "Just remember what I told you, Brynne. Go slowly and steadily. Take all the time you need. Stop and rest if you tire. Clear your mind of all thoughts and concentrate fully on directing your powers through the Staff. You don't need me to guide you this time. You will know when it is done.

"I will leave you now, but I will be within call should you need me. We all will." He placed a light kiss on her cheek. "We wish you good fortune."

Unable to speak, she merely nodded her thanks. Looking around she saw Robin and Blaine, Rienne, Taran, Bull, and Pharikian. Each one willing her to succeed. Drawing another deep breath, she slowly folded herself down upon the ground. Deshan placed the Staff before her and, with a final pat on her shoulder, walked back to the Hierarch.

She was alone with Rykan's Staff.

Chapter Seventeen

Closing her eyes, Sullyan tried to ignore her friends' thoughts and prayers. She needed a blank mind, no distractions to deflect her purpose. Concentrating on her psyche, she surrounded herself with power, seeing and feeling the twists, loops, and helixes of her shimmering, unfathomable, pattern. Reaching down through the vast layers of her strength, she probed through her soul, finally finding the black, insidious mass that was the last residue of Rykan's poison.

As she touched it, nausea swamped her and she nearly pulled back. She had done this before with Deshan, but now, alone and with the terrible task stretching before her, she was dismayed by the poison's hold. It had spread through the fabric of her soul like roots through soil, and she realized she would have to sever each filament separately and oh so carefully. This was going to take some time. She would have to isolate each strand, turning it back on itself before she could use the power of the Staff to finally burn it out.

Lowering her head, she breathed deeply and slowly, all memories and feelings falling away. She could sense nothing. Neither hot nor cold, neither Earth nor Air. There were no sounds but the beating of her heart, the slow pulse of blood through her veins. Blood that was part Albian, part Andaryan. Hybrid blood that might enable her to succeed.

Exhaling strongly, she stretched out her damaged left hand, spreading the fingers wide. On the next inhalation she picked up the Staff.

The silver and ceramic of the Staff began to glow blue-green. Little coruscations ran along its length and it grew warm to the touch. She extended her mind gingerly, merging her own power with the remnant of Rykan's. The Andaryan link in her blood proved true, but the shock she received almost made her drop the device. She exhaled sharply in pain and clasped the Staff in both hands, holding it tightly against her breast. As she channeled more and more of her own strength through it, the glow increased, spreading a nimbus of power about her. It filled the neutral construct with an eerie, phosphorescent light. Oblivious to it, she began to painstakingly isolate each minute thread of contamination in her soul.

It took over an hour, during which time she was forced frequently to rest. Each thread she severed caused her pain, and the last few, the strongest few, caused so much that she could not bite back her cries. Hot tears ran down her cheeks, and she could sense the strain Robin and Blaine were feeling from the effort of maintaining the construct. Even Pharikian was suffering. But it was almost over.

Laying the Staff down, she bowed her head, rocking gently, hugging herself to ease the pain. Her breathing was ragged, and she knew that unless she could regain some measure of control this last and most strenuous effort would fail. If only, she thought, if only one of her friends could lend her some strength. But they couldn't reach her in this neutral place, and she couldn't reach out to them. She felt so alone, so afraid. They were all relying on her, all willing her to succeed. She could feel the pressure of their expectations. More tears came as she thought about them, and she tried to take strength and comfort from their love and support.

Gradually, her breathing slowed as the pain within her eased. She felt as if someone had thrown a blanket of balm over her, offering her a soothing and restful place to be. Soon she was able to raise her head and prepare herself for the final effort. As she did so, she caught a brief glimpse of a pale-faced Rienne, watching with love and concern from Taran's side.

Sullyan straightened her back and reached out, taking up the Staff once more. She clasped it firmly, gathering her will, her metaforce, and her strength. She needed more power from the Staff, much more, and she took a few steadying breaths. Swiftly then, giving herself no time to think, she flung her energies through the Staff, building the power, stoking it, imbuing the device with all the strength she could muster. The artifact glowed brighter and brighter, surrounding her in a blinding halo of light.

She dimly heard Pharikian's warning to Robin and Blaine, urging them to focus. They knew they could not allow the construct to fail. No matter what happened, they must maintain it at any cost. Even when they were sure the power had dissipated, they were to wait until Deshan made sure all was safe before dissolving their meld. If they lost control of the structure with her still inside it, she might become irretrievably lost.

The power was rushing to a crescendo and Sullyan knew the Staff could contain little more. This was the point of balance between too much power and not enough. She knew this was her final chance. She could never force herself to bear this much pain again. Reaching down through her psyche, she touched the terrible blackness deep within her soul. It felt alive, she could swear it moved. Sickness crawled within her at the memory of how it had come to be there. Could it feel the closeness of Rykan's metaforce, contained within the Staff? Was it reacting to the presence of its maker, as it had on the palace Tower before that final battle?

Shaking herself free of the memory, she focused on forging a channel through her soul. The logical part of her mind screamed against opening herself this way, making herself so vulnerable. Yet it was the only way she could get the Staff's energies to where she needed them. Already she could feel the power burning her, and pain began to rise. Her breathing quickened, her lungs unable to draw enough air. Her strength was depleted after the work she had already done, yet this was precisely when she needed to be strongest. The needle of force she was creating out of the energies contained in the Staff could as easily destroy instead of heal if her touch wasn't sure. Yet how could she hold it while her body was wracked by such pain?

Shudders of agony bled through her, each one causing her to gasp. There was rhythm to the pain, a sort of cadence, and her unconscious mind latched on to it, allowing her to breathe within each lull. Accepting the agony was the step she needed to take in order for her body to resume its natural function.

At once, her mind cleared. The pain was still there, but its power to distract her was gone. She was alone with the open channel to her soul, at the end of which was a living darkness such as she had never seen. Poised to oppose this darkness was a tight, flaring needle of metaforce, aimed at the heart of the mass.

It had to be now.

At the end of her endurance, Sullyan envisioned the Staff like a bow and the power an arrow. Drawing it back like an archer, she released her hold. The needle of power shot straight and true toward the poison in her soul, and her perception followed. She braced for the impact, watching with strange detachment as the poison boiled and swirled as if trying to avoid the approaching force. Heat and pain increased immeasurably and she opened her mouth in a silent shriek. The flaring arrow plunged headlong into the poison, vaporizing it on contact, sending waves of unendurable nausea flooding through her body.

She doubled over, gripping her belly, her lungs burning with the need for air. The pain rose higher, searing through her nerves, and she began to panic. The force she had unleashed continued on, raging through her soul. It would kill her if she left it unchecked.

Panting, whimpering with pain, she collapsed to the ground. She had to relinquish all her senses but one if she was to save herself from death. Sight, touch, hearing, smell, and taste vanished like they had never been. All that remained was her metasense, that sense of psyche she had nurtured all her life, the sense that allowed her to connect with the primal forces of her existence.

Free now from physical pain, she was able to fix her awareness on the glowing aura that marked the needle's trail. She should never have loosed it entirely, but it was too late to berate herself now. Now she needed to extinguish it before it extinguished her. The channel through her soul was still open and she plunged her metasenses deeper and deeper, hurtling deeper into her psyche than she had ever dared to go. Twisting, turning, looping, the force had burned its way along every nuance of her personal pattern, altering and remaking some of its structure. She suddenly realized it must stop at the center. Stop, or push through into the Void, taking her awareness with it.

Unfamiliar as her pattern now was, she had to reach and seal the center against this alien force. With luck, she could use her knowledge of Rykan's pattern—the origin of this force—to help her, but first she must reach her goal. She must not allow this final, spiteful remnant of Rykan to be her undoing.

The anger that rose at Rykan's memory provided the energy she needed to reach back to the Staff. It still contained some energy. She could use this to throw her mind ahead of the needle and strengthen the center of her soul against its attack.

This last extravagant use of metaforce took all her remaining awareness. She barely had time to flood the center of her soul with an impenetrable barrier before the needle of force struck, the impact flaring brighter than any light she had ever known. The backlash assaulted her awareness, and she was lost to black oblivion.

*****

The intense light that had blossomed inside the structure faded, revealing Sullyan's body immobile on the ground. Horrified, Rienne cried out and started forward. Taran grabbed her arm, preventing her from rushing toward the substrate structure.

"Gently, Rienne. Let Deshan check her over. It could still be dangerous, and we don't know if the purge was successful yet."

Rienne relaxed into his hold, reluctant but realizing the wisdom of his words. Her eyes were on the Andaryan Master Healer as he entered the structure where Sullyan lay. Deshan kneeled beside her and laid his hand on her brow. There was an agonizing wait while he probed her, and more tension still when he beckoned Pharikian to join him. Robin and Blaine stood firm, holding their end of the tunnel steady, while the Hierarch anchored his end and joined Deshan.

The two of them laid hands on Sullyan and stayed there in silence. The longer they stayed the harder Rienne shook. She longed to run to them, to lend her aid, but Taran's grip on her arm was sure. All she could do was wait.

Then she saw it. The slightest movement of Sullyan's hand on the ground. She tensed, praying for her friend to wake up. The Hierarch placed his arm under Sullyan's shoulders, gently lifting her into a sitting position. Her head lolled against his chest, her eyes still closed, and Rienne held her breath. But then those golden eyes opened and life returned to her features.

Rienne heard a deep sigh from Robin and saw his body sag. He straightened quickly, mindful of his duty. Her eye was then caught by a strange expression on General Blaine's face—an intense look of relief that seemed excessive, even under these extreme circumstances—but she had no time to ponder it. The Hierarch lifted his eyes to the two Albian men and nodded. Joy flooded Rienne's heart. Surely this could only mean it was safe to release the structure because the purging had been successful? She let out her own pent-up breath in a thankful rush.

Once the three men had dismantled the structure, Robin and the General approached the Hierarch. He stood, cradling Sullyan in his arms. Taran released his hold on Rienne and she ran to Sullyan's side just as the Hierarch set her down. With Rienne's shoulder for support on one side and the Hierarch's arm around her waist on the other, Sullyan managed to stand. She looked as weak as a newborn foal. She smiled and nodded at the concerned faces around her, too exhausted to speak. Needing more information, Rienne raised questioning eyes to the Andaryan Master Healer.

He obliged her. "I am pleased to report that the purging has been successful. I can detect no signs of the poison within Brynne's soul. The process, however, has completely drained her energies, and there is also some damage that will need time to heal." Noticing Rienne's stricken look and Robin's fearful frown, he hastily continued. "The damage is not too severe and certainly could have been worse. The poison corroded some areas of Brynne's soul, and these will need time to mend and refill with her personal essence. With sufficient rest, this process will happen naturally. The energy contained within the Staff, however, left some scarring as it seared through the poison, and Brynne will need help if she is to recover the full use of her psyche."

Robin stiffened. "Are you saying Sullyan's powers could be affected for life?"

Deshan gave him a mock stern glance. "Young man, you didn't listen. I said she would need help to recover, not that she wouldn't recover."

Rienne laid a soothing hand on Robin's arm. "She will have all the help she needs, Deshan. I can assure you of that."

"I have no doubt, my dear. Right now, what she needs is rest. Someone should help her to her chamber and then leave her to sleep."

Robin immediately came to Sullyan's side. He swept her up into his arms and kissed her tenderly before walking away. She laid her head on his shoulder and fell instantly asleep.

General Blaine shook hands with both Pharikian and Deshan, thanking them for their help and cooperation. Pharikian agreed to take the artifact back to Andaryon until the time came to destroy it. Taran and Bull also shook hands with the two Andaryans, but handshaking was too formal for Rienne. She gave each man a heartfelt hug, tears of love and gratitude standing in her eyes. Sullyan's safety when the Staff was destroyed might still be a concern, but she pushed that to the back of her mind as she watched the two Andaryans cross into their own realm.

*****

It was late evening in Port Loxton, Albia's capitol city. In the north quarter of the city, Loxton Castle was quiet behind its protective wall, most of its inhabitants abed. Apart from the sentries and servants, the corridors were deserted. Lamplight showed under only a few of the chamber doors on the second floor, where most of the private suites could be found.

One such chamber was situated within the east wing of the castle. The entire wing had been taken over two years ago by Queen Sofira, after her wedding to Elias. Accustomed to the freedom of her father's palace in Bordenn, Sofira had refused to share Loxton Castle's central portion with people such as Elias's Chamberlain, Lord Kinsey, or his First Minister, Rendan Levant.

Privacy was of supreme importance to Sofira. As High Queen of Albia, she felt it was her due.

A fire burned in the generous hearth opposite the chamber window. The heavy drapes were partially open, showing a faint twilight over the castle grounds. Lamps shimmered brightly in wall niches, yet somehow shadows lingered. In a chair close to the fire, the Queen, heavily pregnant with her second child, sipped from a crystal goblet of fine dark wine. Her back was stiff and straight, her honey-blonde hair drawn tightly away from her face. Her hard grey eyes were unfocused and the sipping of the wine was mechanical.

Facing her sat a dapper figure dressed in dark clothes. His face was swarthy, typical of the men from Albia's southern provinces. His eyes, a darker grey than the Queen's, rested on the angular countenance before him, assessing and reflecting on her mood. Between his fingers he twirled a goblet, only now and then pausing to taste its contents. The atmosphere was pensive, broken only by the crackling fire.

Eventually, Sofira raised her eyes. "I fail to see what we can do now, Hezra. Surely our cause is lost?"

He placed his goblet on the table and laced his fingers. This was a discussion they had held before. "I pray not, Madam, as I have told you, although it is severely compromised."

"But how are we to proceed without our outland ally? His aid was crucial to the master plan."

Baron Hezra Reen sighed. Clearly, she still doubted him. "His death is indeed regrettable, although I still feel he would have caused us trouble once he had taken the throne. However, he was not the only one—"

"I thought you said the other one was useless? He didn't have the same standing, you said, so how could he ever provide us with the commodity you say we need?"

The Baron took a healthy swallow of wine. It was a rich southern vintage, far superior to the eastern wines Elias favored. Sofira had a good supply of Beraxian reds, her private cellar kept stocked by her father's vintners. Being the Queen's countryman and confidante had many advantages, the Baron reflected.

"I doubt he could, yet I am loath to lose touch entirely. He might still have value as a spy, despite not being part of the demon ruler's court. I intend to let him stew for a while before renewing the contact, let him reflect upon the income he has lost. I have often found that gold, or more likely the lack of it, has great power to stimulate creativity."

He smiled at her and her lips twitched in response. She was not given to smiling, so this indication of her approval was welcome.

"We may have lost a central player, but remember—we still have the artifact."

Her lips thinned instantly. "We don't, though, do we? We don't know where it is or what might happen to it. And without the outlander lord, we can't get more ore to make another."

The Baron shook his head. "The manufacture of another device does not feature in my plans, Madam. I doubt even Albia's Treasury could bear another such drain. I am hopeful that the fear of the existence of another device will keep them all guessing. Although the youth fears us well enough, I doubt that even Commander Izack could 'persuade' him to go through that again. The experience did nearly kill him, and I want him alive awhile yet. No. I have another scheme for obtaining what we need."

She frowned. "Then it is even more essential to recover the original. What if someone finds out how it was made? What if they discover your involvement? What if they turn it against you?"

Reen froze. There it was again—that subtle reminder that should things go awry, he was alone. "Your involvement," she had said, not "our involvement." His anger rose, but he forced it down. This was a risk he had accepted when he first presented the plan to her, the risk that should he fail, he alone would take the blame.

Quelling his prickling irritation, he held her gaze. He had no intention of failing.

"They cannot discover our involvement, my Queen, and neither can they turn the weapon against us." She was not the only one who could play games with words. "We do not have their blasphemous 'gift,' so it is powerless to affect us."

This was, of course, not entirely true. They had both heard reports of the damage sustained by the village of Hyecombe. Yet Reen knew Sofira was more concerned about an attack on the mind than she was about houses being blown down.

"But what about the Sullyan woman? What if she can sense who made the thing? Surely that will lead them right back here? If we are ever to be rid of these people, rid Albia of their taint forever, we *have* to get the weapon back. As much for our safety as our plan."

She was right. He could feign indifference to the threat Sullyan posed as long as he liked, but the truth was he had no idea what she was truly capable of. Could she discover the mind behind the creation of the artifact? Was there a way she could unravel its construction, find some small clue that would lead her back here? This concern took precedence in his mind, overshadowing Sofira's unconscious acceptance of responsibility.

"I agree, Madam, and I have already decided how to discover what has become of the weapon. Once we know where it is, we can make plans for its recovery. Our remaining contact in the outlander realm may yet prove useful. First, though, I need a reason to go to the Manor. Do I remember you saying the King intends to visit soon?"

She calmed, and he relaxed. The subtle control he had practiced over her ever since his arrival at her father's court had worked its charm once more. He blessed the chance that had brought him into her circle.

"Yes. He has some promotions or battle honors or some such to give out. It's to do with those men who saved that village from the demons. Elias can't stay away from the place for too long. He still feels obliged to Lord Blaine for helping him take the High Throne, I suspect."

Hmm, yes, there's another man who will bear watching. I could do without all these military types with arcane powers getting too close to our King.

Aloud, he said, "That is all to the good, Madam. As you cannot accompany the King in your present condition, you can request my presence at his Majesty's side when he travels to the Manor.

That should give me ample opportunity to ask some questions and listen to gossip. And I have another plan, one which will increase our knowledge of what these people are up to and allow me to devise a way of discrediting them in the King's eyes. Allow me to refill your glass while I tell you."

He stood and took up the decanter, his eyes meeting hers. As she held up her glass for more wine, she smiled.

Chapter Eighteen

Rienne and Robin worked with Sullyan for some days, lending her strength and helping her heal the scarring the Staff's cauterizing power had left. Sullyan was amazed at how fast the void in her soul had refilled with her natural essence—deep, relaxing sleep was the key to that process—but the scarring had affected large portions of her psyche pattern and some of the structure had actually changed due to the trauma it had endured.

During this task, Rienne finally learned the real value of her bond with Sullyan. As an empath, she was unable to initiate contact with Sullyan's mind. Once linked with Robin, however, she could use his strength and knowledge to bind herself to Sullyan's psyche, leaving her free to use her healing skills with no further effort. Rienne directed Robin's, and sometimes Sullyan's, powerful energies to where they would do most good, suffering no draining of her own essence in the process.

In this manner and under Sullyan's direction, Rienne was able to remove the majority of the scarring and restore her friend's psyche to its original condition. She also learned the complex swirls, helixes, and switchbacks of the pattern as well as if it were her own. The day soon came when Rienne found nothing more she could heal.

This was a blessing, for word had arrived at the Manor that King Elias intended to visit. The General summoned Sullyan and Robin to his office to discuss the matter, and he also wanted to hear Sullyan's thoughts on the next step regarding the Staff.

Blaine indicated the chairs in front of his desk, and both officers sat. He steepled his fingers and regarded them.

"Do I take it you are now fully restored, Major?"

She inclined her head. “I cannot pretend all is as it was before”—she glanced down at her left hand—“but all is as well as it can be. I am fit to resume my duties.”

He nodded. “Very well. As you know, his Majesty has scheduled a visit. He was impressed by what he heard concerning the siege of Hyecombe and may well decide to issue battle honors. However, there is another reason behind Elias’s visit. Pharikian has initiated talks with Elias in the hope of cementing better relations between our two realms. It is Elias’s wish that we host the first of these talks here at the Manor, and so the Hierarch of Andaryon and his retinue will visit at the same time as the King.”

He fixed his eyes on Robin’s, causing the young Captain to frown. “The Hierarch has informed Elias in great detail of the parts both you and Sullyan played in thwarting Rykan’s attempt on the throne, and also of his suspicions concerning Rykan’s intentions for Albia had he succeeded. Pharikian has apparently praised you both very highly, and the King wishes to reward you.”

Robin’s eyes grew wide. He opened his mouth to speak, but Blaine wasn’t finished.

“I must also tell you that the Hierarch has informed King Elias that your powers are now sufficient to support Master status. The King has expressed a desire to be present when your confirmation ceremony takes place. Therefore, we will conduct it sometime during this visit.”

Robin flushed. He didn’t quite know what to say. Sullyan sat grinning beside him, clearly delighted with the news.

“General … sir … I am flattered,” Robin managed. “This is a huge honor—”

“Quite right, Captain, and I trust you will not let me or Sullyan down.”

Sullyan reached out and laid her hand on Robin’s arm, pride shining in her eyes. “He will not, Mathias.”

Nodding, Blaine took a breath.

“Now, Captain, we have another matter to discuss. Captain Parren’s behavior during the siege of Hyecombe. I’ve had Captain Baily’s and Sergeant Dexter’s reports, and I can tell you that if you wish to pursue the matter, we have enough evidence for a disciplinary hearing, maybe even a martial court. With the King already scheduled to visit, this would be an opportune time. What are your feelings?"

Robin didn't have any feelings one way or the other. He now had far too much on his mind to worry about a waste of food such as Parren.

"I just want to forget about it, General. There's too much bad blood already between us, and I have no interest in bringing a charge against Parren. I'll leave the matter of his conduct to Colonel Vassa, if it's alright with you."

The General raised his brows, but clearly understood the young man's reluctance to deal with Parren's spite. "This is your last chance, Captain. If you don't pursue the matter now, it will be considered closed." Robin made a gesture of rejection and stayed silent. Blaine nodded curtly. "Very well. I'll pass your comments to Vassa and leave the matter to him." Dismissing the issue, he included Sullyan in his regard. "You have three days to prepare for this state visit, and I will expect your company to participate in a display in the main arena. Let's show Elias and Pharikian exactly what we can do!"

They smiled. The General's expression turned serious and he cocked his head at Sullyan. "One last issue, Major. What is to be done with the Staff?"

She glanced down at her hands, choosing her words. "Now that I have recovered my health, we should delay no longer in undertaking its destruction. I will contain the weapon within a substrate tunnel and cause it to self-destruct."

He nodded. "And will you need help, as before?"

"I will need to focus all my attention and energy on the Staff. There will be none to spare for maintaining a Veil construct."

Robin spoke up. "Why does it have to be you, Sullyan? Wouldn't it make more sense for Pharikian to destroy it? He is a Senior Master, after all."

She gave him a smile. "Yes, Robin, but he is also the ruler of Andaryon. There is danger involved in working with the Staff, we already know that. We cannot take the risk that something will go wrong. I did not go through all that pain to rid Andaryon of Rykan's threat just to endanger the throne once more! Much as I would like to hand the responsibility to someone else, I fear I have no choice."

He hung his head, ashamed he had mentioned it. She briefly clasped his hand, acknowledging his concern. Blaine cleared his throat.

"When, Major?"

She raised her eyes. "As soon as we may. Certainly before the King arrives. Every day that weapon remains in existence is one day too long for me. Surely its maker is searching for it? I expect Pharikian could be persuaded to arrive a day early." The General inclined his head. "Shall I contact him and make the arrangements?"

"Very well, Major. I will leave it to you. We will be at your disposal as before."

*****

In the pre-dawn light of the day before King Elias was due to arrive at the Manor, a small party of Albians waited in the open countryside below the ridgeline. Of Sullyan's friends, only Cal was absent.

Sullyan stepped forward and bespoke the Hierarch, receiving his permission to proceed. General Blaine and Robin accepted Pharikian's contact, and Sullyan, Bull, Taran, and Rienne stood watching while they created a trans-Veil structure between the two realms. Sullyan knew they all felt that same odd shift of time, the feeling they had done this before.

When all was in place, she stood at the Albian mouth of the tunnel and watched as Pharikian strode into its center. Reaching the place of neutrality, he stooped and placed the artifact he carried gently on the ground. He straightened and caught her gaze, the intensity of his stare conveying his love and trust. There were no words this time—they had already been said. The only uncertainty was how the Staff's destruction would affect its surroundings.

As soon as the Hierarch returned to his position beside Deshan and all the watchers were protected under shields of Earth, Sullyan entered the structure. When she reached the structure's center, she bent down and picked up the Staff.

There was no flickering blue-green light. In fact, the Staff did not react at all. It contained very little in the way of energy because Sullyan had already drained it. It was now simply an empty repository for metaforce.

Not knowing how long the process might take, Sullyan sat upon the ground. She laid the Staff in her lap and briefly checked that Robin, Pharikian, and Blaine were ready. Then she cast her metasenses into the artifact. She had thought long and hard about the best way to do this. The Staff's construction meant it would be almost impossible to break or damage by physical means, so the only sure way was to overload it, causing it to shatter from the inside from a surfeit of metaphysical forces. The heaviest and strongest element was Earth, and so Sullyan intended to draw on that power, pouring it into the Staff until she breached its capacity and it burst.

The advantage of this plan was that Earth was an abundant force. She could summon it from the ground almost indefinitely. The only restriction was her own limitations. As Master-elite, her control over Earth went back many years, and she was confident she would never lose her hold on the element, no matter how the Staff behaved. The only question in her mind was whether the materials present in the Staff would exert an influence over the forces that filled it. This influence, coupled with the risks involved in detonating that much power inside a substrate tunnel, was the only unknown Sullyan faced. She also had to defend herself against the detonation itself.

Reaching into her restored psyche, Sullyan surrounded herself in her pattern's familiar folds. She experienced the same glowing feeling she always did when immersed in her own metaforce. Amber and puissant, it flowed around her, buoying her soul. She smiled, at one with her own existence. A tendril of power flowed out, connecting her to the ground beneath her. Immediately, she felt the thrum of Earth—the solidity of bedrock, the rhythm of molten lava deep, deep underground. Images flashed through her mind of great, volcanic upheavals, long periods of static inactivity, the sudden heat of a steam vent forming, and the tiny rustling sounds of roots through soil. This was Earth, this was the Power that shaped the World, and it was hers to command.

Unbidden, the memory of Taran's reaction when he first experienced the level of power she controlled crept into her mind. She clearly recalled her own amazement at such dizzying feelings of supremacy. It was the glory and the danger of the Artesan gift, and it made the development of self-control so vital.

Having permitted herself that brief, savoring moment, Sullyan turned her attention to channeling the Earth power into the Staff. She envisioned it as a deep receptacle, one that could soak up immeasurable amounts of force. As the power levels rose, the familiar blue-green light began to flicker over the ceramic casing and the artifact grew warm in her hands.

*****

The Hierarch kept a close eye on what was occurring inside the construct. He felt Sullyan increase her pull on the element of Earth and saw with satisfaction how the Staff greedily accepted wave after wave of power. The light was increasing, causing the entire tunnel to glow, and he gestured for Deshan to step farther away. Blaine and Robin did the same for the onlookers at the Albian end.

As the minutes paced on, the thrum of Earth power grew stronger until it could be felt in both realms. The tunnel was beginning to resonate with the rising beat of Earth, and he wasn't sure how this would affect its stability. Little coruscations of light flickered along its length, a sure sign of outward pressure, and he increased his grip, forcing it back under control. He had already anchored it deep into the rocks beneath the Citadel Plains, but he checked those ties again, shoring them up against any sudden pull. Satisfied, he turned back to Sullyan.

*****

The flow of Earth power moved faster and faster as it disappeared into the maw of the Staff. Sullyan was surprised at the amount the device had taken, was still taking. Like an infinite void, the small artifact drew in and swallowed every vestige of power she could raise. This was way beyond her experience, and she felt an almost envious awe of whoever had fashioned such a potent, voracious thing. What must their capacity be like if they were capable of envisioning such a device, let alone creating it? What control must they have to be able to manipulate such forces and shape them into such a delicate-looking object?

She wondered what that person's mind would feel like. It could not be like hers, for she could never imagine a need or desire that would lead her to conceive such a weapon. Surely the Staff's creator must be a monster, someone flawed, truly a renegade Artesan? Surely no sane person would be capable of bringing into existence such a terrible thing?

And still it sucked up power. Sullyan was beginning to tire. How much longer could this feeding go on? She was aware of the tunnel's trembling, the deep shudders that rumbled through the ground. She trusted Pharikian, Blaine, and Robin to hold the structure firm, but spared a moment of concern for the wider effects of her work. How far would these tremors reach? She could not bear to think she might damage the Manor.

This worry gave her strength, and she made a strenuous effort to limit the field of her power stream. Obedient if sluggish, the Earth power responded, but its narrower stream rushed faster than ever into the Staff's eager maw. Now she could see some effect. The weapon grew hotter, and its light began to blaze. This was closer to how it had felt when she had used it last time. Finally, she was reaching its limit.

The light flaring from the Staff was becoming too bright for her eyes. Taking it into her left hand, she held it away from her, shielding her sight. But the dazzling nimbus suddenly pulsed out from the weapon, blossoming to fill the entire length of the tunnel. She was caught in a space made of blinding white light.

The beat of her heart increased, gaining tempo with the rush of Earth power. She was connected to the stream pouring endlessly into the Staff, and her blood froze when she realized she couldn't pull out. Refusing to panic, she reached for her psyche, the breath choking in her throat when she found she couldn't touch it. Fear rose like bile, swamping her in nausea, and the panic that had threatened broke loose.

She struggled, straining to cut herself free from the element of Earth. But the force had subtly changed and she was no longer in control. Somewhere along the way the Staff had taken over and locked Sullyan's personal forces into the stream. Now she was irretrievably linked, and nothing she did could break her free.

Her body gave a great judder and she realized she was floating. There was nothing beneath her and nothing above. A scream of sheer terror forced its way out of her throat, but there was nothing to hear. She was pure Earth power, primal element, and there was no destination but the Staff. Whiteness engulfed her, both inside and out, and her awareness bled into it until nothing was left.

*****

Rienne, watching from the circle of Taran's comforting arms, saw the Staff flare brightly. She saw Sullyan hold it to one side, trying to shield her eyes. She watched, alarmed, as the tunnel turned opaque, cutting Sullyan off from their sight. She shivered. How she wished it were Cal here with her giving her comfort, but he was still recovering in their rooms at the Manor. She glanced up at Taran, but his attention was fixed upon Robin standing next to General Blaine. She felt Taran stiffen and followed the line of his gaze. The General and Robin had shifted slightly, the angle of their bodies suggesting great strain. Rienne's heart began to thump, and only then did she realize she could no longer feel the thrum of Earth power. What was going on?

"Watch out!"

The roar came from the General, and Rienne gasped as Taran spun her around and forced her to run. She had no time to protest or look back at what was causing the ominous creaking that grew shriller with every stride she took.

"Get down! It's going to—"

A massive boom rolled over Rienne, throwing her to the ground. Taran tumbled on top of her, wrenching her arm as he was flung head-over-feet. The rushing sound turned into a whirlwind that whipped at her hair and clothes, pelting her with bits of twig, soil, and small stones, flinging bundles of shredded leaves in her face. She rolled onto her belly, raising her arms to cover her head, and prayed it would stop.

The ground bucked as another loud boom sounded, but then everything went quiet. Unsure if it was over, Rienne cautiously raised her head. When things remained still, she pushed herself to her knees and looked back over her shoulder. General Blaine and Robin were staggering to their feet, and she could see Bull helping Taran to rise. The Adept had a nasty bruise on his temple, but he seemed alright.

"Brynne?"

The sound of her own voice surprised Rienne. She hadn't intended to speak. She strained her eyes, but there was no sign of the trans-Veil tunnel. No sign of Sullyan, either. All she could see was Blaine and Robin standing there, staring at something on the ground.

No, not *on* the ground. As Rienne rose with Bull assisting her, she could just make out what looked like a depression in the earth. She stumbled closer, Bull and Taran trailing her. Just as she got close enough to see, Pharikian and Deshan appeared out of a portway some distance away. They sprinted toward the Albians, none of whom could believe their eyes.

A huge crater, its steep sides and smooth floor glittering with a blue-green sheen, had appeared where the tunnel had been. Rienne stared at the faces around her, each one mirroring her confusion and fear. A light pall of dust rose into the air from the crater, but of Sullyan there was no sign.

Chapter Nineteen

It was a grim party that assembled in General Blaine's office later that morning. Pharikian and Deshan sat with their heads bowed, untouched fellan by their sides. Both had drawn faces, fatigue having taken its toll. The General sat behind his desk, taking refuge, Rienne thought, in the familiar. Bull and Taran sat close to Robin, both watching the stricken young man carefully. He was holding himself together for the moment, but Rienne could only wonder how long his strength would last. He had already pushed himself to his limits helping the two Andaryans scour the Veils for signs of Sullyan. They had found nothing, not even the tiniest clue, and when they had finally admitted defeat, Robin had had to be forcibly dragged back to the Manor.

For herself, Rienne took what comfort she could from Cal's embrace. He was being very attentive. His presence was a support, but even his loving care couldn't ease the ache in her heart. She couldn't begin to imagine what would happen now.

The Hierarch spoke into the strained silence, his voice sounding harsh and old. "Will you send a runner to King Elias? Will he cancel his visit?"

The General lifted his head, his eyes unfocused. His hand strayed automatically to his mug, fingers wrapping around it as if seeking answers from the warmth.

"I have already sent a runner to intercept his Majesty's party, informing him of today's events. I don't expect him to cancel, though. Major Sullyan's … disappearance will not affect the Manor's routine."

"What?"

Robin's sharp tone made Rienne jump. The young man

had straightened from his slumped posture and now stared incredulously at the General.

"How can it *not* affect the Manor's routine? You can't seriously expect us to carry on as if nothing has happened? You can't expect us to put on a show for the King, entertain him and line up for inspection, and just forget the fact that we've *lost* her?"

His words caused a lump to rise in Rienne's throat. An image flashed in her mind, the memory of that empty, smoking hole in the ground. They had lost her. Sullyan was gone. It was impossible to believe.

Blaine cleared his throat and stood. Everyone gave him their attention. "Your Majesty, gentlemen, that is exactly what I expect. We have our duties. Major Sullyan would be the first to acknowledge that. The arrangements for tomorrow still stand. Once the day is over, we will resume our search for the Major."

Robin leaped to his feet. "And in the meantime, she could be anywhere, suffering gods know what!" Bull tried to restrain him, but the Captain flung him off. "Well, I for one don't intend to abandon her. I don't care if it takes the very last ounce of strength I possess—I will not stop looking until I find her. Or die trying!"

Robin stalked from the room. He managed to avoid slamming the door, and Rienne was almost sorry. The noise would have been a distraction.

"I'll go after him, General," offered Bull. "The strain has affected his judgment. He didn't mean that bit about abandoning her."

Blaine made a weary gesture and Bull left the room. The General sat back down, lines of worry etched deep on his face.

Pharikian sighed and caught his eye. "No one will abandon her, Lord Blaine, not until we have done everything we can think of. We will not give up, I can assure you of that."

Blaine nodded and his shoulders sagged. "Will you return to Andaryon now, Majesty? I am sure you need to rest. And Elias would understand should you wish to postpone tomorrow's trade negotiations. He will be as disturbed as the rest of us by today's events." His gaze went to the door through which Robin had disappeared.

Pharikian and Deshan stood, the Hierarch seeming to have lost some of his vigor. "We will return tomorrow as agreed, my Lord. You were right; Brynne Sullyan would not thank us for allowing this situation to interfere with improving relations between our realms. Especially if this was the intention of the Staff's creator. We cannot permit renegades to dictate our actions."

"I agree, Majesty, and thank you. I know King Elias will appreciate your dedication. All will be ready for you on your return. The Manor is honored to host this most auspicious occasion."

Blaine summoned an honor guard and left with the two high-ranking Andaryans, personally escorting them from the Manor. Rienne, with Cal and Taran, made her way to their suite of rooms, heart sore for Sullyan and wondering what would become of them now she was gone.

*****

Baron Reen sat his pacer just to the rear of the King's horse. Elias's honor guard ranged around them, alert as ever for signs of danger. They had made good time since leaving Loxton Castle, cutting the normally three-day journey down to two. There was an eagerness to Elias that had been absent at the Castle, and Reen could only assume that the Queen was right, that Elias enjoyed his visits to the Manor. The Baron supposed any excuse to take a break from the everyday business of ruling Albia was welcome, and Elias was bound to feel gratitude toward the man who had helped him quell the civil rebellion ten years ago. By all accounts, Prince Elias, as he was then, might well have been killed along with King Kandaran had Mathias Blaine not championed his cause.

What favors might Blaine secure from a grateful King? What liberties might such a favored man take? What influences might he exert? Surely those influences could extend to gaining the King's tolerance toward those with arcane and blasphemous powers? Or was it Elias's own inclination to tolerate them?

These thoughts took the Baron's mind from the tedium of the journey. He preferred a carriage to riding horseback. It was far more dignified. Why Elias felt the need to expose himself to the weather like this, Reen could not understand. But then, he understood little about Elias. His Queen, on the other hand—ah, she was a different story.

Just ahead of the Baron, the thirty-year-old King Elias sat his charger with ease. He was dressed soberly, his dark red riding cloak only subtly trimmed with gold. His left hand held his reins lightly, while the other rested on the pommel of his sword. He glanced about him constantly as he rode, adding his vigilance to that of his Guardsmen. Although he had lost some of the tension he often exhibited at the Castle, his body still radiated alertness. Reen might have his suspicions concerning the piety of Sofira's husband, but he knew he should not underestimate Elias's lively mind.

When the young Elias unexpectedly succeeded in reclaiming his murdered father's throne, Reen knew that many influential lords were dismayed by both the acuity of the new King's mental faculties and the liberality of his attitudes. Some of these lords had been involved in Kandaran's murder, and many of them came to regret the untimely death of his father. Elias discounted nothing that might be useful to him, refused to be blinkered by prejudice, and laughed in the face of superstition. He was also a shrewd judge of character. Most of his closest councilors supported him wholeheartedly, and those who did not learned very quickly to guard their tongues if they wanted to keep their positions.

Yet the machinations of lords and councilors interested Reen very little. He needed no other support than that supplied by his position as Sofira's mentor and confidante. No. Reen's interests lay in protecting and promoting Albia's foremost religion, the Faith of the Wheel. He was a regular visitor to Port Loxton's Minster, the seat of Albia's Matria Church, and counted Arch-Patrio Neremiah among his closest friends. He and the Queen attended every service the Arch-Patrio led, and Sofira did her best to see that Elias attended too.

It seemed to the Baron that Elias found far too many excuses not to attend. Surely Albia's High King should set a better example to his people? How were they to convince the populace to attend services if their King rarely did? And how could the Church encourage faithfulness, loyalty, and piety in its followers if the King showed favor to those who practiced blasphemous and arcane arts?

His horse snorted and snatched at the reins, and Reen made an effort to unclench his fists. He hadn't realized he had let himself go that far. He really ought to be more careful. He took a deep breath, trying to calm the anger in his breast.

He started as he heard a cry from up front. Elias's hand went up and the entire company came to a halt. Reen nudged his cob to the side so he could see past Elias. A man in combat leathers drew rein in front of the Guardsman and bowed his head to the King. "Urgent message from General Blaine at the Manor, your Majesty."

The Commander took the leather-bound packet the rider offered and passed it to Elias. Reen tried to edge his horse closer, but Elias shielded the parchment with his body so Reen couldn't see. It didn't take the King long to read, and what he read clearly didn't please him. His movements as he re-rolled the parchment and passed it back to the Guardsman were abrupt.

"Please return to the Manor with all speed and tell Lord Blaine that we will be there as soon as we may. The arrangements are not to be changed."

"Yes, your Majesty."

The messenger inclined his head, wheeled his horse, and galloped away. The King gestured to his honor guard and they picked up the pace, urging their mounts to a canter. Reen's stocky cob was not built for speed and it lurched with every stride. Reen cursed it even as he mused on the contents of the message. Clearly it was serious, otherwise it wouldn't have been grounds for altering the arrangements the King had made. Maybe it was something Reen could work with, a reason to get the King away from the Manor earlier than he intended. Maybe it even concerned Elias's subversive ideas for trading with outlanders. Perhaps something had happened to the demons.

Reen could only pray that it had. This dangerous notion of the King's could well provoke another civil rebellion. Reen intended to do all he could to prevent such an agreement taking place. His plan to stop all such trafficking only lacked one final, crucial detail ….

Chapter Twenty

The Manor personnel rose early on the day of the King's official visit. Robin, who had spent much of the previous day and night scouring the Veils for Sullyan, was forced to call a temporary halt to participate in the preparations. His anger had faded to a dull but persistent ache in his chest, and he went through the motions of his duty with scant interest.

He drilled the Major's company mercilessly in their parade march, as much to divert his mind as to familiarize his two new recruits with the procedure. General Blaine had given permission for Taran and Cal to join the company as honorary members, but despite receiving all the help and encouragement they could wish for, they needed constant practice. Robin kept the company so busy that none of them were aware of the arrival of the two monarchs around midmorning.

Elias's party arrived first. The welcoming ceremony went smoothly. The horses were led away, the honor guard was shown to their quarters in the barracks, and Elias was ushered into the Manor.

Baron Reen followed Elias as the King strode eagerly through the corridors and up the sweeping stairs. The General's manservant showed them into the pleasantly appointed third-story hall where Blaine himself stepped forward to greet them. Reen observed how the King clasped Blaine's hand warmly and spoke to him as an equal. Clearly, the General was still exerting some kind of influence over the most powerful man in Albia. Reen would have to make the Queen aware of this.

The second man in the room was introduced as Colonel Vassa, the former Lord of the Downs. He was known to Elias, but Reen had never met him. He did know some of the man's history; how he had lost his family and his holding to outland raiders, and how Blaine had mustered the locals to fight back, thus saving the Downs, an important agricultural area, from being ravaged by outland brigands. Lord Blaine had suffered severe injury during this time and reportedly nearly died. It was thanks, so the stories went, to a small child named Sullyan that he had survived.

Reen didn't believe this tale for an instant.

Elias barely had time to introduce the Baron when one of the sentries appeared at the door to announce the imminent arrival of the Hierarch of Andaryon. Reen saw Elias's head come up eagerly. The two monarchs had only communicated through messengers thus far, so Elias would be looking forward to indulging his curiosity. Open as he was to new ideas, Elias was intrigued by the Hierarch's unprecedented initiation of these talks. Not much was known about the Fifth Realm in normal circles, and Reen wanted to keep it that way. He wouldn't stand a chance if Elias learned about the Andaryan mines that produced rare gems and metals not found in Albia.

Footfalls could be heard in the corridor outside, and the General's manservant opened the door, bowing low as a tall, patrician figure entered the room, followed by a young page and another man. Reen felt nausea swirl in his stomach at the sight of the outlander king. He was older than Reen had expected, and quite thin, and there were deep lines on his face. But what affected the Baron most were the creature's alien eyes—shockingly yellow with slit pupils like a cat's. He nearly choked with revulsion and had to feign a light cough.

Fortunately, the outland ruler didn't notice. The other man with him, a much shorter man with a long face and a hooked nose, spared Reen a speculative glance. The Baron drew himself up and ignored him.

General Blaine stepped forward and greeted the outland king. "Welcome back, Majesty. I trust your honor guard has been housed to your satisfaction?"

Pharikian inclined his head. "Their quarters are more than satisfactory, Lord Blaine, I thank you."

Blaine then turned to include Elias, and Albia's High King came forward to make his counterpart's acquaintance. The two monarchs shook hands cordially and took a moment to size each other up. Elias spoke first.

"Majesty, I am pleased beyond words to meet you in person, and intrigued by your suggestion that we should conduct talks. In my opinion, such a meeting is long overdue."

"I agree, your Majesty. May this be the first of many."

Not if I can help it, thought Reen. *Don't get too enamored of each other. This could be a very short friendship.* He managed to nod politely when presented to the outlanders, and was puzzled when the second man turned out to be a healer. *Why bring a healer to a trade meeting?*

But the healer, it appeared, had not come for the trade meeting. Instead, he asked the General if he might speak with either Captain Tamsen or Healer Arlen. Neither name meant anything to Reen, but the request clearly didn't surprise Blaine, who called in one of the swordsmen stationed outside the hall.

"Please take Master Healer Deshan to Hal Bullen. He will know where to find Healer Arlen."

"Very good, General. Master Healer, please follow me."

The short man with the hooked nose laid a hand on his ruler's shoulder and nodded to Blaine and Elias. "I wish good fortune on your talks, gentlemen."

He followed the swordsman from the room and Reen waited for someone to explain. No one did, and he wondered if it had something to do with the message Elias had received yesterday. No matter. He was sure he would have an opportunity to find out later, if it was important. Blaine ushered Elias and the outland king toward comfortable chairs at one end of the room while Colonel Vassa turned to Reen and offered to guide him around the Manor. The Baron was irritated at being so blatantly excluded from the monarchs' meeting, but could hardly protest. He agreed with scant grace and allowed Vassa to precede him from the room. A tour of the Manor facilities was preferable to making forced conversation with Vassa, and he might overhear something of interest.

*****

Rienne sat in one of the small rooms in the infirmary, trying to shake off the strange headache she had suffered ever since waking that morning. She had no recollection of having spent a disturbed night. Indeed, they had all slept deeply, exhausted by the events of the day before. Yet she felt hagridden, as if nightmares had plagued her slumbers. Images flashed into her mind at random moments; a raging fire, a dark tangle of trees, the face of a boy, crumpled in either pain or fear. None of these images meant anything to her and the sharpness of them faded fast until only a vague awareness remained in her mind. It disturbed her, and so she had come to the infirmary seeking solace.

The Manor's infirmary had become as familiar to Rienne as the cottage in Hyecombe she had shared with Taran and Cal. In the short time she had been here it had taken on the feel of somewhere she belonged, a place where she was valued and needed. The other healers had accepted her without hesitation, and her skills and willingness to work at whatever tasks she was given had earned her their respect. Her association with Robin and Sullyan had gained her a special place in the eyes of many of the fighting men. Normally, just being here gave her a sense of security.

Not today, though.

She was too acutely aware that everything had changed. Their presence here—hers, Taran's, Cal's—had been dependent upon Sullyan. But Sullyan was gone, and while Rienne could imagine a scenario where the Manor might accept her as a permanent member of its ranks, she wasn't so sure about Taran or Cal. So what would become of them? They would return to Hyecombe, she supposed, back to the life they had led before, and she would go with them. But would they be welcome? Could they ever rebuild their lives there? She didn't think so. She didn't even think she wanted to. Far too much had changed.

She roused from this somber musing when Bull entered the small room. She saw the man accompanying Bull, and her heart lightened for the first time since yesterday's shocking event.

"Deshan!"

She rose and stepped into his embrace. He held her for a while and then released her, holding her arms to look into her face. What he saw made him frown, but he spoke softly enough.

"Did you not sleep last night, my dear?"

She shook her head. "I slept well enough, but somehow I feel like I didn't. I have a nagging headache that not even willow will ease."

Bull took his leave to check on Robin. Rienne sighed and turned back to Deshan.

"I don't suppose you have anything stronger than willow for a headache, do you? I had such odd dreams last night, and they don't seem to want to let me go. They weren't even dreams, really, just strange fragments and images. Some of them were quite frightening."

Deshan raised his head and captured her gaze. "What images? In what way were they frightening?"

She struggled to explain what she had experienced while he watched her face with an expression she couldn't interpret. "They were so unconnected, and quite intense. It was the intensity, I think, that bothered me so. I can't clearly recall one single image now, but the sense of foreboding or danger they gave me won't leave. It's as if I'm being stalked by something, but each time I look over my shoulder, there's nothing there. I wish it would stop. I'm exhausted enough as it is."

Taking a small pouch from his bag, Deshan stood and looked around. "Is there somewhere quieter than this, my dear? More private? I can give you something to soothe that headache, but you will need to lie down for a few minutes in order for it to take effect."

She rose wearily and led him to one of the smaller treatment rooms. He walked beside her with his hand in the small of her back, almost as if he was pushing her. She could swear she felt eagerness in the way he strode along, but when they reached the room and he prepared the herbs for her, his movements were as smooth and assured as ever. She accepted the tasteless potion and drank it in one swallow. All she wanted was to lose that headache.

*****

Although the parade practice had kept Robin's mind from sinking completely into the black mire of depression that threatened to engulf him, still he found time to fret about what the day had in store. The King's inspection, the parade march, and the giving of battle honors were routine, and Robin was well aware that others besides him deserved recognition for what had occurred at Hyecombe. But how could they be so cruel as to put him through a test for Mastery at a time like this? How on earth could Blaine or the Hierarch expect him to concentrate? His whole reason for living had suddenly been taken from him, just when he thought he and Sullyan could finally have a future together.

Fate was just too brutal, and he knew he couldn't cope.

After releasing his tired but much improved company with instructions to grab themselves a bite to eat before the afternoon's events, Robin went back to his quarters. Closing the door firmly behind him, he collapsed into a chair. There was a half-full glass of Bull's favorite liquor on the small table beside him and he scooped it up, nearly spilling some in his fatigue. He knocked the spirit back in one go, grimacing at the fiery burn. A sob threatened to escape the confines of his throat, but he forced it down. He had to hold himself together for his men.

A knock came at his door and he groaned inwardly. Couldn't they give him a moment's peace? He stayed silent, hoping the visitor would go away. After another rap, which he also ignored, the door opened to reveal Bull's anxious face. He stepped inside when he saw Robin, and closed the door behind him.

"What is it, Bull? Can't it wait? I just need a few moments to myself."

Bull crossed the room and sank into the chair opposite Robin. He had brought a plate of food, which he set on the table. He eyed the empty glass. "I saw you come in, and thought you might need something to eat. Pharikian and Deshan are here."

Bull waited, but Robin didn't speak. He sighed. "I'll go if you want. I just …."

Robin opened his mouth to tell Bull to go, but the big man's woeful expression and sorrowful tone stopped him. Bull would be feeling Sullyan's loss just as deeply, and Robin had no right to deny his friend some solace. Instead, he reached out and poured more liquor into the glass, shoving it across the table.

Bull took it and mirrored Robin's earlier actions, draining the glass in one gulp. Robin reached for the bottle again, but Bull shook his head.

"I don't think you ought to have any more, lad. It's going to be a busy day."

The heavy blackness in Robin's heart surged upward and he snapped, "Don't tell me what to do! What are you, my mother? Leave me alone!"

Bull looked taken aback, making Robin immediately ashamed of his outburst. "I'm sorry. I'm strung tighter than a crossbow at the moment and I can't seem to help snapping. I wish today was over."

"Not much longer. There's only the parade and promotions to get through."

Robin stared hard at him. "And one other thing!"

Bull ducked his head. "Yes, well, even under these circumstances you ought to be proud of that. Not many people achieve Master level, and it's something Sully worked hard on. Don't throw all that effort away. Just think what she'd say if she knew you weren't proud of yourself."

Robin sighed. "Wasn't humility one of her watchwords? Dammit, Bull, I'd give anything to have her here yelling abuse at me for feeling like this. I'd suffer any amount of temper and foul language if only she was standing here in front of me. I just can't believe she's gone."

"I know what you mean." The big man hung his head. "I remember how angry she was after your duel with Parren, and that vicious dressing-down she gave me when I disobeyed her orders not to follow her into Andaryon."

Robin nodded. Every man under her command loved Sullyan for her mercurial temper. It was the reverse side of her unique care for them, and weathering her storms of anger was one of the hazards even the lowest cadet learned to accept. They all knew her fury was as just as it was swift, and she never bore a grudge.

Bull sighed. "We'll just have to make the best of it, lad. There's still some hope. No one's given up yet. Let's not hold the wake—"

"—before the bloody funeral!"

As he finished Bull's favorite saying, a small but genuine smile touched Robin's lips. He leaned over and clapped the big man gratefully on the shoulder. Bull nodded meaningfully at the untouched plate of food. Robin grimaced, but obeyed the unspoken order. Once he had eaten as much as his overwrought stomach could take, the two of them made their way out to the parade ground to prepare for the ceremonies to come.

*****

Rienne lay on the bed in the small treatment room, waiting for Deshan's potion to take effect. Her headache seemed to be getting worse rather than better, and she was beginning to fret. She couldn't miss the afternoon's ceremonies. She had to be there to support Robin, Taran, and Cal.

Deshan had taken the chair to one side of the bed and Rienne tried to turn her head toward him. She was going to ask how long it would be before the herbs began to work, but her neck muscles wouldn't obey her. Panic rose within her, but before it could take hold, a warm wash of contentment flooded over her. Deshan's comforting tones sounded somewhere inside her mind.

Just relax, Rienne. You are quite safe. I want you to think about the dreams you had last night. Can you do that for me?

As soon as the word "dreams" was mentioned, the images from her nightmares swam before her eyes. Like flickering flames, they danced for an instant on the edge of her perception then vanished. She couldn't hold on to them long enough to make sense of them.

Concentrate, my dear. There could be clues in these pictures. We just have to work them out.

She felt no irritation at Deshan's commanding tone, just a willingness to do as he said. The next time an image came into her mind she clamped hold of it, refused to let it drift by. It was a dark image, full of shadows which slowly sharpened to become a tangled glade of close-grown trees. What did it mean? It was nowhere she recognized and she felt no pull toward it.

Let that one go, Rienne. Try the next.

She released her hold and waited for another image to fill her mind. This one was easier to hold on to, or maybe she was getting the hang of it. She had never done anything like this before and knew, somewhere deep in her subconscious, that it wasn't all her own doing. But that wasn't important. The pictures were the important part, and it was vital that she examine each one. Concentrating harder than she had ever been able to do before, she gave herself over to the task.

Chapter Twenty-One

A succession of unfamiliar images scrolled past Rienne's inner eye. There were faces—a youth with a terrified expression, two older men—and there were places. The tangled forest glade showed up frequently, but Rienne had no idea why. There were images of a raging fire accompanied by feelings of terror but also of glorious power. At first, Rienne thought the fire images might relate to Sullyan's duel with Rykan, but then she realized her error. Sullyan had certainly felt the terror when Rykan defeated her and trapped her hand in the Firefield, but there had been no glorious use of metaforce.

These images seemed to belong to someone else, someone she didn't know.

All the while Deshan sat beside her, his presence resting quietly within her mind, not interfering, only guiding. She felt no urgency, no sense of frustration, simply a willingness to continue this search through her dreams. The headache had cleared completely and she felt calm and in control. So calm that a tune was playing in her mind, keeping time with her heartbeat. She hadn't noticed it before and couldn't have said when it first started. She felt herself smile, although whether physically or inwardly she didn't know. It was a lovely tune, a familiar tune, and she began to hum the melody.

She sensed Deshan's attention was focused fully upon the tune. This didn't worry her, didn't pull her away from the song. If anything, her immersion deepened until nothing existed but the song. It buoyed her soul and wrapped her heart, its words gradually becoming clearer.

Earth speaks in tones of soil, wood, and stone

Where had she heard those words before? She knew them intimately, yet couldn't place their origins.

An echo that runs through all that we are

She felt herself carried along on the gentle rhythm, her heart still keeping time, and knew it would lead her somewhere safe, somewhere she wanted to go.

Its presence and power sustain on their own

Power was certainly sustaining Rienne. She felt like she could exist this way forever, never needing sleep, food, or drink. The only thing missing was—

But your love gives life meaning, your heart is my home

Ah, yes. Love.

*****

The Manor's parade ground was huge, a rectangular space of packed earth stamped flat by the passage of countless boots and hooves. There was a permanent pavilion at the end of the south side, and this had been decorated with the banners and colors of both visiting monarchs. They fluttered gently in the light breeze, picked out by the weak spring sunshine. As Reen stalked along next to Vassa, behind the General and the two monarchs, he breathed deeply, trying to purge the feeling of uncleanness the outlanders' proximity gave him.

The General showed Elias and the outlander king to their seats. Vassa moved to stand just behind the demon while Reen stayed as far away as possible, taking a stance to the left of Elias and Blaine. The banners and flags suggested a festive air, but Reen could swear there was a somber underlying note. His fanatical gaze strayed frequently to the Hierarch's face, an unhealthy light glowing in his eyes as his holy mission burned in his heart.

Tearing his gaze away, he gnawed on frustration. Surely there was someone here open to persuasion? Someone who could be bribed to pass him information? But they all seemed so loyal and so at ease with these blasphemous beings among them that he was beginning to think he wouldn't be able to initiate his little scheme. He was still brooding on the problem when the parade fanfare blew.

*****

Mounted on Torka, Robin led his men onto the parade ground behind Colonel Vassa's formation. Despite his mood, he spared a thought for Taran and Cal, both highly nervous on their horses behind him. Cal still wore bandages on his mending arm. Thankfully, they kept their heads and remembered their drill, and everything went off smoothly.

All the companies managed to end their sequences at the same time and in their correct places. The sound of their choreographed salute echoed across the parade ground. They stood stock still while King Elias acknowledged their homage and accepted their renewed Oaths of Allegiance. Even the horses behaved.

Once they were stood at ease in their serried ranks, King Elias and General Blaine moved down to the platform jutting out into the parade ground. The trumpeters sounded the royal fanfare, triumphant notes rising high into the air. Sergeant-Major Harker, a strongly built man of medium height with a bullhorn voice, moved out from the ranks of Vassa's troops and came to stand beside the platform. He began barking out names, and those summoned came forward to receive their battle honors for meritorious conduct during the repulsion of the demon invasion.

The last two names were a surprise to everyone, not least to the men concerned. Taran and Cal were astounded to find themselves included in the ceremony, receiving their honorary ribbons from the King with pride and slightly embarrassed bemusement. The heartfelt cheers of Robin's company rang in their ears as they returned to their mounts. Both were grinning inanely.

The next name to be called was no surprise to Robin. Sergeant Dexter had proven himself more than deserving of promotion to Captain, and his youthful face was a picture of pride as he received his single thunderflash rank badge from the King's own hands. The cheering that followed was not restricted to Robin's command, as Dexter was a popular man.

Then Sergeant-Major Harker called out three more names, and

grooms ran forward to take the horses' bridles. Robin realized that young Tad had somehow managed to wheedle a groom's place, and the lad grinned widely as he took Torka's reins from Robin. He, Baily, and Parren approached the royal presence. The King commended them for relieving the siege of Hyecombe and presented their battle honors. Parren shot Robin a venomous look, but Robin, in no mood for his spite, ignored the man.

The King did not step back once the honor ribbons were bestowed, nor did he release the three men before him. Instead he turned around and accepted the rank badge General Blaine passed him. Then he stepped toward Captain Baily and, to the small man's utter amazement, promoted him to Lieutenant-Major.

Even then, the King was not done. Blaine handed him yet another rank badge, and this time he stepped toward Robin, regarding the wary confusion in the young man's eyes with open amusement.

"Captain Tamsen, by courtesy of his Majesty, the Hierarch of Andaryon, I have been fully informed of the part you played in protecting his throne from a challenge by the rebel lord, Rykan. A challenge which, had it succeeded, would have had far reaching ramifications for our own realm. For this service and for your loyalty to Major Sullyan, I hereby promote you to the rank of Major."

Robin was stunned. He had expected to be rewarded—Blaine had told him as much—but not like this. The roar of approval greeting the King's statement was deafening, but Robin couldn't feel any pride. He was suddenly and overwhelmingly certain that his promotion and Dexter's was due to one thing only: the vacancy left by Sullyan's disappearance.

The thought turned his heart to lead.

Robin could barely move his arm to salute the King as Elias pinned the double-thunderflash rank insignia to his jacket. Dismissed, all three men walked back to their mounts, Robin hardly feeling the daring pat on the back he received from an adoring Tad. He barely noticed and certainly didn't worry about the lethal look that Parren, passed over and furious, directed at him.

*****

Baron Reen watched the parade with scant interest. Military men showing off their horsemanship and fighting skills didn't stir his breast. The horns and drums that accompanied such displays hurt his ears. A man's ability to march in step with another man wasn't something Reen admired, so instead he let his eyes roam idly over the faces of the many men before him.

Most of them were quite young, he realized. Most of the King's Guard at Port Loxton were veterans, men of some years' experience, but some of those here were scarcely old enough to be apprentices. Of course, he remembered, the Manor was a training ground for the King's forces, and many of these were probably cadets. *An agreeable age*, he thought, his interest suddenly piqued. *Maybe I should look a little closer ….*

*****

Rienne's heartbeat was tied irrevocably to the gentle strains of the song playing through her soul. Deshan had stopped asking her to concentrate on the images and instead allowed her to float wherever the song would take her. It spoke to the elements of her being, calling on each in turn, confirming her existence within the Great Wheel of Life.

Water's music gives birth to the soul

Its essence surrounds us, feeds all that we are

The hard rain, wild sea, the softness of snow

Runs deep within us as love itself flows

Something buried within the song began calling to Rienne, beckoning her, urging her gently on. She floated, serene, untroubled by thoughts of danger or fear, enveloped by her own empathic psyche. Nothing touched her. Never had she known such feelings of security and belonging. Was this what Sullyan felt whenever she used her powers? If so, then Rienne could well understand what had driven Taran to persevere for so many frustrating years.

Such glorious sensations were surely worth all the failures and perils he had endured.

Fire of the sun pours warmth through the leaves

Life's cradle of heat gives us all that we are

Light for our eyes and the life that we see

Kindling true friendship, your love kindles me

Friendship and love. Rienne had been fortunate enough to experience both in her life, friendship and love deeper and more meaningful than many ever found. Cal was her life mate—no matter that they were not yet wed—and she had bonded closer with Sullyan than she could ever have imagined. She simply could not conceive of a life without the younger woman, and this thought pierced the aura of calm around her, sending a sudden pang like fire shooting through her heart. Overwhelming sorrow flooded her, drowning her. She flailed, and Deshan held her, using his own powers to support her as desperation swept through her.

*****

Standing next to his horse, Robin heard General Blaine murmuring to the King. Both men left the platform, returning to their seats as the assembled companies performed a mass salute. Blaine then conferred briefly with both Elias and Pharikian, and Robin saw the tall Andaryan ruler nod. He stood and accompanied Blaine toward the platform. Sergeant-Major Harker gestured to the trumpeters, who blew another stirring fanfare. In his best parade ground voice, he boomed that the Hierarch of Andaryon, Senior Master Artesan, would now preside over matters concerning those of his craft.

Breathing heavily, Robin tried to compose himself. He had been dreading this moment, and his convictions concerning his promotion had not eased him. He knew he wouldn't be able to concentrate. He didn't want this, he wanted to be elsewhere. He wanted to be searching for Sullyan. But he was trapped. In need of support, he glanced about for Bull, but the big man seemed to have disappeared. Instead, all he saw was the murderous anger in Parren's accusing eyes. He failed to suppress a shudder.

Cal and Taran were called forward to be officially confirmed in their status by the most senior member of their craft. Despite knowing it was coming, they were highly nervous, but Pharikian was merciful, demanding no outward show of their prowess. Placing a hand on each of their heads in turn, he merely confirmed and announced their status—Taran as Adept, and Cal as Apprentice-elite. Giving him the obeisance due a Senior Master, they quickly returned to their places.

The moment Robin was dreading had arrived. Leaving Torka once more in Tad's care, he moved unsteadily to stand before the Hierarch. Pharikian, seeing his pale and stricken face, looked on him with sympathy.

"Major Tamsen," he said, and Robin started at the unfamiliar rank. "I would not normally condone putting you through such an ordeal at a time like this, but General Blaine has assured me that it was Brynne Sullyan's wish that I raise your status. You have earned it, son. It is your right.

"However, as you are now entering the final stages of Mastery, I cannot simply confirm you as I did Adept Elijah and Apprentice-elite Tyler. The ancient codes of our craft require you to prove your ability before us all. I would spare you this if I could, but it is not possible. Do you understand?"

"I understand, Majesty, but I most respectfully beg to decline the test. My mind is not ready."

Such a breach of protocol widened Pharikian's eyes. "I'm afraid it's too late for that. You cannot refuse the test."

Robin felt sick. Sensing his distress, Pharikian leaned forward, his heart in his eyes. "You are capable, young man, believe me. Just complete the test Brynne set you and it will be over. You owe her this. You cannot let her down!"

Robin had no choice. Bowing his head, he tried to hide the resentment in his eyes. He knew he didn't have the physical strength for this, and the last thing he wanted was the humiliation of failing in front of everyone. He knew without looking that Parren's burning gaze was fixed upon him. He felt the weight of the thin man's hatred like a lead yoke on his shoulders. Parren was willing him to fail, and Robin knew he would get his wish. He felt crushed, badly in need of support, and once more looked around for Bull. But the big man was nowhere in sight.

Resigned, he stepped back as Pharikian gestured to Blaine. The task Sullyan had set him all those months ago was the breaking of a Firefield, and Blaine had been chosen to cast it in her absence. The General strode toward the edge of the platform, eyes hard, face stern, and Robin felt him gathering his will and his rarely used strength. Although most of those in attendance were not Artesans and couldn't see the Firefield clearly, there were still amazed gasps as the glittering lines and fiery grids materialized around Robin. Blaine might not often use his power, but he was a Master still. His touch was sure.

Robin hastily tried to gather his friable wits. If only he could find the strength to deal with this quickly, get it over and done with. He spent some time examining the structure, looking for flaws in its construction. He had dared to hope that Blaine might leave him a small loophole that he could use to his advantage, but he soon realized his error. Blaine was a General as well as a Master Artesan, and his integrity would never permit him to do such a thing. Especially not with the King and a Senior Master looking on. No matter how sympathetic he might be, Blaine had a reputation to protect.

Robin accepted he would have to do it the hard way. He felt Taran's and Cal's eyes on him, willing him to succeed, and he wished he could take some strength from them, for his own was woefully inadequate. His shoulders slumped.

*****

Robin's hunch was correct. Captain Parren was watching him avidly, praying hard for his failure. Nursing a bitter rage for the thoroughly humiliating experience of being publicly excluded from the promotion list, Parren laid the blame squarely on Robin. The vicious tongue-lashing he had received from Vassa over his behavior during the siege of Hyecombe, and the Colonel's efforts to impress upon him how grateful he should be to Robin for dropping any formal charges, had done nothing to change Parren's opinion. He had been told he owed the continuance of his military career to Robin's forbearance, but this held no meaning for him. Just the opposite, in fact, for in Parren's eyes Robin's failure to bring charges proved what Parren had always suspected. Robin was weak and spineless. Now he had even more reason to despise the man. As far as Parren was concerned, Robin had always hidden behind his unnatural powers and Sullyan's skirts.

Despite his impotent fury, Parren nurtured a nugget of satisfaction. Sullyan, at least, had got her just desserts. Parren's heart had rejoiced on overhearing the men of her company bewailing her loss. They were all as weak as women for consenting to follow her lead. He would never have demeaned himself so far as to take orders from a woman. Women had no place among fighting men, and the Manor would be stronger without her. He ignored the fact that he had often been forced to obey Sullyan's orders—albeit with sullen reluctance—and that she had surpassed his undeniably considerable weapons skills long ago.

All that was in the past. Her absence, he knew, would leave Robin vulnerable, and Parren had indulged his vicious nature by concocting some very pleasing plans. King Elias's unexpected actions, however, had shattered Parren's dreams of vengeance, for a Major was well above a mere Captain's reach. The very thought of this gross injustice caused Parren to seethe with rage. Sitting stiffly on his horse, he glared murderously at Robin, now and then casting a sullen frown at the small, swarthy man standing on the platform behind Elias. For some reason, the man kept staring at Parren and seemed to have found something to smile about.

Chapter Twenty-Two

Grief swamped Rienne, and she floundered. It was too much. Never had she experienced grief like this. It was almost as if she could feel the anguish of two people, her own and someone else's. The song still pounded through her veins, and she was powerless to assuage the grief that rose with its tempo.

Air with a soft sigh or raging with force

Filling the spaces of all that we are

She felt herself raging with the force of a mighty gale, a tornado of bitterness sweeping through her soul. Deshan was carried along with her, whether by will or by chance she could not tell. His strength sustained her, finally enabling her to dampen the almost uncontrollable bitterness with a milder emotion.

Tempests and zephyrs, the clouds upon their course

Its voice sings so sweetly when love is the source

It was then that Rienne realized she could see a thick, pearly light. It was like trying to peer though soft wool. She could even feel its tendrils on her cheek. And now she was walking—when had that happened? She could hear her own footfalls, or was it just the beat of her heart?

And where had the song gone? Its strain had disappeared, cut off as if it had never been. Rienne felt bereft, as if she had suddenly lost everything that made sense of her life. A sob worked its way up her throat, pushing irresistibly outward. The tiny sound broke into the void left by the song, its echo bouncing back toward her.

Then another echo sounded, and another, but Rienne hadn't let out any other sobs. So where had those echoes come from?

Urged gently by Deshan, Rienne moved forward. The echoes came louder now, originating from somewhere to her left. They were not sobs, as Rienne had first thought. They were far too regular. A heartbeat. Someone else's heartbeat. She turned toward it, drawn unerringly as if tied by a cord.

The beats grew louder and faster until Rienne was nearly deafened. Her whole body shuddered in time to the throbbing, her own heart linking to the sound and racing in time. Something odd was happening within her. She could feel the presence of another person, as if someone else besides Deshan had suddenly entered her mind. Yet this was different, more intimate than Deshan's link with her psyche. This was like being two people inhabiting one body.

Now Spirit rise up and join all these as one

The core of our being, of all that we are

The song returned abruptly, playing like thunder in her ears. She could feel another pair of hands, see through another pair of eyes. Another heart beat inside her breast, and this heart was hurting, fearful and lost. A terrible grief leached out from it, threatening to swamp Rienne's soul. But Rienne was a healer and knew how to give comfort. She reached out with her own heart, pushing love against the grief, comfort against the loss. Wrapping her psyche around the heart, she calmed its frantic beat.

The source of all loving, the heart's labors done

Gradually, she felt something respond. Something that felt familiar. Not knowing why it was important, she knew she must make physical contact with this presence. It was vital to connect on all levels, not just the metaphysical. She reached out a hand into the pearly light, and gave a soft gasp as fingers appeared, seeking hers. They stretched and touched, and suddenly grasped, holding tightly to Rienne's hand as if she were a lifeline.

Drawing on the hand, Rienne saw an arm appear, and then another hand reached out. She took it, the fingers cold but warming as her blood pulsed warmth into the skin. Flawless hands, slender hands with amber skin—she knew whose hands they were.

When two Spirits join, when two souls sing one song.

Rienne drew Sullyan's unresisting body into a close and loving embrace.

*****

The men were beginning to fidget. None of Robin's attempts to break the field had made an impression. He had expected as much and was beginning to despair. He didn't need this, not now. He didn't know what else to do. He was going to have to admit defeat, plead ill-health or something, anything, to get out of this with at least a shred of dignity. He just wasn't strong enough. He didn't have the will to concentrate, not even to end his humiliation. Slumping with misery, he saw the anguish in Pharikian's eyes even as he opened his mouth to plead with the man.

His words never emerged. Pharikian turned his head, frowning as a disturbance sounded at the far end of the parade ground. All heads turned that way, but Robin couldn't see what was happening. There was noise, lots of it, and for a panicky moment he thought they were under attack, especially when most of the troops on the parade ground suddenly drew their weapons. He couldn't move because the Firefield was still intact, steadfastly maintained by Blaine even though the General's attention was also focused on what was happening. Robin was about to call out to him when the people on the parade ground moved back, parting to either side as if a scythe had swung their way.

Robin gasped when he saw the distinctive translucent shimmer of a portway appear over the parade ground. His blood froze. Who would open a portway this close to people? It was madness. He could see the consternation in Blaine's eyes, but the General was powerless to oppose the structure while his psyche was caught up in the Firefield. Their only hope was Pharikian.

He turned to the Hierarch, expecting to feel the man exert his will and prevent the portway from opening. Yet Pharikian had a smile on his face, and Robin's heart shivered within him. Was it possible …?

Jerking his eyes back to the spectacle, Robin held his breath. The portway ceased its shimmer and hung immobile, exquisitely controlled with no leakage whatsoever. It would harm no one unless they blundered into it by mistake, and everyone was keeping a very safe distance from it. Then its color changed, bleeding from grey to red, and a figure appeared within it.

Robin's throat was so tight it was painful. His lungs pleaded for air, yet he didn't have the wit to breathe. All his focus yearned toward the portway, all his hope and strength willing this miracle to happen. When Deshan stepped out onto the parade ground, Robin staggered from disappointment. What was Deshan doing there? Then Rienne stepped out, and his whole body tensed. Rienne held someone's hand, and when another figure appeared dimly through the structure, Robin felt his heart stop completely.

There was an instant of complete silence when Sullyan emerged from the portway into the sunlight of the parade ground. The structure behind her vanished with a soft sigh of air, and the sigh was replaced by a great clamor of welcome from her company, which quickly spread to the rest of the men. Robin's heart restarted with a lurch, sending him forward almost into the Firefield. He had to clench his muscles to stop himself being burned. He stood in shock, gasping for breath, while Rienne and Deshan escorted Sullyan through the cheering men and up to the platform.

She was unsteady on her feet, he could see that, and looked a little dazed, but otherwise she seemed unharmed. Elias and Pharikian approached her and she went down on one knee. Elias moved swiftly to raise her, his hand beneath her elbow to help her stand.

"Your Majesties, please forgive my late and dramatic entrance. It was not my intention, I assure you."

Elias snorted. "Under the circumstances, Major, there is nothing to forgive. We are all very pleased to see you safely returned."

Bowing her head, she released his hand and turned to Pharikian. The Hierarch held out his own right hand and she took it in both of hers, pressing it lingeringly to her cheek before kissing the royal amethyst. He said nothing. The moisture in his eyes and the expression on his face told all.

Completely forgotten by the cheering crowds milling around the Firefield, Robin stood forlorn and stunned. He could not have moved even had he possessed the strength, for it was not permitted to break a test for Mastery without the permission of the senior Artesan present. Fortunately, Pharikian recalled the task at hand. Nodding toward Blaine, he gently alerted Sullyan to what was taking place. She caught Blaine's eye and smiled at him. He shook his head in relief.

When she finally faced Robin and met his eyes, the pang of love that shot between them made her sway. It very nearly brought Robin to his knees.

"Sullyan!" he whispered, stretching out a hand as if he could reach her. His fingertips brushed the Firefield and sparks crackled sharply in the air. He snatched his hand back. "*Sullyan!*" he pleaded more urgently.

She was clearly fighting with her own emotions, struggling for breath. In such charged and awkward tension, she did the only thing she could.

"Captain—oh, your pardon," she said as she caught sight of the double thunderflash on his breast, "*Major* Tamsen. I do believe you are under test."

Her forced smile begged him to forgive her.

He was astounded, unable to believe she would prolong his agony. There were murmurs among the crowd, and even Rienne looked concerned. But this was the only way. Doubtless, Sullyan knew Robin would never forgive himself if he failed now.

Her voice gaining strength, the light of love never leaving her eyes, she said, "You have been set a test, Major. Are you going to let me down?"

Swallowing painfully, Robin acknowledged his dilemma. He was going to have to complete the test if he wanted to hold her in his arms once more. But he was still in trouble. He really didn't have the strength, and the shock of her incredible re-appearance had only drained him further.

"Major," he said, trying to pitch his voice for her ears alone, "I can't do it. I couldn't get the hang of breaking it the way you did. I never have. It just won't work for me."

Cocking her head, she regarded him. "Oh, Robin, I did not make the rules. I never said you had to do it my way. Find your own path."

Her words struck something inside him. For some reason it had never occurred to him that there were other ways to break the field. She had used her hands as a focus for interrupting and dispersing the power, but that had never worked for him. Was there something else that might? He narrowed his eyes in thought, searching for an answer. Then, slowly, he began to smile.

He held out both hands, palms upward. Drawing on his will, concentrating on the space between his hands, he called forth a shaft of Fire and held it there. Molding it to his will, he forged it until it became a glowing, flaming sword across his hands.

Sullyan nodded, pride shining in her eyes. "Yes, my love!"

Taking the hilt of his creation in both hands, he raised it high above his head. He saw Taran grinning, and knew the man recognized the powerful overhead stroke Robin used to bring the fiery blade whistling around him. He wasn't the only one to let out a joyful cry of triumph as it connected with the Firefield in a shower of sparks, shattering the glowing cage completely.

*****

The cheers and roars of approval were deafening. Ignoring them all, Robin broke with protocol again. Without waiting for Pharikian's formal confirmation, he sprinted for the platform, leaping the steps to gather Sullyan into his arms. Under the circumstances, the Hierarch forgave the new Master his impetuousness.

Sullyan was fighting for breath when Robin finally released her. Her terrifying experience had drained her, and she was being supported solely by the stubbornness of her will. Her body was trembling with emotion.

Robin was also unsteady as he stood by her side, his face pale and his heart thumping. He had no breath for speech. To give them time to compose themselves, General Blaine came forward, offering the new Major and Master Artesan his congratulations.

Robin shook his hand and returned the General's grin. Then Blaine turned to Sullyan and laid a hand on her shoulder.

"You witch! You always did know how to make an entrance."

She covered his hand with her own. "Believe me, Mathias, that was one entrance I would much rather not have made."

King Elias stepped into her view. "I think we'd better get on with things, my Lord. The … Major looks like she could do with some rest."

His slight hesitation made her frown, but his next act stretched her eyes wide. Extending his hand to Blaine, he accepted a rank badge. Then he moved around to face her and spoke in formal tones.

"Major Brynne Sullyan. For services rendered to the Crown of Albia, both here and in the Fifth Realm of Andaryon, for actions beyond the call of duty, and in recognition of your skills and unwavering loyalty, we hereby accord you the rank of Colonel."

To her utter amazement, he pinned a triple-thunderflash rank insignia to the dress jacket she wore. Giving a small gasp, she stared at him. Then, remembering protocol, she saluted as best she could.

Elias returned her homage with a smile. Lowering his voice so that only she would hear him over the resurgence of cheers from the men, he told her, "There is a matter which we need to discuss privately, but it can wait until you're stronger." She bowed her head over his ring, her eyes brimming. "Besides," he continued, "I believe your ordeal is not yet over."

She gave him a puzzled glance. He didn't speak again, moving away as Blaine and Vassa came over to offer their congratulations. Once they were done, the Hierarch approached her.

"My child," he said gently, "I am so very glad to see you returned, but we will share our joy later. Now, there is another matter over which I must preside. You may think it inopportune, and I ask your forgiveness, but this is actually a very appropriate moment. This is your natal day. Twenty-four years ago today, almost to the hour, your mother gave you life. Because of this, all four elements are in concord with your psyche. And so, Brynne

Sullyan, Artesan Master-elite, I have decided to set you your final test of Mastery."

Robin gasped in protest and stepped forward, but Sullyan waved him back. "No, Robin, his Majesty is right. Today is a very appropriate day. As he says, twenty-four years ago today, I was born. A short while ago, thanks to Deshan and Rienne, I was reborn, for they showed me the way back when I could not find it. And so, this is a doubly special day."

She turned back to the Hierarch. "I accept the trial, Majesty. What is your test?"

Pharikian smiled down at her, approval in his eyes. "It is very simple. I merely require you to demonstrate your Mastery over each of the four elements."

Sullyan inclined her head before turning to Robin. "Will you help me? I feel I need a little strength."

He frowned as he bent forward to take her arm. "Are you sure this is a good idea?"

She gazed up at him, fathomless love warming her soul. With a gentle hand, she caressed his cheek. "It will be alright, Robin. I just need your support for a while, that is all. As I always will."

Unable to refuse, Robin lent her some strength. As she moved to the platform railing another crescendo of cheers greeted her and tears came to her eyes. Eventually, an expectant hush fell. Sullyan felt her pupils dilate as she concentrated her will.

For a moment, nothing happened. Then the massed men on the parade ground began to shift as they realized they could feel a tremor beneath their feet. Horses stamped and snorted. The air in the arena grew hazy, becoming opalescent. Those in the pavilion, and especially those who were Artesans, could see the telltale shimmer of Earth's puissance rising from the ground, arcing upward to be held in place like a shield over the area. Sunshine slanted through the pearliness, and the men glanced around in amazement. Some even reached out as if they could touch the haze that flowed and shimmered before their eyes.

Then the air grew moist as Water condensed out of the atmosphere. It didn't settle on the ground or their clothes—rather it hung over their heads like a dome of droplets, glittering in the sunlight like miniature stars, casting tiny, perfect rainbows through the pearly shimmer. The effect was quite stunning.

Sullyan breathed deeply, knowing Robin was keeping an eye on her. He held tightly to her arm to support her. She was becoming rapt in her expenditure of power, and ignored the drain on her energies.

Her pupils were as wide as they could go, and even Pharikian was impressed when she called Fire while still maintaining control over the other two elements. Her Fire came in the form of a myriad of tiny flashes of lightning, sparking within the misty cloud. They shattered the miniature rainbows, which reformed again and again. Sullyan smiled despite the tiny beads of perspiration gathering on her brow. Was it from the strain of being lost in the Veils, or the effects of controlling so much power? She neither knew nor cared. This was glorious.

A sound began to swell. It started gently, like a sigh, growing in depth and tone until it thundered like a rushing waterfall. The misty dome of Earth and Water began to shimmer, rolling and bulging like some giant bubble. The flags and banners around the arena snapped and streamed as a powerful warm wind caught them. Dust motes swirled among the rainbows, gyring into the air.

Sullyan closed her eyes, feeling her energy drain. Robin stirred beside her. “Enough!” he hissed. She didn’t reply. She couldn’t afford to break her concentration. She needed to reaffirm her control over her powers, and she needed to experience once more the dizzying elation of glory that only came with testing one’s power to its limits.

Reaching deep within to her final reserves, she spread her fingers, arms at shoulder height. The wind she had called raced sunwise around her display, spinning the mist, Fire, and Earth-shimmer up into an elegantly twisting column. It reached for the sky, extending hundreds of feet before abruptly snapping upward, vanishing into the blue.

There was stunned silence. Then her audience burst into wild acclaim, roaring their approval and stamping their feet. Sullyan slumped, panting, caught immediately by Robin. Pharikian, his eyes full of loving admiration, approached her. There was an expression of intense pride on his face.

To Sullyan's embarrassment, the Hierarch of Andaryon, Timar Pharikian, Senior Master Artesan, knelt before her and accorded her the brow-lips-heart salute owed to the Mastery she had shown. Then he stood and confirmed her status. Every Artesan present accorded her the same homage and she waved her acknowledgement, her vision blurring with tears.

Pharikian stepped closer and put an arm around her shoulders. "That was an astonishing display, child. Especially coming so soon after your recent traumatic experience. I will want to hear the details, but first you need to rest and take some sustenance." He turned to the two men behind him. "Your Majesty, General Blaine, might I suggest we go somewhere more private?"

The General inclined his head and gestured for Colonel Vassa to lead the way back to the Manor. Elias walked beside Sullyan as Pharikian turned her to follow them, his arm still around her shoulder. "I don't want the details yet, but I have to ask. Did you succeed in destroying the Staff?"

She glanced up at him. "Oh yes, the device has been completely destroyed."

Nodding in satisfaction, Pharikian led her from the parade ground.

Chapter Twenty-Three

The party walking away from the pavilion spared not one glance for Baron Reen. His presence was clearly not required, and certainly didn't warrant concern. At any other time this would have caused him severe irritation, but not now. Right now, he could hardly have cared less if no one thought of him ever again.

He was frozen in place, his hands gripping the back of a chair. He stared at nothing, his eyes wide, mouth agape. A tremble began in his fingers that slowly climbed to his shoulders. As it reached his chest, the thumping of his heart sped up.

Words echoed around his mind, the woman's voice scouring his nerves.

"The device has been completely destroyed."

He lurched as nausea rolled in his guts, his fingers losing their grip. One hand flew to his mouth as bile suddenly rose in his throat. He doubled up, swallowing painfully, but the battle was lost. His plans, his world, maybe his very existence, had been wiped away by those simple, terrible words.

"... completely destroyed."

Swaying to one side, Reen flailed for support. He was dizzy, he couldn't focus his eyes. His legs refused to hold him as he stumbled toward the back of the pavilion. His stomach heaved again and he collapsed to the grass, explosively losing his lunch.

*****

The senior officers' hall was a large and airy room. It occupied the entire width of one wing and boasted full length windows along one wall, giving stunning views of the Manor grounds.

The wood-paneled room was comfortably appointed with

plenty of easy chairs and couches. It boasted two large hearths, one at either end, which brought welcome warmth to the walls and flagged floor. A long refectory table laden with all manner of foods sat along the wall opposite the windows, and the spicy aroma of fresh fellan pervaded the air.

The room was busier than usual as there were people present who would never normally be invited through the door. Robin had the right since his promotion to Major, but Bull, Cal, Taran, and Rienne had all been included at Sullyan's request. Colonel Vassa, General Blaine, Timar Pharikian, his page, and Master Healer Deshan made up the full complement.

Sullyan was feeling weak and had not been able to hide this from Deshan. She only got as far as the nearest couch before he firmly ordered her to sit. Bull and Robin waited on her hand and foot. Realizing the futility of protest, she accepted their attentions with good grace. Once everyone else was comfortably seated and served with fellan, General Blaine opened proceedings by formally introducing Sullyan's companions, ensuring that Elias was aware of their talents and status.

Since his unprecedented acceptance of her Oath of Allegiance at Loxton Castle eight years ago, Elias had followed Sullyan's career with great interest and knew some of her history. The events of the past few months, however, needed fleshing out in greater detail, and Blaine quickly dealt with them, inviting comments from Robin as necessary. He glossed over their suspicions concerning the Staff and a possible plot against Artesans, as there was a pressing matter to be dealt with.

Once Blaine fell silent, Elias glanced at Sullyan. She was curled on the couch beside him, Robin at her feet as usual. The sandy-haired monarch smiled warmly.

"Colonel, are you able to recount your experiences now? We are all intrigued by what happened. We don't want to tire you, but some of us have a most urgent curiosity."

He glanced at Pharikian, who nodded.

Sullyan took a breath and placed her cup on the small table at her elbow. It was instantly refilled by Robin, who knew it would take a deal of strong fellan to get her through the next few days.

Thanking him with a glance, she laced her hands around her knees while she ordered her thoughts. Then slowly, mainly to give Elias some points of reference, she recounted her experience of using Rykan's Staff to purge his poison. Once Elias understood some of the Staff's properties and capabilities, she told him the tale of its destruction.

Elias was fascinated, and when she was done, he asked Rienne for her account of how she had found Sullyan's psyche. The healer gave him a shy smile.

"I hadn't planned to go searching for Brynne at that moment, your Majesty. In fact, I wasn't feeling too well. I'd had a bad night and was still suffering with a headache my herbs couldn't cure. So when Deshan came to see me, I asked him for something stronger. It was while I was waiting for his potion to work that I somehow slipped …" She stopped and stared accusingly at Deshan. "You planned for that to happen! You didn't give me a headache cure—you drugged me!"

Cal rounded instantly on Deshan. "Is that true? Did you drug Rienne without her knowledge?"

The Master Healer smiled calmly. "I came today with the intention of testing whether Rienne's unique bond with Brynne could be used to track Brynne's psyche." He cocked his head at Rienne. "I apologize, my dear, for my little deception, but I needed you fully relaxed. I feared that if I told you, tension and anxiety would cloud your mind and prevent you from being open to your link with Brynne."

Rienne waved a hand, dismissing his apology. Cal, however, wasn't mollified. She ruffled his hair and he subsided. Then she related how she had used the music she had heard to help her find Sullyan's psyche.

Elias shook his head. "I see that there is much I do not understand, and probably never will. We shall leave it at that, and simply be thankful for the strong ties of friendship." He leaned back on the couch, appreciatively sipping the fresh fellan Bull handed him. Then his gaze fell on Pharikian. "So then, tell me about this artifact—the Staff. How did your Lord Rykan get hold of it? Where did it come from?"

Pharikian pursed his lips. "We cannot fully answer that, Elias. We have no clear evidence as to its origins, only guesses. And we only have theories as to how and why it was made."

"Tell me your theories then, if you will."

The Hierarch relayed all the information and discussions he and Sullyan had had before the Staff's destruction. He finished by telling Elias how certain he was that no one in Andaryon had created the device.

Elias's sharp blue eyes narrowed in displeasure. "Are you saying the Staff was devised and made here, in Albia?"

Pharikian spread his hands. "It is pure speculation. We offer the theory simply because it is the only one making any kind of sense. None of the other realms have ever given us cause to think they would conspire against Artesans, and I doubt whether any of their nobles would be wealthy enough to afford the raw materials. In Albia, however, not only do you have many wealthy and influential nobles capable of funding the device, but also—and I beg your pardon, Elias—Artesans are generally reviled. It would be perfectly possible for such a powerful Artesan to exist here without anyone's knowledge. I can easily credit that Rykan found, or was found by, an Albian ally.

"Those are our theories, and only one question remains. Do you have any thoughts on who could be behind such a plot? We need to identify them quickly, for they will likely be furious at the collapse of their plans, not to mention the destruction of such a rare and costly artifact."

Elias's eyes hardened. He clearly didn't like what he had heard. Sullyan could see that Pharikian's all-too-plausible theory had put him on the back foot. He had not expected such a hypothesis and was unsure how to respond. Yes, there were plenty of self-serving and ambitious nobles in Albia and although the King bestowed close—and unwelcome—attention on some, he could not keep an eye on each one. This was precisely why he had appointed Blaine as his General-in-Command after the civil war, ordering him to inspect, shake up, and re-fortify every garrison in every province. Elias quite rightly didn't intend to suffer his father's fate, and was not so naïve as to believe that every lord who had been involved—or had approved of—King Kandaran's murder had been killed, bound over by treaties, or rooted out and exposed.

Although Elias could name no immediate suspects, he would know that Pharikian's theory could quite easily be fact. He could express his willingness to accept it in principle, but she thought he probably wasn't quite sure yet how far to trust his brother monarch. Their respect and liking for each other, mutual and instant though it was, was young. She hoped he had no wish to jeopardize its growth, yet she could see he wasn't inclined to discuss any of his realm's underlying problems.

She turned to Pharikian. "Majesty, King Elias needs time to assimilate what he has heard and, if he feels it politic, make some discreet enquiries of his own. After all, this is a delicate matter which requires careful handling. In the meantime, we, as Artesans, need not be idle. If there is a highly ranked and undiscovered Master Artesan in Albia, we need to find him. We have our own resources for that. And if, as we suspect, he was coerced, then he might need our help. Nothing more need be decided at present."

Elias regarded her, his face slowly clearing to reveal a smile. "Colonel Sullyan, I can see why you are valued as a diplomat. I am fortunate indeed to have found such a talented Envoy. That was very tactfully put.

"Timar, I beg your indulgence. I do not wish to belittle the problem or seem unconcerned, but I have received no hint of a threat to Albia or its Crown. You are suggesting that someone with great political power as well as vast wealth has thrown their weight behind this plot, if that's what it is, and we need to establish that before we go looking for culprits. I need time to consider the implications of such potentially damaging investigations."

Pharikian inclined his head with no trace of disappointment. Sullyan thought it was what he had expected, and that he would have said the same himself.

Stirring beside Elias, her soft murmur broke the silence. "There is yet another consideration. One which has not yet been raised or discussed."

Both monarchs sharply turned their heads. Regarding each, reluctant to voice her thought, she said carefully, "Due to the enormous cost and rarity of its components, we have assumed that the artifact I destroyed was unique."

Pharikian's face paled and Elias frowned, still not fully aware of the Staff's significance.

Staring into the Hierarch's wide yellow eyes, she said, "What if there is another?"

It was the one question none of them had even considered, and she almost regretted voicing it. Up to now, only she had felt the full force of the artifact. Taran had handled and used it briefly, and had experienced the pain and terror of its alien forces, but his experience had been fleeting. Now that they knew more about the device and its potentially lethal purpose, however, the possibility of a second weapon affected almost everyone in the room. There was an instinctive, almost physical, drawing-together, as if for protection.

"We *must* find out who is behind this," she said.

Chapter Twenty-Four

It was some minutes after the monarchs had left that the Baron emerged from behind the pavilion. White-faced and shaking, he glanced in disgust at the square of finely-worked linen in his hand. Once pristine white, it was now soiled with vomit. He cast it to the ground before wiping his hands fastidiously on his robe, brushing bits of grass from the rich fabric.

They had destroyed the Staff! It was unthinkable. Rykan, damn his lying tongue, had told them the Staff was indestructible. Well, that just served them right for trusting the word of demons and outlanders.

Reen took a few cautious breaths and straightened his back. This was a complete disaster, and he wasn't quite sure yet just how bad it might be. The Queen would have to be told, and he winced as he imagined her frightened and furious reaction. She would be distraught at the thought that Elias might discover her involvement. But he wouldn't. They had been clever. The letter was safe, all their safety measures firmly in place. Elias had no reason to suspect his Queen.

So. How to salvage something from this dreadful mess? Reen still had his master plan, the plan he had devised once they had learned of Rykan's death. He also had his secondary plan, much more important now that the Staff was gone for good.

He cast about the arena, where all who remained were men on cleanup detail. The one he needed to speak to was nowhere in sight, but thanks to Vassa's tour earlier, Reen had a good idea where he might be found. Slowly at first, but then with steadier steps, he moved away from the pavilion.

There was only one figure at the horse lines when Reen arrived, and the Baron gave a small smile. As he had thought, his quarry was not in the mood for company. That was all to the good. He waited silently, not troubling to hide himself but not intruding either. He was a man who knew how to bide his time.

The object of his scrutiny was unsaddling a grey stallion at the picket rail, his rapid, jerky movements and muttered curses betraying his anger. He tugged at the cinch buckles, giving the stallion's belly a punch when they wouldn't come loose. The horse grunted and sidestepped, and the lean man yanked on its halter rope, cursing aloud. Reen smiled and subtly shifted his body.

The movement alerted the man, who raised his head, staring straight into Reen's gaze. He frowned. "What do you want? I'm busy."

The Baron didn't reply. Rudeness was nothing less than he had expected. He chose not to take offence at the young man's attitude or reprehensible lack of manners. This embittered young man might just hold the key to success, so his initial interview had to be conducted with care. Despite his crushing disappointment, overwhelming anger, and justifiable fear, Reen was not about to throw this opportunity away by allowing his emotions to rule him.

The man went back to unsaddling his horse while Reen eyed him. He was now patently ignoring his noble visitor. Having decided on his opening gambit, Reen said, "Captain Parren, would I be correct in thinking that you were unjustly slighted today?"

Parren's head came up sharply, his strangely empty eyes narrowing. The Baron, who was affecting interest in the grey stallion, flicked him a glance, pleased he had succeeded in capturing the young man's attention. Absently, he brushed the stallion's nose.

"How do you know my name? Who are you?"

Once again, the Baron chose to ignore Parren's rudeness. He also ignored the question. "I had heard that the liberation of those poor villagers was mainly your doing, yet you barely received the King's recognition for such a courageous act. Was it then not true?"

Parren drew in a breath then paused. Instead of the angry retort

Reen was sure he wanted to make, he replied tersely. "I was involved in the relief of the village, yes."

Reen wanted to shout for joy, but calmed his leaping heart. He looked Parren in the eye. "Oh, come now, there's no need to be modest with me. You did all the hard work and took all the risks, yet received no reward. Why should that be?"

Parren leaned against the stallion's flank, his saddle over one arm. He regarded Reen suspiciously. "Why are you asking? What is it to you?"

The Baron damped his growing irritation at Parren's abrasive and disrespectful manner. He had found the right person, and it was up to him to handle the situation correctly. One wrong move and he could lose this potentially valuable ally. A much-needed lesson in good manners and respect for his betters could wait.

He gave a casual shrug. "I recognize injustice when I see it, that's all. The other two Captains received honors and promotion for their part, yet you were blatantly and publicly passed over. Why would the King do that?"

Parren's expression soured and he spat in the dirt. Had his commanding officer seen him, the offense would have been punishable by the removal of privileges. Considering Reen's rank, it might even have merited more stringent disciplinary action. Clearly, Parren was beyond worrying about disciplinary action.

"My face doesn't fit," he said harshly. "They stick together, these witch-lovers."

Reen eyed the livid scar running down the side of Parren's face. "Ah, yes," he murmured, feigning comprehension, "I have heard this before. They conspire together to further their own interests and deny those who are more deserving."

Parren frowned, showing the beginnings of a reluctant interest. "I gather you're not in favor of these so-called Artesans, then?"

Certain of his man now, Reen threw caution away. "*Artesans!* That's nothing more than a fancy name for practitioners of evil, of unnatural crafts! There are those who would see every last one of them eradicated from society, especially from any position of power. But it is very difficult to discredit them when they can sense they are being watched. You have seen for yourself how they have beguiled the King. He is completely under their spell."

Still wary of the Baron's intentions, Parren continued to stare. Reen, however, knew he had hooked his quarry. All he needed to do was prime him.

He deliberately held Parren's gaze. "Would you count yourself among those who feel that Albia would best be served by eradicating these abominations—these Artesans?"

Parren's expression shut down immediately and he turned his head away. "That's uncomfortably close to treason, and whatever my personal feelings, I'm no traitor."

"Of course you're not, and you've nothing to fear from me." Reen hid a private smile. This abrasive young man was so suspicious! "I've already told you what I think, and I have much more to lose in my position than you do in yours, believe me."

"What do you want?" Parren's irritation surfaced once more.

Reen leaned forward conspiratorially. "What we need, young man, are like-minded and intelligent people prepared to watch and report to those in a position to act. People who will help stamp out this cult of witchcraft before it spreads once more. You have seen for yourself today that our King does not know his own mind. He has been manipulated into giving them his support. He is not to blame. He was very young and impressionable when Lord Blaine helped him regain the Crown, and it is natural that he should feel gratitude toward the man. But Blaine has already been more than adequately rewarded for his support. General-in-Command of the King's fighting forces ought to be sufficient for anyone, let alone someone of the middle nobility. But in exerting his evil influence to gain the King's endorsement of the Artesan cause, Blaine has overstepped the mark and shown his true allegiance. We feel this is a dangerous development. Who knows how much further he might persuade Elias to go?

"No, Captain, this state of affairs cannot be tolerated. We who are loyal to the Crown are obliged to do our duty, however uncomfortable it may be. Anyone who helps release our King from his thrall will eventually win his gratitude, and the gratitude of all Albia besides."

As it was designed to do, this impassioned speech reassured Parren, whose essential nature now reasserted itself. "And apart. from gratitude, what reward might there be for someone willing to undertake such a dangerous mission? It would be extremely perilous considering how powerful some of these people are."

The hook was in. Inwardly Reen was laughing, but he replied seriously enough. "The reward for loyal service would be great, although much would depend on the personal ambitions of the informant, as well as the quality of the information. But opportunities for advancement would be many, for our cause has some powerful adherents. Some of them hold—what shall I say?—exalted positions at court."

As he said this, he looked Parren full in the eyes, completely capturing the young man's attention. Lowering his voice, causing Parren to lean toward him, he added, "Where resides our greatest benefactress."

Parren's gaze was held long enough for him to fully realize the import of Reen's words. Seeing shocked comprehension dawn in those pallid green eyes, the Baron continued. "As you see, Captain, I spoke nothing less than the truth. The potential for favor and advancement is bounded only by the limitations of the informant."

He could see that Parren was well and truly caught. The implied lure of gold and power had done its work once more. Still the young man hesitated, and Reen had to admire his tenacity. There must be a core of deeply-seated distrust in Parren's soul to make him still suspicious after all Reen had said.

"That's all well and good, but you don't know what these people are like. They're powerful—they're untouchable! They can read minds and sense things before they happen. How on earth can normal people fight against that?"

A valid point, thought Reen. If Parren had been even mildly nobly born, and able to overcome his selfish and abrasive nature, he might have made a useful courtier. Still, a sword didn't have to be made of the finest steel to kill a man. Iron worked just as well.

Keeping his voice low, he said, "Do you think we haven't thought about this? Do you think we don't have plans in place?

There are ways to fight arcane powers, you know. These so-called Artesans are not invincible."

"But—"

"Do not presume to question me!" Reen deliberately let his anger show, knowing his quarry was caught. "It should be enough for you to know that there are ways. You are a simple Captain. Judging by today's events, you are likely to remain so to the end of your days. Think yourself fortunate that you have been given an opportunity to rise far above your lot in life. Are you willing to take a stand for what you know is right, or will you creep cravenly away? Which do you want, Captain? Acclaim and glory, or a wasted life?"

Parren remained silent and Reen said no more, confident he had done everything necessary. He moved slowly away, but after a few steps he added over his shoulder, "Think about what you have heard. There is no doubt in my mind that you were unjustly slighted today, and that you deserve far more than you received. We could easily redress that situation, but the decision—and your future—rests in your hands. Should you wish to speak with me further, send a runner to Baron Reen.

"Captain," he emphasized the title, indicating that it could easily be more impressive, "I bid you good day."

*****

Before departing for Port Loxton early the following day, High King Elias had one more surprise for Sullyan. In a private meeting, much to her astonishment, he revealed his plans to build a college dedicated to the training of Artesans. The college would be situated within the Manor grounds, for the specific reason that Elias wanted Sullyan to be its administrator.

Once she recovered from her amazement, the prospect filled Sullyan with elation. Yes, it would mean extra duties on top of her other commitments, but Elias assured her he had already spoken with General Blaine and that he was willing to grant Elias his wish. She could hardly refuse when providing such training had been a long-held personal desire. Elias left, promising to begin work on the new college building as soon as possible, and also to give serious consideration to the theories he had heard concerning the Staff.

Elias was of the opinion that once news of the college was made public, some rats would be flushed from their holes. That is, if the Staff's destruction hadn't already accomplished this. He agreed to set up a network of informants to watch those nobles he considered most likely to rebel. Elias's new and rapidly widening runner system—a stable of Oath-sworn and dedicated messengers answerable solely to the King—would ensure secure and private communications. Until they had some solid evidence to act upon, there was little else the King could do.

Pharikian and his entourage left at the same time, the two monarchs taking a most cordial farewell. The Hierarch took with him a list of possible trade items. He and Deshan bade Sullyan an emotional farewell, extracting a promise that she and her friends would visit before too long.

Just before the King's departure, Baron Reen received a hastily worded request. Smiling malevolently, he managed to find time to meet once again with a certain disaffected young Captain. They spoke in secret, conducting a curt but mutually satisfying interview at which a certain amount of gold changed hands. They parted, one more than satisfied with a weighty purse tucked into his jacket, the other feeling more optimistic about the future of his plans.

Reen just had one more act to accomplish. He deliberately sought out the newly promoted Major Tamsen. Robin was surprised when the swarthy, dapper Baron chose to congratulate him on his recent successes. He was more surprised when the man made a point of shaking Robin's hand, nearly crushing it in the process. The Baron unnecessarily prolonged the handshake, and his expression was curiously intense. When he finally clapped Robin on the back and moved away, the Major stared after him, a frown on his face. But then he was called to attend his duties and soon forgot the strange encounter.

The Baron rejoined the Albian royal party in his customary position at Elias's elbow. He could not precisely be described as pleased by recent events, but he was at least sufficiently satisfied to be his usual caustic self as Elias's entourage set off for the three-day return journey to Port Loxton.

*****

Two days after the King's departure, a visitor came to Sullyan's chambers. Robin was about his new afternoon duties as a Major, so she was alone when Taran tapped deferentially at her door. She welcomed him and took him through to her private rooms, where sunshine slanted warmly through the windows and the sounds of men drilling could faintly be heard outside. She could guess what was on his mind. She had been waiting for this, and had he not come to see her, she would have sent for him before the day was out. She would not preempt him, however, and was content to let him speak his mind in his own time.

Sitting opposite him, she sipped her drink. She knew he was watching her. She could clearly feel the strong undercurrent of desire that he always tried so hard to suppress. It seemed that his feelings for her were as deep as ever. There was nothing she could do about that, and she hoped that his emotions—and his embarrassment over them—would not get in the way of this conversation. Sensing him gathering courage, she dragged herself out of her thoughts.

Taran took a breath and said lamely, "You're looking much better now."

She resisted the impulse to laugh. "Why, thank you, Taran. I feel much improved."

He glanced down before forcing himself to look at her. His aversion to what he had come to say was so strong it was almost visible. "I suppose it's about time we left the Manor." He was unable to hold her gaze and his eyes slid away. "Our part in all this is over now. There's nothing more we can do to help. We shouldn't presume any longer on the General's goodwill."

Falling silent, he stared down at his cup.

Sullyan sat very still. Casually, she asked, "Would you return to Hyecombe?"

His shoulders sagged and moisture gleamed in his eyes. "I … I don't think we could. I'm sure Rienne would be welcome, but I doubt if any of them would be pleased to see me or Cal. Not after what happened."

She tucked her legs beneath her. "Then where would you go?"

Taran looked thoroughly miserable. "I don't know. We'd have to look for somewhere else, somewhere we're not known. It won't be easy, but Rienne's skills will help. I expect we'll find somewhere."

She remained silent for a moment longer before saying softly, "So, Adept Elijah, with no place to go to, why would you want to leave?"

His head snapped up and he frowned, his eyes still limpid with tears.

She was unable to curb her grin any longer. "Oh, Taran! Have you learned no better of me than that? You are a loved and a dear friend, as I have told you more than once. Did you not believe me? I owe my life to you and Rienne, even to Cal for his great courage in holding out against Sonten's torment. Had he not, the Staff might well have been lost. Did you think I would not reward such sacrifice, such service? Did you really think I would abandon you, especially now, when the King has given us such support? But perhaps I have read you wrong. Do you not want to stay here and learn?"

His jaw dropped and he stared dumbly at her. Her smile grew wider, her amusement rising, and suddenly she was laughing almost helplessly. He hurriedly shut his mouth, shaking his head with a rueful grin. On impulse, she rose from the couch and crossed to him. Before he could react, she kissed him on the cheek. Startled, he responded, but she quickly drew back.

"Ah, forgive me, Taran, I should not have done that. Listen, my friend, and hear me well. I love you much as I love Rienne and Bulldog. It is a deep love, a true love, but it is not quite the love you desire. I am an emotional creature. All Artesans are, as well you know. We cannot help but sense the thoughts and desires of those closest to us, and your desires are very clear to me. No, do not be embarrassed. True love should be treasured, not suppressed, however inappropriate. But it should also be channeled and controlled.

"So let me speak frankly. Should you decide to stay with us, your life would not be easy. We would have to work very closely together, and you would have to remember that my heart is already pledged. I would never betray Robin, and you would have to accept that. But if it helps you, then let me say that the true love of my friendship is yours. It is my dearest wish to have you stay and help me run the college, for I think we could be a good team. I have already spoken to Rienne, and she has given me her answer. Now it is your turn. What do you say?"

Taran continued to stare at her, his hands trembling. It was clear he could barely believe what he was hearing. His breath rasped in his throat as he spoke.

"This is … overwhelming. Only a few months ago, I was a directionless drifter, untutored, afraid. Now, everything I ever wanted is being offered to me. Well, almost everything. Sullyan … Brynne, I—" His voice broke, his emotions spilling over. Unable to finish, he buried his face in his hands.

Sullyan regarded him with quiet sympathy before fetching him a clean cloth and a fresh cup of fellan.

"Shall I take that as a yes, then?"

Chapter Twenty-Five

There was one final occasion of note that summer. A few weeks after work had begun on the new college building, a formal message arrived for Sullyan from the Hierarch. Bearing his royal seal and also the seal of Duke Marik, it informed her of the coming marriage of the Princess Idrimar to Duke Marik. All their friends were invited to attend, and Sullyan, Robin, Rienne, and Cal were also invited to share the festivities in the most personal way possible, by agreeing to take their own life mate vows on the same day.

Overwhelmed by the generosity of this offer, there was no refusing.

It lacked but a week to Midsummer Day when the party from the Manor rode out. Sullyan and Robin led the way on Torka and Drum, followed by Cal and Rienne, both mounted on horses gifted to them by the General. Rienne's was a pretty spotted mare with a gentle mouth and even paces. Cal's was a tall iron-grey with a black mane and tail. They were followed by Taran, Bull, General Blaine, and Captain Dexter, and they were surrounded by twenty men from Sullyan's own company.

To his unconfined delight, young Tad, who had recently been accepted as a cadet, was also there. His official title was squire, but he had been included because Sullyan had sensed the first stirrings of an Artesan's power in his adolescent mind. On hearing this, Robin had stared at her in astonishment. He was even more surprised when she added, "I do believe you have your first Apprentice, Major."

The young lad nearly fainted with joy when Robin told him the news. Already bursting with pride at becoming a cadet, Tad could hardly believe his good fortune. He would be the college's first student, but more important to Tad was being chosen as Robin's Apprentice, as he would now spend much of his time in his hero's company.

Riding in a happy daze, Tad watched Robin construct the trans-Veil tunnel over the river. The party passed through in good order, emerging into scorching summer heat on the Citadel Plains.

Commander Barrin greeted them formally, personally leading the honor guard which escorted them to the Citadel. The lower town had been forewarned of their coming, and the Albians—Sullyan and Robin in particular—were greeted with great acclaim. Hearing their cheers, some even chanting her name, Sullyan could not help contrasting this entrance with her first arrival, when she and Robin had been subjected to suspicion and unfriendly stares. Now, it seemed that most of the trades people and residents had left their tasks to greet them, and the noise of their welcome followed the Albians through the streets.

Three days were spent in preparation before the wedding procession finally wound its way out of the Citadel gates, heading for the stone circle on the hill. The gnarled and ancient monoliths were adorned with garlands of summer flowers and wreathed with twined leaves. Their majestic heads reared toward the sky, looking like venerable wise men spreading approval over the party. Flowering branches were positioned by each great stone, and the gently convex lawn was strewn with bright petals.

A canopy of rich purple silk had been erected at the center of the circle, where Timar Pharikian stood. He was clothed in ceremonial robes, the gold gauze cloak he wore shimmering in the sunshine. His golden crown with its tangwyr crest glittered with fire opals on his brow. He smiled warmly at the three couples standing hand-fast before him, and the musicians and cheering fell silent.

Pharikian approached his daughter and her lord, taking up their right hands. He spoke traditional words of binding, loyalty, and acceptance, and they repeated his words for all to hear. Turning to each other with clasped right hands, they proclaimed their vows. Then they knelt and Pharikian called on Baron Gaslek, who approached bearing two gold rings, one set with amethysts, the other with fire opals.

Taking the fire opal ring, Pharikian gave it to Marik. The amethyst he gave to Idrimar. Ty Marik, Duke of Kymer, was confirmed in his position as second Heir to the Throne as he slipped the fire opal ring on Idrimar's finger. He then accepted the amethyst from his bride and the marriage was done. While they stood and embraced, the whole Citadel could be heard voicing its pleasure as the horns of Pharikian's heralds proclaimed the royal marriage.

Then it was the Albians' turn. Robin and Sullyan, Cal and Rienne approached Pharikian together, listening while he spoke a variant of the traditional vows. These they repeated and then spoke their own personal vows, each to their partner. Then they knelt before Pharikian, and he laid hands on their heads in blessing as rings were exchanged.

The heralds' silver horns rang out again, the people's cheers added to their clarion voices. Three couples embraced, celebrating their union with kisses under the summer sun.

There was much feasting and celebration that night, for the royal wedding was as much a state occasion as a personal commitment, symbolizing not only the joining of two people very much in love, but also the unification of Cardon and Kymer with Caer Vellet.

There was, however, one among the invited guests who did not wish any of the happy couples well. A tall, black-haired noble from the north, this man did not approve of the proposed trade agreements between Andaryon and Albia, and he certainly was not well disposed toward the Albians present. Standing with his son on the edge of the crowded ballroom, he tried to hide his disapproval. Now was not the time to draw attention to himself. He needed to think very carefully about his next move now that both men responsible for the rebellion were dead.

One of these he mourned, even though Rykan had slighted him. The other, he most certainly did not. Sonten had been a sycophant and a usurper, and the northern noble had rejoiced on hearing of the General's demise. Death by the very artifact Sonten had tried to control was a fitting fate for so grasping a man. Yet, despite losing his most powerful rival in this power game, the noble had also lost a potential source of income. This displeased him. It would have given him much satisfaction to force Sonten to pay him for keeping his treachery secret. The General's gold would have filled the hole in the noble's coffers left by Rykan's untimely demise.

However, that opportunity was gone. Of more immediate concern was the loss of contact with Rykan's Albian ally, the Baron. The northern lord was desperate to re-establish the link, and his continuing failure had darkened his already sullen mood.

Glancing sourly at Kethro, his Artesan son, he wished for the thousandth time that the boy had inherited his father's quick wits and ambition. One or the other might have sufficed, but the boy seemed to lack both. Rather, he had his mother's insipid nature, and this angered the noble. Why, he thought irritably, couldn't his son have been more like Tikhal's heir, Rand? Now there was a young man whose attributes matched his inheritance.

This festive occasion, however, was not the time to allow his grudges to get the better of him. Tearing his gaze away from his son, who was watching the dancing and probably trying to screw up enough courage to ask one of the young ladies to partner him, the Lord beckoned imperiously to a wine bearer. He was forced to swerve abruptly aside as a laughing pair of dancers whirled past him, nearly colliding with his arm. He cursed and scowled in disapproval, barely acknowledging Cal's apologetic nod. His outraged expression drew a curious glance from Cal, but the young Albian was apparently enjoying the day far too much to allow a stranger's disgruntlement to depress him. With Rienne giggling in his arms, Cal continued the dance.

The northern Lord glared at the Albians with hot eyes. He dragged his son across the room, attempting to disguise his hatred by joining in the celebrations. He knew his thoughts were making him morose, and he couldn't allow his demeanor to draw unwanted attention. Once his plans were fully realized, however, it would be a very different story.

*****

The midsummer sun did little to warm the atmosphere in Queen Sofira's solar. Her mood, depressed ever since the Baron's return from the Manor, was not susceptible to the pleasures of sunlight. She was living in a constant state of fear, and the attentions of the Baron did nothing to assuage it.

That morning, despite the advanced stage of her pregnancy, she had attended the Minster and listened to a lengthy sermon from Arch-Patrio Neremiah on some new aspects of the Faith his clerics had discovered in the archives. Normally, Neremiah's pious tones and air of certainty had a soothing effect on Sofira, but lately all he did was irritate her. What was the point of him harping on about the importance of Albia's primary Faith when she, High Queen and wife of Elias, couldn't even get her husband to attend? Her failure in this and her fear of discovery dispelled any comfort she might derive from her loyalty to the Church.

There was a tap at her door, and she listlessly turned her head. "Come."

It opened to admit the Baron. She frowned at his air of suppressed eagerness. Lately, he had been as dour as she, so this was something new. Faint hope stirred her as she watched him approach.

He bowed to her and kissed her hand. His touch made her tingle, as it always did.

"Madam, I bring news that might help lighten your mood. May I sit?"

She glared at him for acting so formally when there was no need. They had known each other far too long to stand on ceremony when alone. She waved him irritably to a chair and pushed a goblet and decanter toward him.

"What news, Hezra?"

He irritated her further by pouring wine and sipping it before speaking. So, he wanted to play games, did he? Well, she could play them too.

"I didn't see you at the Minster this morning. Had you forgotten about the new tenets Neremiah found?"

The Baron glanced at her over the rim of his glass. "I had not forgotten, Madam, and I apologize for my absence. I will attend the evening service. I had other things on my mind this morning."

"Well? How long are you going to make me wait?"

He gave her a sly smile and her heart gave a jump.

"I decided recently that the time was right to re-establish ties with our remaining outlander contact."

She gasped, outraged. "And you did not think to tell me this before?"

He held up a placating hand. "I did not want to raise your hopes, Madam. It has been some time since we last spoke, and I did not know whether he would still be amenable to aiding us."

"And was he?"

"Oh yes, Madam. I would hazard to say even more so than before. So much so, that I outlined our plan."

She scowled. "Was that wise, at such an early stage?"

"I had to gain some kind of indication as to its feasibility, Madam. I needed his insight into their customs. I am pleased to say that I see no reason why the plan should not work. In fact, it might even be superior to our original scheme. I really can't see how anyone could interfere with it once set in motion. Not even your husband's favored Colonel Sullyan."

Sofira's hard grey eyes narrowed at the name. "But you are still going to deal with her?"

"Yes, indeed. She's too dangerous, too close to the King. To that effect, the letter I received this morning from our associate at the Manor was most informative."

She raised her brows, pleased to hear that her latest expenditure of gold had at least bought them some advantage. "I take it he was able to provide us with answers to our questions concerning the destruction of the Staff?"

She saw the tightening of Reen's facial muscles and knew that no matter how brave a face he maintained before her, the Baron still felt the same fury as hers at that catastrophic event. Only the complete success of their plan would ever wipe it away.

"He was, Madam, and in some detail. I think you will agree

that he has more than earned his gold when I tell you that I now know exactly how to accomplish our goal."

He raised his goblet to her and, as she did likewise, the same dark smile twisted both their lips.

The End

Glossary

Albian Characters

Baily. A Captain at the Manor under Colonel Vassa.

Bethyn Sullyan. Brynne Sullyan's mother, now deceased.

Brynne Sullyan. A Major at the Manor under General Blaine.

Bull, aka Bulldog, aka Hal Bullen. Major Sullyan's aide.

Cal Tyler. Taran's Artesan Apprentice and lover of Rienne Arlen.

Dexter. A Sergeant at the Manor under Captain Tamsen.

Elias Rovannon. Albia's High King.

Goran. Master cook at the Manor.

Hal Bullen. See 'Bull.'

Hanan. Chief Healer at the Manor.

Harker. Senior Sergeant Major at the Manor.

Hezra Reen. An Albian Baron from High King Elias's court.

Hyram. General Blaine's valet.

Izack. Baron Reen's personal Commander.

Jerrim Vassa. A Colonel at the Manor.

Jessy. Sister to Robin Tamsen, now deceased.

Kandaran. High King Elias's father, murdered during Albia's civil war.

Kinsey, Lord. Chamberlain to High King Elias.

Mathias Blaine. The Manor's senior officer and General-in-Command to High King Elias.

Morgan Sullyan. Brynne Sullyan's father, now deceased.

Neremiah, Arch-Patrio. Senior cleric of Albia's Matria Church.

Parren. A Captain at the Manor under Colonel Vassa.

Paulus. Elder of Taran's village, Hyecombe.

Rendan Levant, Lord. First Minister to High King Elias.

Rienne Arlen. A healer and Cal Tyler's lover.

Robin Tamsen. A Captain at the Manor under Major Sullyan.

Sofira. Queen to High King Elias Rovannon.

Solet. The Manor's stablemaster.

Tad Greylin. Young kitchen boy at the Manor.

Taran Elijah. An Artesan who is desperate to learn his craft.

Andaryan Characters

Aeyron Pharikian. The Hierarch of Andaryon's son and Heir.

Almid. One of a pair of giant twins, members of Ky-shan's pirate band.

Anjer, Lord General. Officer in overall command of the Hierarch's forces.

Arif. A Lieutenant in Rykan's forces.

As-ket. A member of Ky-shan's pirate band.

Barrin. A Lieutenant in the Hierarch's forces.

Corbyn, Lord. One of Lord Tikhal's northern nobles.

Deshan. The Hierarch's Master Healer, also a Master Artesan.

Ephan. A General in the Hierarch's forces, overall commander of the Velletian Guard.

Falina, Lady. The wife of General Kryp.

Gaslek. An Andaryan Baron, secretary to the Hierarch.

Heron. Sonten's Artesan Commander.

Hollet, Lady. The wife of General Ephan.

Idrimar Pharikian. The Hierarch's daughter.

Imris. Lord Sonten's young Artesan messenger.

Jaskin. Sonten's nephew, killed by Taran.

Jay'el. Son of pirate leader Ky-shan.

Kester. One of a pair of giant twins, members of Ky-shan's pirate band.

Kethro. Artesan son of a northern noble.

Ki-en. Younger member of Ky-shan's pirate band.

Kryp. A General in the Hierarch's forces.

Ky-shan. The leader of a band of pirates from Andaryon's eastern seaboard.

Norkis. Senior page to the Hierarch of Andaryon.

Rand. Artesan son of Lord Tikhal.

Rykan. Duke, Lord of Kymer province, and aspirant to the Andaryan throne.

Sonten. Duke Rykan's ambitious general. Lord of Durkos province.

Tikhal. An Andaryan Lord, also known as the Lord of the North. Pharikian's premier noble.

Timar Pharikian. The Hierarch, Supreme Ruler of Andaryon.

Torien, Lady. The wife of Lord General Anjer.

Torman Vanyr. Commander of the Velletian Guard, the Hierarch's personal Guard.

Ty Marik. Count of Cardon province under Rykan.

Xeer. A member of Ky-shan's pirate band.

Zolt. A member of Ky-shan's pirate band.

Realms of the World

First Realm—Endormir

Endormirians are sometimes known as 'Roamerlings' because of their itinerant habits. They are small and slim, dark skinned, with brown or black eyes showing hardly any whites. The Artesan gift runs only through the males, and gifted males always become clan-leaders. As Endormir suffers from severe winter conditions, its people cross the Veils into the other realms for the winter months, where they are well known as traders.

Second Realm—Sinnia

Sinnians are tall and milk-haired, with pale skin. They live in clans and were once nomadic but now live in settlements. All are born able to control their metaforce up to the rank of Adept and are thus considered 'sports'. Their race often produces highly gifted musicians and storytellers.

Third Realm—Relkor

Relkorians are small, fierce and stocky, notorious for raiding the other realms for slaves to work their mines and quarries. Their Artesans, both male and female, invariably become slave-lords.

Fourth Realm—Albia

Albia is the human realm. The Artesan gift runs through both male and female lines, each gender being equal in potential. The craft is currently out of favor due to raiding by both Relkorian and Andaryan Artesans. Albians widely believe that all Artesans use their powers only for gain and control.

Fifth Realm—Andaryon

A warlike race characterized by eyes with slit pupils. They fight constantly amongst themselves, vying for position within the Hierocracy. The Artesan gift passes only through the male line and females play a minor and downtrodden role. Only the most powerful Artesan can become and hold the rank of Hierarch. Their battles for supremacy are governed by strict, ritualistic laws.

Terms

Artesan. A person born with the ability to control metaforce and Master the four primal elements.

Brine rum. Strong liquor, drunk by pirates on Andaryon's eastern seaboard.

Codes of Combat. Strict laws governing any conflict between Andaryan nobles.

Demons. Derogatory term used in Albia to describe those of the Andaryan race.

Earth ball. An explosive sphere of Earth element formed by an Artesan for use as a weapon.

Fellan. A dark, aromatic and bitter beverage brewed from the seeds of the fellan-plant.

Firefield. A barrier formed from the primal element of Fire, through which only Artesans can pass. Fire fields formed by those of inferior Artesan rank can easily be destroyed by those of a higher rank.

Firewater. Incredibly strong liquor.

Free traders. Another term for pirate.

Kingsman. Term used to describe members of the High King's fighting forces.

Matria Church. The Minster in Port Loxton, seat of Albia's primary faith, the Faith of the Wheel.

Metaforce (sometimes also called life force). The force of existence pertaining to all things, both animate and inanimate.

Perdition. A state of non-being for the soul–a place where souls with no ultimate destination reside.

Primal elements. Earth, Water, Fire and Air. There is a fifth element, Spirit, although many believe this to be a myth.

Primal Sacrament. Andaryan name for the Pact, an agreement brokered between Andaryan nobles. Used to settle wars ending in stalemate, it involves the willing suicide of a powerful Artesan.

Portway. Structure formed by an Artesan from a primal element–usually Earth or Water–which gives its creator access through the Veils.

Psyche. An Artesan's unique and personal pattern through which they can manipulate metaforce and channel the primal elements.

Roamerling. Derogatory term for the nomads of Endormir.

Substrate. The medium in which the primal elements reside, and in which the world and all things have their being.

Tangwyr. Monstrous Andaryan raptor trained to hunt men.

The Pact. (See Primal Sacrament).

The Staff. Mysterious and terrible weapon capable of stealing and storing metaforce. Can only be used by Artesans.

The Veils. Misty barriers separating the five Realms of the World. Only Artesans have the power to move through the Veils.

The Void. Dark abyss at the end of life into which all souls pass before reaching their final destination.

The Wheel. Central principle of the primary Albian faith.

Witch. Derogatory term for an Artesan.

Artesan ranks and their attributes.

Level one: Apprentice. Person born with the Artesan gift and the ability to influence the first primal element of Earth. Able to hear other Artesans speaking telepathically but unable to initiate such speech.

Level two: Apprentice-elite. Has some skill in influencing their own metaforce. Has attained Mastery over the element of Earth. Able to initiate telepathic speech but only with Artesans already known to them. Able to build substrate structures, identify a person by the pattern of their psyche, and counter metaphysical attack to some degree.

Level three: Journeyman. Has Mastery over Earth and is able to influence Water. Able to build portways and travel through the Veils. Has some skill in using metaforce for offence. Also able to initiate psyche-overlay and converse telepathically with any other Artesan. Possesses some self-healing potential.

Level four: Adept. Has Mastery over both Earth and Water. Able to build more complex substrate structures such as corridors. Able to influence where such structures emerge. Possesses stronger offensive and defensive capabilities. Able to merge psyche fully with other Artesans. Increased healing abilities.

Level five: Adept-elite. Has Mastery over Earth and Water and is able to influence Fire. Possesses great healing powers which can even aid the ungifted (with their permission). Able to initiate powersinks and merges of psyche. Able to construct such structures as Fire-fields.

Level six: Master. Has Mastery over Earth, Water and Fire. Able to control the power of an inferior Artesan against their will. Control over personal metaforce now almost total. Possesses incredible healing powers.

Level seven: Master-elite. Has Mastery over Earth, Water and Fire and is able to influence Air, the most capricious primal element. Able to absorb a lesser or even equal-ranked Artesan's power and metaforce provided some link or permission (however tenuous) can be found.

Level eight: Senior Master. Has complete Mastery over all four primal elements. Able to absorb another Artesan's power by force, even sometimes without a link. Possesses a high degree of metaphysical (and usually spiritual) strength.

Level nine: Supreme Master. It has never been fully established whether this rank actually exists. Supreme Masters are supposedly able to influence Spirit, largely regarded as the mythical 'fifth element.' Ancient texts refer only to the possibility; no mention has ever been found of a being attaining Supreme Mastery.

Sport or lay-Artesan. Freaks of nature, sports are thought to be able to control their own metaforce from birth, to whatever level of strength they inherently possess. As they receive no training their working is often undetectable. They are also believed to be able to 'hear' the thoughts of those around them; gifted or ungifted, and directly, not through the substrate.

Cas Peace

Cas Peace was born and brought up in the lovely county of Hampshire, in the UK, where she still lives. On leaving school, she trained for two years before qualifying as a teacher of equitation. During this time she also learned to carriage-drive. She spent thirteen years in the British Civil Service before moving to Rome, where she and her husband, Dave, lived for three years. They return whenever they can.

As well as her love of horses, Cas is mad about dogs, especially Lurchers. She enjoys dog agility training and currently owns two rescue Lurchers, Milly and Milo. Milly has already had some success in the agility ring, and Milo will begin competing in late 2011. Cas loves country walks, working in stained glass and folk singing. She has also written a nonfiction book, *For the Love of Daisy*, which tells the life story of her beautiful Dalmatian. Details and other information can be found on her website, www.caspeace.com.

Lightning Source UK Ltd.
Milton Keynes UK
UKOW05f0402150813

215364UK00002B/69/P